The Dartington Bride

The Dartington Bride

ROSEMARY GRIGGS

DAUGHTERS OF DEVON

Cover design and cover artwork by Bob Cooper.

Troubador Publishing Ltd
Unit E2 Airfield Business Park,
Harrison Road, Market Harborough,
Leicestershire LE16 7UL
Tel: 0116 279 2299
Email: books@troubador.co.uk
Web: www.troubador.co.uk

ISBN 978 1 80514 299 7

British Library Cataloguing in Publication Data.
A catalogue record for this book is available from the British Library.

Typeset in 11pt Adobe Garamond Pro by Troubador Publishing Ltd, Leicester, UK

Chapter One

The Regicide

1559 France

'Ton père a tué le roi!' screamed the woman from the doorway. 'Your father has killed the king!' I stirred on the bed and my eyes flew open. Snatched from my dreams in a heartbeat, I strained my ears. Again, those words. 'Your father has killed the king,' but softer, quavering, less strident. The third time the voice was hardly more than a breath, cracking and breaking as the words dropped into the silent room like slivers of ice.

In the clammy heat of that night I had thrown the bed covers aside and my shift was clinging about me, the crumpled linen wound around me like a shroud. Caught between sleep and waking, I scrambled wildly to pull the velvet coverlet right up over my head. Knees curled up, I made myself as small as I could and tried to shut out the thumping noise thrashing in my ears. It was the sound of my heart banging like a drum.

Curiosity got the better of me and, trembling, I peeped out. A shaft of moonlight fell on the ghostly face of a woman framed in the doorway. A scream fought its way up to my voice box but no sound came. I swallowed hard and forced myself to look. She wore Clotilde's clothes, the same green kirtle and crisp clean apron Clotilde had on when she put me to bed. But the woman was not Clotilde. My Clotilde had twinkling brown eyes set in a merry face as round and rosy as a Normandy apple. She had a soft, silvery voice as even and contented as a cat's purr. The woman framed in the stone arch, the not-Clotilde, had put on a white mask; she had bulging, goggly eyes and a gaping mouth. She shook her head from side to side and twisted her hands in her apron as she croaked out the words again in brittle little gasps.

'Your father has killed the king!' So said the not-Clotilde.

'Vite, Clotilde! Vite! Dépêche-toi.' Other servants scurried in, pushing past her, frantically waking my sisters, shouting that they must dress quickly. I shrank back behind the hangings and tried to hide in the great bed.

All the shouting jolted her into action. The not-Clotilde stumbled forward, rushed to my coffer, picked up a cloak and heaped underwear and sleeves and caps and gowns onto it all higgledy-piggledy. She snatched the necklace from the little wooden casket by my bed, added that to the pile and knotted the cloak round it all. Somehow she got me into some clothes; not the pretty blue dress embroidered with pearls; not my best shift with the blackwork collar. Instead, with rough hands, the not-Clotilde bundled me into a plain shift and an old woollen kirtle. She was about to pick me up when I found I could scream.

'Diane! I want Diane!'

The not-Clotilde groaned as she bent to retrieve the doll and tied the ribbon round my middle. Diane was always getting lost and this precaution saved a lot of searching.

The not-Clotilde grabbed me and clasped me to her chest, running through unlit passageways close on the heels of a scurrying maid. The maid's hand trembled so much the candle she carried sputtered and all but died, only for the flame to revive and cast even more grotesque shadows on the old stone walls. That brought me out of my mute terror. I found my voice again and shrieked and kicked and hollered. But the not-Clotilde just gripped me more tightly as she ran on. Her breathing was ragged and wheezy by the time we were down the steps and out of the door. Strong arms hoisted me up onto a horse. I held tight to Diane the doll with one hand and rubbed the plump little fingers of my other hand up and down the familiar soft silky fabric of her gown.

The blanket they used to secure me in front of Alain du Bois, Papa's serjeant-at-arms, was scratchy and rough. Alain had a prickly beard and his breath smelled of ale and onions. I heard muffled voices, then the hooves hammered on the cobbles, metallic echoes that lingered long in the still night air. I clutched my doll as she bumped along under the blanket. After a while I rested my head on Alain's chest and eventually the steady beat of his heart must have lulled me to sleep.

I woke with a start, plucked from a lurid dream of a white-faced goblin chasing after me. Alain du Bois tightened his arm round me.

'Fear not, *ma petite*,' he soothed. 'All shall be well.'

I peered out from under the blanket. I looked down and saw strange shadows on a mossy track. I looked up and saw light filtering through a canopy of leaves high above my head. I sniffed; a woodsy, earthy smell mingled with horse and sweat and leather. Whatever Alain said, all was not well. Instead of waking in my comfortable bed I was on a horse in front of him and we were riding through a forest.

My five-year-old brain simply couldn't make sense of it. I gulped down a great breath of air and tried to remember what had happened the day before. I had been naughty. I remembered being cross about something, very cross indeed. It came back to me in a flash.

'Why can't I go?' I had wailed.

'Your turn will come, Roberda,' my Clotilde had replied. 'There will be other tournaments, other festivals when you are older. Your parents don't want you mixing in the crowds and catching this sickness that rages through the city; not at your age.'

'So why can Jacques go? Won't he get sick? I hope he does!' My voice had risen to a satisfying screech.

'Roberda! That's a wicked thought!' Clotilde had scolded. 'He and Gedeon are much older. Your sisters aren't complaining.'

'Well, why does Papa have to go to the stupid tournament anyway?' I'd demanded.

'You know very well your father is Captain of King Henri's Scots guard just as your grandfather, the Comte de Montgomery, was before him. The guards go everywhere with the king and your papa leads them.' Clotilde's voice had gone all soft and dreamy. She'd stopped folding shifts into the coffer and sat down with a sigh. 'Of course he must be there. He's such a fine chevalier, is your papa. Gabriel de Lorges! He'll be so handsome in his uniform! Just think of it! The Place des Vosges all dressed in its finest colours to celebrate peace with our enemies and your papa riding out on his white horse.'

'Well, I don't care about that,' I'd replied sullenly, curling my lip in scorn when I saw the silly grin on her face.

'Now, Roberda, it's a great celebration. The king's daughter Elizabeth has married Philip of Spain and his sister Margaret has married Emmanuel Philibert, Duke of Savoy.' Marriage was something that happened to we girls when we were old enough, even girls of the Royal blood.

'Marriage! Ugh! I hope it's a long, long time before that happens to me,' I'd shouted, stamping my little feet hard on the floorboards. 'It's just not fair. Everyone will be there; everyone except for me.' That wasn't quite true, of course. I had known very well my sisters would not be allowed to go either. But by then I'd wound myself up into such a fit of angry spite I hadn't cared about telling the truth.

As I sat huddled in front of Alain Du Bois I bit my lip. Telling lies was a sin, wasn't it? My tummy felt a bit strange as I clutched Diane the doll even tighter. Perhaps it was all my fault. I had so wanted to see Papa ride out in his shining armour on his great white horse all hung about with banners and embroidered skirts.

It had felt so good to scream and stomp around until I knocked one of Maman's finest platters onto the floor. Clotilde had scolded me and called me Gabrielle. Clotilde had never, ever called me that before. She always called me Roberda. Even Maman only used my first name when she was really, truly angry. So I must have been very naughty indeed.

Still pinioned in front of Alain I squirmed round until I could see the horse following us. I stared at the woman clinging on behind the rider. It was the not-Clotilde. So it hadn't all been a dream. I turned my head aside to avoid Alain's smelly breath.

As the horse picked its way along the narrow track I huddled down under the coarse blanket and cuddled Diane the doll. How I loved her! I wouldn't go anywhere without her. She had a bright red dress with a stiff hooped skirt and improbable yellow hair. It didn't matter that she was a little mannequin the tailor sent to Maman to show her the latest styles. It didn't matter that Maman pressed her lips together and shook her head when I announced that the doll was called Diane. She was my special friend. Papa had a special friend too and her name was also Diane.

I knew this because when I went to the kitchen to dip my finger in the honeypot I heard the cook say that Papa spent ever so much time with his friend Diane. So I thought she must be a very special friend.

My brow puckered as I tried to puzzle it out. Papa's special friend couldn't be Madame de Poitiers, the one who dressed all in black and white, nor was she Diane, the king's daughter. Papa's friend must be another Diane, someone who didn't have time to come to court, for I had never seen her.

Distracted by those thoughts I drifted back to sleep, only waking when at last we stopped at an inn for food. If you could call it food. I watched my sister Charlotte valiantly spooning the lumpy broth into her mouth. But it was not to my liking at all. I pushed the pottage away and a great greasy dollop spilled onto the rough sun-bleached boards.

'It's horrible! I won't eat it,' I yelled, pounding my fists on the table. The not-Clotilde sighed and cleaned up the mess with a cloth before wiping her hands on her apron. 'If the child doesn't eat soon she'll be ill,' she muttered, 'and then we'll all be in more trouble.'

'She'll eat when her belly gnaws hard enough, woman,' Alain du Blois replied with an impatient jerk of his head. 'We can waste no more time here. See if you can tempt her at the next inn.' I kicked and screamed, but his arms were strong. He picked me up and set me on the horse again.

I was tired of jiggling along in front of Alain du Bois. What did I care if the countryside was parched for want of rain? What did I care to see the men toiling in the fields, bent near double with their sickles flashing and swishing? What did I care if the peasant women in their madder-dyed kirtles looked like so many poppies among the corn? If that was all Alain could think of to distract me, he'd do better to think again. I just wanted to go home.

My Clotilde had still gone away. The not-Clotilde rode beside us, clinging on behind a soldier, clutching a bundle wrapped in woollen cloth tight to her side. Her wild staring eyes were fixed on the back of the man's head, but every time a twig snapped under the horse's hoof I saw her flinch and dart anxious glances over her shoulder. I did not like the not-Clotilde. She frightened me. But it was the not-Clotilde who put me to bed when we stopped for the night at another grimy inn. It was the not-Clotilde who wrung her hands as she tried to coax me to eat. How I longed for marchpane and gingerbread! The truth was, my tummy was really hurting. I had never been hungry before.

My brother Jacques had watched the joust, being so much older. He whispered the story as, on the next day, we sat in the grimy parlour of the next inn. This time Alain du Bois had brought me bread and a honeypot and my tummy felt a bit better. I thought I might try some pottage later. Refusing food wasn't getting us sent home.

Jacques was puffed up like a peacock and determined to tell his tale, despite being told to hold his tongue.

'King Henri wore a black and white ribbon, the colours of Diane de Poitiers,' he hissed. I wondered why the king did not wear the queen's colours, but Jacques gave me a hard stare, so I didn't ask. He didn't tell us whose favour Papa had carried.

'The king is very old,' Jacques said, speaking a little louder and grinning as Alan du Bois frowned at him. 'At least forty, and he's getting a bit fat. But ho, ho, King Henri thought he could still joust as well as anyone.' He paused and ran his tongue over his lips.

'Well, the first time Papa rode out in the lists he was so careful; he managed not to harm His Majesty. Just had him swaying in his saddle a bit. Oh, you should have seen the king smile when in his next tilt he defeated his new brother-in-law, the Duke of Savoy. But it came near the end of the day and still no lance had been broken. So King Henri insisted there must be just one more contest. I saw the queen try to persuade him to have done, but his blood was up. He'd nearly fallen in the first round and wanted to prove a point. So he challenged Papa again.' Jacques paused again, flicking his eyes round to check we were all listening.

'You could see Papa wasn't happy. But he could not disobey. He had his squire make ready. This time Papa's lance went straight and true and King Henri took a blow to the head. I climbed up onto the bench and saw Papa trying to withdraw his lance from the king's helmet which had been forced wide open. Papa's lance had shattered and a great shard of wood had pierced King Henri's eye.' Jacques' grin had become a sneer as he brandished a stick wildly at us. I shuddered and put my hands over my ears.

'I don't want to hear any more,' I sobbed. If the real Clotilde had been there I knew she would have whisked me away and given Jacques a good ticking-off for frightening me so. But the not-Clotilde just looked on with her mouth set in a thin black line.

'They've taken Papa to a tower in the old city walls because he's killed the king. That is why we fled from Paris in dead of night,' Jacques said, and all his bravado melted away as his voice trailed off. 'I don't know if we'll ever see him again.'

'Enough,' hissed Alain. 'Don't speak so loud. We don't want to draw attention. Who knows what retribution may be coming after us.' I didn't know what retribution was, but it sounded nasty.

We travelled on, Alain and the other men in plain jerkins of rough wool with no emblems on display. I coughed and spluttered as we cut through rough country lanes where the horses kicked up the dust. I fidgeted and plucked at the scratchy blanket which had become so damp with sweat it was sticking to me.

'I want to get down,' I wailed. But Alain only held me tighter.

In Paris everything was all right, I thought. *We lived in a fine house and everyone was happy. Papa strutted around in his fine uniform; everyone saluted him and he laughed a lot. Maman and all the ladies of the court glided around in their glittering gowns like swans on a shimmering lake.*

The not-Clotilde said Maman was following more slowly in a litter, in her condition; whatever that was supposed to mean. My sister Elisabeth had been ill, she said, so she was travelling with Maman. I realised with a jolt I had been too frightened and cross to worry about where Elisabeth was.

Out in the countryside the tracks wound through deep woods. There were no church bells to tell the passing of each day. I don't know how many days passed before Jacques told us the not-Clotilde had got it all wrong. Papa had not really killed King Henri after all.

'I heard the ostler at the inn say the king still lives. He's at the Palais de Tournelles. Perhaps Papa will be set free,' he announced.

'They say the king's surgeon, Dr Paré, has been trying out his skills on poor prisoners condemned to death so he can operate on the king's eye to save him,' Jacques said, his grin now ghoulish.

'Tell us more. Tell us more,' Gedeon chuckled, but Charlotte screwed up her face and let out a squeal.

'Don't be so horrid, Jacques,' she cried.

'Perhaps the prisoners were already dead. Perhaps not! Ha! Ha!' my cruel brother continued. 'Imagine that, poking around in all those eyes!' He lunged towards me and jabbed his finger into my face. I turned away, crying, and buried my head in the not-Clotilde's skirts. She wasn't my Clotilde, but she was all I had for comfort.

'Ugh! Stop it, Jacques, it's too horrible!' yelled Charlotte.

'Well, if Dr Paré does save King Henri, then Papa's sure to go free,' Gedeon added, shuffling his feet, and shaking his head. None of us really dared to believe it.

We came to the town of Domfront on market day and the main street was crowded with colourful stalls. Heads turned as our little cavalcade wove through the press and I felt Alain's hand move to his sword hilt. But no one challenged us. The horses puffed and blew as we climbed up towards the towering walls of Château Domfront, a forbidding fortress perched on a craggy rock high above the town.

After a few heated words with Alain du Bois a surly man threw back the gates and we trooped into the courtyard. There were only a few servants about, but Alain said it was a good place to wait for Maman to arrive. I saw him climbing up to the battlements to keep lookout and wished we were all back in Paris.

The not-Clotilde told us that long ago the English had fought the French to see who would hold Château Domfront. Well, they were welcome to it as far as I was concerned. As I lay on my cot the wind crept in and blew the candle out. I shivered and trembled and stared into the pitch black, waiting for the ghosts of long dead soldiers to come out and get me.

Next day the boys teased me and swaggered about, pretending to be soldiers and quizzing Alain about arrow slits and machicolations, whatever they were. We girls just huddled together listlessly. Even Diane the doll couldn't amuse me.

When Maman's litter finally arrived, she clambered out and we all crowded round her in the castle hall. Her face looked strange;

deathly pale with great black rings round her eyes, and she kept rubbing her back.

'I have no news,' she announced, pricking the bubble of our hope at once. 'I will rest for a day of two and then we will all go on to Ducey together.' Alain shook his head. But he must do her bidding, so a few days later, we set off again. The air was thick and heavy that day and I felt a trickle of sweat creeping down my backbone before we were out of the courtyard.

'Make haste,' shouted Alain, looking up at the darkening tops of clouds that might soon grow into thunderheads. 'Like as not this weather will break. We don't want to be caught in a storm. We'll stick to little-used paths. We'll have many streams to cross. Make haste before the rain comes and puts them all in spate!'

The sky was black as tar and thunder was rumbling some way off as, round a turn in the track, we came to a place where the river gushed under a crumbling old bridge. A mill hung precariously over the water and the mill wheel creaked and groaned as it turned in the narrow mill leat. I pulled a face and wrinkled my nose as an acrid smell hit me. Alain chuckled.

'That's the tanneries beyond those houses!' he laughed. 'This is Ducey! Can you see the house behind that low wall?' I craned my neck to follow his pointing arm.

As our horses clattered through an archway their hoofbeats echoed off the stone walls. Just as we emerged from the shadows the sun broke through the clouds, sending bright slanting beams down onto the ancient house. It was as if a magician had waved a wand and suddenly an enchanted grey-stone mansion had risen up from nowhere. In that very moment Ducey became home to me.

I must have been there before because Maman told me I was born at Ducey. But I had no memory of it. It was not large; certainly not a palace; not grand in the latest style like our house in Paris. But the gardens were lush and green and a tangle of pretty roses grew round the door.

Before we had time to dismount a messenger thundered into the courtyard and flung himself from his sweating horse. He strode past the not-Clotilde to Maman who sat wilting in the litter. She leaned forward and the messenger went down on one knee.

'King Henri is dead, madame. God rest His Majesty and long live King François,' he announced in a loud voice that echoed round the old walls. The not-Clotilde and Alain du Bois exchanged a worried look.

'The doctor did get the wood from the eye, but it was too late. The damage was done. He died on the tenth day of July. God save King François! I have letters for you, madame.'

Maman took the letters and climbed unsteadily out of the litter. She shuffled into the hall, moving slowly, cautiously, like an old woman, with her maids scurrying behind her like chicks behind the mother hen. Once inside Maman flopped down onto a bench. Her face was white as the petals on the rose that grew round the door and had the same silky smooth look. She bent her head over the letters, then looked up and murmured something to the not-Clotilde. Suddenly I saw a slow smile creep across the woman's face and I hardly dared to believe my eyes. My Clotilde was back! There she was, bright merry eyes shining above dimpled cheeks that chased away the ugly lines that had sat so uncomfortably on her face since Paris. I clapped my hands together and ran to my Clotilde. Laughing, she flopped down beside Maman and took me on her lap.

'God be praised, oh, God be praised,' she kept saying, over and over as she rocked me. 'He is but banished.'

Later Maman called us all together and told us that before he died the king had pardoned my papa.

'King Henri said your papa should have no need of forgiveness, for he merely obeyed his king and performed the acts of a good and valiant knight. So he is set at liberty, but stripped of his post as captain of the guard and banished from the court. But for the king's words he would have paid with his life. He will soon be here.' Banished was a new word for me, but surely it couldn't be too bad for my Clotilde was back and a broad grin lit up Alain du Bois' usually dour face.

Just as Maman had said, Papa arrived a few days later and I learned that banished meant he could not stay long.

'King Henri may have pardoned your papa, but Queen Catherine will not forgive,' Maman explained, rubbing her hand across a stomach that looked much larger than it used to be. 'She has taken the broken lance as her emblem from which she says come all her tears and all her pain. She will never forget.'

I wasn't sure what that meant so I listened in when I heard Papa talking to Maman the next morning.

'François the king is young. His mother will seek to rule this land in his name. But Mary of Scotland's uncles will also seek to hold power over him.' Maman frowned and murmured something I couldn't hear.

'Yes, Queen Catherine … oh, I suppose we must call her Queen Dowager now … she won't like that at all … the Duc de Guise … the Cardinal of Lorraine … there may be trouble. Best that you and the children stay hidden away at Ducey.' I couldn't hear all of what Papa said but I could see he was twisting a ring round and round on his finger.

I crept away to find my eldest sister. Unlike Elisabeth –the dreamy one, always imagining herself a princess being rescued by a knight in shining armour – Charlotte always knew what was happening. She was a great one for listening at doors, and hiding behind the hangings to find out what the grown-ups were saying. I found her reading under a pear tree.

'What's all this about the Duc de Guise and Mary of Scotland?' I demanded. 'She's nice. I saw her once when I tripped up in the passageway at the palace and she helped me up. She talked kindly to me about Diane the doll. She gave me a sweetmeat.'

'You're too young to understand,' Charlotte said with a smile and went back to her book.

'I'm not too young!' I snapped. 'I know she's Queen of Scotland and I know our family came to France a long time ago from Scotland. And I know that's a faraway place to the north of the land of our enemies, the English.'

Charlotte put down her book and gave me a hug.

'Well, sometimes the English are our enemies, but sometimes they're our friends. It's complicated,' she smiled. 'The people of Scotland are our friends because Mary is married to our king, so she's our queen too. The Duc de Guise is her uncle.'

'So why is Papa worried about him? Why did he say we must hide at Ducey?' I looked down at the grass and shuffled my feet. 'It's all so confusing,' I muttered.

'Don't worry. We're safe here,' she soothed. But then she stepped back and frowned. 'You're right though. It is confusing. I suppose the Duc de Guise might fall out with the king's mother. Or Queen Catherine might remember that Papa killed the old king.' She wrinkled her brow a bit more and then shrugged her shoulders. 'Let's forget all about it. I'll race you to the kitchen door.' I hurtled after her and the enticing smell of the gingerbread the cook had been baking chased it all from my mind.

I giggled when the next morning Papa reached out his strong, long-fingered hands and lifted me high above his head. He planted a kiss on my cheek and hugged me tight, then set me down and made his farewells to all the others. Then he mounted his horse and was gone.

After he left, Maman disappeared into her chamber. A few weeks later she showed us our new brother, Giles, who kicked up a frightful din in the nursery at the top of the house.

But I didn't care about that. Ducey was heaven! We had few visitors and didn't have to wear our best clothes every day. We explored the gardens, found hidden pathways, the bank where I just knew I would find wild strawberries in the spring, and sweet-smelling beds of rosemary and lavender where I tried to catch butterflies. One morning Alain found me running between the clipped hedges. His eyes were twinkling in a face as brown and wrinkled as a walnut as he took something from beneath his cloak.

'Now, see what I have brought for you, my brave little one,' he said, with his gap-toothed smile. He set a white puppy on the grass. She wriggled towards me and nothing else mattered in the whole world. I had a new friend. I called her Fifi. What Diane the doll thought of this as she dangled from my waist I really cannot say.

Chapter Two

Exile's Return

1561

I had passed my sixth birthday and Clotilde had added another keeper to the hem of my kirtle by the time Papa came home to Ducey after his travels to the Isles-de-La-Manche, to Venice and to England. Charlotte, ever the fount of information, told me he had come back just as Mary, the young Queen of the Scots, left our shores. The girl who had talked so kindly to me in Paris was now a widow, sent back to Scotland after King François died and his even younger brother became King Charles. Even I knew it was Queen Catherine de Medici who now ruled over us.

On that chilly December morning my sisters and I were dutifully plying our needles beside Maman. Every day we girls had to sit with her and sew. It was one of those things we were supposed to learn so we could grow up and marry someone.

We had brought our stitching down to the hall, hoping to get some warmth from the logs blazing in the fireplace. But needlework needs good light, so we'd moved nearer the windows, away from the fire. The brazier brought in to warm us barely took the chill from the air. Maman's chair was set in front of the curtained entrance to the solar stair and we sat with our heads bent over our work. My fingers were so cold I was struggling to keep my needle moving.

Suddenly a loud crashing beyond the door at the far end of the hall made me jump and my needle drew a red spot of blood. With my wounded finger in my mouth I fumbled about with my other hand, searching for my dropped needle. I found it just as Papa flung the heavy door back with such violence that the walls beside it shook. My mouth fell open and I stared.

The fury who strode past the long table and down the hall with spittle round his mouth, roaring like a mad bull, didn't seem a bit like the Papa I remembered. I could see the whites of his eyes and his nostrils flaring, while his short cape swayed from side to side sending a pewter cup clattering from the board. The offending needle fell from my hand again to twinkle unheeded among the folds of my skirt as I watched him stalk towards us. He planted his feet squarely on the flagstones in front of Maman's chair with his fingers curled tight around his sword hilt, knuckles showing white, as if he was ready to draw at a moment's notice.

'Madame, you meddle where you should not,' he growled, brandishing a letter in front of her face. 'This is from my father. It seems you have written to him on matters that are none of your concern. It is not your business to know where I choose to go first when I return from across the sea.'

Maman turned to Charlotte and whispered, 'I have need of more thread to finish the blackwork on this cuff. Go, take Elisabeth and Roberda with you. Go to my chamber and bring more for me.' Now I could see she had a skein sticking out of her work basket but the look on her face and Papa's lowering presence had us scurrying through the hangings behind Maman's chair. But I couldn't resist pausing to look over my shoulder.

Charlotte clasped my hand and pulled me away. I had my foot on the winding stair that led to the private chambers when I remembered Diane the doll. If something horrible was going to happen I needed to have her with me. I just couldn't leave her behind.

'Let go, Charlotte,' I screeched as I wriggled and squirmed.

'Maman has told us to go,' she said firmly and her fingers pinched my wrist leaving a red mark. 'You must come with me.'

'I don't care what Maman said. I'm not going anywhere without Diane,' I hissed, twisting my arm until I was free of Charlotte's grasp. Determined to run back to retrieve my doll I didn't really pay much attention to the angry voices coming from beyond the hangings. But

I pulled up short when I reached the curtains and peeped between them. There was Diane the doll lying on the floor next to Maman's work basket. But I didn't move to reach for her. I was frozen to the spot as my eyes travelled up from Papa's feet in their fine leather boots to fix on his florid face. I could hear Charlotte tutting as she came up behind me and reached for my hand. I darted a quick glance at her, expecting to have to avoid her grasp again; I wasn't going anywhere. But the eyes of my usually calm elder sister were round as she too took in the scene beyond the hangings and her lips were actually trembling. Elisabeth caught up with us and elbowed me aside to stand stock-still beside me. I heard her gasp and saw her cheeks go as white as my best smock as she clapped a hand over her mouth. The three of us clung together, half hidden, unnoticed.

Maman was cowering like a greyhound when the huntsman cracks his whip. Papa stood over her, leaning so close she must have felt his breath as he spat out a torrent of words I did not understand. I really thought he would strike. His hostile eyes drilled into Maman and he started to raise his arm. We all held our breath. But suddenly Papa stepped back, turned on his heel and marched back down the hall. That was when Maman found her backbone. She pulled herself up until she was as tall and straight as a poplar by the riverbank, elegant in a black gown laced tight across her breast. Her voice cut through the air like a sword; strong, clear and scornful, though it was pitched so low.

'I will speak, husband. Indeed, it is my place to speak. Do you forget who I am?'

Papa, almost at the door, halted mid-step, but did not turn. I could see his fists clenching and unclenching as he squared his shoulders and waited for her next words. Maman's eyes were flashing and I grabbed Charlotte's hand. We waited, mesmerised, hardly daring to breathe.

'Husband, I am Isabeau de la Touche, daughter of François, Lord of Roches Tranchelion, and Charlotte de Maille. I am your true wife.' I gasped. I had never heard Maman speak like that. She didn't hear my sharp intake of breath, but raised her chin even higher and went on. 'I will serve you well in the matter of religion, as in all things. You are returned a changed man, Gabriel, and I am glad of it.' Papa did not move.

'In the past you have shown no scruples in dealing harshly with those who challenge the old ways of worship,' Maman continued. 'But that was in the service of your king, when feats of arms meant more to a young soldier than any point of principle. Now you have studied the new way in England and in Venice. That I know. That I welcome. I too have found much of merit in the teachings of Master Calvin. I have already had all the trappings of popery removed from our home. I have had Pastor Forêt join our household. He teaches the children.' Papa did not turn, nor did he speak as Maman went on in a voice as cold and hard as ice on a pail of water.

'You are done with the old ways of the church, Gabriel. That I understand. But I will say it again, as I did to your father. You must also be done with her.' Papa flinched at that. His shoulders shook a little, but still he did not turn.

'Gabriel, you have no future in the service of the young king.' Her tone was softer now, more reasoning. 'Charles is even younger than his brother now gone to the grave, God rest him. Madame la Reine will never forgive you for the death of her husband. Our family will suffer. Mary of Scotland's Guise uncles want to regain their hold. God knows, they are no friends of the new religion.' Maman paused to draw breath before she delivered her next words with all the force of a command.

'Gabriel, you must answer the call of your friend François de Bricqueville. Join him and offer your sword to Louis de Bourbon, Prince Condé when the time is right for him to lead a force in the name of our chosen religion. The men of Normandy are ready to rise, but they lack leaders. They need strong soldiers hardened in battle. Men like you. You can be a leader of men, Gabriel. But you must give her up.' Papa's head was down now. As he stood with his back to us his hands hung limply at his sides.

'I will be your staunchest supporter,' Maman announced. 'But more than that, I will call on those of my kin to flock to your banner with all the nobles of Basse-Normandie. I will make whatever sacrifice I must to bring about your success, for that will bring greatness to our line. But your association with that woman will not help you. Those of her blood, the de Tavannes blood, will go against you. You must put her aside.'

Papa turned slowly as if in a dream and with faltering steps made his way back towards her. When he reached her he stood silent, hanging his head, as a red flush crept up his cheeks. At last he looked into Maman's eyes. His hand fluttered towards her for a moment, and then fell again as, with an impatient edge to her voice, she exclaimed, 'I ask only that you show me respect and give her up. God knows I've tolerated your dalliance these many years, as any well-born wife must. But now it will damage you. It will damage our children. You must give her up.'

Papa shook his head and mumbled, 'What of the child?'

'You must make provision as many a man has done before you,' said Maman.

Well, that meant nothing at all to me. I had no idea what child they were talking about. I looked at Charlotte, but she gave a little shake of her head, as if she couldn't believe what she was hearing.

Papa looked at Maman hard and rubbed his hand over his face, then heaved a long heavy sigh. All the anger seemed to seep out of him in that sigh.

'Of course. You are right in this, Isabeau,' he said wearily. 'I am not the man who rode out at the tourney that day. I have travelled and studied and met many who have convinced me of the right way. I pray you will forgive my anger this day. My quarrel with you is that when I flew to her before I came home to Ducey, you thought ill of me. You thought old habits die hard, I suppose. But you wronged me, Isabeau. I am changed. I went first to her to tell her she would see me no more. I went to make just the arrangements you seek.' He shook his head slowly. 'There was no need for you to get involved. You should not have raised this with my father. It made me feel a fool. That was not your place, madame.'

Maman's head dropped.

'Gabriel! I did not know,' she muttered. It was Maman's turn to go red in the face as she plucked at the fabric of her gown. There was a long silence, before Papa took a step forward and closed his fingers round her restless hand.

'It is done. Let us put it aside, Isabeau. My father already knows what I have done. I was angry to find you trusted me so little,' he said. 'But I suppose you judged me as the old, carefree Gabriel who'd left you for so long. I am back. I am changed. It is done. Let us speak no more of it.'

Maman brushed a tear from her eye, smiled and nodded.

'I will lead the nobles of Normandy if that time comes,' Papa announced. 'It is not only for the freedom to worship as we wish but there must also be a new way of governance in this land. As you say, those of the House of Guise are keen to seize back power. I will not take up arms against my king, but I will stand against *them*. If need be, I will fight.' Maman nodded again, but seemed to have lost her voice.

'In England I have met many who like us favour a new way,' said Papa. 'They may be able to persuade Queen Elizabeth to support us. She is ever wary lest Catherine de Medici should support the Scots.' As he raised his head I saw a new glint in his eye. He took Maman's elbow, guided her back to the bench and sat down beside her.

'Let us sit together. I have much to tell you.'

'Ah, yes,' Maman replied after she had dabbed her eyes with a kerchief. 'I have heard that the Queen of England is fearful that her cousin Mary of Scotland will steal a march on her, with help from France.'

'Yes, that's so, and I also think Queen Elizabeth is more likely to support us if she thinks she might regain what the English lost in Calais. I was received most kindly at her court, if with some curiosity. I have quite the reputation as the man who killed the king! But I found a good deal of sympathy too. I have made the acquaintance of Lord Robert Dudley, who favours our cause and has the queen's ear. I believe that William Cecil also leans our way, though he is a canny fellow and will do nothing to endanger his queen and country.'

None of that conversation meant much to me. I was just relieved to see that Papa was smiling as he stretched his legs out to get more comfortable and patted Maman's hand. After all that shouting it did seem strange they could sit down and talk together in such a friendly fashion. I thought perhaps that was the way of grown-ups.

Charlotte drew me back and we crept away. As I hurried up the stairs I was full of questions. But no matter how many times I asked Charlotte she couldn't or wouldn't tell me who that child might be. She did say their talk had something to do with priests and churches, something to do with the young king and his mother. But I really did not understand much of it. And I didn't really care. What did it matter to me whether the priest chanted in Latin or not? I was a bit disappointed that I could no longer carry my pretty beads as I had in Paris. Maman had collected them up and put them away in a sandalwood box after Pastor Forêt arrived. But so long as I could play with Fifi in the gardens and whisper secrets to Diane the doll at bedtime, none of it could be of any concern to me.

But soon it did concern me. Our family was pitched into preparations for war. Maman no longer had time to sit with we girls at our stitching. Instead she was forever dictating letters to the scribe and receiving black-clad men who came to talk long into the night with Papa. They were important noblemen and soldiers from all over northern France and beyond. Papa's friend, François de Bricqueville, Baron de Colombières arrived with the master of the city of Saint-Lo. My brother Jacques, strutting round as though he was already a fighting man, couldn't wait to set we girls straight on what was going on. He cornered Charlotte and me in the garden.

'Papa didn't use to care a fig about the mass. Hunting and jousting and serving the king, that was all that mattered to him,' my brother said in that annoying superior tone of his. 'Why, he even rounded up those who took up the new ways in religion when the old king asked it. Only a few years ago he and our grandfather gave lots of money to Avranches cathedral. But that's all changed now. He's done with all the images and all the Latin praters. He's all set to lead others against the Guises and against the fat priests. I can't wait to be old enough to serve alongside him.'

'Well, I just hate all this silly talk about religion and war,' I said, stamping my foot down so hard on the gravel path that stones flew everywhere. It was a bright cold morning and I was itching to run to the swing and have some fun. So, clutching Diane the doll with Fifi yapping at my heels, I left them to it.

As I leaned back on the swing, using my legs to fly higher and higher, I thought how silly Jacques was. He did so want to be a soldier. He was more than happy to take a place in Baron Colombières' household to sharpen up his skills. Gedeon went with him when the Baron left.

After Christmas I hoped our lives would go back to the way they used to be. But in the dark dreary days of a wet February things got even worse. Papa went to Dieppe.

'He's arming a fighting ship,' Charlotte said as we sat pretending to concentrate on our stitching. 'Jacques and Gedeon will join him.' She smiled when I gave a little cheer. 'Papa being away is nothing new,' she went on. 'When we lived in Paris he sometimes went off to fight. But that was always in the service of the king. This is different.'

My gentle, kindly, even-tempered mother brooked no arguments. She insisted we say our prayers every day and made us study with Pastor Forêt. How I hated those lessons. The wiry little man's piercing eyes stared at me through thick spectacles from beneath bushy grey brows. I was sure he could see right into my soul and knew every time I did anything even a little bit naughty. I always ended up wriggling in my seat, which meant I got a telling-off.

'He looks like a half-starved owl,' I wailed to Charlotte after one particularly uncomfortable lesson. 'He makes me feel like I'm the mouse he's going to pounce on.'

'Nonsense!' she replied tartly. 'Maman says he's a good man and we can learn much from him.' But then Charlotte frowned. 'Though I did hear the cook say he was a firebrand preacher of the new ways, whatever that may mean…' She sounded a bit uncertain and bit her lip. I didn't answer. To me he was simply horrid.

The law allowed people to worship in the way they wanted inside their own houses, but even I could see that wasn't much good for the poor people who lived in tiny hovels. So workmen came to consult Maman about the building of what she called a 'sermon' in Ducey, where all men and women could worship as their conscience dictated. It would be run, Maman said, not by priests but by a group of good people of the town. She called them the elders. So the house was full of people coming and going, and with all that going on Maman had no time for us.

After the end of March my mother became even more furious and tight-lipped. I overheard the servants whispering about something that had happened at a place called Vassy. Something about the Duc de Guise and lots of people killed in a barn. Details too dreadful for me to hear. I felt sick when I overheard Clotilde say to Alain, 'Whatever happened there, it's made Prince Condé call on all the Protestant people of France to rise up, to raise troops and to fight. So that's it! War! '

I thought it a strange thing for Papa to be on the side of those who fought against the king. But Charlotte, being so much older than me, told me it wasn't like that at all.

'He isn't really fighting against the king,' she explained. 'It's the Guise family we're fighting against – the Duc de Guise and his brother the cardinal. And we're fighting for the right to follow the Protestant way in religion. They're calling our side the Huguenots – because we worship in our homes, not in the old churches.' She puckered her fair eyebrows together. 'At least that's what I think it means,' she added.

Maman was so anxious for every scrap of information she rushed out to harangue any messengers before they had time to dismount. I copied Charlotte and started listening in on conversations. I crept up behind Alain du Bois one afternoon as he talked to Clotilde. 'The royalist side were taken by surprise,' Alain said with a chuckle. 'They couldn't muster their troops as quickly as we could. It's going well for our side. We hold Tours, Lyon, Blois, Angers, Poitiers and other places too. Master Gabriel helped take Bourges in May, and he's with Prince Condé in Orléans now.'

I tried to remember all those names so I could show Charlotte and Elisabeth how clever I was. I regaled them with all my newly acquired knowledge when we were weaving daisy chains and eating strawberries under the branches of a gnarled old pear tree already hung with tiny swelling fruit. To me they were just names, and I did forget Tours, but I don't suppose they noticed. Charlotte clapped her hands together and danced around, but I wasn't really sure what all the fuss was about. I spent as much time as I could playing in the gardens, where I could usually be found chasing Fifi between the clipped hedges while Diane the doll looked on. Of course, it could not continue.

Chapter Three

Follow the Drum

Summer 1562

'I wish everything could go back to normal,' I moaned, adjusting my position on the swing so I could watch a butterfly with wings like a swallow's tail dancing and dipping among the flat-topped flowers of cow parsley. With so many men away fighting, the gardens had been neglected and great drifts of wild flowers – a glorious riot of poppies, cornflowers and daisies – were creeping into the orchard under the trees where the grass hadn't been cut.

'Maman is always cross these days and Papa's never here. And I hate all the soldiers milling around by the river lighting their bonfires. The air reeks of smoke!' Charlotte smiled as I gave an exaggerated sniff. 'Some of them speak strangely and wear such odd clothes. They frighten me.'

'Perhaps it will soon be over,' Charlotte soothed from her place on the bench. She closed her book with a loud snap. 'From what I've heard, our side is doing well.'

'But what about those soldiers? Why are they here at Ducey? They are on our side, aren't they?' I demanded as my eyes flitted back to a column of smoke curling high into the sky. Charlotte squeezed herself onto the swing next to me.

'Of course they are. There's no need to worry. Papa is gathering troops to follow him into the fight. Some of the soldiers by the river come from a long way away and don't speak in French. They have to be paid to fight. Maman's writing letters to everyone she can think of to raise money to pay them all. Pastor Forêt says…' I pulled a face. 'He says a lot of valuable things have been taken out of the churches and stored on the tiny little island of Tombelaine, to be melted down to pay the soldiers. Do you remember that island, Roberda? We saw it when we went across the causeway to Mont St Michel that time?' I screwed up my eyes and smiled.

'I remember how green the grass was and the salty smell of the sea. Oh, and all the sheep and Mont St Michel shimmering and shining as if it was floating in the sky. And I remember the singing in the church,' I replied dreamily, distracted as I remembered that visit. It had been a welcome break from our routine when we were staying with Maman at Pontorson one summer. 'I don't remember any other island.'

'Well, it doesn't matter. But can you believe it? Papa has set up a mint to make coin on that island! Then he'll be able to pay the soldiers. Imagine making your own coin!'

'I don't care,' I shouted jumping off the swing. 'What's the use of money if it all has to go to pay soldiers? I've had enough of war. I don't want it here at Ducey! I hate it.' I picked up Diane the doll, who had been observing us from beneath a thistle where I'd dropped her in my haste to reach the swing, and stomped off, nearly colliding with Elisabeth who was drifting down the lavender-edged path followed by Fifi. Elisabeth never looked where she was going. I called Fifi and ran off towards the kitchens to see if I could sneak a spoonful of honey while cook's back was turned. Grinning, I licked the spoon and let the syrupy sweet honey, with its hint of lavender, tingle on my tongue.

I felt hot and sticky that sultry afternoon and was heading for a shady spot under the apple tree with my doll when Maman called us into the hall.

'We must prepare for a journey,' she said in the brisk voice she had used ever since Papa became such a great leader. 'News has come that the Royal Army has set off from Paris.' I dropped Diane onto the floor, crossed my arms and frowned.

'What's that got to do with us?' I demanded sullenly. 'Why do we have to go on a journey? I'd far rather stay at home.'

'It is no longer safe here. We have only low walls to protect us.'

'Walls that wouldn't keep out a fly,' murmured Charlotte. 'That's what Alain du Bois said.'

'Well, be that as it may,' Maman snapped, 'the truth of it is that the family of such a great leader as Gabriel de Lorges might be attractive hostages. So your papa has arranged that we should go to St Lo where we will be safe. The people there support our cause.'

'But, Maman, I don't want to go! I just want to stay at home at Ducey and play with Fifi in the gardens.' An awful thought struck me. 'I cannot leave Fifi behind,' I shouted, stamping my feet and flailing my arms about wildly. The words were no sooner out of my mouth when I knew my mistake. Maman put her hands on her hips and scowled at me.

'Gabrielle! You are a foolish, selfish child,' Maman raged. 'Your papa risks his life day in, day out to make a better world for you and all you think of is yourself and that dog! The animal must stay behind. There are more important things to worry about. Now look to your packing, girls. We leave at first light.'

Maman glowered at me then turned towards the solar stair. I saw her clenching her fingers behind her back and knew it was no use to argue.

As Clotilde threw my clothes into a travelling chest, I thought my heart would break. I just couldn't stop crying.

'I have a cousin in the village,' Clotilde soothed. 'She'll take the dog and see her fed for you.'

After lots of hugs and cuddles, Fifi was taken away by Clotilde's cousin, a rather stout woman in a grubby kirtle. I strained my eyes to watch the little white dog with her tail bobbing along until they were out of sight. Then I flung myself on the grass and wept until I could cry no more.

We all lined up ready to go; my brothers and sisters; little Giles and his nurse; Clotilde; three other maidservants; Pastor Forêt; Alain du Bois and the group of loyal guards he led. Grand-père Jacques, safe in his well-fortified mansion near Blois, had sent his newly purchased carriage so that Maman and her youngest children could travel in more comfort.

'I won't go in that thing,' I protested as Clotilde shoved Giles through the door. 'When we went to Pontorson that time the seats were so hard I felt every bump in the road. Every bone in my body ached for days afterwards.' If it had been left to Maman, I knew I'd have been in that carriage for certain. But I thought I might just be able persuade Papa to let me ride. Only a few weeks before he had praised my skill when I'd sat my pony when she'd shied at a rabbit that ran across the path. So when his horse drew alongside I smiled at him just as sweetly as I could.

'Papa, can't I ride my own pony, like Jacques and Gedeon?' I said pointing to the boys, already mounted up, ready to go. 'I'm a good rider. You said so,' I chirped.

'It's good to see you've dried your tears,' he said gently. 'I know you were upset to leave the dog. I'm sorry for that.' I held my breath as he looked earnestly into my eyes. For the first time in a long while I saw his white teeth flash in a fleeting smile.

'All right. You can ride in the mornings but you must go in the carriage when the sun gets high. We can't have you getting tired and slowing us down.'

I turned in the saddle for one last look at my home standing forlorn and abandoned with the windows all boarded up. I had to swallow hard to stop the sobs overtaking me again as I took my place in the long line of riders. Papa rode proudly though the countryside on a huge white horse at the head of a troop of mounted men. Then came the foot soldiers, some of the strange men I'd glimpsed by the riverbank among them, all marching in step to the beat of a drum. Maman's carriage and the wagons carrying our belongings completed the cavalcade.

The sun beat down from a clear blue sky as we rode along well-worn tracks through woods that stretched as far as I could see. Alain du Bois never left my side.

'Hmm! Not many dare to cheer on the great Huguenot army,' Alain murmured as we trotted through a deserted village. The horses' hooves stirred up a great cloud of dust and with the drum and everything we made quite a commotion, but there was no one in sight. 'Cowering behind closed doors, I'd hazard,' he went on. 'Afraid the soldiers might pillage the countryside and rob them of food. They needn't worry. Your father's intent on getting us to St Lo as quickly as might be. No foraging parties will leave the ranks.' I wasn't quite sure what he meant, but it was good to have him there trying to keep me amused by making his white beard bob up and down on his chest as we rode along, always keeping close to Maman's carriage.

With all the soldiers and baggage we were moving at a walking pace and could not complete our journey in one day. So we clattered into the yard of a pilgrim's inn and I spent an uncomfortable night in a bed with none-too-clean sheets before we set out for another long day on the road. At last I saw grey stone walls on the horizon, shimmering in the heat haze.

'That's St Lo – we're nearly there!' Alain told me, grinning and showing the gap in his front teeth. I followed his pointing arm and spotted a small group of riders approaching at speed.

'Coming from Orléans,' Alain muttered and reined in.

I screwed up my eyes, but I couldn't make out what colours they wore. Papa signalled to the soldiers to put down their weapons. I sighed with relief, for that meant they were not our enemies.

We watched Papa ride out to meet them and then the horsemen joined our column as we filed in through the city gates. No one had noticed that I'd ridden all day instead of going in the carriage when the sun was high. I was exhausted and aching and so relieved the journey was over, I forgot all about those riders.

It was when we were safe inside a merchant's house near the Church of Notre Dame that I noticed Maman's belly had grown large again. White-faced and unsteady on her feet, she disappeared to her chamber that first night leaving the rest of us with the servants.

As soon as Jacques and Gedeon arrived they started to question Alain, who was ordering men to guard the doors. I was glad to get away from all their talk of war when Clotilde took me yawning up the stairs. There were two small beds in the stuffy little chamber and I stood uncertainly in my shift, not sure which to lie on.

'You can sleep in this one with Charlotte,' said Clotilde. I supposed Elisabeth would have the other bed that was wedged against the far wall. I was soon fast asleep with Diane the doll tucked in beside me.

The bells clanging close to the window woke me early on that first morning. When I slipped out of bed I found myself face to face with a girl I had never seen before. She was about Charlotte's age and was sitting on the edge of the second bed where Elisabeth still lay snoring softly.

The girl glanced at me then went back to combing out her long auburn hair. As she turned her head, the morning sun streamed in through the little window and caught highlights among those abundant tresses; flashes of colour that reminded me of Maman's amber beads. I stared and felt a strange tightening in my ribcage. My own hair was a nice colour, down past my shoulders and fair like Papa's. But this girl's hair shone in the light in such a surprising way and was so long she could easily sit on it. I forced a smile onto my face and watched as the girl arranged braids around her head and put on a coif of the finest linen, all the time considering me with steady blue eyes. Eyes that made me shiver. They were exactly like my papa's eyes.

'Who are you?' I blurted out the words more loudly than I had intended. Charlotte raised her head from the pillow and rubbed her eyes. She sat up, smiled and in her sweetest voice she purred, 'There's no need to sound so cross, Roberda. This is Béatrice and she will be staying with us for a while.' My sister looked at the girl with such admiration I felt a bit sick.

After prayers with the odious Pastor Forêt we squeezed into the tiny parlour where the girl, Béatrice, joined us.

'Best settle in and look to your needlework, girls,' Clotilde advised. 'We're likely to remain in St Lo for some time.'

'I don't want to sit here and stitch day after day,' I whined. 'Can't I go out and explore the town?'

'Certainly not,' came the reply. 'I have strict instructions that you're to stay within the walls of this house, which Madame has said we are lucky to have at our disposal.' I scowled and looked longingly at the sunlight streaming through the tiny window. The poky little parlour was so small I was sure that, if I stood on tiptoe, I could touch the beams in the ceiling over my head. Béatrice had her head bent over her work as her needle made neat little stitches that soon spread a pleasing, regular pattern of black silk along the neckline of the shift she held lightly in her long fingers. Charlotte was casting admiring looks again. Elisabeth had for once set down her book and I could see from her face she was also coming under the spell of the tall slender girl.

'Well, I still don't know who you are, or what you've got to do with us,' I piped up in a voice I loaded with as much venom as I could muster. I gave her a belligerent stare and went on, 'You're not dressed as a servant but no one has introduced us, so you can't be from any noble family.'

As she turned her eyes on me, her voice was sweet as honey dripping from the spoon.

'I am Béatrice,' she said, as though that explained everything. I fixed my eyes on her in an icy glare. 'Where I come from there was sickness. My mother is dead,' she went on in that sickly sweet voice as she brushed a tear from her eye. 'I am to stay here with Madame de Lorges.'

'I'm sorry about your mother,' I mumbled, avoiding Charlotte's eye. 'But you've got a father, haven't you? Why can't you go to him?' Charlotte gasped but the girl gave a small shake of her head and just went back to her sewing. So I was none the wiser.

During all those long boring days at St Lo my sisters fawned over Béatrice. Every time I came into that horrid little parlour there they sat, heads touching over their sewing. One morning I found them trying a new way to braid their hair; on another they were giggling together over a book.

'What are you reading?' I asked, trying my best to be civil. But they just ignored me and went all quiet, as though they were hiding some great secret. I retreated to the bedchamber and cuddled Diane the doll.

'You're my only friend now,' I whispered, as my tears splashed onto the threadbare bedcover.

We hardly saw Papa. Clotilde looked uncomfortable when I asked her what he was doing. Eventually, at my persistent questioning, she let a few things slip.

'Your papa seems so very angry,' she said, shaking her head. 'Since those riders brought Mademoiselle Béatrice to join us, it's as if he's consumed with grief and he's taking it out on the whole world.' Her fingers plucked at her apron and her eyes went all cloudy. She didn't have that silly grin on her face, the one she usually had every time she mentioned Papa's name.

'It's said his name is heard with terror all over Normandy. They say he had his soldiers sack Mont St Michel and murder all the priests, and had the Bishop of Coutances dragged here on a donkey! It cannot be true. I cannot believe this of him. Your papa is a good man.'

I felt the back of my throat burning and thought I was going to be sick. *Clotilde must have got it wrong. My smiling, gentle papa couldn't have done those things.* I turned away with a shudder as I remembered the heavenly voices that rose up into the towering space of the abbey church when we visited Mont St Michel that time with Maman. I didn't want to think about blood being spilled in that magical place. *Whoever murdered those priests and put that old man on a donkey, it just couldn't have been my papa.*

With eyes nearly blinded by tears, I stumbled off and found Charlotte in the parlour sitting close to Béatrice in the window seat. It might have been better if Jacques hadn't been there slaking his thirst with a mug of ale when I came upon them. But I had to know.

'Clotilde says Papa has murdered ever so many priests and everyone hates him.' I blurted it out and felt my voice rising until it became a high-pitched screech. 'It just can't be true! He'd never do those things.'

'It's what happens in a war, you silly little girl,' Jacques barked before Charlotte could stop him. He put down the pewter mug with a clatter and smirked at me. 'All commanders must be prepared to do such things and order others to do them too.'

'Not our papa,' I yelled as the tears burned my cheeks. 'I'm not a silly little girl, Jacques. I know we want everyone to be able to worship God as they want and that's why we're fighting against the Duc de Guise and all those others. But I don't understand why Papa would get so angry that he did such horrid things. God wouldn't want that.'

Charlotte looked at Béatrice and raised an eyebrow. The girl shook her head. That made my blood boil.

'And I don't see what it's got to do with you,' I yelled, jabbing my finger towards Béatrice. 'He's *my* papa. I don't see what you have to do with anything!' Brushing off Charlotte's comforting hand I picked up my skirts and fled towards the door, only to collide with a white-faced Maman in the passage.

'I've had to struggle down the stairs to see what all this noise is about. Explain yourself,' she scolded as she put a hand to her back. When I mentioned Béatrice I saw the muscles in her jaw clench. But she spoke more kindly than I expected.

'Your papa is a leader of men in a time of war. There are things you cannot understand, my child. You are too young. Things it is best you do not know. You will hear all sorts of stories. Close your ears and do your best to behave with decorum. Believe me, it is the best way.' Her words came out all in a rush, and she turned back to drag herself up the stairs. I ran after her but she turned aside to her own bedchamber. I burst into our room and flung myself onto the bed clutching Diane the doll as I whispered, over and over, 'It can't be true.'

In the last week of July Clotilde told me I had a new baby sister, Suzette. Only a week later, a messenger arrived from Lorges. Grand-père Jacques was dead. I hardly knew my grandfather; he was always away soldiering, so this news hardly touched me. I suppose I was too busy feeling sorry for myself. But then I realised it meant Papa was now the Comte de Montgomery.

Maman struggled from her bed.

'We must make sure the news reaches your papa,' she announced. 'He must return to Lorges and see his father properly buried. It's near the royalist lines, but he must go.'

I had taken to hanging round the kitchens, hiding in the shadows, to catch the servants' gossip.

'Shocking! That's what it is,' the cook proclaimed, a few days later, as he brought down a meat cleaver with a thump. 'He should show proper respect. All he cares about is that now his father's dead he'll have money to pay his soldiers.' I slunk away, thinking he couldn't mean my papa.

'Alain du Bois says the tide of the war has turned,' Charlotte said with a worried frown as we sat again at the tedious sewing next morning. 'He says the royalists have been besieging Bourges for weeks now, trying to take the town back.'

'Well, I just hope it all ends soon. I don't really care who wins any more,' I muttered.

She gave me a stare but went on, 'Alain says Blois has been

ransacked, and that's near to Grand-père Jacques' house at Lorges. He thinks Orléans may be next in line.'

I sat moody and glum, wishing I was in the gardens at Ducey with Fifi. Elisabeth wandered in.

'There's been an outbreak of plague in Orléans,' she announced. 'Lots of people have been dying there for months now. So they won't attack there.'

Hmm, I thought, *didn't Béatrice come from Orléans?*

I found it quite hard to look at Papa who had only just returned from one of his sorties. He sat with a mug of ale in one hand and a document in the other. Maman blew in like a whirlwind, not realising we girls were still sitting on cushions in the corner.

'So your orders have come. You must lead the defence of the city of Rouen,' she croaked, sounding breathless and hoarse. Papa nodded. 'How may I best serve you in this new adventure?'

'It's not the first time Rouen has come under attack since we routed the Catholics there earlier this year. Our men fought hard in July to repel forces led by the Duke of Aumale.' Papa gave a bitter little smile. 'Fort St Catherine kept him at bay! But they've been harrying the city ever since. Now they've turned away from Orléans they'll attack Rouen in earnest. It's a good thing we still have access via the Seine. The merchants of Rouen have good trading routes to England…' Papa's voice petered out as he studied the bottom of his empty mug.

'You will know exactly how to defend the city, Gabriel,' Maman soothed. Papa frowned and turned towards her, as if he hadn't realised she was still there.

'I'm not sure it was such a good idea to have you all here with me. You've only just risen from childbed,' he said with a frown.

Maman narrowed her eyes.

'Let me tell you, Gabriel, there is much I can do in your support,' she insisted with a proud lift of her chin. 'And where else could we go? The lands around Ducey are in hostile hands. Lorges is even closer to royalist strongholds. Even Pontorson is not safe for us.' I remembered visiting my grandfather's solid stone house in Pontorson on our way to Mont St Michel. I had played with Elisabeth on the carved oak staircase. What fun we had slipping and sliding on the polished steps until Clotilde found us and told us to stop lest we fall. Maman had always said how much she liked the place. I'd have given anything to be back there.

Maman swallowed and shook her head.

'God alone knows how the people there fare or if the barn we had made into a temple for their worship still stands.'

'If only there was some word from the English,' Papa muttered, as he poured more ale from the jug. His hand shook and some spilled onto the floor spreading a dark stain on the stone slab. 'I had looked for something by now. The English queen must see we're in urgent need. 'He took a long draught from the mug and wiped his mouth on a crisp white napkin.

After a pause Maman gathered herself.

'Gabriel, our place, my place, is with you. I will write letters on your behalf to the English lords you have befriended. The Queen of England will stand good to her word. I'm sure of it.'

I didn't hear any more as Clotilde came and shooed us out of the room. Béatrice went out first and I noticed Papa's eyes following her. He had a very strange expression on his face as he ran a finger round the inside of the embroidered band at his throat. It was as if he too was becoming besotted with the stupid girl.

The next thing we heard was that we must pack and be ready to leave in the morning. Clotilde's voice carried all the way out into the passageway where we were waiting.

'Madame, you should not be riding out like this so soon. What of the poor babe?'

'I am as fit and well as I'll ever be, woman,' I heard Maman bellow back at her. 'The babe is hale and hearty. My husband has need of me. Make sure all is ready. We leave as soon as the sun is up.' There was no arguing with Maman.

After that we were constantly on the move. Back and forth we went, from town to town, like a shuttle in the loom. Caen, Honfleur, Le Havre, Dieppe, we saw them all more than once as Papa prepared for the defence of Rouen. I lost count of how many different houses we stayed in, how many nights we spent in roadside inns with lumpy beds and scratchy flea-ridden blankets. Wherever we went Alain checked the sentries and tested the locks.

'It's no fun riding any more,' I complained one day as we squelched behind Maman's carriage along roads awash. Storms had set in, bringing summer to an abrupt end. I could feel the wet seeping through my cloak and I was shivering. 'The rain never stops. I want to go home.'

'Courage, little one,' Alain answered. 'It is your father's wish that we go back to Le Havre.' But I could tell from his face that he didn't like it.

On the seventeenth day of September we stood at the quayside to wave goodbye to Papa who stood on the deck of a galley bound for Rouen. He kissed us all fondly – even Béatrice – and told Jacques it was his duty to look after his mother and all of us.

'Still no word from England. They've offered her Le Havre as a foothold on French soil. You'd think she'd go for that … when I was over there I could see how much the loss of Calais rankled.' Papa said, looking down at the floor. 'But still no word, nor any support either!' He screwed up his eyes and looked at the sky. 'The tide's on the turn; I must go.' He bent to brush Maman's lips with a kiss, a display of affection so unusual it made me quite frightened something very bad was going to happen soon. Then he was up the gangplank and waving to us as the galley glided into deep waters midstream to take the incoming tide.

Chapter Four

Under Siege

Autumn 1562

'Stay inside,' Alain warned when he came in from his latest round of inspection of the horrid little house in Le Havre. 'The town's overflowing with soldiers! Thank God that at last the Queen of England has sent the Earl of Warwick and all these men.'

'Not everyone wants English soldiers on French soil,' Clotilde replied with a worried frown. 'Two captains were thrown into the town gaol when we were in Dieppe for saying they wanted no English in their land.' She noticed me listening in and said more brightly. 'Most people here seem happy enough. Perhaps it'll soon be over.' I glanced at Alain and his gloomy face told a different story.

Clutching the books we were supposed to be studying we crowded round the parlour window when a messenger arrived. I turned away, sank down on a bench and threw my book aside.

'It's probably orders to move again. I'm so tired of it all. We ride for days in the rain and then we're stuck in another horrible house with no garden until we have to move on again.' Maman came rushing in.

'That will do,' she said sharply. 'As it happens we will soon join your papa in Rouen.' We all gasped.

'But isn't that where all the fighting is?' Charlotte quivered, glancing from face to face.

'What if it is?' demanded Maman. 'I must convince the

commander sent by the English queen to send urgent relief to your father there. When I have that agreement we will travel downriver to take munitions and supplies to the brave people of Rouen. May God be praised for the Seine! The royalists already control the roads.'

'But why must we go, Maman?' whimpered Elisabeth. Her face was the colour of ash in the grate and she was trembling.

'I won't go!' I shrieked, jabbing my finger towards Maman. 'You've dragged us all over France to Dieppe and back ever so many times. Now you want to take us to Rouen. Are you mad? Don't you know there's a battle going on? Right there in Rouen?'

'It's not for you to question. We will go!' Maman roared. 'Gather your bags at once.' I burst into tears and stumbled towards the stair. I was shaking so violently I felt dizzy and had to rush to the close-stool in my chamber. Then I looked around frantically for somewhere to hide but by now Clotilde was there, already packing our bags.

Clotilde held the pail, my stomach heaved and I nearly fainted, though the galley was still only rocking at anchor. Jacques leaned nonchalantly on the rail.

'You're no sailor, little Roberda,' he sneered.

'I don't ever want to be,' I shouted as I wiped the sweat from my clammy brow.

'Good thing it's such a short journey, and not even on the open sea,' Jacques teased. He turned to Alain du Bois. 'I've counted six huge brass cannons being hauled on board, and arquebuses. They're handing up powder and shot now from those little boats alongside.'

'Not nearly enough!' Alain growled. 'The English seem more concerned to fortify Le Havre than to send aid to Rouen.'

'Look, there's the English commander, Ambrose Dudley, Earl of Warwick,' cried Gedeon. 'He's brother to Lord Robert, the one Papa met.'

I followed his pointing finger to a tall man about my father's age standing on the quayside watching our ship loading. He was dressed in a rich, dark red doublet and wore a feathered cap set on one side over a sun-browned face with a fashionable beard.

'You should have heard Maman berating him!' Jacques laughed. 'If it weren't for her, I don't think we'd have got much help at all from the English. They've come to Le Havre, but they don't want to venture beyond for fear of stirring up the King of France. Our mother was magnificent!'

'I heard the earl say he hoped he would be there if ever Maman met his mistress the Queen of England. He said he was sure that lady would find a kindred warrior spirit in our maman!' Gedeon added, his face shining with pride.

'See the big red-faced Englishman standing next to him? That's Sir Henry Killigrew,' Jacques said. 'He says Rouen will be under siege in two days' time.' I spun round to face him, heart beating fast.

'Under siege? But that's where we're going!' I couldn't believe it. 'Alain says the royalists are hell-bent on breaching the barricades and storming the city. We'll all be killed!' My stomach couldn't stand the motion of the deck or, more likely, terror was gnawing away at my insides. I clung to the gunwale and emptied what was left of my breakfast into the River Seine.

We sailed from Le Havre on the incoming tide as dusk fell, drifting quietly down the broad river as it twisted and turned through low-lying water meadows. Other vessels, decks packed with soldiers, slipped along beside us. Only the soft slap of the oars and the creaking timbers broke the silence as the light faded. Clotilde took us to a cramped cabin where we all had to crowd in hugger-mugger. I slept fitfully on a little cot.

I woke with a start. Shouting, then a terrifying boom that made the boards under my little bed quiver and shake.

'They've set black powder to break through a line of pilings set up by the royalists,' Jacques called from the doorway. 'And they've strung a line of boats filled with sand and stones across the river. We need to break through that barrier too.'

I shuddered.

The air was filled with smoke and I caught a whiff of a sharp unpleasant stink like rotten eggs. It made me feel sick all over again and my fingers dug into the brocade fabric of Diane the doll's skirt. I was drenched in sweat and trembling at the same time, praying the ear-popping noises would stop.

Suddenly my prayer was answered. All was quiet and I could feel the ship moving again.

'We must have got past the barriers. I think the other boats have been less fortunate,' crowed Jacques, 'but we're through!'

Sometime later there was a thwack as the boat banged into the quayside. Alain du Bois carried me down the gangplank. I wriggled until I could take a peek at his face. It was set like stone. We followed Charlotte and Elisabeth. Behind us Giles squirmed to escape his nurse's grip, the baby bawled in the wet nurse's arms and the other servants struggled along with our belongings. Pastor Forêt caught up with us, eyes flitting everywhere as he minced along with his hands pressed together in prayer. In front of us all, Maman marched tall and straight right off the boat with Béatrice tripping along behind her as though she was just setting off for a picnic.

Alain set me down and led me along a cobbled street among smouldering timbers and debris to the lodgings Papa had prepared for us.

'These used to be the royal apartments, right next to the castle,' Alain told me.

'They don't look fit for royalty now,' I cried, casting my eyes round the empty chamber. The floor was bare, no tapestries hung at the walls and lots of the windows were broken.

Through the long days and nights that followed, we children huddled together, sometimes snatching a little sleep on makeshift beds. Most of the time we just waited. Pastor Forêt had us all praying – I suppose it did pass the time. Maman calmly took out her needlework and encouraged we girls to do the same. Béatrice was first to follow suit, sitting there beside Maman, using the light of the small window to work her magic with the needle. I studied her from beneath my brows. She looked as calm as if she was on a visit to some great lady in a well-appointed château, not sitting in a cold dreary fortress under siege. Maman was giving her warm looks. I longed to punch Béatrice on her smug nose!

I returned from my latest visit to the garderobe where the sharp ammonia smell had made me retch again to find Béatrice with Diane the doll in her hands. I saw red. I rushed at her, screeching like a demon.

'Give her back!' I yelled. 'She's my doll. Give Diane back to me!'

Béatrice was taller than I and she held Diane tantalisingly out of my reach as I kicked and screamed, but I had the satisfaction of feeling my left foot thump into her leg a few times. Charlotte jumped from her seat, caught hold of my arms and tried to hold me back. That made me squeal even louder.

'Why do you call the doll Diane?' Béatrice demanded in a voice no longer honey-sweet. 'Don't you know Diane was my mother's name?'

'I don't care if it was! 'I shouted. 'I called her that because she's always been my special friend. Just like the special friend Papa used to have. Her name was Diane too.'

Béatrice gasped. I looked into her cornflower eyes, so like Papa's, and all of a sudden I knew for certain who she was. I made a last desperate lunge, caught hold of Béatrice's arm and dug my fingernails in as deep as I could. She let out a yelp, relaxed her grip and I took my chance to claim my doll. With my prize secure I slunk away and hid under a heavy piece of canvas Alain had thrown over a stack of arquebuses he had in reserve.

I squeezed my eyes tight shut and clenched my fists, but I couldn't hold back the tears. My worst suspicions were confirmed. Béatrice's mother had been Papa's special friend.

I heard Maman scolding the others and Béatrice wailing that I'd made her arm bleed and bruised her legs. I heard Clotilde searching for me, her voice getting more and more insistent. But I stayed in my hiding place, sobbing my heart out, curled up next to a keg of powder. Much later when my empty tummy forced me out I ran to Clotilde. She gave me such a look, it was almost as if she'd turned into the not-Clotilde again. She took my hand in a firm grip and led me to Maman.

'This will not do!' Maman exploded. 'I can't have you shouting and squabbling while your papa is out there.' She jerked her head towards the window. 'You are not a wild child of the woods. You are the daughter of a noble house. You will never again brawl and scuffle with another to the point where blood is drawn. Do you understand me?'

When I plucked up courage to raise my eyes she looked so stiff and starchy, I knew my punishment would be severe.

'Your behaviour caused Charlotte and Béatrice to act in a most unseemly way. They will be punished, but less severely than you. You will have no supper and will spend this night and all of tomorrow on your knees with Pastor Forêt praying for forgiveness and for Papa's victory.' I did feel a bit guilty that the others had got into trouble because of me, but I tossed my head and crossed my arms over my chest.

'I won't apologise,' I insisted. 'It's all because of Béatrice!' Maman sighed, came closer and spoke more gently.

'You are lucky that I do not beat you,' she sighed. 'I understand more than you know. I too have struggled to accept that which you now understand. Béatrice is your half-sister. We women must accept such things. Learn that lesson well, Roberda.'

A day and a night on my knees with the ghastly little pastor certainly gave me a lot of time to think.

In all the time we were cooped up in those cold cheerless rooms, only on one day did I dare to stand on tiptoe by a window and peep out. I jumped back straight away, clapping my hands over my ears to block out the dreadful noise of the guns and the screams. I steeled myself to scrunch over scattered glass, long since blown from the window, and take another look. Spirals of grey smoke snaked up from a jumble of blackened wood, all that had once been fine houses, while wagons, piles of timber, tables and benches were all piled up higgledy-piggledy; a last desperate barrier should the enemy breach the city walls.

I watched as a straggly line of women, old men, even children younger than me picked their way through the debris. Each carried a stone so heavy they could barely lift it. With grim determination they stumbled to the top of the walls and hurled those rocks down onto the attackers, then scurried back down for another. My eyes fixed on one crooked old woman bent near double at the top. As she let go of the huge stone she lost her footing and I could not wrench my eyes away as she tumbled, red skirts and apron flying above her head, until her screams were silenced as she hit the ground with a sickening thump.

Horrified, I flicked my eyes away and back to the top of the wall. One of Papa's soldiers had raised his head above the ramparts to take aim at the besiegers. Perhaps he was an officer, for I could make out a surprisingly white ruff band at his throat. Before he could fire his face erupted, a fountain of blood spurted out and pieces of his ruff scattered to the winds. The hand I raised to block out the gruesome sight froze halfway. Knocked back by the force of the shot, he swayed on his feet and his arquebus fell, bumping down the walls, ever so slowly, until it landed with a crash in the cobbled street. When I shot a look back to the top of the wall his body was bent over the ramparts. Then he was gone. Swallowing down the bile that had risen in my throat I put my head in my hands. I didn't look out of the window again.

'Your face is a white as a bedsheet,' chuckled Jacques, giving me one of his most patronising looks. He was gleefully watching the progress of the siege as though it were just a tourney. 'The royalists have got thirty thousand men! They've dug in with trenches beyond the walls, but we'll keep them out as long as Fort St Catherine holds.' I shuddered and turned to make my escape. But my legs didn't want to work. So I had to listen as Jacques went on, 'The English have sent four or five hundred men. They lost some in the Seine.' *Pitched into the river at those same barriers we only just got through*, I thought.

'I don't care,' I whimpered, but it was as if Jacques hadn't heard me.

'They're trying to get more men down the river,' he said.

'Not sufficient and much too late!' grunted Alain du Bois who had come to stand beside Jacques among the shards of broken glass beneath the window. 'The English should remember the heart of their Lionheart lies in the cathedral of Notre Dame here in Rouen.'

'There's Papa,' Jacques cried, eyes shining. 'See, there, on his white horse; he's rallying the troops. He'll urge them to the barricades if the fort falls,' he went on excitedly. 'He's threatened to shoot any deserters on the spot! He won't give in.' He grabbed my wrist and tried to pull me to the broken window again. My stomach lurched as the stench of powder and rotting corpses drifted in. Somehow I managed to break free and ran, desperately trying to shut my ears to the cries of the wounded and the dying that followed me.

Through it all, Maman sat serenely at her needlework, stately and defiant. Clotilde and the other servants tended Giles and my baby sister. Pastor Forêt prayed a lot. We ate such little food as could be spared – coarse stale bread, hard cheese, a few onions and some wizened apples. The portions got smaller every day. My tummy growled and ached. I would even have relished a bowl of steaming pottage, however greasy it might be.

It was almost a relief when, a few days later, Jacques burst in.

'Fort St Catherine has fallen! But they say that Antoine, Duke of Bourbon, leader of the attackers, is like to die. Took a shot to the shoulder while he was directing the attack. They've sent for Dr Paré. Remember him?' I grimaced and shut my eyes. 'He's the one who tried to save King Henri.' I didn't want to hear any more, but he wouldn't stop. 'Now they're preparing mines to blow us all up while the dowager queen watches from the hill outside the city. She'll want to parlay; she won't want Rouen completely reduced to ashes.'

I put my hands over my ears.

'This is all so stupid,' I shouted. 'I just want to go home.' But no one was listening to me.

It was late in the afternoon on the twenty-first day of October – Jacques told me the date – when Papa appeared, covered in dirt and sweat. I cringed when I saw the blood on his clothes.

'That's it, Isabeau, some treachery has delivered the fort to them,' he said in a shaky voice. 'They've breached the city walls. You could ride a horse through. They're upon us. We can do no more.'

'Gabriel,' she answered firmly. 'Montmorency is leading them. He will not harm women and children, but they must not find you here. Clotilde! Bring the master's razor.' Clotilde scurried off. Her hands were shaking when she passed the razor to Maman.

'Shave off your beard, Gabriel. If you're taken, they will not know you.' So he did and then he pulled off his bloody doublet and put on a rough tunic Alain du Bois held out to him. In no time Papa was gone.

Maman didn't seem surprised he'd left us to wait for the victors to find us. None of us slept much that night. It was barely light when the soldiers banged on the door.

'You must come with us. Marshall Montmorency orders it,' the leader barked. We were marched off to face de Montmorency, the Constable of France. Maman had us all stand round her as she looked the ageing soldier in the eye. The grizzled old man looked hot and uncomfortable in a dark doublet with half-armour over the top.

He studied us one by one. His lips twitched a little when he came to Maman who stood unbowed before him. It occurred to me that Maman must have known him years ago when Papa was Captain of the Guards, when everything had been all right.

'Madame la Comtesse,' he said, with a nod and just the hint of a knowing smile. 'All His Majesty's faithful servants are deeply saddened by your husband's conduct. As for you,' he waved his hand to show he meant all of us, 'you have nothing to fear. Tomorrow you will hear the wishes of the queen. You may expect them with confidence.' I hoped that meant he might appeal to the queen to treat us well. But then I remembered: she would not have forgotten it was Papa who killed her husband. We passed another sleepless night in the dismal draughty chamber that had become our prison.

Charlotte held my hand tight when Montmorency came to our lodgings next morning.

'Madame, you and your children are free to return to your husband. We believe he has escaped to Le Havre. The queen charges you to reason with him. You must persuade him to lay down his arms and serve his king.'

Montmorency must surely have heard the deep gusty breath whooshing out of us all as we heaved a collective sigh. Papa had managed to get away and we were free to go! But the old soldier had not delivered the queen's message in full.

'Madame, you have in your party a girl called Béatrice? Is it so?' Maman nodded. 'Which of you is Béatrice?' he asked with a beaming smile. In another life he'd have looked like a kindly old uncle.

I looked up and smirked as Béatrice stepped forward.

'Ah, yes! You have your mother's bright shining hair. Diane was quite a beauty as I remember,' he said. A sharp tut came from Maman as she shut her lips tight together.

'Mademoiselle, it is the queen's wish that you join her household. You are to sever all connection with your father, the Comte de Montgomery. It is at the request of the king's staunch supporter, your uncle Gaspard de Tavannes. He would have you receive a good Catholic education.'

My mouth dropped open. She was going! Maman made no protest and my heart started to sing. Béatrice didn't look at any of us as Montmorency gave his order.

'Have your belongings packed within the hour and be ready to come with us.'

When later I entered the cramped little space where we had been confined for so long I found Béatrice tearing her hair and throwing things around. Flinging a jumble of our clothes aside in a heap, she turned to me with tears in her eyes.

'The hour is up. The soldiers are here to take me away,' she moaned. 'But I can't find it.'

'Whatever are you talking about?' I demanded.

'*Mon trésor*! It is lost,' she wailed. 'It's all I have of my mother and I can't find it. I've searched everywhere, but it's not here.' She scrambled about on the floor, lifted up the slop pail and spilled its smelly contents over the rushes then turned Charlotte's sewing basket upside down. At last she threw up her hands and sat down on the bed with a thump.

Charlotte took her hand.

'You must go; they are waiting,' she whispered, hugging Béatrice close.

'I cannot,' Béatrice cried.

'You must,' Charlotte insisted.

It suddenly came to me that Maman would not be pleased if Béatrice caused trouble by keeping the soldiers waiting. I might be able to get back into Maman's good books if I offered to help find whatever it was Béatrice was looking for. I think I actually began to feel a bit sorry for Béatrice too. After all, it wasn't really her fault she was who she was and it must be quite frightening to be suddenly whisked away and told you would never see your father again.

'You go down with Charlotte,' I offered. 'Go down, but be as slow as you can, while I carry on searching.' Béatrice's eyebrows shot up and she shook her head slowly in disbelief.

'You? You will search for it for me? You will search for it?' Béatrice spluttered. She stumbled a few steps towards the door, then turned back and stood wide-eyed right in front of me. 'I can't believe you would do such a thing.'

'Roberda will search, won't you?' Charlotte confirmed and I nodded. 'Come.' She led the protesting girl to the door, struggling with the bag Béatrice was too distracted to lift.

I looked again beneath the jumble of clothes and then turned to the second bed to reach under the pillow. As I stretched across I felt something hard beneath my arm. I rummaged under the rough blanket and pulled out a pretty ring on a golden chain. I held it up to the light and saw that the clasp was broken. I'd often seen Béatrice wearing that chain round her neck, often watched those long fingers turning the little ring over and over. With Béatrice's treasure clasped tight in my hand I flew down the stair as fast as I could.

I was almost too late. Béatrice was already in the saddle, perched on a heavy-legged brown mare that was shambling towards the gateway in the wake of two burly soldiers. I called out her name. Béatrice hauled on the reins. When she turned, her eyes looked as big as meat platters. I dodged past Alain and Charlotte, raced across the cobbles nearly tripping over my gown, reached up and pressed the ring into her hand.

'It was my mother's,' she murmured as she slipped the ring and chain into the leather pouch at her waist. Then, with tears streaming from her eyes, she called out as the horse started to move. 'How can I ever thank you? I shall never forget.' The soldiers signalled impatiently for her to keep up and with a flutter of her hand she was gone.

Chapter Five

The Orphan Boy

1563-1566

I was so happy to escape the horrors of Rouen I didn't have time to feel sick as the boat carried us back to Le Havre. We found Papa waiting there and crowded round to hear how he had escaped.

'Some soldiers spotted me leaving the palace. I fought a couple off with my sword but then I had to run for it,' he laughed. It didn't seem to me to be a laughing matter, but evidently Papa was in high spirits. 'What do you think I did? I sprinted for the quay and jumped into the water! It was getting dark and, thank God, they could not see me well enough to shoot me. I was lucky. I swam to a galley with slaves at the oars. With the promise of freedom when we reached Le Havre they agreed to row me back down the river. So here I am.'

With blue eyes shining he greeted each of us in turn. His face felt all scratchy when he hugged me. Then he turned to Maman with a frown.

'But where is Béatrice?' We left Maman to explain and I slept well in the small house near the port, which didn't seem half as bad as I'd thought it before.

After prayers with the little preacher, who was ever more zealous in his desire to instruct us, we all joined Maman and Papa in the parlour.

'I must go to London to persuade Queen Elizabeth to engage more fully in this war, Isabeau,' Papa announced. 'I'll go first to Jersey, where I have a galley I would present to her. Perhaps that will sway her to send it back with more arms and men. You and the children may accompany me to the island and await my return.'

The ship pitched and yawed over the crashing waves and I spent the whole journey with my head hanging over the side, spewing the contents of my stomach into the water to feed the fish. I felt as weak as a day-old kitten by the time we sighted the fortress on top of Mount Orguel.

'Thank God,' I murmured as we docked in St Helier. That earned me a reproving look from Pastor Forêt, but I didn't care. I knew that high on the hill above the town Papa had a house. Not a tiny town house like those we'd had to endure in so many places as we followed him on the campaign trail, but a house almost as spacious as Ducey, surrounded by pretty gardens. Even though autumn winds blew chill and the leaves were falling, it was beyond joy for us children to run about, gulping down great lungfuls of fresh salty air. Oh, the pleasure of swishing our well-shod feet through piles of crisp and crinkly leaves. For a few short weeks we felt safe, we felt free.

After a quiet and peaceful Christmas on the island, on a frosty January morning Maman sat by the window, a message in her hands.

'At last we have news from your father,' she said. 'Not the news we hoped for. His timing could not have been worse. He found Queen Elizabeth sick with the smallpox.' My heart nearly stopped, but Maman's next words reassured me. 'Thank God she has survived, and Papa is well. But many died and many survivors are marked for life. Your papa has returned to Le Havre. He says we may rejoin him.'

Another crossing in winter seas to meet my father sounded mad to me. But this time I didn't waste my breath in protest. By the time we got there Papa was in Dieppe and that was where we went to meet him. I shuddered as I heard Alain du Bois give the order to double the guard on the doors.

'I wish we were still in Jersey,' Charlotte whispered. My stomach rumbled as we watched Maman put her signature to another letter.

'I have written to tell the Queen of England that your father is gone and she must send forces or Dieppe will be lost.' *May woe betide the Queen of England if she does not heed the request of my imperious mother,* I thought.

A few days later Papa stormed in and I could see from his flushed face that he was furious.

'I am recalled,' he growled. 'Condé has accepted terms. It is over.'

'Whatever do you mean?' Maman asked. With her lips curled back and her nose all wrinkled up, she looked at Papa as though he'd crawled out from under a stone. 'Gabriel! We cannot give up so easily!'

'I can do no more,' he sighed. 'While I was in England we suffered a defeat at Dreux. Our men captured Montmorency ... but still we were defeated. We suffered heavy losses. Many were taken prisoner, including Prince Condé himself.'

Jacques jumped in. 'I heard someone fired at the Duc de Guise in Orléans, and that his surgeons bled him, but he's dead.' Trust Jacques to want the gory details. Papa had his legs planted wide apart. He was flexing his fingers.

'It can be no bad thing to be rid of that man,' Maman exclaimed.

'Perhaps, but none of that matters. I am recalled!' he barked. 'There's some sort of agreement, a truce. Condé's been released. He accepted terms that give freedom for worship for some, but only within their own houses.' He turned to Maman who stood wringing her hands beside him. 'Can this be enough, Isabeau? Was it all for this?' Papa shook his head, passed his hand over his eyes and heaved a great weary sigh. And then he said the words I had been longing to hear.

'We will go back to Ducey.'

I was dancing with joy. We were going home!

The countryside looked very different from the woods and neat fields we had ridden through when first we left Ducey. We passed burned-out cottages, villages raised to the ground, ragged tree stumps where the wood had been cut for campfires and fields of charred stubble where new shoots should be showing green. A trickle of poor people stumbled along, eyes cast down, carrying on their backs what little they'd been able to salvage from the lives they lived before the war. I turned my head aside every time we passed a rotting corpse by the road. The thought of Ducey kept me going.

When we arrived, late one afternoon, I felt as though my chest was full of fizzy bubbles, but at the same time my mouth was bone dry. At the gate I put a hand up to shade my eyes and squinted. Then my mouth dropped open. I blinked hard and almost forgot to breathe.

Ducey was a sorry sight. A tangle of brambles covered the walls and the gardens were completely overgrown, weeds smothering the once neatly clipped hedges. Only the white rose flowered valiantly beside the door, thrusting its thorny branches through the muddle.

I handed the reins to a waiting boy and we picked our way through broken platters and shattered glass. A large patch of scorched earth showed where the boards that had covered the windows, and who knew what else, had been piled up and set alight. Inside the house it was even worse. We rushed from room to room. All the twinkling windows were smashed, doors stove in, curtains pulled down, polished floors littered with rubbish left by looters who had ransacked every room. My lovely home, the haven I'd been pining for, was utterly destroyed.

'At least we're safe,' said Charlotte, giving my hand a squeeze.

'Yes, I suppose so,' I replied with a hesitant smile. 'We are home, even if it doesn't look like home just now.' I felt my heart lift. 'Soon I'll find Fifi. She'll be squirming with excitement to see me again.'

It was Clotilde who told me, ever so gently, that my little dog was no more.

'Fifi was caught beneath the hooves of the soldiers' horses,' she said in a voice as soft and gentle as a silk gown on a polished floor. 'Poor little mite! She couldn't get out of the way when the village was overrun.' I felt dizzy and sagged back onto a bench, putting both my hands over my face as I tried to shut it out. But I kept seeing it over and over; my Fifi, my little friend, crushed under flailing hooves.

Dazed and numb, I wept angry salt tears as I tried to sleep in the gutted remains of the maidens' chamber. That night the nightmare came for the first time. I heard the screams and the booming guns. I smelled the blood. I saw the old woman falling from the crumbling walls of Rouen. I saw the soldier with the exploding face. I saw Fifi crushed and bleeding as I tossed feverishly on the bed. It was pitch black when I opened my eyes and sat bolt upright. Befuddled and still locked in the dream, I screamed.

Charlotte crept across from her bed and put her arms around me to try to still my shaking.

'It's all right,' she soothed. 'I'm here. There, there, it's all right. It's just a bad dream. We're home. Nothing can hurt you now.'

Clotilde, woken by my screams, bent over and tucked us in. Her face was wrinkled with a frown as I started to whimper again.

'Hush now,' she crooned. 'Try to sleep.' But sleep would not come. Despite Charlotte's comforting arms, I couldn't shut out the horrible vision; the old woman falling, the faceless soldier and Fifi in a puddle of blood.

So started a pattern. By day I jumped nearly out of my skin at any loud noise; I had stomach ache; my head throbbed. By night the demons of Rouen haunted me.

Clotilde's cousin took me to the little grave under the apple tree beside the swing where she had buried my Fifi. I laid a bunch of bluebells in front of the wooden cross Alain carved with her name. Charlotte and Elisabeth and little Giles stood by solemnly, heads bowed. Pastor Forêt, in an unexpected show of compassion, said a prayer. As we walked slowly back to the house Alain turned to Clotilde.

'I'll find her another puppy. She's been through so much. It might help her heal,' he said. I knew he meant well, but couldn't bear to think of replacing my friend.

'That is a kind thought,' I said, surprising myself with the dignity of my words. 'But I would sooner remember Fifi than have another.'

The nightmares continued. Charlotte and Elisabeth tried to lull me to sleep by telling happy stories. Clotilde brought me bedtime drinks infused with camomile and put lavender bags under my pillow. Gradually I began to understand what Clotilde had been trying to teach me: to put my bad memories away in a box and hide them on a high shelf where I could never reach them. Only then did I begin to sleep a little more easily.

While I struggled to put away my nightmares, plenty of carpenters and joiners were happy to come to the aid of my papa; the man they called Captain. The old walls echoed with their singing and laughter and the sun shone that summer. The gardeners returned and soon the grass was clipped, the flowers bloomed and apples hung from the bough. Gradually, it began to feel a bit more like home again.

But I was worried Papa would not be content to play the part of a country squire for long. One morning I screwed up my courage and tackled him.

'I am sorry to disturb you, Papa.'

'It's of no moment,' he replied, shuffling the papers on his desk so I wouldn't see what he was writing. 'I am merely sending to my lord of Warwick about a consignment of wine for our cellars here in Ducey.' I suspected he might have other reasons for keeping in touch with the English earl.

'Will there be war again, Papa?' I demanded. I had his attention and wasn't going to let the moment pass. The long pause before he replied gave me all the answer I needed. 'Well, Roberda, the concessions towards freedom of worship are not so generous as we might hope,' he admitted at last. 'But let us see how things develop. It may be that the peace can continue.'

I was not going to be fobbed off so easily.

'But will your English friends help us if war comes again?' I asked, feeling very daring to be so direct. 'Will the Queen of England send money and men?'

'That I cannot say. Whatever is in her heart as far as religion is concerned – she may well be as true a follower of the reformed way as your Maman and I – she'll do nothing to put her country at risk. She'll be friends with France if that keeps Spain at bay and vice versa when it suits. I know men in England who are staunch friends. Perhaps in time… But these are weighty matters for you to understand, Roberda. Never fear. Trust me. All will be well.' He patted me on the head and started to shoo me away.

'I don't believe you, Papa,' I shouted, glaring at him. 'I hate war. Fifi is dead because of war. Ducey was ruined because of the war. Can't we stay at home?' He kept his eyes on his papers. 'You'll go off fighting and it will be as bad as last time,' I cried. 'If you do, I'll hate you, Papa.' I ran from the room leaving him shaking his head.

As I had feared the peace agreement that had allowed us to come home soon started to unravel. As the scythes were busy with a meagre harvest, word came to Ducey that Queen Catherine had declared her son Charles, who was now of age, King of France. And by the time the autumn leaves were falling, Papa was away again.

Just before Christmas of 1564 it started to snow. A chill wind wormed its way under doors to nip at our toes and stir up the rushes on the floor, piling them in dank corners and exposing the cold stone beneath. For days on end we huddled at the fireside, cocooned in layers of thick woollen blankets.

One morning a weak and watery shaft of sunlight crept in through the window. Desperate to get out, I pulled on an extra cloak, tied wooden pattens beneath my shoes and pushed the door open. I gasped as the icy air hit my lungs like a punch in the ribs and was soon skittering along the icy path someone had cleared towards the kitchen door.

'Whatever are you thinking of to go outside in such weather!' Clotilde scolded. 'Go back to the warmth. I've never known such cold as this in all my days. When the kitchen maid crept out to feed the hens this morning she found the cocks without their combs. The very crests from their heads froze solid and have fallen off!' I shuddered and rushed back to rejoin my sisters huddling together for warmth.

'Maman,' I said. 'We have a warm fire to sit by. How do the poor people of Ducey manage?' But she merely shook her head and twisted her hands together. I asked the same question of Pastor Forêt, but he had no answer for me either.

The cold driving rains and then the melting snow had the River Sélune bursting its banks. Dirty, brown and smelly, the water lapped up against the walls round our home and damp dank air seeped into our clothing and our beds.

'The fields are under water,' Alain said one morning in early February as he laid his sodden cloak out before the kitchen fire where soon tendrils of steam were rising up from the cloth. 'The winter wheat is rotted in the furrow, there's dead sheep everywhere.'

When spring did come mild winds dried out the land and we rejoiced to see the sun. But Alain said it was too late to save the crops.

'It'll be another poor harvest. Plenty of empty bellies come next winter,' he said gloomily. But we had plenty in our storerooms and ate well.

When better weather came we were allowed to ride out with Alain and an armed guard in attendance. I was bubbling over with excitement and couldn't help grinning as we trotted beneath the trees.

As we came into the village I saw a boy no older than Giles sitting on the ground by the bridge. He scrambled up unsteadily; barefoot, all skin and bone with dull brown eyes, far too large for his haggard little face. Those great hungry eyes held mine, sending a chill down my spine. Alain waved me onwards. I kicked my pony forward but turned in the saddle and looked long at the boy until he was just a tiny dot beside the bridge. All that day I couldn't get him out of my mind.

'It can't be right that we have plenty to eat, all that food in our stores, while a boy in our village is starving,' I muttered to Charlotte. But she went on with her sewing.

Next morning I rose early. I sneaked down the stairs and into the storeroom before the kitchen servants were up and about, found an empty flour bag and collected up some bread and cheese and old apples. With the bag hidden under my cloak I breezed into the dairy to beg a cup of milk from a startled dairy maid. A few drops splashed from her overfull pail, the first of the morning's milking. Last night's pans stood on the cold shelf with their luscious layer of cream on top and I almost forgot why I was there, I was so tempted to dip my finger in. But then I remembered the boy with the huge staring eyes.

'Pour me a mug and put a muslin over the top,' I commanded airily. 'I'll take it with me and drink it in the garden.' The maid complied. While Alain was inspecting the guard there was just time for me to slip through the gate without his spotting me. I dared not run lest I spill the precious milk but, walking as fast as I could, I was soon on the bridge. I looked round desperately, but the boy was nowhere to be seen. I sighed and turned, about to retrace my steps when a small movement caught my eye. I found him huddled beside the wall, weaker than ever. He seized on the food I offered like a ravening dog and then gulped down the milk.

'Do you have strength to walk?' I asked. He nodded. 'Follow me to the château then,' I ordered. He only hesitated a moment. By some miracle we got through the gate without drawing attention. I hustled him round to the barn behind the stables. The horses had been taken to water and there was no one about.

'Up there,' I commanded, pointing to the ladder that rose to the hay loft. 'If you keep to the back and cover yourself with hay, no one will find you.' I watched him clamber slowly up the ladder and sauntered away.

I managed to keep the boy hidden for three days, taking him what little food I could steal each day. At first he would say nothing but with gentle coaxing I discovered that his name was Pierre and his parents were dead. He was the only one of his family left.

I carried on sneaking titbits of food from the table when no one was looking and oh, it felt so good, to see those empty hungry eyes turn to pools of warmth and gratitude.

On the fourth day Clotilde followed me as I carried away my latest offering.

'Whatever are you doing, you foolish girl,' she cried as her head peeped over the top of the ladder. She cuffed Pierre on the ear and dragged him down. 'Come, both of you. You must answer to Madame.' She marched us off to face the wrath of Maman.

Charlotte, Giles and Elisabeth looked on with their mouths open as Maman raised her eyebrows and fixed me with her most ferocious look.

'We have been neglecting our duties to the poor people of Ducey,' I announced in the strongest voice I could muster. I was quailing inside but kept my voice low and steady. 'Yes, we have,' I said, with my eyes on Maman. 'This poor boy was near starved to death when I found him. His parents are dead; his father followed Papa to the fighting and was lost; his mother tried to make a living from her spinning but with so little to eat could not survive the winter. His younger brothers and sisters are all dead. He has no one to care for him. Where is our Christian charity, Maman? Is it not our duty to give help to one such as he?'

I turned to Pastor Forêt, who stood behind Maman's chair with his nose in the air.

'Sir, did you not teach us that in one of his sermons Master Calvin said that the rich must consider the poor as their poor? That we must show our thanks to God by practising generosity? Pierre is of our village; he is our poor!' The pastor flushed red and wiped the sweat from his brow. It was one of the lessons he was always going on about.

Maman's lips twitched and she looked from me to Pierre and back again. I had expected she would beat me for sure, but when she looked into Pierre's eyes I saw her expression soften.

'You should have come to me, not skulked around stealing food and hiding him,' she remarked. I threw up my head, mistaking her quiet tone for anger.

'So will you abandon him?' I cried. 'Leave him to die by the roadside? You and Papa are too busy fighting stupid wars while the poor people starve. When he's well he could work scaring birds in the fields or carrying firewood.' Pierre nodded his head vigorously and to my amazement I saw a slow smile creeping across Maman's face. I heard my sisters and Giles gasp. This was not what any of us had expected.

'You are right. We should aid the poor people. Just this once I will forgive your disobedience. As soon as he's strong enough, he must make himself useful. But this must not happen again. It is not safe for you to take in any passing vagabond.'

'Yes, Maman,' I said, meek as a lamb. But I kept my fingers crossed behind my back. That was one promise I certainly didn't intend to keep. I shot a triumphant look at Pastor Forêt. *Ha! That's taken the irritating holier than-thou-look off your face! You'd better not try to lecture me about Christian charity again.*

The months passed and Pierre grew stronger and was found work in the kitchens. Every time he saw me he beamed. His great brown eyes reminded me of Fifi.

Giles was breached that summer and Suzette was joined in the nursery by another baby, a boy called Gabriel, after my father. Following my small act of charity Maman stepped up her own efforts to aid the villagers. New serving women appeared as Maman found work for those left with no man to provide for them and I often went with her to give out alms or to buy produce from those who had anything to sell.

'The boy is doing well,' said Maman, nodding at Pierre as he carefully stacked the platters one late September afternoon. 'He's proving quite useful. He may stay and offer round the spiced biscuits and refill our mugs while we watch the play.' I clapped my hands together. It was a rare treat for we girls to be allowed to put aside our books and our sewing to wonder and laugh at the juggler, tumblers and minstrels who came to Ducey to entertain us. Soon we were all tapping our feet to their merry tunes and songs. I grinned at Pierre who stood motionless in the shadows, mesmerised by a man who was conjuring up stirring melodies from a little fife while another shook a tambourine. Even Maman joined in the applause when the players took their final bow.

'Bravo! Bravo!' she cried. 'You have entertained us well. You may go to the kitchens for some refreshment before you continue on your way.' They started to pick up their belongings but as Maman was heading for the stairs she called back over her shoulder, 'You may leave all your instruments here. The boy will keep watch.' Charlotte and Elisabeth tripped along after Maman, chatting about the show, but I hung back just beyond the hangings. Keeping myself hidden, I watched Pierre take a furtive look around the hall. Once he was sure we had gone he walked over to the musician's pack and took out the little fife from among the bundle of instruments.

After another surreptitious glance over his shoulder he wiped the fife on his doublet and put it to his lips. At first no sound came at all. I nearly gave myself away by bursting out laughing when his second attempt produced a noise just like the yowl the kitchen mouser gave when Suzette pulled her tail. But then clear notes started to flow, soon a little tune, stumbling at first but then more confident as he worked out how to move his fingers. Pierre played on until sounds from the direction of the kitchens announced the minstrels' return. As swift as an arrow from the bow he replaced the fife and picked up the tray of mugs. He nearly collided with the musician in the doorway.

'Was that you with my fife?' the man asked.

'I'm sorry, sir,' Pierre quaked. 'I did but wish to know how such sounds could come from a stick with holes along it. I have returned it with no damage done.'

'It's all right. I can see that,' the musician laughed. 'But you have a gift, boy, a true gift for music.' Pierre's face turned bright red and he fled.

I rushed out from my hiding place and approached the man who swept off his feathered cap and gave me a most elegant bow.

'How may I be of service, young mistress?' he asked.

'I see you have several of those instruments in your pack. Would you sell one to me?'

'Ah! I can guess why you'd suggest that,' he replied with a smile. 'You heard the boy play?'

'I did. I would buy it for him. Wait while I find my purse.'

'Mistress,' came the respectful reply. 'The coin would be most welcome to clothe my children. But I would forgo it and make a gift of that fife. The youngster has a talent that is rare indeed. He must be encouraged.'

'No, no! You must be paid. Wait here!' I cried, and ran from the hall bumping into Clotilde, sent to find me. '*Vite*, Clotilde! Bring me the leather purse Maman gave to me to spend at the fair. *Vite*!' She looked at me questioningly. 'I need to buy the fife for Pierre,' I explained, hopping from foot to foot. 'Clotilde, he can play so well! He must have it!' After a bit of discussion she agreed to fetch the money and I pressed a few coins into the musician's hand. He doffed his cap and was gone.

Later that day I found Pierre sitting on the grass by the swing. I felt all warm inside to see his face light up when I gave him the instrument. After that I often heard Pierre practising on his fife. His merry tunes drifted though Ducey like dancing sunbeams, cheering us all up. Maman must have heard him too for, to my delight, when next May Day came she gave permission for Pierre to join Papa's musicians. Grinning from ear to ear, he sought me out and shyly offered me a bunch of lily of the valley.

'Will you allow me to present these to you, Mistress Roberda?' he asked as tears welled up in his soft brown eyes. 'I wanted to thank you. You've heard about my new position among the musicians?'

'Of course. I'm so pleased Maman has recognised how good you are at playing that fife!' He stepped back and dropped his chin.

'You don't mind, do you?' he asked, more timidly. I couldn't help but smile.

'Of course not,' I replied and sank my nose deep into the bunch of flowers to drink in their perfume, the fresh scent of spring; light, floral with just a hint of spice.

'Alain du Bois told me how someone gave King Charles a lily

flower as a lucky charm. He says it's now the fashion to exchange them on May morning,' Pierre went on, relaxing a little, although a warm flush smothered the freckles on his face. I felt as though I was walking on air to think how I had helped Pierre. I hadn't yet found another candidate for my own particular brand of charity, but I was always on the lookout.

One morning early in July of the year 1566 Maman held a parchment in her hands.

'This is an important legal document,' she announced with a triumphant smile and I'd swear she grew an inch taller as she spoke. 'Your papa is so often away fighting that he has given me a power of attorney to act in his stead. There is much to set in place to protect everything he has worked for all these years.' After that a string of black-clad lawyers came to Ducey to help Maman seal deals about land and property. Then she started to look for husbands for us all.

Charlotte was first and it didn't take Maman long to secure the marriage contract. My eldest sister stood up beside Maman's choice for her hand on a sunny day at the end of that same July of 1566. Christophe de Chateaubriand, Seigneur de Beaufort and Plessis-Bertrand, was a grey-haired widower and I didn't think him very handsome. But he was certainly wealthy and Charlotte would become mistress of her own grand house. I had no time to get used to the idea before she was hugging me in one last farewell and was gone.

Life settled into a routine at Ducey while periods of uneasy truce were interrupted by more battles. Even when all seemed peaceful Papa was drumming up more soldiers to stand ready to fight again. I wondered if France would ever be truly free of war as the dreary seasons turned.

Chapter Six

The Perfect Knight

1568

'They're coming! Riders! Lots of them!' Giles shouted from his position high on the rooftop. There never was a boy who loved to climb so much as my brother Giles. Tall for his age, he had reached that stage of growth where his legs outpaced the rest of him and he looked like a long stringy bean. With his gangly legs Giles found his way into some very precarious places. He always had a good view of the comings and goings.

I ran to the window of the turret room I now shared with my little sister Suzette. Standing on tiptoe I strained my eyes and soon saw that Giles was right. Maman was on a white horse at the head of a column of riders and at her side rode a knight on the biggest warhorse I had ever seen. Soon they were in the courtyard and the stranger swung his leg easily over to dismount. His black horse, clearly a fiery steed, tossed its head and sparks flew from the cobbles as hooves crashed around. The black-clad knight put a calming hand on the beast's muzzle and soon had him under control while Maman made a more careful descent at the mounting block.

I was mesmerised. My heart was pounding. I felt suddenly hot all over. The knight took off his helmet revealing brown curls that hung to his shoulders, threw back his head and laughed, showing perfect white teeth. Then he turned to Maman so I could no longer see his face.

I had to grab the stone windowsill for support as my legs went weak under me. On that May morning Sir Galahad and Sir Lancelot all rolled into one had ridden into the courtyard at Ducey and I couldn't take my eyes off him. A group of younger men clustered around him. One tall youth carried a banner on which I could make out the words *Finem detmihi virtus* – Let valour be my aim. That sounded to me just the sort of thing a knight from the tales of chivalry I loved to read would have on his banner. The knight took Maman's hand and led her into the hall, out of my sight. I turned from the window and sat down with my back against the cool stone wall, hugging my knees, waiting for my heartbeat to slow.

Maman had been to England to negotiate my marriage to the son of Papa's English friend, Sir Arthur Champernowne. At least that's what Papa had told everyone. I knew my marriage prospects were not the only reason for her visit. She had also been sounding out English support for the Huguenots in Normandy and was back just in time for a double wedding. My brother Jacques and my sister Elisabeth were to marry on the same day. Jacques' bride Pérronelle de Champagne was a tiny dark-haired girl with nail-bitten fingers who brought with her a tidy little fortune. Elisabeth's groom Jehan de Refuge came from a noble family with holdings all over Northern France. Both marriages would bring advantages for my papa. A peace agreement meant it was safe to hold a big celebration. Everyone in Basse-Normandie would be there, at least all who followed our faith.

Sitting on the hard floor of the maidens' chamber I shivered. I would be next. My thoughts turned again to the handsome knight. If he was the one, my husband to be, I'd be the happiest bride in all of France.

Clotilde came huffing and puffing up the stair.

'Help me put on my prettiest gown, Clotilde,' I cried, grabbing her round the middle and dancing her round. 'I want to look my best before our visitors.' There was only one visitor I was interested in.

'Let me go then,' she panted, 'or how will I ever get you dressed?' She bent to take my best kirtle from the coffer.

'Whoever is that knight who has just arrived with Maman?' I asked, all innocence, as she laced me in.

'Why, I believe that is an Englishman of the name Champernon,' she said. I gasped and goosebumps ran up my arms.

Clotilde tutted and shook her head as I struggled into the crimson gown with its fashionable puffed sleeves and high embroidered collar. Out of the corner of my eye I spotted Diane the doll, looking on as usual.

'Don't wriggle so. I'll have the pins in you if you don't keep still,' Clotilde scolded as she fixed the sleeves in place. I shook out the folds of my skirt and soon I was tripping, light as a feather, down the stair to find Maman all alone in the hall.

'Where are our visitors?' I called as I skipped across the room and nearly knocked her from her feet.

'That's a fine welcome home for your maman,' she hissed. She stepped back and took my hands in hers and said, much more kindly, 'It is good to be home. Giles has just taken Monsieur de Champernon to meet your father.'

'He looks such a fine knight,' I exclaimed, hopping from foot to foot. 'So handsome!'

Maman gave me a sideways look.

'Is it agreed, Maman? Am I to wed Sir Arthur's son?' I asked.

'Sir Arthur is a fine English gentleman but he drives a hard bargain,' she replied. 'Your father and I must consider his request for monies and lands as part of the marriage settlement. In the meantime we hope to enlist his support with the English queen.' I sighed heavily. I was just an added sweetener to some wider agreement Papa wanted to reach.

'Now wherever is Elisabeth? Is Charlotte here with her husband?' Maman demanded. 'I haven't even had time to change and now I must greet guests who've just arrived.' She bustled towards the door, looked out and threw back over her shoulder. 'Oh, it's only your uncles, Louis and Jacques.'

I spotted my uncles by the mounting block and gave them a cheery wave. Uncle Louis, resplendent in the dark purple robe he wore as Second Commendatory Abbot of Saint-Jean de Falaise, raised his hand in mock salute. Uncle Jacques, who was not much older than me, burst out laughing and made a most exaggerated bow.

'Ah! The scribe,' Uncle Louis grinned. 'How does your writing progress, Roberda?'

'Not as well as my tutor would wish, Uncle Louis,' I called. 'I fear I am not as diligent as the monks in the scriptorium but I still have the ink horn.' I pictured the rows of monks on their high stools bent over huge parchments as they dipped their quills or with the finest of brushes added the finishing touches to brightly coloured illuminations. When we had visited the abbey years ago, when I was little, before the wars, I'd been so fascinated with the ink and parchments that Uncle Louis had given me a small ivory ink horn, carved with angels. It was one of my most treasured possessions.

Papa rushed up, shook Uncle Louis by the hand and clapped Uncle Jacques on the back.

'We have much to discuss,' he cried. 'This peace won't last long. I'll look for your support.' For all he was an abbot, Uncle Louis had taken to the reformed religion just like Papa. Uncle Jacques had fought at Papa's side. It sounded as though they were going to spend all their time talking about war. So I made my excuses and went in search of Elisabeth who I found on the swing with her blonde hair flying loose behind her shoulders like a shining cloud.

'I'm enjoying my last moments of freedom,' she said with a huge grin. 'Soon I will be a wife and I'll have to cover my hair and behave with due decorum.' Her laughter echoed around the old orchard like the song of a lark in the morning.

'Is he here yet?' I asked. 'Have you seen your suitor, your soon-to-be husband?'

'He'll be here this evening. I'm so lucky! Jehan de Refuge is a good-looking man, a fine gentleman, who dresses in the latest fashion.'

'He must be smitten with you,' I chortled. 'He's converted to the Protestant faith just so he can marry you. Papa wouldn't agree to the match if he hadn't.' I paused and bit my lip. 'Elisabeth, can I ask you something?'

'Of course, little sister,' she said quite kindly. 'What is it?'

'When you first saw Jehan did your legs go all wobbly and did you feel as if you just couldn't draw a breath at all? I've just seen Maman ride in with the most handsome knight I've ever seen and that's how I felt!'

Elisabeth smiled. 'Oh dear, it sounds like you've got a bad case of hero worship. Now don't go getting any ideas about Henri de Champernon.'

'But … but!' I stammered. 'Isn't he Sir Arthur's son, the one I'm going to wed?'

'He's a seasoned soldier who's been fighting the Turk and all sorts. Henri de Champernon's much too old for you!'

'What does age matter? Charlotte is wedded to an older man!' I spat the words out as Elisabeth's eyes opened wide.

'Oh, Roberda! You silly girl! Henri is Sir Arthur's nephew, not his son. And there's another small complication.'

I felt tears stinging behind my eyes but I lifted my chin defiantly. 'Whatever do you mean, Elisabeth?'

'Henry Champernowne, as the English call him, is already married. He has a wife and children in England. So he can't marry you, can he? Sir Arthur's son, the one Maman has in mind for you, is not among the English party. Apparently he's too busy somewhere on the high seas.'

I turned away to hide my disappointment. First she had told me that the valiant knight, the man of my dreams, was out of reach. But worse still, the one I was to marry couldn't even be bothered to come to Ducey to meet me. I stumbled away leaving Elisabeth swinging back and forth, kicking her legs out in front and revealing her garters.

I hid in one of the little arbours among the yew hedges and wept hot, angry tears. Much later, after I had dried my eyes and calmed down a bit, I walked back towards the house. A tall lad with curly dark hair came sauntering towards me; one of the party who had accompanied my handsome knight. He made an exaggerated bow and fell into step beside me.

'May I accompany you, mademoiselle?' he said. His accent was so strange and thick that, even in my misery, I couldn't help but laugh.

'That you may,' said I, 'though how I shall understand a word you say to me I know not. Do you accompany Monsieur de Champernon? What is your name?' I spoke in French, though I had learned some English words from Papa, who spoke that strange language well after his time in England.

The boy reddened and smiled.

'Walter,' he said, and then, struggling to say it in French, 'my name is Walter Raleigh.' I thought it sounded like one of the English words I knew, though that seemed a most improbable name.

'I shall call you Monsieur L'eau, for that is the French name for water,' I said drawling out the word to mimic him and painting on my brightest smile. I had switched to English and the boy chuckled.

'That was a sly trick, mademoiselle,' he laughed. 'Now you must tell me your name.'

'I am Lady Gabrielle Roberda Montgomery,' I announced with a flourish. The boy grinned. He might have barely a wisp of beard on his chin but he really was rather disarming.

'You travel with Henri de Champernon? He seems to me the finest of knights.' I couldn't help it. Even though he was out of reach I simply had to know more about him.

'Henry's my cousin and the bravest man I know,' he answered, puffing out his chest in a way that reminded me of Papa's hawk. 'He's a fine soldier and I'd follow him anywhere! We all would.'

'He's so tall and handsome,' I breathed, allowing myself a brief return to the world of my dreams. The boy chortled.

'Ah! So that's the way the land lies, is it?'

'Now, let me get this straight,' I said with an impatient edge to my voice. My anger was not really with Walter. I was angry with myself for showing my feelings to a mere boy. 'Henri de Champernon who is here talking to my father is your cousin?' He nodded. 'But what of the other Champernon, the one I am to wed?'

'He's another cousin of mine; there are quite a lot of us spread about all over Devon. I've quite lost count of how many cousins I have!' His grin was infectious and I started to giggle. But then I scowled as I remembered his other cousin was too busy to come to meet me.

'Gawen is a lucky fellow and no mistake,' Walter said with a flirtatious smile. 'All of England will be in awe of the beauty of his sophisticated French bride.' I burst out laughing again as he swept me another flamboyant bow.

'Well, sir,' I said, putting on a haughty voice, 'when you see that cousin of yours you might tell him I think it ill he has not yet come to Ducey!' His tone of voice changed and he spoke much lower as he leaned in towards me.

'Oh, mademoiselle, that I will. Old Gawen doesn't know what

he's missing!' I felt my cheeks go hot and had a funny tingling in my chest. I wasn't sure I liked the way he was looking at me, and yet part of me was drawn to the young man whose knowing smile promised something dangerous and exciting. I laughed rather loudly to cover my confusion.

As my laughter died, Clotilde hove into view, bustling along purposefully; on a mission to find me no doubt. She stopped short and threw up her hands when she saw me standing so close to the young man.

'Young mistress! Whatever are you doing dallying here with this young squire! That is not the behaviour your mother expects of you! 'Tis not ladylike! Come, you are wanted inside.' She took me by the hand and led me away as though I were a naughty child.

I was afraid I might be in so much trouble that I wouldn't be allowed to attend the weddings. But after a round ticking-off from Maman – a long and embarrassing lecture about how to behave before young men – next day I was allowed to join Charlotte as we helped our sister dress.

Charlotte and I embraced, for she had arrived late on the previous day.

'You don't look the least bit different, even though you're an old married woman,' I teased. Charlotte took a friendly swipe at me and, giggling, we helped Elisabeth into the wondrous carnation-coloured silk gown, embroidered with glittering gold threads. Satisfied, we stood back to admire the bride. My sister's blonde curls spilled out from beneath a cap with a veil of frothy fabric, such as I'd never seen before. The same gauzy stuff trimmed her cuffs.

'Wherever did you come by this?' I asked fingering it enviously. 'It's so beautiful. Is it cut work or some strange embroidery? The pattern seems to float in the air as if caught in a net.'

'Maman had it sent from Paris,' Charlotte volunteered. 'Queen Catherine brought some from Venice years ago. All the ladies of the court are wearing it. See how the threads are twisted together.' She held up a piece to the light.

'Is it drawn-thread work? Is it worked with a needle?' I asked all agog.

'I really don't know how it's made. They call it lace,' Charlotte answered, smiling broadly at Elisabeth. 'Only the best is good enough for my sister's wedding day.'

We stood beside Elisabeth as she took her vows and then listened to Jacques' booming tones and Pérronelle's whispers. I shot Jacques' new wife an encouraging grin and she blushed furiously. Poor Pérronelle! She looked as though she'd do better in a nunnery than married to my over-loud brother. Then the celebrations began. I was surprised Papa could afford to spend so much on lavish entertainment, but supposed it was to woo others to his cause. I looked up at the band of musicians playing in the gallery and gave Pierre a cheery wave.

I couldn't resist trying to manoeuvre though the throng of well-wishers until I was near Henry Champernowne. Walter, grinning beside him, raised a hand in greeting, but Henry didn't even notice me. He was deep in conversation with my father.

'I will seek the queen's approval. I'll muster as many as I can,' my hero said in perfect French with hardly a trace of accent. 'My uncle will help arm us. He'll provide the ships to transport me and my men to La Rochelle. We'll be back before the autumn.'

Elisabeth went off with her husband. Jacques carried Pérronelle away. All was quiet at Ducey. But the peace that had allowed so many to gather for the wedding celebrations didn't last long. By August Alain du Bois was in charge of our defences at Ducey once again, while Papa was holed up at Lorges with my uncles, planning future attacks. Alain stopped me on the path one September morning as I was helping Clotilde carry a basket of new-picked rosy apples back from the orchard.

'Best keep within,' he advised. 'Things are getting tense again. I'm not sure how safe we are with all these soldiers milling around the countryside.' I made a face at him. 'That Englishman, Henri de Champernon – you remember him? He came for the weddings,' he went on, looking straight at me. 'I hear he's been as good as his word. He has brought a hundred horsemen and is off to join our forces. We need all the help we can get.'

'Well, what of that?' I said raising my head defiantly. I wondered why Alain had felt the need to tell me about the English knight. Clotilde busied herself with the basket. *She must have told him I was sweet on Henri. How embarrassing!* But I hadn't forgotten the first man to tug at my heart strings. Sometimes I whispered to Diane the doll about him in the small hours.

Charlotte joined us at Ducey when her husband went off to join Papa's forces. I was glad of her company. Maman was rushing around trying to manage Papa's lands and Suzette was too young to be much fun.

On a bright morning at the beginning of March Charlotte threw her needlework aside and paced to the window.

'Still no news. No sign of any messengers today,' she sighed, leaning out as far as she dared. I chuckled softly. Charlotte hated not knowing what was going on. But then I frowned. She was right. It had been rather a long time since we last had any word. I watched her twisting her hands together as she peered into the distance. 'Surely we should have heard something by now?' she murmured, pulling her brows together.

'I'm sure all is well. You'll see Christophe riding into the courtyard, all dashing and bold, any day now,' I said, but wasn't sure I believed it. Thinking to distract her I picked up the collar she'd been working on. 'Is this a new stitch?' I asked.

'Béatrice taught me that pattern when we were in Rouen,' she said, peering into my face.

'It's all right, Charlotte. I don't jump out of my skin every time anyone mentions Rouen any more.' She sat down beside me, took my hand and smiled.

'That's good! I don't know how I would have managed without Béatrice. She helped me a lot, you know.'

'Hmm – did she?' I said with a wobble in my voice. Despite my protestations the mention of that war-torn city threatened to trigger an episode of shaking. I took a breath and concentrated on the embroidery, picturing Béatrice's long slender fingers weaving their magic.

'You were so jealous of her, weren't you?' Charlotte asked, her voice thick with concern. I felt the warmth rising in my cheeks.

'Well, perhaps I was! Whatever happened to her anyway?' I asked rather sharply.

'Papa looked for her when he was in Paris. Christophe told me. '

'Did he find her?' I asked, intrigued despite myself.

'Yes, but not in Paris; she's in a convent somewhere in the north, not far from Calais. I've written to her a few times.'

'What? So she's a nun? Really? Béatrice – a nun?'

'Béatrice has taken Holy Orders but she won't be an ordinary nun. Her Tavannes relatives are wealthy. I think she'll soon be in charge of the convent.'

'Perhaps that's better than having to accept a husband chosen for you,' I said. 'Someone who can't even be bothered come to meet you!' It really rankled that Gawen Champernowne had still not found time to come to Ducey. 'I wish I could make my own choice of husband,' I went on. 'I don't want to marry a man who's always rushing off to fight in some war! I don't want to be the shadow behind the elusive Gawen Champernowne. I want to do something for myself; something to help people, as I helped Pierre.'

Charlotte laughed. 'You always were a wilful girl,' she chuckled. 'Béatrice asked after you. I thought you two hated each other after the way you carried on that time she got hold of your doll.'

I glanced across at Diane the doll who still sat in pride of place next to my bed and felt a bit light-headed as I remembered that quarrel and then how I'd pressed the ring into Béatrice's hand as she was leaving.

'Did she?' I muttered. 'Let's go down to the garden. The sun is up.' Charlotte gave me a sidelong stare, but said nothing more.

A few days later the longed-for messenger arrived. We rushed into the hall to find Maman white-faced and shaking.

'What is it, Maman?' Charlotte demanded.

'There has been a setback; a defeat. Jacques, my dearest boy – he's held prisoner. Oh, dear God, what will they do to him?' She shook her head from side to side, and then studied the message again. 'No! No! Some say that your father is lost! No! No! I will not have it so!' She shrieked and let the paper fall to the floor. Charlotte bent and picked it up in trembling fingers and scanned the top page.

'Maman, it says only that Papa's horse was seen galloping riderless from the battlefield at Jarnac. He'll have got away. Someone will have plucked him from danger and lent him a mount,' Charlotte soothed, trying her best to bring some comfort. 'If Jacques is held, then he will be treated well. He'll be exchanged for some royalist prisoner. All will be well.'

Maman snatched the letter from Charlotte's grasp and studied the next page. She took a deep breath before she turned tear-filled eyes on my sister.

'Sit down, Charlotte,' Maman whispered. 'I'm afraid all will not be well. There is more certain news here. Sit down, my dear child.' I could see from Charlotte's rigid face that she already knew the news of Christophe must be bad. She wrested the crumpled paper from Maman and read.

A cold feeling was growing in my belly. What if there was even more bad news? What if Christophe was not the only one to have died on the battlefield? It was heartless and cruel of me when Charlotte had only just learned she was a widow, but I couldn't help it.

'Monsieur de Champernon? What of Henri de Champernon?' I asked.

Maman stared at me with such venom in her eyes that I jumped back as if she'd hit me.

'He's no concern of yours,' she snapped. 'What about your papa? What about your brother? You must save all your care for them. Look to your sister. She needs your comfort.'

I bit my lip, hung my head and muttered an apology. Maman was right. Jacques was a horrid, boastful boy, but he was my brother. I didn't really want to think of him in some dank dungeon among the rats and I couldn't even begin to imagine life without Papa. She was right. I must offer all my prayers for my own flesh and blood.

Two days later Charlotte's bags were packed. I felt quite in awe of the calm and practical way my sister had absorbed the news of her husband's death. Although her face was set in lines of sorrow there was a new air of determination about her. She looked very much like Maman as she clambered into the coach that would take her to Plessis-Bertrand to take charge of her lands. For Charlotte was now a wealthy widow.

'Roberda, will you do something for me?' she asked, leaning out from the carriage's small window.

'Of course,' I replied. 'I'll try, though I'm such a silly selfish thing, I'll probably get it wrong.' I was still smarting after my thoughtless behaviour when the news came.

'It's not much to ask. Will you write to Béatrice? In her last letter to me she said she was anxious about something between you, but hesitated to write to you direct. I don't know what's on her mind, but I've always thought of her as a friend; as another sister. Will you do this for me?'

'Just like you to think of someone else at such a time!' I tried a smile, but it felt wrong. 'Yes, I suppose I can try.'

Before the carriage pulled out of the courtyard a horse pounded in. Maman grabbed the saddlebag, tore it open, broke the seal and scanned the message; all before the rider could dismount.

'May God be praised. It is as we thought. Your papa survives to fight another day. A small injury, nothing worse… He is mustering his forces with Admiral Coligny. No news of Jacques!' she muttered, drawing the page closer to squint at the writing. A stray thought struck me. Maman was getting older. Perhaps she needed spectacles like Pastor Forêt. 'There's more here. Prince Condé is dead! Tavannes crossed the river at Châteauneuf and surprised them. That is why they lost at Jarnac.'

I looked at Charlotte and knew we were thinking the same thing. Gaspard Tavannes was Béatrice's uncle. I wanted to ask what had become of all the English forces. But Maman had already rushed back into the house.

Jarnac did not put an end to the war. Maman gave me regular updates whenever news arrived. At the end of August she called me in from my seat under the apple tree.

'At last, good news,' she announced with a broad smile, pushing back a lock of greying hair. 'Your father has led his troops to victory at Orthez. He's captured the enemy leader and there'll be a prisoner exchange. Even better news; the prisoner to be exchanged is your uncle Jacques. It's not *our* Jacques who's been mouldering in a royalist gaol. He's been with your father all the time.'

'That is good news indeed, Maman,' I replied, as she gave me a rare hug.

It was not until late August, after Papa came home with news of another peace treaty, that I dared send a short note to Béatrice. Her reply came swiftly. It was on her conscience, she said, that we had been bad friends in Rouen. Her vows required that she discharge all earthly debts. I had restored her mother's ring to her. She wanted to repay me. I must remember that if ever she could be of service she would come to my aid. Well, I thought it was all rather silly. How on earth could a nun, even one in charge of a wealthy convent, ever be of service to me?

Hiding behind the kitchen door I listened in as Alain regaled Clotilde with his views of the latest developments as Christmas approached.

'That English fellow – you know the one – rode a big black horse; he went back to England after Jarnac. Came back with a bigger force and saved our army, or so they say. Kept the way clear for our retreat after the battle of Montcontour. Proper hero, he is! He's holed up in La Rochelle, for the winter, I wouldn't wonder.'

'He's safe to fight another day,' I whispered to Diane the doll that night as Suzette snored beside me in the maidens' chamber.

Without Elisabeth and Charlotte, life at Ducey was dull. I took refuge in reading and waited for that winter of 1569 to give way to spring.

I heard Clotilde calling me one June morning as I was helping to pick cherries. I had sampled quite a few and ran my hand quickly over my mouth to wipe away the juice that stained my lips. As Clotilde came near, I noticed the red juice had also dribbled down the front of my kirtle. But she did not upbraid me.

'Whatever is it, Clotilde?' I asked when I saw how her hand shook as she held out a mug of ale for me. Blinking hard she took a breath.

'Come, let us sit,' she said, leading me towards the arbour. 'No one will notice us here.'

'Clotilde? Is there news? Is it Papa?' I asked, taking the mug with my heart thumping.

'There is news,' she whispered with a heavy sigh. We sat down and she took my hand.

'Your papa is well, and Jacques too. But there is news from La Rochelle. I thought it best I tell you away from prying eyes.'

I knew before I heard the words.

'The town was packed with soldiers, all squashed in with the townspeople. A dreadful sickness came; it snatched many lives. The

Englishman, the one who came here; the one you carried such a torch for, though he was never for you. Oh, my dear! He is gone.'

I squeezed my eyes shut.

'No … no… Clotilde, it cannot be so.' She held me in her arms while I sat beside her numb and dry-eyed, shaking my head.

Henry Champernon had never noticed me and yet his death shocked me to the core.

But others had the right to grieve for him, not I. I could not own the feelings his loss had stirred. I must stifle the urge to weep, must never publicly vent my rage at God for taking so fine a man. By day I floated like a cloud from which no rain could fall and the screaming woman and the faceless soldier returned to haunt my nights. I wished Charlotte was with me.

As the summer wore on, with Clotilde's encouragement, I tried to put my few memories of that perfect knight into one of the boxes on the imaginary high shelf, out of reach.

Chapter Seven

Betrothal

Spring 1571

In the month of May, as nodding bluebells carpeted our orchards, Sir Arthur Champernowne came to Ducey. He came alone.

I waited on the doorstep behind my parents as the red-faced Englishman dismounted and swaggered between the ranks of the soldiers Alain du Bois had drilled into a guard of honour.

'But where is his son?' I faltered, my voice no more than a breath. 'Where is Gawen Champernowne? Where is the man I am to wed? The man I must serve till the end of my days?'

'Hush,' Maman hissed.

'But, Maman! Can't he even find the time to attend his own betrothal?' My stomach was clenched into a ball and it was a struggle to keep my voice down. 'Is it really to be a betrothal without a bridegroom?'

'We still have a lot to discuss with Sir Arthur,' Maman whispered over her shoulder. 'Your father would have the wedding in England in the presence of the English queen.'

I choked back a little bark of laughter. I had always known that I would be bait in a trap to secure a wealthy husband who would bring lands and fortune to my family, or a military alliance to defeat our foes. That was the lot of all well-born girls. But my parents were setting a snare to catch bigger game, royal game. They hoped to use my marriage to the son of the Vice Admiral of the Fleet of the

West to secure Queen Elizabeth's support for the wars of religion in France.

I felt my fingernails digging into my palms and my throat hurt as I gulped down angry tears. But I had been well schooled from birth. As Sir Arthur reached the steps, kissed my mother's hand and made his bow to me, I turned on my brightest smile. The corners of my mouth ached with the effort of it and inside I was seething. But I dipped a respectful curtsey and smiled sweetly as I raised my eyes to study the face of the man who might soon be my father-in-law.

In his youth Sir Arthur must have been a handsome man. A faint echo of the gorgeous Henry Champernowne lingered in what must once have been finely chiselled features and a head held high. His abundant brown hair, swept back from a lofty forehead, showed only a trace of grey near the ears. I was cheered to see a crinkled map of laughter lines around his eyes; he must be a man of generally good humour. But for all that I thought I could detect a hint of sorrow, something world-weary, in the striking blue eyes Sir Arthur fixed on me.

'Mademoiselle Gabrielle,' he said in excellent French. 'The reports of your beauty hardly do you justice. My son will be a lucky man indeed to have you at his side.' The look he gave me said more than the gallant, courtly remark. I knew I must accept it. This was the way of our world. A girl like me must expect to be appraised as if she was a prize mare.

I murmured the appropriate response then, on a whim, added 'Sir! It would give me pleasure if you would call me Roberda, as my family do.' Maman looked at me askance but Sir Arthur smiled and nodded.

I followed the party inside and the Englishman accepted a glass of Papa's finest red wine. I stepped back and watched the show of bonhomie unfold. Sir Arthur Champernowne cut a fine figure, dressed to impress, throwing back his wine and laughing with Papa. I hid a little smile behind my hand. His fine black velvet doublet was strained across an ample girth. It was quite apparent that Sir Arthur Champernowne didn't need to add much padding to achieve a stylish peascod belly.

My parents spared no expense. The tastiest dishes our kitchen could offer were served on silver platters. We drank fine wine from exquisite Venetian glassware. Gilles, Suzette and little Gabriel all appeared dressed in their best. Jacques and Gedeon, recalled to lend their presence to the festivities, talked about ships and arms and battles with Sir Arthur. When his nephew Henry was mentioned I saw a shadow cross Sir Arthur's face.

Pierre accompanied me as I sang a French chanson. My protégé had moved on from the fife and was accomplished on many instruments, but especially the lute. A truly gifted musician, Pierre; you could tell he felt the music in his very soul. He ended our duet with a flourish of top notes and I looked up.

'Bravo! Bravo!' cried Sir Arthur, clapping his hands together. 'That's reminded me of happy times at the Court House in Modbury. My father kept a fine troop of musicians there. You sing well, mademoiselle, and the boy plays well. Perhaps, if your father will allow, he may come to England with you when you become Gawen's wife? His music would be welcome in our hall at Dartington.' *Now that would be a fine thing*, I thought, *for I will have but few friendly faces about me in that foreign place.*

As the evening shadows lengthened Sir Arthur was shown to the best chamber and I spent a fitful night full of fears for my future with the as-yet-unknown Gawen.

Next day we rode to the hunt – another opportunity to show me off as a potential bride. I must admit I cut quite a dash with a new saddlecloth sent from Paris which meant I could ride side-saddle just like Queen Catherine.

Papa's huntsman ensured that a fine stag appeared well within bowshot, and Sir Arthur loosed his arrow and found the mark. It was, of course, courteous to allow our guest the privilege of taking his prize, but I always felt a tug of sorrow to see such a noble beast fall. I looked away as the stag was dispatched and stowed on the pack pony. As we made our way homewards, Jacques and Gedeon were loud in their congratulations so I pushed on to get a little distance between us. But as I walked my horse beneath the beech trees a smiling Sir Arthur trotted up and drew his mount alongside mine.

'It's good to see that you ride so well and enjoy the hunt,' he exclaimed with real warmth in his voice. 'At Dartington, where it is my hope you will enjoy many happy years with Gawen, we have a well-stocked deer park. You will be able to hunt as often as you please.' I merely nodded, realising I knew nothing of the home where I might soon be mistress. Maman had been there but she'd told me little of what lay in store for me. My mind raced through wild images of the sort of place it might be. As if he read my thoughts, Sir Arthur continued.

'Dartington was built for the half-brother of a king. In his day John Holland had one of the grandest, one of the largest halls in all England. Of course that was many years ago. But you'll sit in that great hall built to entertain royalty. And in case you're worried it's old fashioned, Mary and I added new chambers and laid out pleasure gardens. It's a pretty spot, high above the River Dart and surrounded by our green Devon hills. I'm sure you'll be happy at Dartington.'

'Sir,' said I, emboldened by his kindness. 'I have not yet met your son. Will he come here to meet me while you come to agreement with my parents?'

Sir Arthur regarded me solemnly as if weighing up his options.

'He is on the sea, doing our queen's work. Even as we speak he is entrusted to carry a letter from the Queen of Navarre to Queen Elizabeth,' he answered at last. 'He's a fine boy. You will do well together.' The last was said with such determination as if by saying it out loud he could make it so. My worries were certainly not set at rest.

On the last day of his visit Sir Arthur asked me to walk with him in the gardens.

'I hope that your visit has been a pleasant one,' I offered, seeking an opening.

'It most certainly has,' he replied, eyes twinkling as he spoke. 'Your father and I are in agreement and have signed papers. The wedding will be in England. I believe I may be able to persuade the queen to allow you to be wed in her private chapel. It will give me the greatest pleasure to see my son joined to so noble a family; a family of Normandy, the land of my own ancestors; a family that shares my passion for the new religion.'

He did not add, though Maman had told me, that he'd stuck out for a substantial sum as dowry.

'Gawen... He has the name of a knight in a story I've read,' I said dreamily, unable to dispel the image of his cousin Henry from my mind. 'Please tell me more.'

'We named him Gawen for his uncle, Sir Gawen Carew. A fine man indeed,' Sir Arthur answered with a proud smile. 'It follows the fashion set when our king named his son Arthur.' I must have looked confused for he smiled and went on, 'Queen Elizabeth's grandfather named his eldest son Arthur. Oh yes, the Tudor Court – the new Camelot. That's where my name came from too.'

I smiled at him, then asked, 'So when will I meet my future husband?'

'As soon as I can secure the queen's permission you will come to England,' he laughed as we reached the arbour where he sat down on the bench and invited me to sit beside him. Sir Arthur turned a quizzical gaze on me. 'You are eager to meet my boy, it seems?'

'Well, it is only natural for a girl to wonder,' I smiled. 'Is he like his cousin, sir?'

'His cousin? You don't mean young Walter?' he chuckled. 'I know he's been here – the young jackanapes.' I could see he had a soft spot for Walter, the boy I'd met briefly when he came to Ducey for the weddings. I shook my head. 'Not Walter? Oh... Do you mean Henry then?' His eyes clouded over. 'Did you meet him?'

'That I did, sir, and never saw so fine a knight.' I couldn't hide the tremble in my voice.

Sir Arthur sighed and there was a long pause.

'That was a dark year; first Henry and then, so soon after, I lost my dearest Mary.' His voice shook and he stared down at his hands. 'Henry was a fine boy ... the Queen of Navarre ... thank God she wrote to Queen Elizabeth. He fought bravely in her country for her cause, so Jeanne d'Albret wrote to our queen to ask her to make sure his family will be treated well. All is arranged; in time Modbury will be theirs.'

'I am sorry to have brought back unhappy thoughts for you, sir,' I said and very daringly I put my hand over his. Another long pause followed and then he spoke again.

'He was my brother's boy, you know. Johnny went to his grave long before his time, chasing all over Europe with my cousin Peter

… Sir Peter Carew. Johnny died in Vienna of all places. Some disease they picked up. Henry was still in the nursery. My father took the boy under his wing. A few years later, when my father died, I stepped in. I brought young Henry up as though he was my own. A boy to be proud of.' He rubbed his chest and his head dropped. After a while he pushed his shoulders back and stood up.

'You are a good kind girl. You and Gawen will do well together,' he said firmly and offered me his arm. We retraced our steps between the clipped hedges in silence.

Sir Arthur rode away, saying he must go to Paris to meet the English ambassador, Sir Francis Walsingham, before he returned to England. Gawen had not put in an appearance. Papa said he was somewhere on the seas off La Rochelle.

'Champernowne would have liked his son to join Count Ludovic who is assembling a fleet for the Indies,' Papa announced with a grin as we sat at board a few days after we'd waved Sir Arthur on his way.

'If he is to go so far away then how will we ever be married?' I gasped.

'Have no fear. As always with the English they falter on grounds of cost. They'd rather dabble in a spot of piracy.' That didn't reassure me much. 'I just hope Sir Arthur can do as he's promised and gain Queen Elizabeth's support,' he went on. 'You, Roberda, you must play your part. You'll go to England later this year.'

The maidens' chamber was all in a muddle; silk gowns and velvet cloaks, woollen kirtles, shifts and kerchiefs of the finest Holland linen, bead-trimmed headdresses and embroidered gloves were scattered all over the beds. Clotilde began to fold the clothes and place them in the coffers while my little sister Suzette looked on. I stood at the window fingering a fine blue-green damask. It was to be my wedding gown.

'Clotilde? Must I go?' I groaned. 'I'll be so lonely in England.'

'Now then! Your mother has said young Jeanne, my cousin's girl, can go with us. Sir Arthur has asked for Pierre to accompany you and I'll be there, so you won't be alone.'

'Just think of it,' said Suzette in a dreamy voice. 'You're to be married in the presence of Queen Elizabeth of England. All the ladies and gentlemen of her court will be there. It's so romantic.'

'No, it's not,' I snapped and bent to pick up the ink horn Uncle Louis had given me. I threw it into the open coffer, earning a cross look from Clotilde.

Suzette picked up Diane the doll from a pile of stockings on the bed. I'd thrown her down in a fit of pique as I watched Clotilde calmly boxing up all I would need for my future life.

'You're much too grown up for dolls now, Roberda,' Suzette chanted. 'Will you leave her behind for me?'

'I will not,' I yelled, snatching the doll and stowing her safely in the smaller coffer. 'She goes with me. She'll remind me of home.'

It was all arranged. Maman was to take me to my wedding in London. Papa might join us there but, as always, his movements were shrouded in mystery. The coffers were full; the last items packed. The next day I would leave my childhood behind forever.

I took one last walk in the gardens, my footsteps dragging as I noticed little everyday things; a patch of bright dandelions that had escaped the gardener's best attention; some unruly dark spikes waiting to be clipped on the yew hedge; the bright russet leaves beneath trees where medlars hung, almost ready; the untidy remains of the robin's nest in the abandoned barrel by the onion bed – a nest as empty as my heart. The robin would return to his nest in spring. But I must leave my home forever.

The gravel on the path scrunched loudly beneath my feet as I trudged along. I paused and let my eyes wander over walls dappled by a burst of autumn sunshine. I sat on the swing, kicked back and forth half-heartedly a few times, then wandered towards the little cross that marked Fifi's grave. With tears rolling down my cheeks I bowed my head. After a while I realised that Alain du Bois was standing a pace behind me. He offered me a surprisingly clean kerchief.

'Dry your eyes and put on a brave face. You're off on a rare adventure. Grasp it with courage, Mistress Roberda. But remember – this time I won't be there to guard you. Be sure that those English look after you as well as I have all these years.'

Chapter Eight

England

November 1571

Pierre's face was white as a dove's wing as he stumbled onto the deck. He reached the side just in time.

'Poor Pierre! Your first time at sea. I wish I could tell you it gets better,' I offered. 'But I'm sorry. Just look at me! I've crossed to Jersey many times but I still end up hanging over a pail, even on a calm sea like this.' The boy could only grunt in reply. Jeanne, who I supposed I must now call my maid, looked in no better case. But Clotilde was clearly made of sterner stuff. I'd even seen her eating the ship's biscuit and poor gruel we were offered with some relish.

'It won't be long now. I think I can make something out through the fog,' I called to the sad pair hanging over the gunwale. Heedless of the persistent light rain that was beginning to soak through my cloak I elbowed Pierre aside.

'Look! There! Can you see?' I called, pointing excitedly to a thin fuzzy line on the horizon. I could hardly keep still as I waited for that blurry line to grow into a smudge as the coastline started to emerge from the mist. I screwed up my eyes and stood on tiptoe, craning my neck for my first sight of England. At first it was hard to make anything out. But as we drew closer, church towers and tall houses slowly loomed out of the gloom, and a neat harbour crowded with boats large and small. Away to the right the sky was thick with raucous seagulls swooping down on fishing boats that were disgorging their catch; the stink of rotting fish almost overpowered the briny smell of the sea. I released my grip on the rail and sighed.

'Why, Southampton looks a lot like the ports we've left behind in France,' I muttered, without realising I spoke aloud. 'Perhaps England will not seem so strange after all.' I was trying hard to convince myself that all would be well. I didn't quite succeed in quelling the queasy feeling in my tummy. This time it was not the ship's motion that had my stomach churning.

As our boat made fast at the quay I saw a well-dressed figure striding towards us, heedless of the drizzle.

'There he is!' I cried and raised my arm to wave wildly, eliciting a cold stare from Maman. We hurried down the gangplank and along the quayside, Maman striding in front, Clotilde, Jeanne and Pierre struggling along behind with our luggage. Sir Arthur doffed his cap and bowed to Maman before taking my hand.

'Welcome to England, Roberda,' he said. My mouth felt dry and I swallowed hard. I had arrived!

'Will you walk a step to the Red Lion Inn on the High Street?' asked Sir Arthur. Maman assented and he led us away from the waterside and the crowds of porters scurrying in and out of the vast wool warehouses. We took refreshment at the inn while Sir Arthur spoke with a group of men, merchants by their dress. I looked up when he raised his voice saying something about a Spanish treasure ship and money for the queen, but I didn't understand his meaning. With a start I realised I knew very little of the dealings of the family I was about to join.

Soon we were on our way, bumping along in a carriage over rough roads much worse than those in Normandy. We stopped at another inn where, over a satisfying supper of beef and bread, I turned to Sir Arthur.

'May I ride tomorrow, sir? Can a horse be provided for me? I can't abide another day in that carriage. I don't want to go to my wedding black and blue!'

'It will be my pleasure to have you ride alongside me,' he chuckled. 'I'll be able to tell you something about the countryside we pass through.'

So next day a grey pony was led out and my introduction to England really began.

'Does this drizzle ever stop?' I asked, as I handed my sopping riding cloak to Clotilde. She grimaced as she hung it before the blazing fire in the chamber set aside for us in the courtier's house where we were lodged that night.

'Mistress, this England does seem a dark and dreary sort of place to my mind. I don't think we've seen the sun since we left France.'

'Never mind, Clotilde,' I chirped, taking her arm and holding on to it. 'Tomorrow we'll be in London and then all the dazzle of Queen Elizabeth's court will surely brighten us up. At last I'll meet my intended and we'll be married.' Maman put down the glass of warmed hippocras she'd accepted to ward off the chill and gave me an enquiring look.

'I hope you are ready to play your part well, Roberda.' Her words had all the force of an order. 'This match with Sir Arthur's boy will bring great advantage to your father. I don't expect to see a sour face when first you meet him. You know you must accept your destiny. The agreement is made and he's a fine young man who will make a good husband for you.'

'Maman! I know my duty. You may depend on me. If truth be told, now I'm here I'm quite overcome with the excitement of it all,' I declared, with a wide grin. Since we docked in Southampton a little germ of excitement had been growing inside me, a strange breathless lightness in my chest that kept me constantly flitting here and there and laughing out loud at nothing. Still holding Clotilde's arm I danced her around the room until we collapsed in a heap, both of us giggling fit to burst.

I took my seat gingerly in the swaying little vessel that bobbed on the murky waters of the River Thames, and smoothed out the folds of my gown of lavender silk; the beautiful blue-green damask was safely stowed in my small coffer waiting for my wedding day. My stomach felt full of butterflies as I squinted at four white turrets glinting in the sun above a mighty tower fortress. I could hear a tremor in Sir Arthur's voice as he told us how, years ago, he'd been kept within.

'My cousin, Peter Carew, got us all involved in a plot against Queen Mary's Spanish marriage,' he said with a shudder. 'The plot failed, of course. Wyatt lost his head, Peter fled to France and they kept me in there for a while. It's not an experience I ever want to repeat.' He shook his head. 'Norfolk's in there now; planned to marry himself to the Scots Queen. Done for, I should think!' Sir Arthur turned to Maman. 'Of course, you know of the affair? Ridolfi? An assassin? No wonder the queen jumps at shadows.'

I fidgeted on the hard wooden seat. Visions of that perfect knight, Henry Champernowne, had been haunting my dreams for days. By the time I stepped from the barge I'd convinced myself that Gawen would look just like his cousin and all would be well. After all, I could see a family resemblance in Sir Arthur and even that boy Walter had a look of him. I hugged my arms tight round my middle and grinned. I was sure the court would be glittering, exciting and gay. Gawen would instantly fall in love with me and we would be happy together.

At Greenwich Sir Arthur jumped out quite nimbly for a man of his age and offered his hand to Maman. I looked up to see a man hurtling down the steps. My heart leaped. *It must be Gawen, impatient to greet his bride.*

But it was not my elusive soon-to-be husband, breathing heavily as he came to a standstill on the quay. It was my brother, Jacques.

'What on earth are you doing here?' I cried. But Maman didn't look at all surprised.

'Papa has left Plymouth,' said Jacques. 'He's taking post horses and will soon be here.' Jacques gave me a mock bow. 'Little sister! I'm come to dance at your wedding!'

'Huh! Have you seen Gawen?' I asked, scowling at him with my head tilted back.

'That I have,' he replied without hiding a note of irritation in his voice. I had no time to quiz him further. Sir Arthur was already leading Maman towards the enormous palace so I picked up my skirts and ran up the steps.

A liveried footman showed us to the cramped chamber my parents had secured in a distant part of the palace. Pierre deposited my coffer in a corner and went off to find the court musicians and I flopped down onto the bed, wondering what I should do next. A knock soon came and Jacques marched in.

'Make ready, sister. You're to meet the queen. Who knows, you might also meet Gawen Champernowne,' he crowed.

Jeanne held the glass as Clotilde put the heart-shaped cap over my neatly coiled shining hair; only on my wedding day would I let it fall loose. I preened until I was satisfied with my appearance and then, with head held high, I took Jacques' arm. I had never seen so many people all together in one building. We made our way through the crush until we came upon Maman with a tall woman in a glittering gown with a jewelled headdress set on bright auburn hair. The woman had her back to me as we approached and I was about to drop into my deepest curtsey when Maman signalled to me.

'This is Lettice, Viscountess Hereford, with whom I have corresponded for years. Her husband served under Ambrose Dudley. You remember? Dudley was in Le Havre. She is a good friend of our cause.' I felt my cheeks grow hot, for I had really thought it was the queen herself. I mumbled a greeting and shuffled from foot to foot until at last Maman made her excuses and we moved on.

I glided along in a dream as we passed between the ranks of ladies and gentlemen, hardly noticing the brightly coloured tapestries hung on the walls. I knew I looked pretty; the glass had told me so. But I was not at all prepared for the admiring glances of all the courtiers.

'Oh my!' Jacques whispered. 'You're causing quite a ripple through the court, little sister. See how their heads turn, how their eyes follow you. Look over there. Even Sir Christopher Hatton is ogling you.' I followed his gaze to a tall man dressed in a particularly fine doublet. 'A pretty fellow!' Jacques murmured. 'Made his name by dancing in a masque, would you believe. Some say he's the handsomest man at court, though others say the queen prefers the Earl of Leicester who stands beside him.' He nodded towards another man dressed in opulent ermine and velvet. 'Robert Dudley's a good ally to have at court and no mistake.' But my eyes rested not on the resplendent Earl of Leicester but on the man beside him. Sir Christopher really was a stunningly handsome man.

Sir Arthur took my hand and led me forward to stand before a gloriously clad figure and I had no doubt it was time to drop into the deep curtsey I'd been practising. I wondered how I could ever have mistaken Viscountess Hereford for the dazzling vision before me. They might both have hair of the same red hue. The Viscountess did have a fine gown. But the Queen of England radiated her magnificence in a way no one could match. She commanded the space around her, drawing all eyes. Everyone else looked faded and dull, just as stars in the night sky are quenched by the luminescence of bright moonlight.

'May I present the Countess of Montgomery and her daughter Gabrielle? – who I am delighted to say is to be married to my son Gawen,' Sir Arthur announced in ringing tones. I kept my head bowed, forewarned that I must not raise my eyes until she spoke. To my amazement she took several steps towards me; came so close that I could see her embroidered slippers peeping from beneath a stunning gown of rich velvet, heavily encrusted with sparkling jewels and bands of gold.

I waited shaking a little until, in impeccable French, she bade me rise.

'Welcome to your new home, mademoiselle,' she said, peering into my face. I felt as though those steady dark eyes could see right into my soul. She gave a little nod like a goodwife who has assessed the quality of goods she will buy at market and found them satisfactory. 'Sir Arthur, I hope your son realises his good fortune?' Then she signalled to Maman, who was still bent in her own curtsey. 'You may rise, Madame la Comtesse. You have a beautiful daughter. Does she sing or play? I might keep her a while as an ornament to my court.' But there was no time for Maman to reply. The Queen of England had many to greet and was already moving on. 'I will look for Monsieur le Comte tomorrow,' she called over her shoulder. It was over so quickly I couldn't take it in. Had she really said I might remain at her court?

I turned and followed Sir Arthur through the crowd, feeling as light as air. I was so excited I tripped and almost fell. It was Sir Christopher Hatton who caught my elbow and righted me. I didn't feel at all threatened when he gave me an admiring look. Instead, feeling heady as if I'd taken too much wine, I returned his gaze and offered my hand. He brushed it with a courtly kiss and I felt all of a tremble as his startling blue eyes twinkled up at me from beneath hooded lids.

'Thank you kindly, sir,' I breathed, favouring him with a rather flirtatious grin.

Lost in the moment, I heard it vaguely, as if from far, far away. Someone called a name; 'Gawen'. Still wrapped up in Sir Christopher's flattering attention it was only when Sir Arthur's voice boomed, 'Roberda. This is my son, Gawen,' that I realised who was standing behind me. Our first meeting had come at last.

Sir Christopher released my hand but I did not turn. Instead I stood motionless, took a sharp breath in and closed my eyes. Unbidden a memory of the face of Henry Champernowne, my perfect knight, flashed into my mind. I took another breath, opened my eyes, and with my heart in my mouth I swung round in a flounce of lavender silk to greet the man I was to wed. A stab of disappointment shot through me as if a dagger pierced my side. This was not the man of my dreams. However briefly, my foolish dismay must have shown clear as day on the face I turned on him. I caught the flash of hurt in steely grey eyes; eyes as cold and bleak as a midwinter sky. Shaken, I quickly rearranged my face and painted on my brightest smile. But too late; the damage was done.

Gawen was not ill-favoured; far from it. Had I not been blinded by my childish fantasy, I would have rejoiced that my bridegroom was a tall, well-built eighteen-year-old, broad-shouldered and with a complexion burnished by long hours at sea. He had the same high forehead as his father, but darker hair, and a long straight nose set into a face only a little too narrow to be called classically handsome. With his lips drawn into a thin line those hostile eyes regarded me sternly. His lips twitched before he made a perfunctory bow. Dressed less flamboyantly than the court gallants, Gawen was nonetheless well turned out in dove-grey doublet and hose, though something in his stance suggested he might be more at home in a plain leather jerkin at the helm of his ship.

I certainly had no cause to react as I did. But Henry Champernowne had raised my expectations and, immediately after that brief encounter with the glamorous Sir Christopher, poor Gawen didn't stand a chance.

'My father bids me walk in the gardens with you, Mistress Gabrielle,' Gawen said as he stood, stiff as a gatepost, beside me. I forced a smile as we walked to the door. As soon as we were outside he dropped my arm as if it was burning him.

Though the sun was bright I felt the autumn chill as we passed into the gardens and was pleased to hear Clotilde pounding along the path behind us. We paused and he stood, legs planted firmly apart, and surveyed the shipping on the river while she wrapped the cloak round my shoulders before withdrawing to a discreet distance. The cold didn't seem to bother Gawen but, from the look on his face, there were many places he'd rather be.

'Won't you call me Roberda? Everyone does,' I burbled, still brimful of excitement. I risked a quick look in his direction and was disturbed to see his lips pursed tight together and his brow furrowed in an angry frown. We walked on.

'I have waited long to meet you,' I quavered, uncertain how I might bridge the icy silence.

'I have been engaged on the queen's business.' He threw an anxious glance back at the palace. I looked round to see Sir Arthur at a window, keeping watch on us. Gawen heaved a heavy sigh and shrugged his shoulders.

'I trust your journey was satisfactory?' he asked after a long and awkward silence.

'Indeed it has been most interesting, for this is the first time I set foot in England. I have not been in a city as large as London since I was a small child. That was in Paris, of course…' My voice trailed away as, stony-faced, he watched a barge manoeuvre its way towards the bank. I shot an anxious look in Clotilde's direction. She smiled, nodded and signalled her encouragement with a little motion of her hand. So I ploughed on with another sally.

'Do you often come to London?' I enquired politely, hoping a more direct question would elicit a more enthusiastic response.

'No, not often,' was all the reply he gave me. I stifled a deep exasperated sigh – well, it was more of an angry moan. I was finding it hard to keep my legs still. If this went on much longer I knew I would start to fidget. I tried another tack, even though my face was aching with the effort of keeping a hard smile fixed on my lips.

'I am so looking forward to seeing Dartington. Your father says it is a pretty place with a spacious hall and pretty gardens,' I offered, then wished I could pull the words back when I realised I was falling into the trap of answering my own questions.

He shrugged again. 'It is well enough. A good base not far from the sea,' he answered before lapsing into silence once more. My patience ran out.

'Pray tell me what is so fascinating about that barge?' I challenged, raising my voice. At last I had his full attention. He whirled round, and I saw a warm flush creep up his cheeks as he ran a hand through his hair. He flicked a glance over my shoulder towards the palace then fixed his eyes on my face. I almost felt sorry for him, he looked so uncomfortable and flustered.

'I must be on my way,' he stuttered. Then, taking a breath, 'I have no practice in the art of conversation with a lady and neither time nor wish to perfect it. No doubt we shall meet on the morrow, for soon we have business to transact.' I stood with my mouth open as he bowed stiffly and marched off towards the waiting barges.

I dragged my feet disconsolately along the path as Clotilde led the way back to the palace. All the joy of my entry to the court and the thrill of my meeting with the queen were stifled, damped down, as surely as if Gawen had thrown a wet blanket over the sparks that should have ignited the start of our life together. I had been foolish enough to show my irritation. It had not been a good first meeting.

Chapter Nine

Marriage à la Mode

November 1571

Clotilde went off in search of refreshment and I slumped in a window seat, plunged into the deepest gloom. But I didn't have much time to wallow in my disappointment. As soon as they were released from their duties, a covey of the queen's ladies, mostly the younger ones who were called the maids of honour, sought me out. I couldn't believe Queen Elizabeth had really meant that I should join this gaggle of giggling girls.

They descended on me like a flock of chattering starlings, shimmering around me, firing questions so fast I couldn't answer.

'Word is that you are to be wed before the week is out, Mademoiselle Montgomery!' quipped a bright-eyed girl.

'Who is the bridegroom, you lucky girl?' shrieked a dark-haired beauty.

'What will you wear?' demanded another.

'Oh yes! Do tell us about the latest fashions in France,' someone called from the back.

I spun round in the midst of the crowd, feeling as though I couldn't breathe. Luckily, a sombre-looking man clad in lawyer's black with a heavy gold chain across his chest came into view. He had a rather plain-faced girl about my own age on his arm. As they advanced the pack of babbling girls scattered, their high-pitched chatter gradually fading away.

He acknowledged my shaky curtsey with a nod and moved on. They had only gone a few paces when the girl took her hand from his arm and whispered in his ear. He nodded and she turned back to greet me while he continued his stately progress.

'Hello! I'm Anne Cecil. That's my father Lord Burghley,' she announced, indicating the retreating figure. 'You're the Count of Montgomery's daughter, aren't you? Just arrived from France?'

I nodded and felt my legs give way under me. I flopped back into the window seat and Anne sat down beside me. She tilted her head to one side.

'I'm glad I could rescue you from that cluster of cats. If you're not used to them they can be a bit overpowering.'

'Thank you,' I replied with a weak smile. 'I've had a long day. I've just met the man I must marry in two days' time. So yes, I'll own, it has all become a bit much for me.'

'You poor thing!' she sympathised.

'Even though I'm to marry, I'm to stay at court with those girls. I don't know how on earth I'll manage,' I wailed, trying hard to hold back my tears. The thought of facing the queen and all those girls again had me quaking.

'It won't be as bad as you fear,' she consoled, patting my arm. 'I've just endured an interview with the queen about my own wedding. She was quite kind, really.' I looked down at my hands and tried to stop my fingers twisting in the cloth of my gown. 'Now, here's your maid bearing food – I expect she's come to take you to your lodgings,' Anne said kindly as Clotilde hurried towards us. 'Perhaps we can meet tomorrow when you feel better? I'm sure my father will allow me to visit you. We're to stay at Greenwich for a few more days.'

We said our goodbyes and I followed Clotilde, who kept casting anxious looks my way.

'A little rest might do you good, Mistress Roberda,' Clotilde advised after she had offered me a mug of ale and some bread and cheese in the stuffy little room. I tossed on the bed, trying to make sense of all that had happened. I was at a complete loss to know how I might mend my fences with Gawen. My dismal mood didn't lift when Maman rushed in to tell me that Papa had arrived and my wedding would go ahead as planned. On the first day of December in the year 1571 I was to become Gawen's wife. I would be married to a man who didn't want me.

'Must it be so soon?' I wailed. 'I'm afraid I gave offence to Gawen when first we met.'

'That's of little consequence now, you silly girl,' she scolded. 'The important thing is the queen has given her consent. It's a sign she's warm to our cause.'

'Can't we at least have some little time to get to know each other?' I asked. 'I want to be a good wife, but it's all so sudden.'

'It must be as the Queen of England wishes, you know that. I think she may have a mind to send your young husband to France. That can only be of help to us. So off you go tomorrow and see if you can charm the boy.'

Though I was exhausted, it was a long time before sleep claimed me.

True to her word, Anne appeared next morning. My mother had gone off to meet her friend Lettice, Lady Hereford, so I could receive Anne without interruption.

'You do look better this morning,' Anne said with a warm smile as she accepted my invitation to sit. 'I did so want to get to know you. I think we will find we have much in common. My own wedding will follow soon after yours.' She went on to tell me she was to marry Edward de Vere and become Countess of Oxford on the sixteenth day of December.

'He's the handsomest young man at court; he even outshines Sir Christopher,' she said with a dreamy look in her eyes. 'I already know Edward well. We practically grew up together.'

'Oh you are so fortunate in that,' I sighed. It was a relief to find someone I could confide in. 'I first set eyes on Gawen Champernowne only yesterday afternoon. I don't think he likes me much.'

'Oh, my poor dear girl,' Anne cried. 'That makes me realise I really am the most fortunate girl alive. Edward was a royal ward and my father his guardian.'

'You are lucky indeed,' I sighed. 'Girls of good family have little choice in the matter of husbands. It is the same in France.'

'I was supposed to marry Sir Philip Sidney but that came to

nothing. But I'm not sorry. It seemed a most natural thing that my father would arrange for me and Edward to be wed.'

Anne must have seen my downcast face for she went on kindly, 'I know you don't know him yet, but Champernowne's a nice-looking fellow; comes from a good family. He's a decent sort, I'm sure.'

'Well, he could do with some lessons in good manners, if you ask me!' I seethed. The more I thought about our depressing meeting, the more I put the blame squarely on Gawen's shoulders. 'I don't know what he can have against me that would prevent him from engaging in polite conversation.'

'I'm sure it will blow over,' Anne consoled, 'and perhaps the queen really will keep you at court for a while and you won't have to be buried in deepest Devonshire with him quite yet.' Clotilde tutted from her chair in the corner as we chatted on, and I began to feel I had found at least one friend in England.

'My mother says I'm to find him and charm him,' I moaned. 'But I don't know where to look for him. The palace is a rabbit warren of rooms and passages. I don't even know where to start.'

'That's easily solved,' Anne chirped. 'I know the palace well. I'll show you around. Should we happen on your intended I'll melt away and leave you together. Your maid can follow to see you well chaperoned.' So we set off along corridors and through magnificent rooms with Clotilde puffing along behind us. But there was no sign of Gawen.

'Let's try the gardens,' Anne suggested. Eventually we came on him down by the river, staring into the water with a face as long as a fiddle.

'Now's your chance,' Anne whispered. 'Let me know how you get on.' As she walked quickly back in the direction of the palace I took the deepest of breaths and caught his eye.

'Shall we walk together, sir?' I asked, as bright as a sunbeam as I approached him with Clotilde a few paces behind.

'I suppose we must,' said he, gloomy as a graveyard on a wet afternoon. 'I am told we are to be wed tomorrow, Mademoiselle Montgomery.'

'Oh, please will you call me Roberda. I would like that,' I said, gazing up at him in what I hoped was a suitably adoring way. I was determined to seem cheerful as I fell into step at his side and placed my hand lightly on his arm. But his next words dashed all hope.

'This wedding is not of my choosing. It's a thing of business between us, no more than that. Don't go getting any fanciful notions about love and such. I'm a soldier and I've been captain of my own ship for years. I'm not used to having women hanging around me.'

'But surely we may grow to love each other in time?' I quavered. 'I will do all I can to make you happy, to be a good wife.'

'Huh! Make me happy? You'd best mend your ways then.' His cheeks flushed red and he was shuffling his feet in the dust, not meeting my eye. 'You seem to me a flighty piece. Oh yes, you appeared quite taken with other men yesterday. I saw how you flirted with Hatton.'

'Sir, you wrong me!' I cried. I raised my chin and glared at him, but I was too angry to see the hurt in his eyes. 'Sir Christopher was merely kind enough to offer me his hand when I tripped. It meant nothing. What sort of girl do you think I am?'

'How should I know?' He turned away.

'Sir,' I hissed, with a tight smile. 'Perhaps we may speak again when you are in a better temper.'

I gathered what was left of my dignity and stalked off, with Clotilde throwing black looks Gawen's way as she scurried after me. Boiling over with rage I missed the door into the palace and came in though the kitchens, causing the cooks and kitchen boys to raise their eyebrows. When I reached my chamber I paced up and down, my breath coming in searing gasps. My new friend Anne found me, red-eyed and spluttering.

'I came to check on you,' she said, distress on her face. 'I hardly need ask how your meeting went.'

'Oh! He is quite insufferable,' I croaked. My throat felt dry and my voice sounded scratchy.

'He'll come round … you'll see,' she murmured.

'But, Anne … he doesn't want to marry me at all. He won't even talk to me.' I threw my headdress into the corner. 'Ugh! I feel so hot in that scratchy thing.'

Anne took both my hands in hers. She called for a cooling glass of cordial and made me drink it. She mopped my sweaty brow with her own kerchief and waited for me to stop trembling.

'There now,' she soothed, when I'd calmed down a little. 'At least I can bring you some good news. The queen has given permission for me to attend you at your wedding.'

'Thank you, thank you,' I blubbered and managed a weak little smile. 'At least I'll have one friend with me.'

'It will be my pleasure,' Anne replied. 'It is an honour to be wed in the queen's chapel. You must try to enjoy it a little. Let's look at your gown and then we can watch the evening's entertainment. If we keep in the shadows no one will see us.'

Clotilde looked up at me from where she'd crouched to adjust the hem of my dress and smiled.

'Beautiful, *ma petite*,' she murmured. 'You're a sight to melt the hardest heart.' I managed a tentative smile in return, a little laugh, but words were beyond me. Anne Cecil reached for my hand and squeezed it, and together the two women ushered me to the door of the chamber. I set out bravely, swishing along the corridor towards the queen's chapel with my hair unbound. Anne had helped me dress in the blue-green damask gown and lent me the prettiest ruff collar. My sleeves were trimmed with pearls and I wore velvet slippers embroidered with little flowers. I should have felt wonderful decked out so for my wedding day. But my stomach was turning over and over, like one of the queen's tumblers who'd entertained us the night before. I had a sour taste in my mouth as I braced myself to give a convincing performance. Anne Cecil squeezed my hand and fell in behind me and I saw Papa waiting at the door, his face wreathed in smiles. Sir Arthur stood beside him, grinning like a cat with its paw in the cream jug. Maman, resplendent in her best court gown, and Lady Hereford smiled their encouragement.

Beyond them all Gawen waited. His eyes did not turn as the splendidly dressed lords and ladies made way for me. I took my place beside him but still he stared straight ahead, one foot tapping impatiently on the brightly tiled floor. I risked a quick peep at him. I felt the bright smile I had painted on my face slipping a little when I saw the cold glint in his eyes.

At last Queen Elizabeth made her majestic entrance and drew eyes away from us. It was over in no time. I mumbled my vows. Gawen said his in a flat voice with no feeling at all. He did not venture to kiss his bride. We knelt before Queen Elizabeth for her blessing.

'You will go to France, young sir, to learn something of the language and customs there, that you may better understand your wife,' she commanded and a ripple of laughter spread through the throng. I knew, of course, that she was really sending Gawen over to France to have him act as spy for Walsingham and Anne's father. 'Now, Madame Champernowne –' a titter among the ladies was instantly stifled – 'Sir Arthur has told me you sing well and play on the virginals, and that you've brought with you a boy who is a fine musician,' the queen continued.

'Yes, Y-y-your M-majesty,' I stuttered, feeling suddenly hot. It was the very first time anyone had used my new name.

'It will please me if you remain at court until the spring to entertain us,' she announced, in a voice that brooked no questioning. As she spoke she gave me such a penetrating stare that I felt even shakier. Then she turned the same look on my papa who, with a beaming smile, gave her a well-practised bow. I wondered if she was keeping me as some sort of hostage against my father's good behaviour.

Everyone relaxed a bit after the queen swept from the chapel in a dazzling cloud of sumptuous silks and glittering jewels. A group of the younger ladies-in-waiting swarmed round me to admire my gown. As I tried to extricate myself I looked for Gawen. He was nowhere to be seen. I shot rapid glances round the room, hoping no one had noticed and, feeling the flush creeping up my cheeks, I took Sir Arthur's arm. When we arrived at the room set aside for the celebratory feast Gawen was already seated and helping himself from a platter.

I sat uncomfortably beside my husband at the wedding breakfast and tried valiantly to engage him in conversation. To be fair he did, at least for a time, make a little effort to play his part before the wedding guests, though his eyes never met mine.

'Tell me about your ship,' I ventured after a few abortive sallies, and at last he came to life. He gabbled off lots of strange shipboard names that were beyond my English vocabulary and I mumbled what I hoped were appropriate responses. We might even have looked as though we were enjoying each other's company, but not for long.

When Pierre came in with some of the queen's musicians they struck up a tune and all eyes turned on us to lead the dance. Gawen just sat there.

'Husband,' I said, trying that word out for the first time and not feeling it applied to us at all, 'we must lead the dance. Everyone is waiting.' But Gawen pushed back his seat and stumbled away, murmuring that he must find the jakes. I gritted my teeth and felt as though my flesh was crawling.

Anne came to my rescue.

'Will you step a measure with me and the other ladies?' she asked, holding my eyes in her steady gaze.

'Gladly,' I answered, beaming. That was the only dance I had on my wedding day.

I felt rather sick as I climbed into the carriage that would take us to the house where we were to spend our first night together as man and wife. Clotilde gave me a weak smile as she took the seat opposite, while Gawen flopped down beside me without a word. I craned my neck for a last glimpse of Anne standing next to Maman to wave us off. Thankfully there would be no accompanying party to see us truly bedded. Anne said that often parents, friends and well-wishers went along to witness the newlyweds safely in their marriage bed; sometimes they even called in a priest to bless the bed. In our case everyone must have had more important things to do. At least I'd be spared all the ribald jesting before we were left alone.

The short journey passed in a strained silence. As soon as we arrived Gawen disappeared into the kitchens beyond the cramped parlour, calling for ale. I dragged my feet up the stairs to the bedchamber, feeling as though my insides were quivering. Clotilde helped me out of my clothes and into the bed before she squeezed my hand and left me. I lay trembling beneath the sheet, waiting for what I knew must happen on my wedding night.

The candle had burned low before the door opened. Gawen lay down on the bed beside me, fully clothed. He made no attempt to hold or kiss me, but remained still and silent as the grave. I clutched the bedsheet so hard I thought my knuckles would crack and steeled myself to make the first move. But when I reached out a hand he shifted further from me.

'Madam,' he said crisply formal. 'I am here only because it is willed by the queen and my father that we be wed. I have no wish for this marriage. It is a matter of business. That is all.'

I took a deep breath and closed my eyes for a moment.

'You seem to see me as akin to the parchment and ink used to seal an agreement – merely part and parcel of some business transaction,' I cried, the words tumbling out of me all in rush. He made no reply.

'But it is apparent that you are reluctant to put the final seal on our contract,' I continued. Still no reply. 'We are man and wife in the sight of God,' I ground out these words between clenched teeth. The effort of keeping my tone civil in the face of his brooding silence was making my jaw ache. I tried once more.

'We were married this day in the presence of the queen and many witnesses.' My voice had started to rise and I felt a cold sweat gathering on my brow, but I would not give up that easily. 'I know my duty as a wife. I am not afraid. Indeed I have looked forward to this night.' Too late I realised my mistake.

'Indeed, a woman such as you would do so,' he muttered.

'I will not grace your loathsome words with a response,' I snapped, balling my hands into fists and beating on the mattress. With a supreme effort I forced myself to lie still.

After another long silence the bed shook as he took a deep breath.

'Look, I have no wish to quarrel with you,' he said, suddenly icily polite, 'it is as it is. My father pressed for this match, not I. I have no need of a wife for I leave for France at first light. Now go to sleep.' My chin trembled as I bit back a retort and felt hot tears on my cheeks. I wrapped my arms around myself and buried my face in the pillow. I did not sleep.

So we started our married life together lying chaste upon the marriage bed. He must have known that I wept futile angry tears that night. But his heart was not melted. Next morning he left me, still a maid. He left me without a farewell. Our contract remained unsealed. A part of me wanted to curl up into a ball and weep, to hide away from prying eyes. Another part of me wanted to vent my anger, to find a way to shame him. No bride should feel so.

Chapter Ten

Gloriana's Court

December 1571

The day after my wedding I crossed Queen Elizabeth's presence chamber with short jerky steps, assumed my position beside Pierre, took a deep breath and gave him a curt nod. My voice wobbled on the first phrases of the French chanson, but Pierre caught my eye as he took up the tune on his lute and swept me along with him. Soon my voice was rising confidently and I almost forgot the Queen of England was there, so wrapped up was I in the magic of Pierre's talent. As the last chord died, the room was silent until Queen Elizabeth smiled and clapped her hands. My heart was racing, drumming in my chest, as the applause grew and we took our bow.

But our performance was not over. The queen motioned for me to take a seat at the virginals and, emboldened by the reception our first offering received, my fingers flew over the keys as never before. But it was Pierre's final solo that held everyone spellbound and brought the loudest applause. Pierre's grin was so wide I thought it must split his face in two. As we basked in the glow of success, I remembered the little waif with the huge eyes I had rescued.

We were asked to perform for the queen most afternoons and Pierre strutted around in a liveried outfit to show he played with the royal musicians. His talent did not go unnoticed.

'She certainly enjoys the boy's music,' Sir Arthur chuckled as Queen Elizabeth led the applause after another performance. 'She might want to keep him at court. Let's hope she'll let him come with you to Devon. My father once had a lot of trouble getting his musicians released from King Henry's court. Had to pay for their keep. Cost him a fortune.' I recognised the kindly concern beneath Sir Arthur's jollity. He knew I would value a friendly face from France at Dartington.

I soon learned to be careful whom I smiled upon when our music drew attention from the young men of the court.

'I don't know why they all think they have a right to look at me so,' I stormed when I met Anne after an encounter with one young man had left me blushing. 'They don't all have Christopher Hatton's charm and good looks, however much they think they do. And I'm a married woman now. I dread to think how Gawen would react if he saw them ogling me.'

'Just play it as a courtly game, laugh it off, and don't ever allow yourself to be alone with any of them,' Anne advised. 'That way you'll avoid any suggestion of scandal.'

After the wedding Papa was locked in long discussions with the queen. He went about with a broad grin on his face and Maman held her chin high. On the sixth day of December they were ready to leave.

'We're going home tomorrow,' Maman informed me. 'Charlotte has cared for your younger brothers and sisters quite long enough. Make best use of your time at court, Roberda. I look to have good reports of you.' Papa gave me one long hug and Jacques bade me a cheery farewell. Sir Arthur left for Devon on the same day.

But I had no time to miss them, for the court moved on the twelfth of the month with a great upheaval. Tapestries, furniture and all were packed up and taken from Greenwich to grace the queen's chambers at Whitehall Palace. Once we were established in the rambling labyrinth of rooms near the River Thames the preparations for Anne's wedding started in earnest. It was to be a triple wedding with two other couples tying the knot at the same ceremony; a much grander affair than mine had been, as befitted the daughter of William Cecil, Queen Elizabeth's chief adviser.

'I'm so excited,' Anne breathed as I helped her braid her hair. 'But I'm very nervous of tonight too.' I concentrated on combing out her hair and avoided her eyes as I answered breezily.

'Oh, it's nothing to be afraid of. He's a fine young man and will treat you kindly.' I kept my eyes down and felt my neck growing hot. I was in no position to give advice. Luckily the moment passed in a flurry of ribbons as I fixed Anne's headdress in place.

Anne looked very sweet in a gown of ivory silk all trimmed with silver thread work and pearls, so that she appeared to shimmer and gleam like a moonbeam as she stood next to the dazzling Edward de Vere in Westminster Abbey. She was so happy that day, but I was not so sure her husband was the paragon she thought him. Although he was marrying my friend, Edward de Vere kept looking at me in a most disturbing way. Worse still, his eyes followed every girl who came near. I really hoped Anne's father would look out for her.

I found it hard to keep still in my seat as we watched the gentlemen of the court ride out to the lists on the day after Anne's wedding. It was the first tournament I had ever attended; none had been held in France since my father's dreadful accident with the king. I dared not bestow a favour, though I was tempted to offer my kerchief to the dashing Sir Christopher Hatton when he rode out against Charles Howard.

Anne made sure I was on the invitation list for the grand dinner and reception given in honour of her husband at her father's house in the Strand. Whisked out of the palace with the maids of honour in a carriage painted with Lord Burghley's arms I joined the throng of well-wishers. After a delicious feast even the queen joined in with the dancing and I had no shortage of partners. After a few dances, as I sat down to recover my breath, the French ambassador, a wiry little man with a nose too big for his face, sidled up and tried to pump me for information about my father's visit to Queen Elizabeth and Gawen's mission to France.

'*Monsieur l'Ambassadeur*,' I simpered, rolling my eyes shamelessly. 'I am but a giddy girl newly wed. I know nothing of such matters.' I tripped off to join Anne and the other girls, leaving him gaping after me.

I missed Anne when she went to her father's house, Theobalds, with her husband. But there was plenty to distract me as everyone prepared for the holiday; Christmastide was marked by twelve days of feasting and merriment such as I'd never known. I laughed until my sides ached and marvelled at the masques and plays, a different one each day. On the first day of January I watched the New Year gift exchanges, though I wasn't important enough for the queen to remember me.

Anne had not forgotten me. I turned the pair of cuffs over in my hand, studying the fine stitching. She had enclosed her gift, worked with her own hand, with a letter. Her father was unwell – an attack of gout – so she'd had to miss the court festivities. I frowned as I read her fulsome praise of Edward de Vere. I was hearing rather different stories about that young man.

At the Twelfth Night revels, my heart fluttered when Sir Christopher Hatton led me out in a dance. But I did not take up his offer to supply me with a slice of the twelfth cake and another glass of wine. His eyes held mine just a little too long and I found myself trembling at the touch of his hand. I pulled away, making a weak excuse that I must return to the other ladies, and watched him from the shadows. Something about that man made me feel weak at the knees. But I dare not take the risk of some tale being relayed to Gawen.

After the holidays Pierre and I were asked to play less often. I tried to close my ears to all the talk of Spain and France and religion and the Queen of Scots. But I couldn't help but notice how the mood changed, how everyone became tense and sombre when the Duke of Norfolk was found guilty and sentence passed. He might appeal, but the odds were he would eventually go to the scaffold.

February passed with dreary weather, and the gaiety of the court remained muted. One morning I almost ran into Lord Burghley as he was hurrying towards the presence chamber clutching a bundle of papers. I couldn't help smiling to see his cap slightly askew and the twinkling gold buttons on his otherwise severe black doublet dancing as he stepped aside. Anne's father righted his headgear and smiled.

'Ah, well met, Mistress Champernowne!' I looked askance at him, not yet used to my married name. William Cecil considered me as he stroked his straggly beard. For all his genial manner I felt his cool green eyes boring into me.

'Sir Arthur has written from Dartmouth,' he announced.

'Dartmouth, sir? Why, where is that?' I asked with a puzzled frown. The English names were all so similar.

'A fine port on the coast of Devon. Sir Arthur is often there. He's Vice Admiral of Her Majesty's Fleet of the West,' he answered with a touch of impatience. His chin jutted out and he narrowed his eyes before the warm smile returned to his lips.

'Of course, you have much to learn,' he said, more kindly. 'News has come from France. Sir Arthur fears the peace will not last long. Your husband is on his way back to England and will look for you in Devon.'

'But how shall I travel there, sir?' I asked, blushing furiously.

'I will arrange an escort to see you safe into Devon and Sir Arthur will meet you in Exeter,' he replied. 'Anne's in London; she'd like to see you before you go. Come to Burghley House tomorrow, stay for a day or two while your people make ready for the journey. I'll send men to accompany you.'

'Thank you, sir, it will be my pleasure to visit my friend Anne,' I assured him with a nod. Very daring, I put my hand on his arm as he gathered his papers.

'Sir, is there news of my family?'

'No news, but I'm sure all is well,' he answered without looking at me. I watched him scuttle away to his meeting then turned and rushed headlong to my chamber to start packing. *Clotilde and the others will be pleased,* I thought. Their time in the palace had not always been easy. Only that morning Jeanne had complained that one of the kitchen boys had been sniggering about her, calling her a French whore.

Two broad-shouldered men wearing the Cecil livery arrived the next morning to escort me and I strutted along between them, eagerly taking in the sights and sounds of the city. This time I was on foot, weaving through streets teeming with merchants, travellers, gentlemen on horseback, priests, roughly dressed men driving pigs and sheep and women struggling along with heavy bundles. All were bustling about their business; no one paid any attention to me. I held a pomander of sweet-smelling herbs close under my nose as the noisome stench of city life hit my nostrils; a pungent mix of woodsmoke, animal dung, rotting fish and cabbages, with an occasional whiff of heady perfume as a fine lady or gentleman passed. There was a deafening hubbub; people yelling and shouting, bells pealing, cows bellowing, pigs squealing, horses whinnying, carpenters hammering, doors banging and cartwheels clattering over cobbles. It felt as though the whole world were in noisy motion; as though all humanity were streaming down the Strand. Between the mansion houses of the rich I glimpsed narrow crowded alleys with filthy water and excrement running down the middle and all manner of stinking rubbish was thrown down from windows above.

Anne greeted me with hugs and suggested we walk in the gardens before the midday meal. I was quite speechless as we wandered among fruit trees just beginning to bud against brick walls. Close-hedged spiralling paths led us though ornamental parterres all overlooked by a mound and a banqueting house.

'Your father's gardens are even grander than the queen's!' I laughed as we climbed the mound and looked out over the orchards and green fields beyond.

'Hush. You mustn't say that,' Anne chuckled. 'But come, look through here.' She led me past a bowling green and a tennis court tiled in red and white.

'It's splendid, Anne,' I whispered. 'And you look so happy. How is your husband?'

'He's the finest man in the whole of England,' she said, glowing with pride. But then a shadow crossed her face. 'My father says he presses too hard for his kinfolk. This business with Norfolk and the others seems to have upset everyone,' she said. She blushed and twisted a lock of hair round her finger. 'But let's not think of that,' she said, brightening. 'Let's enjoy our time together, for Father tells me you're off to Devon in a couple of days.'

'I am. A new life awaits me,' I replied. 'I feel breathless just thinking about it.'

Our time together flew by. Anne's husband was not in evidence; I wasn't sure if she knew where he was. Her father was always busy at court or holding secretive meetings in his study, so Anne and I could enjoy each other's company in peace. She showed me her wardrobe of beautiful gowns, many trimmed with the finest lace and pearls. We discussed the latest fashions and shared sweetmeats and talked long into the evenings in the candlelit parlour – I never saw a house so brightly lit as Burghley House – but as we shared confidences

I omitted to reveal the dismal details of my wedding night. When it was time to leave we exchanged embraces and promised to write often. Heart pounding, I took my place in the carriage which had brought Clotilde, Jeanne and Pierre and all my belongings ready to start our journey to the West.

We made frequent stops, seeking lodgings with friends of Lord Burghley's. As we travelled further from the city the crowds of poor people at the roadside, some openly begging, thinned out. But the rain was relentless. Clotilde pulled a face as the carriage splashed through a ford running high with dirty brown water.

'I do hope Devon is a better place than this,' she moaned. 'I mislike this country more and more as each day passes.'

''Tis the season, that is all,' I said, hoping it was true. 'When summer comes I'm sure it's as merry a place as France.'

Sir Arthur met us on the road as Exeter's city walls came into view.

'Welcome to Devon, my dear,' he beamed. 'We'll be on our way tomorrow, but first I want you to meet someone.' We made our way to a small house close to the magnificent cathedral that towered over the city. A well-dressed woman met us at the door.

'This is my sister, Gawen's Aunt Katherine,' Sir Arthur said, eyes twinkling.

I guessed that Katherine Raleigh must be a little older than her brother, but the years had treated her well. Only a few grey hairs showed beneath her cap and she was slender as a girl. With a warm smile she invited me to sit while Sir Arthur went off in search of Master Raleigh. She quizzed me gently about France and my family over spiced cakes and ale. Then she looked me directly in the eye.

'And how do you like your husband?' Taken by surprise, I hesitated a little too long before I replied. The older woman nodded and smiled.

'Ah, such is often our lot. I have been fortunate indeed to find a man like my Walter as my second husband.'

'Walter? So the boy I met in France is named for his father?' I enquired.

'Indeed he is, and he's the apple of his father's eye too. As I said, I've been lucky with my second husband. My first was not so easy, but I have fine children to show for my patience.' I swallowed hard as she went on. 'Gawen is a young man bent upon achieving great things in war or at sea. My best advice to you, my dear, is not to expect too much of him. You have a fine place at Dartington, gardens and orchards to oversee, a household to run. Give your attention to that. I offer you this as no doubt you'll miss your mother's guidance.' I gave her a feeble smile and nodded.

'Arthur's been lost since his Mary died, though his girl Bess does well,' she went on. 'She'll be glad of your company. Now, let us sit here by the fire and you can tell me all the court gossip, while my husband and my brother put the world to rights.'

That night I heard the watchman call 'All's well' more times than I could count, as wild images of the home I must share with Gawen flitted through my overactive imagination.

My eyes snapped open at the knock on the bedchamber door. A shiver ran through me as the door swung open and the candle Clotilde carried cast giant shadows on the wall. I leaped from the bed and darted across the oak floorboards to the window. It was that time between night and day when dreams linger, when chimney stacks silhouetted against a pearly dawn can seem like castles in the air. I took a deep breath, gave myself a shake and let my hopes fly out into the soft morning air.

'Sir Arthur is already up, mistress,' Clotilde croaked, irritation making her voice grate. 'He's set on having us all on the road before cockcrow,' she grumbled. She found a space for the candle on a large chest and helped me into my clothes, complaining all the while that I wouldn't keep still. I pushed past Jeanne on the stair as she bumped a bag down and nearly knocked Pierre off the bottom step in my hurry to reach the kitchen. An enticing smell of newly baked bread had set my stomach rumbling. After a hasty mouthful, we mounted up in the street. Sir Arthur gave a cheery wave to his sister who leaned out from an upstairs window to bid us farewell.

'We'll see you at Dartington soon,' he called to her, then over his shoulder to me, 'no carriage today! We'll cover the distance faster on horseback.'

'That suits me well, sir,' I laughed. 'I've had more than enough of that carriage.'

The horses slithered on stones still touched by morning dew as we passed bleary-eyed tradesmen setting up for the day before we rattled out of the city over an ancient bridge. A sweet breath of spring hung in the air and the small birds were singing their hearts out. I felt light as one of those birds, borne up on a wave of hope and anticipation.

The sun was high and Exeter far behind us when we rode into the bustling market town of Newton Abbot. The hubbub reached our ears long before we came near the market square, where stalls clustered around a little chapel were doing a brisk trade.

'Why, mistress, it's much like the markets in France,' Clotilde called as her eyes roved over bolts of cloth, crusty loaves of bread, heaps of vegetables and stalls laid out with cheese and fish. Well-to-do matrons in fine woollen gowns were haggling over prices, while drably dressed women struggled with heavy baskets on their arms.

'Watch out,' shouted Pierre, as a man pushed a barrow loaded with sacks of grain across our path. My pony snorted and threw up her head and her hooves rang on the cobbles until I had her under control again. Pierre grinned as I steadied her, and clutched his precious lute tight to his chest lest any thieves took a fancy to it.

Clotilde's face was a picture as she held her nose with her fingers as an unpleasant stink wafted across from tanners' pits that must lie beyond the cramped tenements.

'What a dirty, noisome place!' she sniffed.

A girl in a faded blue kirtle stood a little apart from the crowds, jealously guarding a basket of flowers. Above the din her voice rose clear.

'Primroses! Bright primroses! Three bunches for a penny! Fresh heather from the moors to bring ye luck, good mistress!' I fumbled for the purse that hung at my girdle, thinking a bunch of the sweet flowers and a sprig of heather would look well pinned to the front of my gown. But Sir Arthur spurred his horse forward, giving wide berth to a fight broken out between two young men. I would have to do without my posy.

We stopped but a short time to refresh ourselves at an inn before we pressed on along an ancient trackway.

'This way will shorten our journey,' Sir Arthur called cheerily. I grinned back at him and felt my pulse quicken. Sir Arthur had boasted that the countryside of Devon was the greenest, the most beautiful in all the world. But however hard I peered between my pony's ears, my view was blocked by high banks topped with thickset hedges bursting with vibrant green. The deep Devon lanes twisted tantalisingly ahead, leading me to a mysterious new life.

As the day wore on I found it more and more difficult to keep my hands steady on the reins. My heart was turning somersaults within my breast and the creaking leather shrieked loud in my ears as I shifted impatiently in the saddle. In an attempt to keep myself calm I brought my pony alongside Sir Arthur's rangy bay and plied him with a stream of hopeful questions. He spoke warmly of his love of Dartington but his bright smile faded when, with a heavy sigh, he told me how, with his wife, he had brought the long-neglected estate back to life.

'It will be for you and Gawen to see it through now.' His voice trailed off and he lapsed into silence until we approached a village.

'This is Staverton!' he announced, giving his shoulders a little shake as if to rid himself of lingering melancholy. We passed low cottages where women seated at their spinning in the doorways scrambled to their feet to bob a curtsey, and beyond a solid square-towered church and an orchard – and I saw the River Dart for the first time. We followed the course of the river, its blue-grey waters snaking lazily between low banks fringed with scrubby trees. I hauled on the reins and paused to watch a speckled fish, no more than a silver dart, glimmering briefly in the crystal-clear water before it found a hiding place among the stones on the river bottom. Sir Arthur signalled impatiently to me to move along and, to my surprise, after we'd passed a substantial mill he turned his horse into the stream and splashed across.

'It's quite safe. Tide's down,' he called as I gingerly encouraged my mount to follow. 'It's usually passable so long as the river's not in flood; by far the quickest way to Dartington; you'll come to know it well.' Halfway across I turned in the saddle to see Clotilde perched behind one of Sir Arthur's men, her face as white as chalk.

'Don't worry, Clotilde,' I called brightly, waving an arm downstream. 'The river is as calm as a shining mirror.' As Pierre guided his own mount into the water, I smiled to see Jeanne's knuckles showing white as she clung on behind him.

'Not far now,' Sir Arthur called over his shoulder. His face was much brighter, as if a curtain had been lifted.

A deeply worn track led us along the edge of dense woodland and up a gentle slope past stands of thick-trunked oaks. I pushed my weight down into the stirrups and tried to raise myself up from the saddle so I could look ahead. My pony, already skittish as she picked up my nervous excitement, took exception to this unexpected manoeuvre and shied, nearly pitching me into the dirt. Sir Arthur grinned as I righted myself.

'This is all our deer park,' he declared with an exuberant sweep of his arm. 'Just a little further and we'll be home.' He pressed his mount to a trot and my pony picked up speed behind as if she too knew she was on the homeward stretch. Breathless, I craned my neck to get first sight of my new home. But I slumped back in the saddle as we drew nearer. I had imagined a splendid entrance, perhaps a turreted tower, not an archway between two crumbling buildings. The unmistakable stench of cattle was strong as we clattered into a huge cobbled courtyard. 'I've plans for a gatehouse and better use for these old buildings by the arch. But it suffices for now. I'm surprised John Holland, the man who built our hall, didn't pull 'em down and make a grand gateway here.' Sir Arthur puffed out his chest to explain further; it was clearly a subject he loved.

But I couldn't keep my eyes on Gawen's father any longer. My gaze was drawn to the far side of the courtyard where a flag fluttered jauntily in the breeze above a squat tower that rose above grey-stone walls and a slated roof. As I stared at the tall windows a cloud suddenly blocked out the sun, casting the hall into deep shadow, as though a veil had been thrown over the roof and draped down the walls in menacing folds. I felt the hair rise at the back of my neck and a chill ran down my spine. I shuddered, gave myself a shake and sighed with relief when the sun peeped out again. The windows shone as warmly as before and I told myself it was just a silly fancy.

'Holland needed space for all his retainers; all his men-at-arms. The half-brother of a king must have quite a train of followers. So first he built these lodgings to house them all. We keep a more modest staff here now. Many rooms are used only for storage,' Sir Arthur explained, as I noted the lines of two-storeyed buildings, each with an outside stair and a chimney, that edged the cobbled court.

I slipped from the saddle at the mounting block and a groom stepped up to take the reins. Smoothing my riding gown I gathered myself to face the line of people waiting before the door. A round-faced girl about my own age picked up the skirts of a rather fine gown of tawny silk and bounded forward to greet Sir Arthur, flashing a brilliant grin at me.

'I'm Elizabeth, Gawen's sister, but everyone calls me Bess,' she gabbled. 'It's going to be wonderful to have you here. My father says I may call you Roberda. Is that all right? Come on, let's go in.' She bounced off towards the door but I hesitated. The others were waiting in silence all in a line, with empty eyes fixed on some point far in front of them. I took a breath, beamed my brightest smile and, in my very best English, I pronounced the words I'd been practising for this very moment.

'Thank you all. It is so very good of you to greet me. I look forward to getting to know you.' Not one of the Dartington serving people smiled back. No one curtseyed or doffed their cap. They just remained rigid and unmoving like a line of sentries standing guard.

Seeing my confusion, Bess took my hand and drew me in through an arched doorway into a porch beneath the tower.

'Watch out for the king's deer,' she giggled, pointing upwards. I looked up and there in the middle of the vaulted roof, where the ribs met, was a carving of a chained white hart upon a painted rose. 'I'm sure my father has told you all about John Holland? He's the one who built Dartington. Well, that's the sign of his brother, King Richard.'

'So you live in a house fit for a king,' I laughed.

'Oh, it's ever so long ago. But I'm rather pleased my parents left that deer in his place when they built the rooms above the porch. I used to love looking at it when I was little. Come on, let's go in.' Bess reminded me of a busy little bee, happily buzzing from flower to flower, never still. The smiling welcome shining from her face was balm to my injured pride after the strangely hostile reaction of the Dartington staff.

Chapter Eleven

Mistress of Dartington Hall

Spring 1572

My mouth fell open and I froze on the threshold, letting my eyes drink in the splendour of Dartington Hall. A soaring forest of carved oak beams supported the huge span of the roof high above my head. I slowly let out my breath as I watched the banners fluttering gently from the beams and took in the stone corbels, each with an angel bearing the arms of some great knight on a painted shield. Wispy tendrils of smoke rose from a fire smouldering in a fireplace even larger than the one Papa had at Ducey and long tables stretched the length of the hall, enough space to seat a multitude. I could see why Sir Arthur was so proud of this place. It was as splendid as the queen's Great Hall at the Palace of Westminster.

Lost in wonder, at first I did not notice Gawen. My husband was well built and tall. He looked over the heads of most men. But he faded to insignificance in the grandeur of that lofty hall. He had almost reached me before I realised he was there, a sharp-featured little man hovering at his elbow.

I thought I caught a momentary flicker of recognition, even of welcome, in Gawen's steel-grey eyes when he paused in front of me. But if I did it was gone as soon as it came. His fingers felt cold as he took my hand, as courtesy demanded, but he turned quickly away so I could no longer see his eyes

'My wife is tired from her journey,' he announced in a lordly voice. 'Rist, will you see my lady to her chamber. Father, we must speak. There is news from France.' Undeterred, I put my hand on his arm.

'Is there news of my family? I have heard nothing since they left me in London months ago. Did you bring letters from my mother?' He shook my hand away as a horse shakes to rid itself of a fly and rapped out a short reply.

'I did not. Go with Rist, if you please. I must speak with my father.'

Such a curt dismissal quenched all my hopes, all the joy I might have taken in my new home, as surely as if he had thrown a pail of water over me. My head dropped and I came within a hair's breadth of meek obedience before a vision of my mother rose up in my mind; Isabeau, Countess of Montgomery, mistress of her household, imperious and commanding. *I'm her daughter. I'm mistress of this household now. I'll not be told when I'm tired and sent to my room!*

I threw back my head, drew myself up in imitation of Maman at her formidable best, forced my lips into a smile and whirled around.

'How kind and considerate you are, husband,' I said, honey-sweet, but firm. 'But I am not at all tired and would see more of this household which is now mine to manage. Master Rist, is it?' I favoured the rodent-faced servant with a withering stare. 'If you please, conduct me to the kitchens and the storerooms. I take it they lie beyond the passage?' I'll swear I heard Sir Arthur stifle a chuckle, or perhaps it was Bess. Rist looked questioningly at Gawen.

'As you wish,' my husband ground the words through clenched teeth, then recovered himself a little. 'Yes, Rist, off course, you must do as your mistress orders. Bess, will you go with them?'

'Oh yes, brother, I wouldn't miss this for anything,' she chortled as we passed through the opening.

'Do the gardens lie that way?' I asked brightly, pointing to a door that stood ajar. Rist grunted in reply. As I stepped forward I felt a rush of wings over my head. A swallow was making a nest high on the wall just within the door lintel. 'Well, well. I see others are making a new home under this roof,' I laughed. 'Be sure not to close this door, Master Rist. Some say birds in a house bring bad luck, but I deem it an honour to share my home with this pretty fellow.' Bess gave me another encouraging smile, but Rist looked at me as though he thought me mad.

I stepped outside and found myself in a second courtyard to the rear of the hall. Mellow grey stone walls enclosed a pretty knot garden with beds planted with flowers. The far range of buildings looked neglected, but the effect was rather charming. To the left of the door an area had been left unplanted, save for an apple tree. Away to the right, past the hall, I could just see a church tower rising up in the shadow of an enormous yew tree.

I walked a few paces enjoying the sweet, lemon-tinged fragrance of early apple blossom. Out of nowhere, two boys came hurtling along the path, giggling and laughing, egging each other on to run faster. They veered sharply into the doorway and nearly knocked Rist off his feet.

'Scurvy little imps!' he growled, as they ducked under his flailing arm.

'Now, Rist,' said Sir Arthur, who had ignored Gawen and come to stand beside us. He watched the boys' retreating figures as they burst out through the other door and raced across the courtyard. 'Let 'em be. Boys will be boys! They're the cook's lads, aren't they? As likely a pair as you'll ever find! Good for them to let off steam a bit. They already practise at the butts every Sunday. Soon they'll be put to work or to fighting for the queen.'

Rist grunted and Sir Arthur gave me a searching look.

'It would do my heart good to see another Champernowne youngster running through these gardens,' he said with a sigh. I felt my cheeks flaming and suddenly found the flagstone path beneath my feet fascinating. *Not much chance you'll get your wish,* I thought. *With a husband who's always away on the sea or in France and doesn't seem to even notice he has a wife, I wouldn't hold your breath for a grandchild.*

Sir Arthur left us to follow Gawen who had already stomped off, I knew not where. Rist shrugged his shoulders and scowled as we turned back towards the hall.

'Sir Arthur and Lady Mary had this all planted anew,' he grunted, raising his head to glower at me. 'I trust you will not order any changes.'

'I will walk in the gardens tomorrow, Master Rist, and then we shall see. Now, where is the buttery?' I asked, quite determined to keep the obnoxious little man firmly in his place. He looked more like a rat every time I glanced at him. Bess's eyes, bright as a starling's, darted between us and a little smile hovered about her pretty lips. She was clearly enjoying Rist's discomfort.

We retraced our steps and Rist indicated one of three arched doorways. I made an elaborate show of counting the butts of ale standing on the cool stone floor beyond the first door and ran my finger along the boards to check for dust.

'The pantry, Master Rist?' I asked, just as haughty as my mother. He led me through another door into a room hung with joints of beef, a feathered goose, barrels of dried fish and several rabbits. All appeared in order. I asked about the cellars, the brewhouse and the bakehouse as we made our way towards a cavernous kitchen, sensibly set at some distance from the hall lest fire might spread. An old woman crouched before one of the massive fireplaces. Her grubby cap was knocked slightly awry as she put a hand to her brow before she took up a long-handled spoon to stir a bubbling pot. High above, fish and hams were hung to dry in the smoky air and a fire blazed high in a second fireplace where a red-faced boy turned a spit. My mouth watered as the smell of roasting beef reminded me it was a long time since I'd eaten.

I noticed the servants flicking anxious glances my way as they busied themselves preparing food for the next meal. I stopped a scullery maid hurrying in from the direction of the pantry to question her about the stained and patched clothing she wore.

'Your name?' I demanded imperiously. The girl's face coloured and she looked at the floor.

'Alice,' she mumbled. 'I'm Alice Blackaller, mistress.'

'Where is your apron?' I enquired, pointing to the brown smudge on the front of her kirtle.

'I left it off on account of it being so hot in the kitchen,' she stuttered. Her chin quivered and she looked frantically over her shoulder. Rist waved an impatient hand and she scuttled away.

'I would have all Sir Arthur's serving people cleanly arrayed as they go about their work, Master Rist,' I ordered, giving him my haughtiest stare. 'Will you have new aprons and caps made for all in need and make sure they are laundered regularly? Now, I have seen enough for today. I will see the brewhouse, the gardens and the orchards tomorrow. Then you may bring me the account books.' Rist gave me a sullen nod as he led me back towards the hall. Bess grinned conspiratorially.

'That was well done!' she whispered and I grinned at her.

'This staircase?' I asked as an afterthought, turning back towards the heavy oak outer door. 'Here, this stair tucked behind the door. Where does it lead, Master Rist?'

'Above was Sir Arthur's chamber when he and Lady Mary first came here. He had a fine plastered ceiling added and put new windows in. Now he's moved to the new chambers beyond the hall. The rooms now serve as my lodging, mistress.' His stare was hostile, as if daring me to order him to find other accommodation.

'That is quite in order, Master Rist,' I replied smoothly. 'It is fitting that as steward you are close at hand, by the door.' I followed him through the empty hall.

Sir Arthur had spared no expense in remodelling the family chambers. We climbed several short flights of newly installed carved oak stairs with dog-legged turns leading us this way and that. 'Sir Arthur took them old stairs out,' Rist informed me. 'Proper dangerous they used to be. All them worn-out stone steps.' He paused to recover his breath then led me along a landing to a small room, hardly more than a closet. I peeped inside and saw that on the opposite wall another door stood open, revealing a spacious bedchamber. I walked to the window and peered out at the gardens below.

'This is the room set aside for your use, mistress,' Rist informed me. The emphasis he placed on the word *mistress* made it sound odd, as if the word was stuck in his throat. 'Sir Arthur and Master Gawen have rooms to the other side.'

'Thank you, Rist. I trust Pierre, the musician who travels with me, has been allotted suitable rooms?'

He gave me a sullen look, but nodded and, in a voice that left me in no doubt of his disapproval, he replied, 'As Sir Arthur ordered it, mistress.'

'Thank you, Master Rist, that will be all,' I announced, frowning as I watched him slithering out of my sight.

'Don't worry,' soothed Bess. 'He's always like that. Miserable little man. Never paid much attention to anything I said, though I've had to manage things since Mother died. I expect you'll want to rest now. Here are your maids. Tomorrow we can explore the gardens together. I can't wait!' Clapping her hands together, Bess skipped off, happy as a lark, leaving me to fall on the tray loaded with food that had been left for me.

'Come, Clotilde. Come, Jeanne. There's plenty for you here too,' I said softly. 'It has been a long day and there's no need for you to go seeking out the kitchens.' Clotilde huffed and puffed a bit, but at my insistence sat down to share the meal before they started to unpack. The truth was I was glad of their company. Only after my appetite was satisfied did I admit to myself that, although I was rather tired, I must prepare myself for a visitor. It was my first night under this roof and I expected my husband to come to my chamber. I felt sure it was time for us to truly become man and wife.

'I think I'll retire now, Clotilde,' I said with an exaggerated yawn some little time later. She placed the pair of sleeves she held in her hand into a coffer and closed the lid with a snap and turned to Jeanne, who was busy folding my clothing.

'You may finish arranging the mistress's belongings in the morning.' She gave the order in her usual even tone. 'Now, Mistress Roberda, which shift will you choose?' she whispered with a knowing smile.

'My best one, of course; the one with all the fine blackwork embroidery,' I answered with a nervous grin. Once I was clad in my shift, Clotilde freed my hair from its braids and let it spill down my back. I clambered into the bed and stretched my legs into the welcoming soft cocoon of fine linen sheets and a deep feather mattress. I fidgeted, sat up again and arranged myself in what I hoped was an alluring position on the pillows. Clotilde and Jeanne went quietly to their truckle beds in the outer room, leaving the candle burning as I waited.

The night was warm for April and I'd left the window open just a crack. Muffled sounds crept in; distant voices; a door banging; pots and pans rattling; far away a dog barking. Footsteps rang out then melted away as the quiet of the night settled in and the house slowly came to rest. After the clamour and noise of London and the royal court, the silence of Dartington wrapped around me like a velvet cloak. In the stillness of that April night, lying in an unfamiliar bed, all I could hear was the steady, if rather rapid, beating of my heart. I waited. I waited. I stared up at the candlelight flickering on the carved tester above my head. I shuffled around, flung the covers off, then wrapped them tight. I waited and I waited. But still my husband did not appear.

In the quivering light of the guttering candle I could just make out Diane the doll regarding me from the shelf where I had placed her as a reminder of home. I felt a hollow lump in my chest and drew my knees up to my stomach, wrapping myself in the embroidered counterpane for comfort. The candle flame died and angry tears began to flow down my cheeks as I accepted the bleak truth. My husband had chosen to leave me lonely.

I pulled the covers up and closed my eyes tight, willing myself to sleep. But the sky was tinged with rosy light before at last I drifted off. When I awoke the sun was up and I was still alone.

I sat up and pressed my hands to my temples. I had hoped that in this, his own home, we might find joy in each other. A nagging voice sounded in my head; *it must be my fault he has no desire for me.* I ran my hands through my hair and clenched my jaw as bleak thoughts raced through my mind. Sir Arthur had made it quite clear he wanted a grandchild. If my husband had no wish to do his part, he might have a long wait.

I clutched my stomach and felt my cheeks burning. Everyone would know that my husband shunned my bed. There can be no secrets in a noble household. Servants are ever present. Every movement in that great house would be noticed and any juicy gossip seized upon by people with little else to think of.

Clotilde greeted me with a long face and I slipped from the bed.

'Oh, Clotilde, this is not as it should be! Have I given offence to my husband? Does he find me unattractive?' I quavered. She put her hands on my shoulders, gave them the gentlest of squeezes and looked square into my face.

'You are as beautiful a bride as any man could wish for. You know that in your heart. Madame la Comtesse, your mother, has prepared you well for the role you must play. Oh no, 'tis no fault of yours.'

She spat out the words harshly in a voice I remembered from my childhood; the voice she only used when someone had really annoyed her. 'There is no accounting for the ways of men,' she barked. 'Your husband will no doubt see the error of his ways in time and come to treat you well.'

Clotilde's eyes flashed and her nostrils flared. But then she took a breath and I saw the mask of servitude drop into place to smother her anger. She took another breath, gathered herself and picked up my gown.

'Forgive me. It is not my place to speak so, my lady. Let me help you dress, so you may take up your duties as mistress of this place.'

Humiliation and anger are two playmates that often run hand in hand. As Clotilde struggled to lace my gown, anger raced ahead and took me in its grip. I felt a sudden pounding in my ears as my heart beat faster and faster. I stamped my foot, let out a roar.

'I'll show that husband of mine!' I shouted, pulling away from her. 'To leave me lonely on my first night under this roof! I'll show him!'

'Let me fasten your gown before you go anywhere!' Clotilde now wore a worried frown. I marched out of my chamber to the top of the stairs, intent on finding my husband. Clotilde caught up with me and put a hand on my arm.

'Perhaps best to wait until your anger has cooled a little,' she cautioned. 'Words spoken in heat often come back to bite you.' I thumped my hand on the banister rail so hard it stung. But I allowed Clotilde to draw me back into my chamber where I stood fuming beside the bed.

'Do not fret so. All shall be well.' Clotilde's soft voice was an echo from my childhood and, when I saw the genuine concern in her wise old eyes, I fell sobbing into her arms.

'There now, there now,' she soothed. 'Let this pass and show how well you manage this household. Act as the woman you wish to be. The woman any man would be proud to own as his wife.' My sobs gradually subsided and I felt my heartbeat slowing as I saw the sense in what she said.

A little later, when I was calm again, I set out to complete the tour of my new home, collecting a rather grudging Rist on the way.

He followed in my wake saying nothing as I inspected the remaining rooms, holding my head high. Whenever I turned an icy gaze on him the horrible little man had the insolence to regard me with narrowed eyes and a jaw set as firm as a doorpost. He bowed stiffly and left me outside where Bess was watching from the knot garden.

'Oh, it's so good you're here,' she burbled as we walked, swishing our gowns along to release waves of heady scent from lavender bushes which I noticed had not been trimmed of last season's growth. 'I've done my best, but things have definitely gone downhill a bit since Mother died,' she conceded, plucking a head of spent lavender and rubbing a perfumed hand down her gown. 'Let's hope you soon have Rist licked into shape.'

'I'm afraid Master Rist doesn't much like me, nor I him, if I'm honest.' I paused for breath and registered Bess's raised eyebrows. 'It seems none of the other servants welcome my presence either.'

She pursed her lips together for a moment.

'You've only just arrived. Be careful of Master Rist. I know I've complained about the little weasel, but he does hold a lot of sway with the others.' I swallowed and looked at my feet.

'I'll be glad of your company, Bess. For I'll own it's a lonely path for a young wife.'

Bess gave me a sideways glance and we walked on in silence until we reached the apple tree at the end of the path.

'You'll have more company soon. My father is hosting a gathering later this week. The Seymours of Berry Pomeroy, of course!' Bess scowled. 'He is angling for me to marry the Seymour boy.'

'Well, as far as I've heard they're a wealthy family. You could do worse. Wasn't one of them the wife of old King Henry?'

'Yes, and Edward Seymour of Berry Pomeroy is the eldest living son of her brother; the one who was Lord Protector. Of course Protector Somerset lost all in the end; lost his head too!' She drew her hand across her throat with a grin. 'But the estates were restored. The problem is that most of their wealth was settled on the children of the Protector's second wife, not those of the first. So the one here in Devon was left in want of his full share. Father says the dispute will run on forever.'

'But why ever would the Protector cut his eldest son out of his inheritance?' I asked. Bess's face dimpled and she gave me a sly look.

'Oh, it sounds as though there was a mighty scandal. But no one will tell me the truth of it. All I know is that Protector Seymour's first wife – now let me see, what was her name – ah yes, Katherine; it was Katherine Fillol – well, she ended her days shut up in a convent.' She flashed another look at me, but then her face changed. For the first time since I'd met her, Bess's smile slipped away and her tone was sharp. 'If I'm to marry into that family I think I've a right to know the ins and outs, but Father won't tell me. Says it's not fitting!' I didn't quite know how to reply. I didn't want to appear critical of Sir Arthur, though I sympathised with Bess entirely.

'My theory is that Katherine Fillol was very young when she married the Protector,' she continued more evenly. 'I think she must have had a dalliance with someone else and questions were asked about who the boys' father was.'

'Oh my goodness! To think a man could shut his wife up in a nunnery because he thought her unfaithful!' I said, my voice rising as the shock registered.

'Well, it seems that's one way to extricate yourself from an unwanted marriage; if you're a man, that is. By taking to the church, Edward Seymour's mother freed her husband to marry again. She died soon after.'

'Poor woman! How awful!' I cried.

'Men will treat we women so. We used to have a king who had few scruples about getting rid of unwanted wives,' she shuddered.

'I have heard of it. To think he would actually have women he'd professed to love beheaded. Just because they didn't give him the son he craved.' I shuddered, feeling a chill crawling up and down my backbone.

'Don't think of it,' she advised. We walked a few paces in silence. But Bess couldn't keep quiet for long.

'The Seymour estates here in Devon alone are not to be sneezed at. Edward of Berry Pomeroy didn't get the titles, but he did get some of the lands. My father thinks it's a good match for me. So that's it.' A wave of sympathy washed over me.

'Of course it'll be years before it happens,' Bess went on. 'The son's only about ten years old!' I gave her hand a little squeeze. 'Well, it can't be cured, so I suppose it must be endured,' she said stoically. 'Isn't there something in that poem by Langland a bit like that? Anyway, I don't think the negotiations are going well. Seymour's angling for lands as well as money.'

'Oh dear! It took a long time for my parents to reach agreement with your father,' I offered, trying to sound reassuring. 'I'm sure it will be resolved.'

'It sounds as if old Seymour doesn't think I'm good enough for his boy. That hasn't gone down at all well with my father,' she explained. 'That's why he wants to show you off. His son wedded to the beautiful daughter of a French count in the presence of the queen! It might just impress Lord Seymour.' She shook her head. 'Of course, in the end it will all come down to money and property. It always does.'

Our walk had taken us to the bowling green and we took a seat on a bench conveniently placed to view any game that might be in progress. We watched the laundry maid spreading new-washed clothes on the bushes. Before long Bess chirped up again.

'Anyway, tell me. How do you like my brother?'

'If I saw more of him I could give you a truthful answer,' I replied, unable to keep the bitterness from my voice.

'Don't be too hard on him. Gawen's all right, though he's not as much fun as my other brothers, I'll grant you that.' I must have looked surprised, for I had met none of them. 'Oh, I've got such a parcel of younger brothers,' she laughed. 'Charles and Philip, George and Edward. Not one of them at home. All off learning to be lawyers or soldiers or some such. Perhaps you'll meet them at Christmas. Everyone used to come home for Yuletide when Mother was alive.'

'You must miss her very much,' I said gently.

'Yes, and Father does too,' she answered, staring down at her hands. 'It's affected him more than he will admit. He used to be forever smiling. Now he's often sad and his face doesn't seem to fit any more. Ever since Mother died he's had very little patience with Gawen. They keep falling out. I think my brother's always felt he had something to prove; always overshadowed by that paragon, our cousin Henry Champernowne.'

That name again! And I felt the warmth stealing up my cheeks.

The family gathered to eat at midday in the parlour behind the hall with the steward, bailiff and other staff in attendance, arranged below the salt in order of their importance. I trailed in behind Bess and couldn't help but notice a fair-haired man taking his place beside Rist. In truth, I'd challenge any woman not to give him a second glance. The stunningly handsome man at the steward's side turned towards me, blue eyes sparkling, and considered me much longer than was appropriate, an impudent smile playing around his perfect mouth. I made a great show of taking my place between Sir Arthur and Gawen, but my husband barely acknowledged my smiled greeting.

'Who is that man seated beside Master Rist?' I hissed at Bess, who sat opposite me. 'I've not seen him before.'

'That's John Gatchell,' she whispered. 'He works closely with my father. Goes with him to meetings. Acts as scribe and courier.' I took a peek down the table and found his eyes still on me. My skin felt tight, as though something was crawling all over me, and I made a mental note to avoid the man as much as I could. There was something dangerous about this John Gatchell.

I placed the napkin carefully over my shoulder, rinsed my fingers in the proffered bowl, and helped myself to a small portion of meat. An explosion of tangy spices; a fusion of cinnamon, mace and pepper, hit my tongue. I was surprised to find such a tasty dish served at an everyday meal. Sir Arthur clearly liked his food well flavoured. He turned to me and patted my hand.

'I trust you slept well and have found your chamber comfortable?' I could have kissed him. It was just the opening I needed if was to draw attention to my lonely state and shame my husband.

'Sir, my chamber is most pleasant and well furnished,' I said before casting my eyes down. 'But I myself slept little last night, for I was sadly lonely in that great bed.'

It was probably unwise; probably not what Clotilde would have advised. But I didn't care. I wanted to make sure that Sir Arthur knew it was not I who stood in the way of his precious grandchild. I felt Gawen's eyes boring into me. My father-in-law's face grew red and he thumped his fist down on the table making the servants all look up from their food. Eyes swivelled, necks craned to see what was going on. No doubt they were all hoping for a tasty titbit they could gossip about afterwards.

'We have discussed this many times,' Sir Arthur spluttered, leaning across me and jabbing his finger at Gawen. 'You know my wishes.' I saw the muscle in Gawen's jaw twitch and his face grew dark as a thundery sky in August.

'Sir, we have indeed discussed this before, but the fact remains. The dowry is still not paid.' My mouth fell into a great round 'O' and I stared at him aghast.

'Montgomery is a man of honour. He has given his word.' Sir Arthur ground the words out between his teeth and continued to hiss at Gawen, right across me, in sharp clipped staccato sentences. 'He fights for a just cause in France. It is the cause we also espouse. It is the cause your cousin died for!' I could see the veins standing out on his flushed face and I was afraid his fury might spark a fit of apoplexy. 'That cause drains a lot of coin from Montgomery's coffers. More may be needed soon. He's waiting to see if the truce will hold. To be sure all are really free to worship as they please in France.'

Gawen blustered and cursed.

'Now listen here!' Sir Arthur shouted. 'I'm quite sure Gabriel Montgomery will play his part in the matter of your marriage in due time. I expect you to play yours to the full now.'

The air between the two men crackled as they glared at each other. It was Gawen who gave ground first. He pushed his seat back, sending it crashing onto the stone floor, and stalked off, muttering as he went. I gasped. I was sure I heard the words *annulment* and *divorce*.

I bowed my head and chewed my lip. Blinded by the glamour of the court, excited by the prospect of a new life as mistress of a grand house in Devon, I had completely failed to understand why Gawen was reluctant to share my bed. He was looking for an easy way to escape an unwanted contract. I was but a pawn in the game, to be disposed of, sacrificed, if need be. Perhaps he thought to send me to a nunnery like Protector Seymour's first wife.

I was smouldering with resentment, my veins throbbing. It was all I could do not to scream. I flashed my eyes at my father-in-law who, having mastered his own anger, sat nonplussed at the head of the table with eyes cast down. It was only then I noticed the noise, a growing hubbub as the servants exchanged their own interpretations of the scene my foolish words had provoked. Guffaws and laughter cackled about me. I tried to swallow, but felt as though I had a great lump of apple stuck in my throat. To think of that hateful crew, already hostile to their new French mistress, picking over the bones of Gawen's words! How the likes of Rist would enjoy my humiliation.

Sir Arthur, may God bless him, took command. He clapped his hands and beckoned to Pierre who sat in the corner with his lute.

'Silence,' he thundered without meeting my eye. The murmuring dropped a notch or two then petered out completely. 'We will have music. Keep your peace now and give ear to Master Pierre.'

I drooped on the bench, wringing my hands, wondering if I should write to Maman. But gradually the haunting tune that flowed from Pierre's skilled fingers caught my attention; an air of such lilting beauty it soon had everyone spellbound. The last note quivered in the air, and as they drifted from the parlour carrying platters and mugs to the kitchens everyone was speaking of the music. I had never heard that air before. I would never forget it.

A few days later – after I had spent more lonely nights worrying about Gawen's talk of annulment and divorce – the Seymours arrived. They came with ever so many neighbours and a parcel of Champernowne relatives; so many I simply could not put names to them all.

A mighty feast was spread in the great hall amid much noise and jollity. After the meats were cleared we were served delicately flavoured fish and hearty pies, highly spiced dishes and loaves of good manchet bread. There was plenty left over for any poor beggars who came to Dartington's door that night. Much good wine and ale had been quaffed and some had spilled onto the cloth by the time the servants scurried around offering sweetmeats and sugared subtleties.

'Now for the sugar banquet,' boomed Sir Arthur. 'We'll stay at board today but soon I'll have a banqueting house built beyond the garden. Like the one Cecil's going to have at Theobalds. He showed me the plans. Such gardens! It cost him a pretty penny entertaining the queen there for ten whole days last year.' His grin grew wide as he nodded towards Lord Seymour. 'Sometimes I'm quite pleased we're too far from the court to expect a visit when she's on progress!' Edward Seymour forced a wry smile to his lips. Bess had told me all about the elegant mansion he had raised at Berry Pomeroy. Perhaps he'd done so in hope the queen might one day visit and he might get back his inheritance.

I looked shyly round for a familiar face and found Mistress Raleigh regarding me over a cup of Rhenish wine. Sir Arthur had brought the best from his cellar to impress his guests. I approached her and made my curtsey.

'No need to stand on ceremony, girl,' she cried. 'We're family now. Tell me, how do you fare with Gawen?' Katherine Raleigh was not one to mince her words.

'Well enough,' I answered. 'Dartington is such a fine place, do you not think so? The gardens are so well laid out for both pleasure and to supply the kitchen and still room. We had such gardens as these at my home in Ducey.' I prattled on, hoping to turn the conversation.

'As bad as that, eh?' she interrupted, with a twinkle in her eye. 'God has blessed you with more than your fair share of beauty. You must set to and use your charms on that nephew of mine.' I felt the blood hot in my cheeks as she drew me close and whispered in my ear. I gasped, but she laughed loudly. 'All will be well and my brother will soon see a grandchild in the cradle.' Walter Raleigh senior, engaged in deep conversation with Sir Arthur's lawyer, looked up at his wife with an indulgent smile. I felt a pang of envy for that look. It told of enduring love, devotion and understanding between the elderly couple. I looked across the hall to see Gawen giving me a hard stare. Once again I slept alone in the carved oak bed.

Next morning everyone was up early for the hunt. I rode out beside Gawen who sported a fine black doublet and was seated on a fiery black courser. I allowed myself a fleeting thought that his cousin Henry had carried off that look much more convincingly. The young Edward Seymour, Bess's intended, sat stiffly in the saddle trying not to look bored with the proceedings, while his father gave me a long appreciative look. I kicked my pony forward sucking in my breath in irritation. *Why must all men look at me so?* I thought. *I didn't choose to be born with fair curls and dimpled cheeks. Why must I always suffer their insolent stares?*

The hunt went well. Edward Seymour the elder brought down a stag and everyone was in good humour. That evening a lot more of Sir Arthur's finest wine disappeared rather quickly.

I glanced up at Pierre with the other musicians in the gallery and felt a warm glow of pride. They launched into a merry tune and I wondered if anyone would ask me to dance. To my surprise the first was Gawen's cousin, Sir John Gilbert, Katherine Raleigh's eldest son from her first marriage. Katherine had a quiverful of boys – three with the family name Gilbert and two named Raleigh – and it seemed all shared the same smouldering good looks. She had told me how proud she was when John had received his knighthood the previous year. Now he spent much of his time at Greenway Court which lay downstream of Totnes on the River Dart. He was approaching middle age, and country life and good living clearly agreed with him. I noticed that his doublet was straining a bit as we stepped the measure slowly, exchanging pleasantries as we passed. As the last notes died he took my hand and raised it to his lips.

'My mother was right,' he said, with a twinkle in his eye. 'Gawen is indeed a most fortunate man!' Sir John's look was kindly, not at all threatening, and I was pleased to receive such a gallant compliment. I smiled and dimpled as I curtseyed.

There was something vaguely familiar about my next partner who I guessed must be another of Gawen's many cousins. *All these Devon men are so tall and handsome,* I thought as he grinned broadly. I gave a little chuckle as he took my hand.

'Have we met before?' I asked, gazing up into clear blue eyes.

'That has not been my pleasure,' said he in an accent that jogged a memory. The family likeness was clear, although this man was broader in the shoulders and had a full growth of beard.

'Are you another of Mistress Raleigh's boys?' I asked as he put his hands to my waist to spin me in the dance. He grinned again, nodded and stepped back, interrupting the other dancers in our set.

'That I am. Carew Raleigh at your service,' came the booming reply as he swept me a bow.

'Then it must be your brother I met in France,' I cried and felt a warm blush creep up my cheeks as I remembered that encounter when I was a young maid at Ducey. 'I called him Monsieur L'eau,' I giggled. 'For the way he said his name. To my ear it sounded just the same as your English word for water.'

Carew Raleigh gave a booming guffaw that turned all heads.

'Ha! That's good! He's a rare fellow is my brother Walt!' and, still laughing, he spun me round in time with the music. I rather enjoyed the attention and laughed with him. But as we came to a breathless standstill I noticed Gawen giving me an ice-cold stare. I flashed him a smile, hoping he might step up and lead me in the next set. But Gawen showed no inclination to dance. I shrugged my shoulders and waited for my next partner. Later Gawen and his father had their heads close together in deep discussion.

'Go to then, boy,' Sir Arthur roared, as Gawen gave a curt nod. Sir Arthur clapped his son on the back and every head in the hall lifted. Katherine Raleigh winked at me when my husband followed me as I retired for the night.

Gawen stalked after me, boot heels clacking as he clomped up Sir Arthur's fine new stairs. He marched past me into the bedchamber, waving Clotilde and Jeanne aside with an angry swish of his arm.

In the outer room I cursed the complicated attire fashion dictated I should wear.

'What's taking you so long, woman?' he bawled through the open chamber door. Clotilde fumbled again with my laces and at last, clad only in my shift, I walked into the bedchamber, closing the door softly behind me. Gawen's features were blank as he stood beside the bed, but his jaw looked tense.

'I could see from your performance in the dance that you know your business well, madam,' he said in a flat voice.

'I had much rather have danced with you, husband,' I answered as sweetly as I could manage.

'I do not dance. Oh no, I do not dance to anyone's tune," he said bitterly. "And yet here I am; your husband! Here only to do my duty on my father's orders.'

My first instinct was to shrink back, quivering against the door, to try to make myself as small as I could. But then my mother's voice sounded in my mind. He spoke of duty. Well, I knew well the duty I had been brought up to fulfil. Gawen was my husband and a man like any other. I gathered my courage and walked slowly towards him, smiling as I loosened the ties at the neck of my shift.

'Then let us try to make it a pleasant duty,' I murmured. He heaved a long sigh wrenched from somewhere deep within him and closed his eyes.

'So, it must be done,' he breathed. After what felt like an age, he opened his eyes again to look on me as my shift fell to the floor. No endearments ever passed his lips, no words of love. Gawen treated me as well as he could, as we learned together the secrets of the marriage bed.

Chapter Twelve

Bright Summer's Lease Cut Short

Summer 1572

The visitors were long departed. Eight days had passed and I'd spent no more lonely nights. It was hardly light when I woke to find Gawen sprawled across the bed, snoring lightly. He stirred when a shaft of early light touched his face.

My husband rubbed his eyes and regarded me lazily. He looked so contented that I thought he might speak, might give me some words of love on that last morning before he left with his father. But as he sat up and pulled his shirt over his head, his face took on the stern look he usually presented to the world. He searched for his boots, tutting and cursing.

'I must be away,' he grumbled, with a boot in his hand. 'I'm recalled to serve Walsingham. I'm to go first to La Rochelle, then on to Paris.'

'Will you see my father? 'I asked.

'Yes, I would think so. He'll come to Paris for the wedding in August,' came the short reply as he bent forward and fumbled to tie the points of his hose.

'And my brother, will you see him also?' I teased. 'Will Jacques be there to dance at the wedding of Princess Marguerite of Valois to Henry of Navarre?'

'Hmm! That I don't know. And I don't care either,' he snapped, delving beneath the bed for the second boot. In those nights we'd shared, Gawen had sometimes let down his guard a little, and I'd not been surprised to learn he had a poor opinion of my brother. Jacques could be an impossible idiot, full of his own self-importance.

'I doubt that this wedding will do much good,' he continued bleakly.

'What do you mean?'

'Many don't favour this show of religious tolerance. Most of the citizens of Paris stay true to their old Catholic ways. More to the point, it's been a bad year over there. Crops failed. People are hungry.'

He sighed and sat awkwardly on the stool to pull his boots on. As he straightened up he paused and tapped his fingers impatiently on the polished lid of the bedside coffer. Then with a shrug he set off for the door, but had to come back to retrieve the cap he'd left by the bed where I lay still savouring the lingering warmth of his body. He ignored me, picked it up and muttered to himself as he turned it in his hand,

'Hmm ... my father will go to Paris,' he murmured. 'Admiral Coligny's made progress with the king, but the dowager queen's another proposition entirely ... support's needed in the Low Countries...'

He must have caught sight of me lying there with a puzzled look on my face, for he turned on me with vicious words.

'What would you, a woman, understand of these things? What can you know of war?'

I opened my mouth to tell him I had once been right in the heart of a city under siege, that I had seen war first hand, but I bit back the words. The image of the soldier with no face swam before my eyes and my chin quivered. I took some deep breaths to calm myself. How I yearned for a touch of his hand, some show of sympathy for my distress.

'A plague on this wedding! Pah! Walsingham and Cecil have work for me. I'd rather be at the helm of my ship. But there it is. The less you know the better.' I should have heeded the rough, impatient edge in his voice. But as Gawen flipped his hair back and set the cap on his head I stretched out a hand.

'No more, you hussy,' he snapped. I shrank back and pulled the bedsheet up. Gawen's eyes were like hard slivers of ice as he turned a piercing look on me.

'I've wondered where you learned all those tricks, madam. Perhaps I'm not the first you've known.'

Those words hung in the air between us as he stomped out of the door.

I was up in time to say a rather frosty farewell. I pressed letters for my mother and Charlotte into Gawen's hands and he had the grace to promise he would see them delivered. I'd enclosed another short missive for Charlotte to pass on to Béatrice to tell her of my marriage. I didn't think it likely my husband would convey a message to a nun.

Bess hugged her father before he walked slowly to his horse and heaved himself into the saddle. We watched from the steps until the two figures on horseback faded to nothing but fuzzy blurs framed in the archway. I was not sure whether I would truly miss my husband.

With Gawen and his father away I was free to enjoy that first summer at Dartington with Bess. She was always bubbling over with mirth, hatching some scheme or outing for us. At first I demurred.

'I must look to my duties, Bess. I'm determined to stamp my mark on the household. I'll never gain the servants' respect if they think me a giddy girl.'

'You've already put Rist on his mettle,' she laughed. 'He has them all well drilled in their work.' She was right. Dartington now ran itself. Fruit was picked and preserved, ale brewed, bread baked, the storerooms full, the gardens well tended and fresh linen always to hand.

'Come on,' she laughed. 'Let's have some fun.' So I gave in to her pleading and, with no one but Clotilde to notice that our needlework lay untouched in our work baskets, we roamed the gardens and woods.

'I can't believe I'm seventeen,' Bess chuckled one morning as we wandered along a winding path through the bee-loud gardens.

'So am I. It's a good age to be on a summer's day. Race you to the apple tree!' I chased her along the paths until we collapsed in the arbour to catch our breath. I put my head back and drank in the heady, woody scents of lavender, hyssop, thrift, marjoram, savory and thyme.

'Wasn't it clever of Mother to mix marigolds, sweet william and gillyflowers here?' Bess said. Then her bright smile faded. 'But she never finished her garden.'

'I'm sorry, Bess,' I murmured, with an understanding nod. 'I know you miss her very much.'

'It's not so bad now you're here,' she said with a grin.

As the days became warmer we often ventured into the piny shade beneath the trees that clothed the hill behind the old hall, finding secret glades where we could sit on the soft spongy grass unobserved. We wove daisy chains and garlands and danced under the trees.

It was joy to linger late into the night on balmy summer evenings while the old walls around the garden court echoed to haunting airs of Pierre's own devising.

'Who would have thought that ragged boy I rescued from the bridge in Ducey would have such talent?' I laughed as one of the laundry maids followed him with her eyes. Pierre's curly hair and ready smile made him a favourite among the women servants and visitors alike.

'His playing is divine,' Bess purred, settling back on the garden bench as the tune I'd first heard at that disastrous meal on my second day at Dartington drifted round us.

'This is my favourite,' I beamed. 'It makes me feel I could fly up to the heavens. I'm so pleased Pierre didn't stay at Queen Elizabeth's court.'

'Father's given him a supply of paper and ink so can set down his new compositions,' Bess commented. 'Says it's a trick the boy learned from the court musicians.' I looked at Pierre and felt a warm tingling glow.

Devon put on its best face that summer; the weather was fine, the days sunny and warm. The hay was cut early in the meadows where we wandered among the wild flowers, while in the uncut wheat fields vibrant poppies left vivid red brushstrokes on nature's masterpiece of golden ears dancing beneath a cornflower sky.

'Let's ride to Totnes,' Bess said one sunny morning. 'We can go to the tailors and see if any new styles have come from London.'

So the stable boy brought round the horses and we had a fine time promenading up and down the town's steep hill and resting in the cool shade beneath the red walls of St Mary's Church. How I preened as the ladies of the town bobbed their curtseys, keen to make the acquaintance of the new mistress of Dartington.

On another day we rose at dawn to ride through the leafy lanes all the way to the Seymours' mansion at Berry Pomeroy. We hammered on the huge door, to be answered eventually by a wizened old man who scowled and peered at us through narrowed eyes.

'There's no one home. You should have sent word before you bothered to come. They're all away in Dorset.' So I only caught a brief glimpse of the grand mansion that might one day be Bess's home.

Our happy excursions were curtailed only a little when Sir Arthur returned from Paris at the end of July having come home via the court in London. He looked at me enquiringly, but I shook my head. Those few nights I had shared with my husband had not given rise to a new life within me. His grandchild was no nearer making an entry into the world.

Sir Arthur brought the excitement of a letter from my friend Anne Cecil. Clearly still besotted with her husband, Anne remained at her father's house and, reading between the lines, she saw little of Edward de Vere. I read snippets out to Bess as we sat in the garden.

'The Duke of Norfolk has at last gone to the block, despite all his pleadings.'

'That's old news! Even in deepest Devonshire we get word of great events like that,' she commented.

'Anne says everyone thinks it was the Queen of Scots who led him to it. I expect that's her husband's defence of his noble kinsman,' I added, shaking my head. 'I can't believe that the kindly girl I remember from the corridors of the palace could turn into such a scheming seductress. But according to Anne, people say she's inspired ever so many plots, and would happily kill her cousin without a moment's pause.' I scanned the rest of the page.

'I think these questions are prompted by her father,' I whispered to Bess as I folded the letter. 'Since I have no knowledge of any of my husband's doings in France, I can't give any secrets away.'

On Sundays we promenaded past the spreading yew to worship

in the little church tucked away behind the hall. Sir Arthur, who was as staunch a follower of Master Calvin as my mother could have wished for, said by attending church we were setting a good example to the servants, estate workers and tenants. It was no hardship for me; in truth I found the simple service quite soothing.

As the three of us emerged from the cool shade of the porch into the sun one August morning, Sir Arthur hailed an elderly gentleman.

'Roberda? Have you met Master Melhuishe who has leased the parsonage?' I shook my head, remembering the sprawling building that lay to the north of Dartington Hall. Master Melhuishe leaned heavily on a cane as he lifted his cap, revealing a fine head of winter-white hair.

'I am honoured, Mistress Champernowne,' he declared with a beaming smile.

''Tis my pleasure to meet you, Master Melhuishe,' I replied, as polite as could be. 'But pray tell me who is this at your side?' The well-dressed younger man – perhaps he was in his twenties – turned, removed his cap and blushed right up to the roots of his sandy hair. But then, to my amazement, he greeted me in perfectly enunciated French, with no trace whatsoever of that impenetrable Devon accent.

'*C'est un plaisir de vous rencontrer*,' he said, keeping his eyes on the grass beneath his feet. 'A pleasure to meet you. I have been fortunate enough to travel and spent some time in Paris.'

'Well, it is a delight to meet someone who can converse in my own language, sir,' said I. 'Perhaps we may see you at the hall at some future time?' He nodded and murmured his thanks, shuffled his feet and pulled his hat down low over his face. Sir Arthur stepped in.

'Of course, young Melhuishe. You and your father are welcome to join us after supper one evening. Perhaps when my son returns. I'll have it arranged,' he boomed, for all to hear.

As we made our way back to the hall, Bess put her hand on my arm.

'*Pardonne-moi*! I didn't realise that you missed speaking French so much, Roberda. Perhaps I should have tried harder,' she said. Her attempt at French in a terrible accent had me tittering.

'You mistake me.' I laughed. 'It is best that we two always speak in English, for how will I ever learn your strange way of talking if I cling to my own tongue? I've forbidden Clotilde and the others to speak in French too, or they will never adjust to life in England. But it is refreshing to find someone with whom I could speak the language of my birth from time to time.' I didn't add that it was equally refreshing to meet a young man so bashful there was no chance he'd ever give me the unnerving look so many men felt entitled to bestow on me.

On a hot sultry day later that August Bess and I were out walking. The leaves were still, the air so oppressive and heavy it felt as though the sky was pressing down, trying to smother every living thing. An irritating trickle of sweat was creeping down my back by the time we came to a place where a clear fresh stream bubbled up from the limestone below, forming a little pool before it disappeared again.

'Everyone says it's a holy well,' smiled Bess. She bent down and thrust a hand into the spring, allowing the cooling droplets to trickle through her fingers. She cupped her hand and, giggling fit to burst, splashed water over her face and then over me. 'The water is so cool and refreshing. Let's take off our stockings and paddle. No one will see us! If we make a wish, perhaps it will come true.' So we untied our garters, wound down our stockings and cast them aside to dip our toes into the cool, sparkling water.

'Don't tell,' Bess chirped as she wriggled her pretty pink toes in the flowing stream. 'You must keep your wish secret or it won't come true.' So I closed my eyes and wished Gawen would return transformed, head over heels in love with me with no more of his dark moods.

When we'd had enough, wet gowns clinging to our legs, we picked up our stockings. Carefree as the swifts that flitted in and out of the narrow windows high up in the church tower we hitched up our skirts and ran barefoot down the hill like village urchins. We collapsed onto a little bench overlooking the graveyard, a favourite spot where the blackbird's fluting song could always lift my heart. Still laughing we spread out our wet skirts to dry in the sun. I leaned back on the bench, lazily watching the oxeye daisies dancing in the light breeze through half-closed lids. Suddenly I felt a nudge in the ribs. Bess sat bolt upright beside me, shading her eyes with a hand.

'Look at that!' she exclaimed, pointing into the distance and screwing up her eyes. 'Can you see? That cloud of dust? Look! Whoever it is, he's at full gallop. We'd better go and see what's to do.' We hurried to pull on our stockings, gathered up our skirts and ran pell-mell from the churchyard. By the time we erupted into the courtyard a groom was leading a sweating horse towards the stables.

We were still full of the joys of that sunny day, chatting and whooping with laughter as we came into the hall. But our idle prattle died on our lips, all our mirth caught in our throats, at the sight of Sir Arthur slumped in his seat with his head in his hands. A paper lay on the floor at his feet.

He hardly stirred though he must have heard us, but sat hunched over, slowly shaking his head from side to side. Bess and I exchanged anxious glances and waited. At last he lifted his head and his hand fell from his brow revealing tear-filled eyes. He stuttered out the terrible news.

'A massacre! A massacre! Paris! St Bartholomew's day! Thousands dead!'

I grabbed Bess's hand and we both stared blankly at him as he shrank back into his seat and closed his eyes.

'Surely she would not stoop to this?' he mumbled picking up the letter in shaking hands to study it again, as if searching for some other meaning among the words. 'So many gathered in the City … the wedding went off without much bother … a bit of a fuss when Henry of Navarre didn't go to the nuptial mass, being of our persuasion.' He paused, took a breath and tried to start again.

'Did they think Coligny was gaining too much influence?' His voice trailed off again. 'Perhaps he pushed too hard … wanted them to side with Orange against the Spanish in the Netherlands… But no, surely not this … so many dead?'

I looked at Bess who was hovering over her father.

'But, Sir Arthur, whatever has war in the Netherlands to do with people dead in Paris and Admiral Coligny? Sir? Please? Can you tell us exactly what has happened?' I coaxed him gently, as if I was talking to a toddler reluctant to go to his bed, though I struggled to stop my foot tapping impatiently. At last he sat up straight and squared his shoulders.

'All I can glean is that someone took a shot at Admiral Coligny outside his house. It was after he'd been at the king's council meeting at the Louvre Palace,' Sir Arthur's voice was harsh and strained. He brought his fist down hard on the table. 'This smells of the Duc de Guise! I saw when I was last in Paris how desperate he was to get the country back to his Catholic ways! So desperate to claim power for himself! God's blood! I wouldn't put it past him to be plotting with Spain.' His face turned purple and a bubble of spittle formed at the corner of his mouth. 'We've had more than enough trouble with the Guise family and their meddling with the Queen of Scots,' he stormed. 'Of course, Guise blamed the admiral for his father's death at Orléans all those years ago. Oh, yes! I can see he'd be desperate to get Coligny out of the way!'

'But, Sir Arthur, was the admiral wounded?' I demanded, my tone now sharp. I wondered why he was taking so long to spit out the details.

He sighed wearily. 'This report says the admiral was recovering in his house when some villains broke in and killed him.' He sagged back into his seat. 'After that it sounds like all hell was let loose; as if that shot set a match to a fuse under a great keg of black powder. All the pent-up resentments spilled out and exploded on the streets of Paris. Everyone who didn't wear the white cross, every Protestant they could lay hands on – killed.'

'I can't believe it,' Bess breathed. 'Surely some were spared?'

'It seems they went mad.' As he took my hand a cold stone sunk into my belly. At last I realised why he was struggling to find the words. 'I'm so very sorry, my dear.'

'Papa? My papa was going to Paris! What news of my papa?' I screamed.

'We have no definite word. All is confusion. But many are lost.' His words hit me like cannon shot. My brow was suddenly strangely hot and clammy. I felt my legs give way beneath me. Then everything was black.

When I opened my eyes, still feeling groggy and bleary, I was lying on my bed with Clotilde bending over me, holding a damp cloth to my forehead. Beyond the door I could just make out a muffled conversation; a man speaking low.

'Ordered my horse … ride first to Exeter … send word as soon as we know. Take care of her.'

A woman replied but I couldn't make out what she said. The man spoke again louder, gruff and stark and I was in no doubt it was Sir Arthur.

'No; we've heard nothing from Gawen either.' A door slammed. I curled into a ball, hugging my knees to my stomach and screwing my eyes tight shut. Before the blackness descended again I saw the old woman falling, falling head over heels, over and over with her skirts flying. She was falling from the walls of Rouen. I saw the soldier at the top of the wall. This time he was wearing the face of my papa.

I don't know how long I lay there, drifting in and out of consciousness, as the effects of the drink they forced down me took hold. It may have put me to sleep but it did not stop my desperate nightmares. In rare lucid moments I wished I could stay awake and escape those lurid images of death and destruction. But fitful sleep kept claiming me and the horrible dreams held sway. Sometimes I woke with a start to see Clotilde patiently knitting in the shadows, humming a tune she used to sing to me in the nursery. Sometimes it was Bess who took my hand and held a cup to my lips. One time I stirred to find Clotilde placing Diane the doll beside me in the bed. My fingers found again the soft fabric of the gown my childhood playmate still wore. I'm not sure if it was hours or days before I was back in my senses.

Bess burst in as a shaft of morning light fell across my pillow.

'Listen to me, Roberda. May God be praised! My father has sent a message.' She bent over me, took hold of my arms and tried to shake me awake. 'Wake up! There is news. Roberda! Good news! Your father escaped!' I sat up and rubbed my eyes.

'Best read it for yourself,' she exclaimed. 'Words spoken by one who was with the queen at Woodstock when the news came.' She held out a piece of paper.

'No! You read it, Bess. My eyes won't focus yet. Read it to me,' I cried.

'It says … *these French tragedies, and ending of unlucky marriage with blood and vile murders, cannot be expressed with tongue to declare the cruelties… None of any name of the religion is left living, but such as fled and escaped their pursuers, as the Count Montgomery, who was pursued two whole days by 200 horse, and yet escaped, and is come into Jersey*. Oh, I can't read the next bit, someone else I think – *also being pursued, is yet escaped…'* Bess threw the paper down. 'This is the best news, Roberda!' she yelled triumphantly. 'Don't you understand? He has escaped! God alone knows how. He must be one of only very few who survived.' She set down the paper and clapped her hands together, then picked it up anew and her brow puckered as she studied the spidery writing once more.

'But there is more. It says nowhere in France is safe for the Huguenots.'

'I don't understand,' I murmured uncertainly. 'I thought it all happened in Paris?' Bess took my hand gently, sure she now had my attention.

'It seems the violence has spread to other towns. We must pray that all your family will be safe.' I clung to her and at last I could weep. There was hope where none had been; my father lived. But yet there was more to fear; Maman and my brothers and sisters were in grave danger. I clung to Bess as she rocked me in her arms and stroked my hair. It was a long time before I realised I had not asked what had become of Gawen.

All we could do was wait. The days dragged slowly by as summer's warmth gave way to the first hint of autumn chill. There came a September morning when the sky grew dark and the walls were pressing in around me. I donned a heavy cloak and, strapping Jeanne's wooden pattens to my shoes, headed out through the gardens and up the slope between the trees.

I was near the top, looking hopefully towards the track, when the first drops of rain pattered down; at first no more than a soft whisper that grew to a steady plip-plopping from the leaves leaving a sprinkle of dark teardrops on the path. I drew a breath deep into my lungs, savouring that first sweet smell of rain as it soaks into the grateful earth. So many childhood memories belonged to that smell; summer at Ducey; the joy of running for cover when the heavens opened on a scorching hot day; Alain du Bois picking me up in his strong arms to carry me back to the house lest we be drenched; Clotilde at the door with a dry kirtle.

Perhaps I stood too long trying to wrap myself in the warmth of days long past. Shivering I gathered the cloak around me and scampered back towards the house. I was caught in a sudden torrential downpour halfway down the hill. Pelted with hail as sharp as needles of glass, I was soaked to the skin long before I reached the door. Just as in my childhood memory, Clotilde met me there and helped me change out of my wet clothes. I joined Bess in the little parlour, picked up my sewing and regarded the cuffs I was embroidering with a sigh. I would need to redouble my efforts if I was to have the stitching finished so I could offer them as a gift for Maman or Charlotte. I could hardly dare hope they would be safe and I would see them again.

That night one of Devon's worst early autumn storms raged in from the sea. A furious wind howled round the old walls, rattled the windows and sent boughs crashing to the ground. A white-faced Bess knocked at my chamber door and climbed into bed beside me. We clung together, eyes tight shut, as thunder loud as a cannon's roar shook the house. Later we drifted off to sleep as driving rain battered the window glass. It was pitch black when Bess grabbed my hand and sat up to listen. I heard it too. In the room below a bench clattered and scraped across the floor, then we heard muffled voices. Intruders! Someone had braved the wild weather to come to Dartington.

Chapter Thirteen

Refugees

Autumn 1572

I crept down the stairs, setting my bare feet gingerly on each creaking board, grabbing frantically at the velvet coverlet I'd wrapped round my shoulders in case it slipped and knocked something flying. A few steps behind me Bess was struggling to get her arms into a fur-trimmed bedgown while Clotilde tiptoed in front wielding a heavy candlestick. A quaking, white-faced Jeanne brought up the rear as she tried to hide in Bess's shadow.

We paused at the foot of the stairs and Clotilde put a finger to her lips. A low hum of voices was coming from the parlour. Clotilde edged up to the door, pushed it open a crack and we peeped in. A man was bent forward over the fire, an iron poker in his hand as he stirred the embers. He had evidently been at it for a while for, as the door swung back, I saw flames licking up the soot-blackened fireback. A musty smell of damp wool tickled my nostrils as a trail of steam rose from the sodden clothing of a second man who had his back towards us, hands stretched out towards the fire. We all held our breath and watched as the first man straightened up and pushed the other aside. For an instant I hoped it might be my papa. He removed his broad-brimmed hat and shook the water from his cloak, sending droplets spitting into the fire. Only when he turned did I realise it was Gawen.

'What on earth are you doing arriving here in the middle of the night?' Bess shouted as she stormed into the room. 'You gave us a rare fright!'

I remained on the threshold, trying to cover my disappointment with a brave face. Before Gawen could answer the other man dropped his own sopping cloak on the floor and spun round to face us. I stepped back and my hand flew to my mouth. My brother Jacques was regarding me with his familiar sardonic grin.

'What ho, sister! Thou art well met!' he chuckled, with an exaggerated pretence at an English accent before he continued in French. 'You look as though you've seen a ghost. It's me! Your favourite brother, seeking shelter in this foul English weather.' I noticed Gawen's right eyebrow twitching upward, saw how he forced his lips into a wide, rather menacing smile. I stretched my hand towards him, but Gawen recoiled, glanced at Jacques and went on in a voice that failed to hide his contempt.

'Aren't you pleased I've brought this fine fellow to visit, my dear? He'll be with us for a while, I'm afraid. We only just made it. The road's a quagmire!' Gawen stopped short. He'd realised all at once that four women stood before him.

'Not a word of this,' he growled, glaring at Clotilde and Jeanne, then back at me. 'None must know that your brother is come from France.' At last I remembered my wifely duty, though my voice wobbled a bit as the words tumbled out.

'Husband, it is such a relief to have you here safely. You may trust my maids. None of us will say anything. But why such secrecy?'

Jacques and Gawen exchanged glances and, for once, were in agreement.

'Best you don't know too much,' Gawen said, taking my hand at last and drawing me further into the room. 'What you don't know, no one can discover from you. These are dangerous times. None must know that Jacques is here.'

Jacques nodded. 'I'll make pretence to be an Englishman!'

I threw up my head and a mocking little titter escaped before I could hold it back.

'Don't be such a fool, brother. No one would ever take you for an Englishman! As soon as you open your mouth you'll be discovered,' I scoffed. 'Sir Arthur sent word that Papa has escaped. You can at least tell me if it's true. Is Papa safe?'

They looked at each other again. Jacques shrugged and stepped to the door, peered out, then closed it softly. 'Do not breathe a word, but yes, he escaped to Jersey. He was pursued. We must be on our guard. They will seek him out.'

'And Maman and our brothers and sisters?' I whispered.

'We must wait for more news. We can tell you only of our own escape. Nothing more,' Jacques said bleakly, then putting a finger to his lips he whispered, 'Listen! Someone comes!'

It is in times of need that I realise my mother's blood runs in my veins. I felt my muscles tighten as I looked my husband in the eye.

'I'll deal with it,' I hissed, and stepped to the door. Once outside, had the matter not been so desperate, I'm sure I would have laughed out loud. There stood Rist barefoot, with his skinny white legs protruding from beneath a crumpled nightshirt and his sparse grey hair sticking out at all angles from a tasselled nightcap. He gaped vacantly at me.

'Master Rist. So, you are awake at last? My husband has returned with a man who serves my lord Walsingham. I am surprised you did not hear them come,' I said sharply, giving him my most glacial stare.

'I heard nothing, but then I sleep heavy, mistress,' he yawned. The candle in his hand wavered and a fat dollop of wax fell and landed with a splat, right next to his gnarled toe. Rist righted the candle and cleared his throat. I could see the cords in his neck standing out above the collar of his nightshirt while his Adam's apple bobbed up and down.

'This will not do, Rist!' I scolded. 'We cannot allow any passing vagabond to creep into our hall. From now on we must have a watchman stationed by the door, if I cannot rely on you.' The little weasel shifted from foot to foot and lowered his eyes.

'Now,' I went on, in full imperious flow, 'go to the kitchens and find something for Master Gawen and his companion to eat. Bring a jug of hippocras too.' I waited until he'd taken a few steps then called, 'And, Rist? Walsingham's man has a raging fever. He'd best stay isolated until we can be sure he's not afflicted by some foul disease that will spread among us.' Rist peered at my face, which was probably flushed with the excitement of the night's proceedings. He took a step backwards and his left hand fluttered across his chest, as though to ward off any infection I might already have contracted.

'Clotilde alone will serve them in my husband's chamber until we may be sure. Give out that all must stay well away for fear of contagion. Now hurry, man! When you return just knock and leave the tray at the door if you please.' He hovered in front of me just a little too long for my liking. I wondered if he really believed my story. 'Well? What are you waiting for? Go!' I shooed him away, flapping my hands as if he was a chicken that had strayed into the vegetable patch. Rist stalked off, his shoulders as rigid as if he had a yoke across them.

You'd have thought they hadn't eaten in a week to see Gawen and Jacques tucking into the platter of meat pasties Rist somehow spirited from the kitchens. I plunged the heated poker into the jug of spiced wine and a strong aroma of cinnamon wafted around as I poured two mugs of the warming brew. Later, well fed, warmed by the fire and clad in dry clothes, Gawen opened up a bit when I asked what had set things off on that dreadful day in Paris.

'You know of the first attempt on the admiral's life? Well, it seemed Coligny would recover. King Charles sent his own surgeon to see to the wounds which did not seem serious. The king even sent guards – he said it was to keep the admiral safe until the assassin was brought to justice. Huh!' Gawen lapsed into a silence that Jacques was only too pleased to fill.

'All a ruse!' he declared, bristling with anger. 'A lot of our leaders went to Coligny's chambers. That was only natural. I might have joined them had my father not sent me on another errand. That gathering was misinterpreted. More likely, deliberately presented as a sign there was a plot to overthrow King Charles. There was no such plot! They were unarmed!' Jacques' face contorted and a string of French oaths came spitting out of his mouth.

'At first we thought the Duc de Guise was behind it,' Gawen continued. 'The would-be assassin struck from a house that belonged to Guise so the man was likely in his pay. But the murder that followed was on the orders of the king himself!' He paused to give us time to take that in. 'Coligny was attacked at his prayers, stabbed to death and thrown from a window.'

'Many of our leaders – good soldiers, noblemen – all massacred either within the Louvre Palace or out in the streets,' Jacques croaked. 'All on King Charles's orders!'

'And then a wave of violence broke over Paris.' Gawen shuddered. 'Townspeople, soldiers, those who had come to see the wedding; all caught unawares; killed in their beds. Women and children too; none were spared.'

Bess's face was white, her eyes bulging. I was amazed to see my husband, the hard-nosed soldier, wipe a tear from his eye.

'But how did you escape?' Bess murmured the question so quietly I wasn't sure if he'd heard her. He stared blankly into the fire a moment longer before he threw back the last dregs of his wine.

'I came across Jacques in the street outside the ambassador's house. It's in an awful part of the city, full of the stench of the tanners' and dyers' shops; Walsingham says he can't afford a more prestigious address. So at first we were not in the thick of the attack.'

Jacques' chin quivered and his eyes grew wide. My brother's usual bravado had vanished; he seemed deflated, smaller, just like a pig's bladder that shrinks when it collides with a sharp stone as the boys kick it around.

'I'd heard all the noise and commotion,' he said, his usually confident voice sounding gravelly and broken. 'Oh yes; I'd heard it. How I wish I hadn't. I shall never forget it.' He paused and shook his head. 'A church bell sounded. Gunfire! Screams … it's those screams that'll live with me forever.' With all his arrogance melted away Jacques looked like a lost boy, yet strangely aged all at the same time. He continued with eyes fixed straight ahead. 'I was on my way to Father's house. A man in his thirties, a man of substance for he was well dressed, came hurtling down the street. Ran right into me, nearly knocked me to the cobbles. Grabbed me as if he'd never let me go. Moaned and whimpered and started to beat his hands on my chest. I've never seen terror like that on anyone's face before. Not even in the heat of battle.' Jacques swallowed rapidly and glanced at Bess. 'I took the stranger by the hand and we set to running, but soon he fell. I lost him.' Jacques passed his hand over his eyes and let out a heavy sigh. 'What could I do? I ran on and thanks be to God Gawen secured a place for me at the English ambassador's house. I hid under the stairs until things quietened down.'

'There were so many of us crammed into that little house. Lots of Englishmen; Sir Philip Sidney trying to calm Mistress Walsingham and her young daughter Frances. Plenty of Frenchmen like Jacques were given shelter there too,' said Gawen gravely. 'They say Briquemault sneaked past the royal guards into the embassy disguised as a butcher and hid in the stables. But later he was arrested and taken away for trial. Three Englishmen and another Frenchman were dragged out and killed in the street.'

'Walsingham did his best,' Jacques murmured. 'The next day he sent out a servant to the king and demanded protection. Got it in the end. Eventually the king sent guards to protect the embassy while the madness went on.'

'It spread through the city like wildfire and went on for more than three days.' Gawen uttered the words slowly, shaking his head, as though he still could not believe it had really happened.

I sank down onto a bench and felt the room tilting round me. Shaking violently I saw the walls of Rouen, the soldier's face as it exploded, the blood, the old woman falling. It was only Bess's arms around me that brought me back from the brink of blackness.

'Hold fast. You're safe here in the parlour at Dartington,' she crooned, rocking me in her arms. Bess had learned the trick of calming me and my heartbeat slowed as the visions receded.

'What ails you, sister?' Jacques barked. 'You were not there.'

'She is well, good sir,' answered Bess with spirit. 'But 'tis a shocking story! What you have told us, sir, such deeds would upset any woman and many a man too.'

Once I had recovered myself I saw them safely ensconced in Gawen's chamber and crept back to my own bed. But it was too late for sleep. Disturbing images were running through my brain; too many, too vivid. I needed to be busy. So I was soon giving curt orders to Rist and his crew. The apple store must be cleaned and made ready; woollen cloth must be fetched from Totnes to make new clothes for the house servants; the miller's bill must be paid; Rist must accompany the shepherd to see which ewes would be culled and which sent to the fair. In short, any task I could think of that would take him out of the way.

I don't think we could have kept up the pretence that Jacques was ill for long, but luckily we didn't have to. Only two days later Sir Arthur rode into the courtyard at the head of a formidable troop of men. Called up from the muster lists, they were all kitted out with billhooks and the like. A few carried arquebuses. Sir Arthur declared they would drill and march and keep guard on all roads that led to Dartington.

'They will arrest any Frenchman who comes within five miles of the place,' Sir Arthur declared as he pulled off his boots in the hall. 'Roberda? Your brother is here and safe? Others in need of refuge will be with us shortly. You take my meaning?' He grinned as he saw understanding dawn on my face. 'Oh, such disguising and tricks we have employed to bring them here. We must keep careful watch lest they are pursued. Call Rist, if you will.'

Rist scowled when he learned how many guests were expected and I saw him ball his hands into fists at his sides as I gave him his orders. But he took a breath and shuffled off to instruct the servants to make ready.

It was just before dark the next day when the coach wheels bumped roughly over the uneven stones in the courtyard. I could hardly keep still as the carriage groaned to a standstill and the door creaked open. A tall woman clad in a simple gown of dark homespun wool stepped down. A white coif was just visible under a heavy hood pulled down over her face. It was only when she threw back the disguise that I recognised her.

'Welcome to my home. Welcome to Dartington, Maman,' I announced, before all pride and decorum left me and I ran into her arms. She held me for a moment then stood back so that she could study my face.

'You look well, daughter,' she said crisply, as though we had just met for an afternoon of cards and had only been parted a week. As I wiped the tears of joy from my eyes I caught sight of the other woman, struggling to descend the steps with a sleeping boy in her arms.

'Charlotte!' I screamed, not caring that my mother winced. 'Is it really you? Surely that child is not Gabriel?'

'Yes, and yes,' she replied with a grin as she set my seven-year-old brother on his feet. He ground his fists into his eye sockets for a moment, then stood up straight and made a bow.

'I was just resting my eyes a bit,' he said with an endearing grin.

'A very good precaution against all the dust from the roads, young Gabriel,' I answered, offering a sop to his wounded pride.

'We are all here but for Elisabeth who stays with her husband. He knows well how to dissemble to keep them safe.' I couldn't help but notice the edge in Charlotte's voice and must have looked puzzled for she went on, 'Jehan now professes he is a true Catholic. He's a fickle fellow! But here are Gedeon and Giles and Suzette. And here is Pérronelle with her girls. No doubt they're eager to see their father. Is Jacques here?'

I looked around to see a second carriage drawing up and right on cue my brother appeared. I saw a flash of a Jacques I didn't recognise as, with love and pride shining from his face, he lifted his daughters off their feet and carried them into the hall. Pérronelle pushed back a lock of hair that had escaped the woollen cap she wore and looked round anxiously before following him to complete their family reunion.

'But where is Papa?' I asked.

'Following in an oxcart with the servants lest anyone recognise him,' Charlotte said with a wide grin. 'I don't think he cares much for travelling with the lower orders, but needs must!'

I ushered everyone into the hall and called for Rist, who appeared bearing a flagon of ale while a bunch of serving women erupted from the direction of the kitchens and scurried off to make sure all was prepared for our guests. Rist shot me an accusing look, for now he knew I hadn't told him the truth about Gawen's companion. I sighed. It had been necessary, but it had probably done nothing to improve my relationship with the steward.

My mother was to have the best chamber overlooking the gardens and she soon commanded that space as her own; so much so that before long it became known as the Countess's Chamber. She demanded that a desk be set up forthwith and as soon as she'd changed into clothing more appropriate to her rank she was writing letters.

'Maman wields that pen as mightily as many men wield a sword,' Jacques commented as we stood in the doorway watching her fill pages with careful strokes of the quill. 'She has it arranged that any letter bound for France shall go via Jersey to maintain the pretence she is still there.'

Dartington's resources were stretched to the limit to cater for so many at such short notice. Sir Arthur said we must not send out for large quantities of additional food or that might give away we had numerous unexpected mouths to feed. So the first meal was rather a meagre one. Charlotte and I had a lot of catching up to do, and after everyone had eaten we settled down to talk. Bess made to leave us alone, but I bade her stay. I wanted my new friend and my favourite sister to get to know each other.

'Are your estates in France safe?' I asked, not forgetting that Charlotte was a wealthy widow with acres of land to her name.

'We believe so, yes,' she replied. 'I don't think there can be much to worry about on that score or Captain Leighton would not be so keen to make my acquaintance.'

'What? You have a suitor?' I chortled.

'Don't get excited. He's only an English soldier who was in Rouen. I can't see what on earth he would have to offer me, though he might gain much in return. It's a match I will never agree to. But it does no harm to have him keen to keep in Papa's good books!'

'Oh, Charlotte, you have become a scheming minx,' I laughed.

'We left Jersey on a boat so full of refugees I though it must sink under the weight of us all,' she said. An edge of concern had crept into her soft voice. 'When we docked at Southampton it was hard to push our way through the throng of passengers who flooded down the gangplank and wandered about uncertainly on the quayside.'

'So many? But what will they all do in England?' I asked. 'Where will they go?'

'That I don't know. For the moment they are just relieved to be safe,' she replied.

'They'll go to London. It's a big place,' said Bess. 'I expect they'll find employment.' The thought of all those misplaced souls in an unknown land troubled me. I remembered how difficult it had been for Clotilde and Jeanne when we were in London. Not everyone would be as welcoming as Sir Arthur Champernowne.

My father arrived next morning in an oxcart weighed down with sacks of grain. How I laughed to see him dressed as a miller with flour all over his rough tunic and sprinkled in his beard. I scanned the faces of the ragged people who piled out from their hiding places in the cart, searching for one I longed to see. But Alain du Bois was not among the bewildered Frenchmen and women who stood scratching their heads behind Papa. The only face I recognised was that of the odious Pastor Forêt, prayer book in hand, his customary self-righteous expression intact despite the rags he wore as he stepped from the cart with his nose in the air.

After Papa had changed his clothes and eaten, I was on the edge of my seat as we all waited to hear his story.

'I was disturbed from sleep by an apparition in my chamber!' Papa spoke in sonorous tones that sent a chill down my spine. 'A man stood over my bed, dripping wet and with blood pouring from a wound to his head.' He paused dramatically, then, sure of our rapt attention, 'At first I could make neither head nor tail of what he said,' he admitted. 'I tried to calm him, called for assistance for his wounds. But he waved my help away and gabbled out his warning that I must flee.' Papa stared into the fire for a long moment, before he went on. 'By then I could hear the rioters. He urged me to go, saying they followed hard on his heels.'

'Thank God he warned you in time,' I gulped. 'Thank God!'

'But for that brave man who swam the river to warn me I would have been lost. I dare not wait to thank him, to dress his wounds or to see him safe. I don't know what became of him…' Papa paused again, rubbed a hand across his brow and shook his head before gathering himself to continue. 'We barely had time to take to our horses; fifty or sixty of us; all who had lodged in the Faubourg St Germain. If the city gates had not been barred, the Duc de Guise and his men would have caught us. By the time they found the keys we'd put some distance behind us. May God be praised for a fleet-footed horse!' He took a sip of ale.

'They say you were pursued?' prompted Sir Arthur.

'Two hundred on my tail! Riding hard beside Guise himself! But we outran them! In time they gave up the chase and we reached the port in safety then took ship to Jersey. The rest you know.'

'And what of you, Countess?' Sir Arthur asked.

'I was at Ducey when I heard the news. It was great good fortune that Charlotte and Pérronelle and the children were with me.' She smiled at Pérronelle, who as usual sat quietly, like a little mouse hiding in the corner. 'Gabriel was already in Jersey. Reports of massacres were coming from so many cities.'

For once my domineering mother looked shaken. Her voice was thick with emotion as she went on. 'We travelled on byways and back roads with a strong escort. No one troubled us until we were near the port.' She sighed, turned her head away and was silent.

'So what happened then, Countess?' Gawen demanded. She hesitated then went on in a shaky voice.

'Our scout spotted a group of horsemen wearing the Guise colours. Alain du Bois led a group of our men away as a decoy. They made a lot of noise and left a clear trail. The rest of us continued secretly by another road and were soon on board ship.'

'But what of Alain du Bois and his party? Were they caught?' This time it was Jacques who rapped out the question. Maman's chin started to quiver and she hugged her arms round her stomach. I had never seen her look so uncomfortable.

'We dare not wait long,' she faltered. After another long pause she added in a small voice I could barely hear, 'Alain and his men did not come.'

I jumped up from my seat and stood before her.

'What? You did not wait for him? You left Alain behind?' I shrieked.

'I had no choice. I had the children with me,' Maman spluttered. 'Word came to us in Jersey that Alain and his men fought hard. But it was hopeless. They were outnumbered. I am sorry. Alain was lost. Another good man is dead in the cause of our religion.'

I barely registered Clotilde's anguished scream. A sudden pain stabbed my chest as though I had been run through. My mother's last words registered. Blinded by tears I spun round.

'You are mistaken in that, Maman. Alain did not die for your precious religion!' I snorted. I heard Maman gasp, but that rasping intake of breath was not going to hold back my words. 'He laid down his life out of loyalty to you, Papa,' I cried, whirling round to jab my finger in his direction. 'And he died for love of this family. Alain did not die for religion! He died for love!'

The air in the room felt brittle enough to snap. My mother raised her head and glared at me, turned on her heel and left the room with Papa close behind her.

Messengers came and went, men carefully chosen who could be relied upon not to say anything about my father's whereabouts. My family settled in at Dartington. Pérronelle kept herself to herself with her children, but Suzette often joined Charlotte, Bess and me at our sewing. As for the boys, Jacques had Gedeon and Giles practising with their swords most mornings, and in the afternoons they rode out across the estate, sometimes accompanied by Gawen. Meanwhile, young Gabriel was left to his own devices and struck up a rather unsuitable friendship with the cook's sons and the three of them ran riot whenever they had a chance. Had I not been so angry with Maman I'd have taken it up with her; as it was, I said nothing.

One morning early in October we were seated in the window, heads bent over our needlework. Mine was not progressing at all. In my misery at the news of Alain's death I was merely putting on a show of threading my needle to hide my tearstained face.

The parlour fire was lit and my father had joined Sir Arthur, Gawen and Jacques to consider the latest despatches which were spread in confusion all across the table. Maman stormed in and thrust a letter under Papa's nose.

'The Comte de Retz dares to suggest that if you swear you will never disturb the peace of France again you may return to your properties!' Maman snorted, brandishing the rolled-up missive as though it were a knife. 'But he says our son must be sent to King Charles's court and all my other children taken from me and put in the custody of some other woman! No doubt to be instructed in the worst of Catholic ways!'

'Thank God we have Jacques safe in England,' Papa fumed as he paced up and down. 'Pah! They would hold him hostage just as they keep the King of Navarre and the young Prince Condé confined.'

'Ah yes, they say those two have been forced to convert. Forced to hear the mass,' Sir Arthur confirmed.

My father crossed the room in two strides and sat down on a bench, but was on his feet again in an instant, heading for a different seat. I remembered something Anne Cecil had told me about the caged beasts kept in London's Tower. How they were continually pacing up and down next to the bars of their prison. That is just how Papa was. Up on his feet again, he ran his hands through his hair, now shot through with silver, and came to a brief standstill in front of my mother.

'Isabeau! I must see the Queen of England.'

'For the moment is it not safer to remain here?' The way she said it made it more a statement than a question.

'I must test the water to see what she will offer,' Papa insisted. He was pacing up and down again and setting everyone on edge. 'I sent my servant but she told me to remain in Jersey.'

'That was surely just for show. She knows where we are,' Maman said firmly. My father threw up his hands.

'We need ships and men. The chance is there for the taking…'

'Look here. Queen Elizabeth wants to keep any support she might give to the Protestant cause secret,' Gawen interrupted. 'She doesn't want to upset the French too much.'

'You're right, my boy,' Sir Arthur nodded. 'Her greatest fear is an alliance between Catholic France and Catholic Spain. Emboldened by a French alliance, Philip of Spain might seize his chance to support the Queen of Scots. That I could not stomach. I've never minced my words where the Spanish and their religion are concerned.'

'I suppose that's why she dangles marriage with the French king's brother as a prospect, but always keeps it just beyond reach,' Maman mused. My father's lip curled.

'Robert Dudley is our strongest ally with the queen,' he growled. 'I shall put on my disguise once more and join him.' Sir Arthur raised his eyes to the rafters and drummed his fingers on the tabletop. It was plain as day he didn't think that a good idea.

'I have taken the risk of writing to the queen at great length, seeking her approval that I raise volunteers to relieve La Rochelle. We of the reformed faith are all in the same boat. The monstrous deeds in France could set a fuse to threaten us in England. I've dared to set out the case in the strongest terms,' Sir Arthur said wearily in an attempt to calm my father down. 'It is best we await a reply.'

Papa was having none of it. 'No. I'll not wait. You've been most generous in your hospitality, but now I must be on my way.'

Maman fluttered her hands, then drew herself up to her full magnificent height.

'Go if you must. But do not even consider what Retz has

suggested.' Papa crossed his arms over his chest and frowned at her. That put Maman's back up.

'You may be assured of one thing,' she raged. 'I will always have my children in my own keeping! I will hold them close whatever may befall, wherever I may go!'

I set aside my needlework and bit my lip. I did try to keep the words back, but it was no use.

'Just as you dragged us into that hellhole in Rouen?' I cried, leaping to my feet. 'What sort of mother would put her children in such peril?' I did not wait for a response. Instead, with angry tears streaming down my cheeks, I bolted for the door.

Charlotte and Bess found me sobbing into my pillow.

'Well, it's true, isn't it? I've always looked up to Maman. Always thought she was so strong, so valiant.'

'Well, she is certainly a most impressive woman,' Bess agreed.

'I've done my best to be like her, to live up to what she expected of me. But now I can see. It's all her fault!' Bess opened her mouth to speak then closed it with a snap.

'Well, what sort of woman would take her children into a town under siege?' I blazed.

'It was war. We were too young to understand,' Charlotte soothed.

'How could she have left Alain like that? She'd been here under this roof for days and she didn't tell us. Poor Clotilde – she's distraught.' I rapped out the words as my hands flew this way and that. Bess took hold of my hand as anger, disappointment and all-consuming grief threatened to send me back into that dark place where a woman fell from crumbling walls and a soldier had no face.

'Did you care for him, this man Alain du Bois?' asked Bess gently, perhaps hoping to distract me from Rouen. I closed my eyes. A memory of that night-time flight from Paris lay buried deep, hidden away but never quite forgotten; Alain du Bois with his strong arms around me, keeping me safe. He had always kept me safe, right up to the last time I saw him in the garden at Ducey.

'He gave me a puppy,' I wailed. Bess patted my hand. 'He served my father all his life. He was strong and kind. He smelled of beer and onions and horses and there was a big gap in his front teeth when he smiled, which he did a lot.' Charlotte sat down beside Bess on the bed.

'Come now,' she coaxed. 'It won't do to get so upset. Alain was a kind man. He was a good man. But your carrying on like this won't bring him back.' I looked up. Clotilde had approached the bed, red-eyed and twisting a kerchief in her fingers.

'How could she do it, Clotilde? How could she sail away knowing he was somewhere out there in the hands of our enemies?'

'Like any mother she sought to protect her own, I suppose,' Clotilde answered, her voice barely more than a whisper. 'But Madame de Beaufort is right,' she breathed. 'All Alain wanted was for you, for all of us, to be safe and happy. He would not want you to spoil your life in grief.'

'But it's not right, Clotilde,' I protested. She looked into my eyes.

'His loss is hard for me to bear too. He was the best friend I ever had. We won't forget him, but we must endure.'

'I swear I knew nothing of it until now,' Charlotte sighed. 'But even had I known, I don't suppose I could have done anything to change her mind.'

'She cares only for her wretched church,' I growled. 'She has the zeal of a convert and that hateful little pastor feeds her passion.' I swung my legs over the side of the bed, slipped to the floor and marched to the window. Outside the sun glinted on leaves turning to russet and gold against a sky of purest blue. *Alain du Bois would never see the beauty of an autumn garden again. All because of my mother.*

'I can't forgive her this! It was bad enough that she took we children into danger so many times. Alain was always there to protect us,' I groaned. 'But now she's got him killed and left him to rot by some lonely roadside.'

'I'll write to Béatrice and see if she can find out more,' Charlotte offered.

'It's too late, isn't it?' I muttered, with a sigh. 'Oh, I know Maman thinks she does it for love. I know she thinks she does God's will. I know she and Papa love us. But when we were little she was always busy and Papa was never there. Well, even when he was at home he was…' I searched for the right word. 'Papa was … distant. But Alain du Bois, he was always there.'

Chapter Fourteen

The Physick Garden

Winter 1572

My father went in disguise to see the Earl of Leicester in hope the queen would grant him an audience. We were all under orders to keep up the fiction that he'd never been in Devon; that he'd been in Jersey or Guernsey all the time. Nor was I to admit to anyone my mother was in my house. In truth she was very much in evidence, interfering with my running of my household. Sometimes she even countermanded orders I had given. Charlotte did her best to keep the peace between us, but I could not forgive.

In the midst of my grief for Alain, my husband returned to my bed. I'll own that did give me solace, but not because he had suddenly become more loving. Simply having his warm body there beside me brought me some small comfort. Gawen and his father spent hours in Sir Arthur's study. I intercepted Rist one morning as he was carrying a jug of ale and fresh-baked biscuits.

'Refreshments for the master,' he announced pompously.

'Thank you, Rist, I'll take them in myself,' I ordered.

'No need, mistress,' he replied, and made to push past me. It occurred to me that he wanted to eavesdrop on their conversation, so I insisted and got a belligerent stare from the steward as he handed over the tray. I found Sir Arthur seated at his desk with Gawen pacing up and down.

'Ships all prepared and ready to sail to aid the people of La

Rochelle, and no word from Burghley!' Gawen complained. 'It's the last refuge for many Huguenots, and they need our help.'

'Aye! They're good people; staunch Protestants. Your cousin Henry knew them well.' There was a wistful note in Sir Arthur's voice and a faraway look in his eyes.

'I'm sure my father is keen to bring aid to La Rochelle,' I commented, thinking it best to steer Gawen's thoughts away from Henry Champernowne and his valiant adventures. I was beginning to understand how important it was to Gawen that he gained a reputation as a solider that might one day eclipse the memory of his cousin. And I was acutely conscious that Henry Champernowne had two sons to succeed him at Modbury.

'That's if your father can persuade the queen to support him,' Gawen rasped, flashing an angry glare at his father. 'Perhaps then I shall have my share of the action. I've had enough of slinking about France spying for Walsingham. I wish I could have joined Drake when he set out to raid the Spanish Main. Word is that he was wounded but not seriously. He'll not give up. He'll attack Nombre de Dios, capture their gold and treasure. He's a good man is Francis Drake.' I stifled the little growl that crept into my throat at the thought of the puffed-up little sea captain. He'd visited us once and his self-importance had irritated me, but Gawen was always going on about him.

Since my outburst Maman and I had exchanged hardly a word. I stopped and listened at her chamber door sometimes and heard her pen scratching away, but could not bring myself go in and make my peace with her. The wound was too raw.

I was in a hurry that December morning, intent on setting the servants to work to check our supplies against the coming festivities. I flew down the stairs and bumped right into Maman at the turn, sending the packages she was carrying flying. We both bent to retrieve them and our heads banged together. She stepped back, pinch-mouthed and unsmiling and I bent again and picked them up. I turned the carefully bound missives over in my hands and read the addresses inscribed in her familiar scrawling hand.

'So, you write to my lord of Leicester and to your friend Lettice who is now the Countess of Essex? No doubt you write of some new plot to pitch my father ever deeper into danger? All to do battle for your religion!' The taunt was out before I knew it. To my surprise I saw a hint of a smile hover near her lips. It was no more than a weak little grimace, but it was there. When she spoke her tone had no trace of anger.

'I have come to think there may be something in what you said to me, Roberda. It may not always be in the best interests of my children to be at my side. It may be years before we can go back to France. My boys are growing. They need to continue their education. I write to seek places for them.' I stifled a little gasp before I handed the packets back to her. Just at that moment a shout echoed from the hall below, followed by the sound of running footsteps. I looked down and caught sight of young Gabriel tearing, hell for leather, after the cook's eldest son who was hooting with laughter. It was my turn to offer a smile.

'It does seem that Gabriel might find benefit in giving more time to his studies,' I laughed, and a tiny crack opened in the barrier that had grown between us. 'Shall I give your letters to the messenger, Maman?' I offered. She nodded and I swear I saw a tear glistening in her eye. But her back straightened and, in a proud rustle of silk, she turned and headed back up the stairs with determined tread. Neither of us was quite ready to fully embrace the olive branch.

As I handed the packages to that day's messenger who waited, booted and spurred for his journey, a thought struck me. It might be some time before Maman had an answer and it was by no means certain that any of the English nobles would take young Gabriel. Perhaps we could do more to educate the boy while he was at Dartington.

A bright sunny day is a rare gift in the dark and dreary depths of an English winter. Determined to enjoy the morning sun, having completed my round of the kitchens at lightning speed and donned my warmest cloak, I was soon stepping out in the direction of the parsonage. The elder Master Melhuishe greeted me warmly and invited me into his book-lined study where a dog lay before a blazing fire.

'Why, Master Melhuishe,' I exclaimed, rubbing my cold hands together before the flames. 'I had no idea you had so many books! This is quite a library.'

'Christopher is the one who loves to read, Mistress Champernowne. I struggle to make out the text these days. He often reads to me. Ah, here he is.' I smiled. His words called to mind a cosy scene, the young man reading to his father before the fire on a winter's evening. Still smiling I turned to greet Christopher who carried a bound volume in his hands. He blushed furiously and passed it to me.

'I've been reading William Turner's *New Herbal,'* he confessed. 'It's a wonder. The medicinal uses of so many herbs and plants described so clearly. If you ever think to set out a new physick garden up at the hall then I would certainly recommend you study it.' He cleared his throat and blinked as he gave me a nervous smile.

'I wonder if I could?' I mused, flicking though the pages, momentarily distracted from my purpose. I handed the book back to Christopher with a smile.

'I hope you will forgive my boldness,' Christopher's father interjected. 'But we have heard of your grief at the loss of your faithful servant and friend. Dare I suggest that the creation of a new garden would be an admirable project to ease your grief? Lady Mary had thought to have such a garden with herbs for the still room, but she was taken from us before she could have the ground prepared. Perhaps you might consider it. Activity can act as a welcome balm at such times.'

Suddenly the idea of laying out a new garden and filling it with medicinal plants was very appealing.

'Thank you, sir, it is a kindly thought,' I exclaimed, clapping my hands together. 'Create a new garden… Do you think I could?' Both men nodded. 'I would like to try. I will seek permission from Sir Arthur.' Then, remembering my mission, 'Christopher, I came to ask if you might take on a task for me?' The young man's colour deepened and he nodded vigorously. 'My young brother Gabriel is missing his tutor who did not travel with the party from France.' I smiled. 'To be frank, Gabriel is running out of hand and needs to get back to his books. My mother hopes to settle him in some great household or at a place of learning in England. But that will take time. Would you consider acting as his tutor in the meantime? He has fallen behind in his Latin. He has quite forgotten how to hold a pen and, above all, his command of the English language is in much need of improvement.

It would be better if he did not rely entirely on the servants' children for that or he will pick up that unspeakable Devonshire burr. I know that you've studied at Cambridge and travelled widely. Your command of French is second to none. I can think of no one better for the task.'

'If you truly think me equal to it, then I would gladly try,' he said, green eyes all a-sparkle.

'A capital plan,' commented his father. 'Now will you take some refreshment?'

We spent a pleasant time sipping cider by the fireside. As I rose to take my leave, Christopher held out the *New Herbal.*

'Here; take it. You can start to plan your garden. Do not think to return it until all is complete.' I took the book, feeing its weight in my hand. 'But it is heavy!' Christopher exclaimed with another nervous smile. 'Perhaps I may accompany you to your door?' So we walked back together and it was pleasing to see the usually diffident Christopher striding out confidently beside me as we chatted about plants and gardens and how herbs could be used to create all sorts of remedies. I was so engrossed in our talk that I failed to notice Gawen until we were almost on top of him.

'I will ask my mother then? I am sure she'll welcome the suggestion. I will send word,' I declared as he put the book into my hands. 'And thank you again for this book. I shall speak to Sir Arthur immediately.' Christopher bowed and smiled. I thought I detected a spring in his step as I watched him go.

'What was all that about?' Gawen demanded, glowering at me.

'Merely that Master Melhuishe has lent me a book,' I said with a forced smile. 'Also, if Mother is agreeable, he will become tutor to my brother. You cannot fail to have noticed Gabriel runs wild with the cook's boys instead of attending to his studies.'

'I don't see why any of that warranted his walking so close with you all that way.'

My eyebrows shot up.

'Whatever do you mean?' I asked. 'Surely you're not jealous?'

'It is not seemly for a wife of mine to walk abroad with another man.'

'But it is only Master Melhuishe who will soon be tutor to my brother,' I retorted.

'Even so, it is not the behaviour I expect. What is the book?'

'A book about plants, that is all.' He took the volume from me and turned the pages as though searching for some secret message. My patience snapped.

'I did not expect to face the Inquisition on such trivial matters,' I fumed, snatching the book from his grasp to sweep past him as he stood glaring after me with arms crossed over his chest.

I went first to my mother's room. Her face lit up when I explained my solution to the problem of young Gabriel and she readily agreed that Christopher become his tutor.

'Tell him he may start immediately and we will make sure of appropriate recompense.' I was almost out of the door when she called me back. 'Thank you, Roberda,' she said solemnly. 'You have shown wisdom and sensitivity in this matter.' I felt my cheeks grow warm. For the first time she had spoken to me not as a parent to a child, but as one woman to another.

I bounded down the stairs, full of new energy, and found Sir Arthur at his desk, surrounded as usual by papers, account books and maps.

'What have you there that's brought such a bright smile to your face?' he asked. I explained about the herbal and the idea for a physick garden. 'Why, that is a splendid plan, my dear,' he gushed. 'Absolutely splendid! I know just the spot behind the kitchens. Come, I will show you. I'll be glad to get away from all these despatches. The day is fine, let us walk in the gardens.' He took my arm and, having picked up our cloaks, we walked to the grassy area behind the kitchens where the laundry maids often spread the linen to dry.

'My dear wife Mary thought to have a herb garden here, but she was denied the time to complete her plan.' Sir Arthur's eyes misted over and he turned away, pretending he was looking hard at the soil. 'The light is good and the soil not too fertile. I believe many herbs thrive best in soil that is not too rich?' He straightened up. 'We could raise some steps, set out beds and include every sort of useful herb and plant. There are new ones coming all the time as our explorers return from across the ocean. My sister's boys all have a great interest in gardens – picked it up from their mother, no doubt. I'll put my head together with them to see how best we can help.'

'I'm sure the laundry would dry as well elsewhere,' I laughed as a gust of wind picked up a smock from a bush and blew it onto the grass. 'Could we name the garden for your late wife, sir? Would *Lady Mary's Physick Garden* please you?' My chest swelled to see his smile. 'And, sir? Could I place a stone here in remembrance of our faithful servant, Alain du Bois?'

'Of course. Of course,' he said as he took my hands and planted a kiss on my cheek. 'As soon as spring comes we'll get to work. Now, shall we walk a little further?'

We climbed the hill beneath the spreading branches of fine old oaks still waiting for a strong wind to dislodge the last tenacious russet leaves. At the top of the hill we came to Sir Arthur's favourite lookout.

'I had a bench set here so I can take in that view,' he smiled, indicating the vista of rolling hills that spread as far I could see.

'Beautiful,' I breathed. 'It's as though a bolt of green cloth has been carelessly thrown across the landscape. And the little white dots everywhere. So many sheep!'

'Devon's wealth has grown on the backs of sheep for hundreds of years,' he declared, pushing his chest out. 'Our wool and woollen cloth is second to none.'

'Sheep graze on the salt marshes in the bay near Mont St Michel,' I murmured. 'The meat is the finest.'

'You're not homesick?' he asked, anxiously scanning my face.

'No, sir, not at all!' I assured him with a shake of my head, 'Why, how could I be homesick with this to gaze on? I love this place. I don't miss France, not even Ducey. My childhood there was not easy … the war … all of that was but prelude to my life's work here. I'm so excited to start work on the new garden.'

'A good project indeed and you already have the household well ordered. It's a credit to you.' His face was as bright as a sunbeam as he came to stand beside me. 'I'm so pleased to see you happy here. You've become a true daughter of Devon.'

All my irritation with his son was long forgotten as Sir Arthur and I turned and walked back to the hall arm in arm. It was not often I had Gawen's father all to myself and I was determined to make the most of it.

'Sir, is it true that many people from France have sought refuge in London since the dreadful deeds of St Bartholomew's Day?' I asked.

'Yes, indeed,' he agreed.

'I do wonder how they will fare in a strange land. Will all of those poor souls have such a pleasant welcome as we have received here at Dartington?'

He gave me a quizzical look. 'I believe that most of those arrived in London are physicians, doctors, printers, and such like. Men who have a trade should soon find work.'

'But, Sir Arthur, what of the women left behind? The ones who've lost fathers, sons and brothers in the fighting. Those left with no man to provide for them, struggling to keep their children fed. Would they be welcomed here?'

He regarded me steadily. 'My goodness! I had not thought of that. I can see no reason why they would not, if they are prepared to work and fit in with our ways,' he replied affably. 'Do you doubt it?'

'When I was at the court in London, Clotilde and Jeanne were not well treated. Not being proficient in the English tongue it was hard for them to argue their case. It may be the same for others. I wish we could do more to help them.' He tilted his head to one side and the warmth of his kindly smile made my heart swell.

'It is good that you are so thoughtful of others,' he said.

Chapter Fifteen

Tides of War

Christmastide 1572–November 1573

Christopher Melhuishe took his duties as tutor seriously. He soon had Gabriel working hard at his books every morning and, provided the weather was fine, in the afternoon he continued the lesson with walks around the estate or excursions to local towns. I preened myself in the knowledge that my instincts had been correct. Christopher was proving an excellent teacher.

At the Christmas feast Bess's young brothers, home for the holiday, sat in a line, all moulded from the same clay. Full of fun, they made Gawen seem even more dour and stern. I was disappointed to learn that Katherine Raleigh and her family were celebrating the season in Exeter. But Sir Arthur extended the usual hospitality to his tenants and neighbours and, with my father returned and all my family with us, we were a large party. Papa was like a coiled-up spring, pacing up and down or huddled in a corner with the menfolk as they plotted a rescue mission for La Rochelle. How I wished they would let it all rest.

We feasted well, Pierre excelled himself with the other musicians and we had jugglers, fire-eaters and travelling players to entertain us. Each day a plentiful supply of leftovers found their way from our table back to the kitchens from whence sounds of merry-making and singing could often be heard as the staff enjoyed the holiday.

The third day of Christmas was still remembered by some in

Devonshire as Saint John the Evangelist's feast day, much to the annoyance of Pastor Forêt who thought all saints' days should be expunged from the calendar. It was perhaps fitting, since St John was supposed to have survived drinking poisoned wine, that Sir Arthur's cellars were mercilessly plundered. After the wine everyone moved on to ale and, when it was growing dark, I noticed the flagons were running low. Not wishing to call the servants and disturb their Christmas fun, I decided to go to the buttery myself for a refill. But when I turned the tap, not a drop of ale flowed. I pushed with all my might, trying to rock the barrel forward, but it was no use. A new one must be tapped and that was something I couldn't manage alone. I would have to disturb the servants after all.

The shrieks of raucous laughter grew louder as I approached the kitchen door and someone burst into song, a rude ditty not fit for my ears. As I pushed the door open a crack and peeped through I felt a flush of heat come to my face.

The cook was bawling out the bawdy song, swaying on his feet with his great fat belly wobbling from side to side, slopping ale down an already stained doublet. Three dishevelled serving women slumped on the floor surrounded by a jumble of chopping boards, bowls, cooking pots, knives and spoons – all swept from their proper places on the tabletop. Gaming pieces were scattered all about and as I watched unseen a man cursed loudly and leaped to his feet, sending an upturned barrel flying. Another man jumped up to stay his hand before he could punch his opponent. A dog, sniffing among the bones and half-eaten pies that lay across the rushes, yelped and cringed under the table as a boot made contact. Across the room, John Gatchell lolled on the settle, his arm draped over the laundry maid's shoulder. I couldn't tear my eyes away as he set down his mug and pulled her towards him. His hands were all over her as he kissed her on the lips.

A chorus of strident cheers went up and Rist appeared wearing a long open robe with full skirts that he held bunched in his hand to form a tail behind his back.

'Rist! Rist! Rist!' the chant went up. He grinned, showing all of his blackened teeth, and clambered onto the table.

'So, Master Rist,' called Gatchell. 'I hear you have new duties as valet to Monsieur le Comte! Do you help him on with his clothes? There are things we'd like to know about the Frenchman! Come, tell us do.'

'Tell! Tell! Tell,' came the chant as Rist strutted along the board, turned and minced his way back, with the bundled-up cloth swaying from side to side behind him.

'Aye, 'tis true. I am close to Monsewer,' he snickered. 'Oh I know all his secrets I do! And thereby hangs a tail!' They all hooted with laughter as he paraded up and down, waggling the coat behind his back.

That was too much for me. I exploded from the shadows screaming like a demon.

'Get down this instant, you odious fool,' I shrieked, elbowing my way past the women, who scrambled to their feet. A guilty hush crept over them all.

'How dare you behave so, you ungrateful crew,' I scolded. 'Sir Arthur has provided you with good food and a holiday from your duties. It seems to me he has also provided far too much cider and ale. He will hear of this.' I swung round and was about to flounce out by the way I came when Gatchell caught my eye.

'And shame on you, Master Gatchell,' I fumed. All heads swivelled. 'Have you quite forgotten you have a wife at home? I will not tolerate such goings-on in my household. Is that clear?' As I stalked back to the door I almost set my foot in a pile of stinking vomit.

Shaking with rage I slammed the door behind me and hid in the screens passage, trying to get my emotions under control. Gawen found me there.

'I was wondering what had become of you,' he said accusingly. I blurted out a garbled account of what I had witnessed. He threw back his head and laughed.

'That's an old one – the French having tails! Hah!'

I gasped. 'Was that it? Such insolence! I don't see why you find it so funny,' I rapped back, my hands gesticulating wildly.

'Calm down. What do you expect? Why would someone like Rist have any love of the French?'

'Whatever do you mean?' I faltered. Gawen suppressed another burst of merriment and looked me in the face.

'Rist's father died at the Siege of Boulonge with old King Henry. Died at the hand of a French sniper, though it could just as easily have been the bloody flux!' I took a step back, and my hand flew to my face. 'To people like Rist the French are the 'old enemy' and they've grown up making fun of the French. It's what they do.' His shoulders shook as laughter got the better of him again.

'I hadn't thought of that…' I murmured, then, more loudly, 'but it's no excuse for what I saw!'

'Come on, Roberda. It's best forgotten,' he coaxed. 'I'll own it was a cruel jest, but I think we must show some tolerance. It's Christmas, after all.'

'Tolerance? Tolerance?' my lip curled. 'We shall see what your father has to say to tolerance. They have insulted his guest and they must pay.'

'Come on,' he said. 'I tell you, it's best you overlook it. What a man does and says when he's in his cups often seems foolish to him come the morrow. Rist will be full of apologies. Of that I'm sure.'

'Bah! He had better be! I was quite prepared to allow them their fun. No one minds a little drinking at this season. But this is too much. Such insolence! Such lewd behaviour! I'll not have it.'

'Lewd behaviour? What do you mean?' he asked. But I would say no more. I wasn't quite sure why Gatchell and the girl had upset me so much. I didn't want to discuss it with my husband.

Next morning the kitchen was clean and tidy. Rist had a sour look on his face when I called him to account for his antics. He stood before me with his arms crossed over his chest.

'Master Rist. I know what happened to your father and can well understand you might bear a grudge against the people of France,' I said, trying to arrange my features in an expression of sympathy. The thought of a man dying on the battlefield reminded me of Rouen. Rist stared as I gave a world-weary sigh. 'Look, I may be young, Master Rist, but I have seen more than you could ever imagine. Wars are grim, cruel and wasteful. They leave many bereft and I doubt they ever solve our problems. Your father fought loyally, but that was King Henry's war. That time is gone. My father is a guest in Sir Arthur's home and you owe him your respect as much as you owe it to any other.'

I may as well have addressed my words to the wall. Rist's face remained blank, his shoulders tense.

'Now, go about your duties,' I ordered. He walked away, straight-backed and defiant still. After much thought I decided not to raise the matter with Sir Arthur. It would only add fuel to the fires of Rist's resentment.

As the holiday ended and the village women took the decorative greenery from their spinning wheels, my father was on the road to London, saying he was weary of his idle life.

Charlotte had more knowledge of my father's whereabouts than I, for she helped Maman decode some of the dispatches he sent.

'Everyone's afraid of spies. Lord Burghley and Walsingham have ciphers and Papa has taken to using them too. Maman's not so quick to interpret them as I,' she bragged. 'It sounds as if our papa is on better terms with the queen. He's gone with her on a little progress. Just places close to London where they can talk more freely.'

The dreary unrelenting rain that fell in the dark days of January and February made life difficult for my laundry maids, but it did not keep my husband at home. He returned for short interludes, only to be away again on some business in Plymouth.

On one of his brief visits Gawen came to my chamber looking as excited as one of Sir Arthur's hounds that has just picked up the scent, dancing around with a grin stretching from ear to ear.

'It's good to see you smile,' I said as he sat on the bed to pull off his boots. To my amazement he stood up, stepped across the room and took both my hands in his. My heart skipped a beat as he stood back to gaze into my face.

'I am happy. I have my chance to lead the expedition to relieve La Rochelle. Your father has agreed that I will share command.' He reached out and touched my cheek in a rare show of tenderness that gave me new hope for our future together.

At the end of March they took ship for the port.

By then, plans for my new garden were taking shape. Sir Arthur, who had brought back drawings from his nephew Adrian Gilbert, set the gardeners to work to lay out the beds and prepare the soil while I made lists of plants.

The sun was bright and no April showers threatened as I stepped out briskly through the archway to make my way to the parsonage. Old Master Melhuishe had been suffering from a cough so I'd added a syrup of feverfew and black pepper to the basket of honey cakes I carried on my arm. I hoped the fresh air might make me feel a little less queasy. My errand accomplished, on my return I was alarmed to find the gates were bolted and not one, but two heavily armed soldiers barred my way, only to admit me with smiles once they recognised me. I hurried into the hall where I found Sir Arthur with Gatchell, who gave me a sly sneer as he accepted a package. I did not deign to acknowledge him as he swaggered off.

'The men at the gate, sir…' I started.

'Just a precaution; a rumour that a man has been sent to England to kill your father. Now don't you fear. I've no doubt it's nothing more than foolish talk, but we must be on our guard. Your father isn't even here, but I've made a show of it,' Sir Arthur explained. I swayed on my feet and squeezed my eyes shut. Sir Arthur took my hand. His reassuring tone was calming and my heartbeat slowed a little.

'Thank you, sir, I know you will do what is best. I was a little alarmed, that is all,' I replied. Sir Arthur's forehead creased and his brows came together.

He patted my hand and with a voice full of concern he asked, 'Are you quite well, Roberda? You look rather pale.'

'Oh yes, I'm well, thank you,' I murmured. 'Just a little tired from my walk.' I made my excuses and escaped to my chamber where I lay down to rest.

As the days grew warmer and the blossom began to fade on the cherry trees I still felt unusually tired and took to lying in late of a morning.

Towards the end of May, Charlotte bounced in and pulled back the bed hangings.

'What? Still abed? Whatever is wrong with you? I have news. Papa's in Plymouth! Jacques is here and we are all going to Queen Elizabeth's court.' I sat up, felt the wave of nausea coming and slipped from the bed. I just reached the close-stool in time.

'Sick of a morning? Tired? Can it be that you also have news?' Charlotte gasped.

I climbed back onto the bed and hugged my arms round my stomach.

'You do know what's been wrong with you these last weeks, don't you?' Charlotte coaxed as she squeezed my hand.

'Yes,' I moaned. 'I just didn't want to believe it.'

'I've no experience and I'm sure it must be frightening. But you'll be all right. Look at Maman and all the children she's brought into the world. And she was usually fighting a war at the same time! Oh Roberda! You can't keep it secret any longer.'

I looked her full in the face. 'I know. It's time to tell everyone. But what is all this about going to court?'

'Jacques is on his way to report to Lord Burghley. Papa thinks if we women go to the queen she might listen.'

'That doesn't sound likely to me.' I frowned and grabbed her hand as the realisation came to me. 'But is Papa back in Plymouth? What does that mean? Are they all safe?'

'I suspect Sir Arthur has been trying to keep you in the dark until things were more certain. He's been concerned about you. I think he's guessed what's amiss. Oh, Gawen will be so pleased when he gets home!'

I wasn't so sure about that.

'Hmph! Now, Charlotte, you'd better tell all you know,' I demanded.

'Better that you come down to hear it from Jacques himself,' she answered. 'Now where is Clotilde? You must get dressed quickly.'

They were all gathered in the great hall. Dressed in leather jerkins with swords at their belts my brothers, Jacques and Gedeon and Giles, stood to attention before the fireplace. Beside them, Maman fiddled with the pearl necklace at her throat while Christopher Melhuishe tried to melt into the shadows behind young Gabriel, whose lesson had been interrupted. Charlotte and Bess squeezed into the window seat and Sir Arthur was perched on the settle.

I shifted from foot to foot and my eyes darted round the hall. I ventured one trembling word: 'Gawen?'

No one could mistake the sharp edge of irritation in Jacques' voice when he snapped back at me. 'He's all right; he's with Papa in Plymouth, en route to Jersey.' He placed his hands on his hips and scowled at me as he quickly brought us up to date with events since they set sail for La Rochelle.

'My husband suggests we women go to Queen Elizabeth and plead with her for more support,' Maman declared, waving a square of folded paper. 'My lord of Leicester has offered a place for you, Gedeon.' Gedeon's face shone with joy. 'I await replies about you, Giles, but the Earl of Essex will take young Gabriel into his household at Chartley as companion for his own son Robert.' The child looked anxiously at Christopher. 'You and Robert Devereux will get on splendidly, my boy,' my mother reassured. 'Master Melhuishe, will you accompany us ? You may return to your father once Gabriel has got to know his new tutor.' Christopher blushed and nodded assent. 'Make ready, girls. We will set out immediately.'

Sir Arthur, who had been watching me anxiously, cleared his throat.

'I think it may be best if you remain here, Roberda,' he said. Maman's eyebrows shot up and she peered at me through narrowed eyes.

'But you know Cecil's daughter quite well. That might be of use to us,' she snapped.

My headdress had slipped back and I pushed a curl of hair from my face as I swallowed hard. Sir Arthur reached over and took my hand.

'Am I right?' he asked gently. I could only manage a nod. 'You must stay with Bess and take care of the child you carry,' he twinkled. I squeezed his hand and felt the tension seeping out of me.

'You did not tell me,' Maman cried in a voice laden with accusation and disappointment. 'Well, be that as it may, we must make ready.' She bustled off without giving me the barest hint of a smile.

'Don't worry, she'll get over it!' Charlotte soothed as we watched Maman's stiff back disappear from view.

'It's a pity; I thought we were getting on a little better. But there it is,' I sighed. 'I'd have liked to send word to Anne, but I've had no time to write. I'm not sure how she fares these days as Countess of Oxford. Will you visit her and see how she is?'

'Of course. Is there anything else I can do for you?'

I hesitated and looked over my shoulder to check we were not overheard.

'I've heard there is a strangers' church where those of France worship. Could you go there? I'm worried about those left behind; the women with no provider, the ones left to manage all alone when their husbands, sons and fathers all followed Papa and his like to war. I want to do something for them. I want to know if the people at the church have any means of finding those in need.'

Charlotte put her head on one side and smiled.

'You're not serious? Women in your condition are given to fanciful thoughts. What on earth could you do?'

'I am not fanciful! I am determined!' I insisted, pushing my shoulders back. 'Look what I did for Pierre. All that talent would have been lost if he'd perished. There must be many children like him, left to starve because mothers can't put food on the table. I will do something for them, though as yet I'm not sure what. Find them employment here perhaps. I think Sir Arthur might be willing to help.'

'You look just like Maman! Like her, you're looking for a cause!' she laughed. 'All right. I'll see what I can do. Now I must pack.'

They left next morning accompanied by Sir Arthur who said he would add his voice to their entreaties. Gawen saw no need to visit his wife, so I had no opportunity to tell him my news.

Dartington was empty and quiet that summer. Perhaps we were a little less carefree, perhaps our excursions became a little less adventurous as I grew larger and more ponderous. But Bess and I enjoyed another summer together without hindrance from the menfolk. I spent many happy hours overseeing the gardeners as they planted and tended my new garden. The stonemason from Staverton arrived with a small carved stone with the legend: *In memoriam: Alain du Bois, a good man*; and a larger one proclaiming: *Lady Mary's Physick Garden*; and set them up at my direction.

I was sweltering in August's heat when a carefully worded note came from Maman. She said nothing of Papa's whereabouts, no doubt fearing her message might be intercepted. They were lodging with a respectable widow and expected to remain in London for some time. Gabriel had settled well at Chartley. There were good reports of his proficiency in French and Latin. Sir Arthur would soon be back with us with more news.

He appeared as we sat in the garden enjoying the late afternoon sun.

'This is coming on,' he declared, smiling broadly. 'Lady Mary's Garden; she would have been so happy to see it.' I called for refreshments and he settled down on the bench beside me.

'You look well,' he said and gave me the latest news. I found it difficult to raise much enthusiasm for my parents' continuing attempts to get aid from the English queen.

'What of my husband?' I asked, shifting my position as the baby delivered a hefty kick.

'He will be here soon. Do not fear. He'll be back before your time comes.' I wasn't sure I was that concerned whether he was there or not.

October came; winds ripped the leaves from the trees. Sir Arthur found me in the parlour one wet afternoon.

'I'd hoped your mother might be back by now to help you. Bess won't be able to manage on her own so I've sent for my sister. You remember Katherine, don't you?'

'But of course,' I laughed. I couldn't think of anyone I'd rather have with me when my time came.

I did not have long to wait. I felt the first pain while I was walking in my garden. Katherine Raleigh, who had only just arrived, saw me wince and whisked me back to my bedchamber without delay.

Chapter Sixteen

Fulfilment

November 1573–1574

On that autumn afternoon in the year 1573 my world shifted on its axis forever. Nothing would ever be the same again.

'Look, Clotilde! See my little girl!' I breathed. The baby opened her eyes and my cup of joy overflowed. 'Hello, little one!' I whispered, and felt as though I'd known her all my life. I wanted to hold that moment forever, gazing into those shining eyes, touching those unbelievably delicate fingers, drinking in the new baby smell of her. With shaking hands I pushed back the cloth and smiled to see wisps of fair hair sticking up at jaunty angles like a halo round her little head. She was perfect.

As I rested on the feather pillow, the autumn sunlight dappling the bright green bedcover looked brighter, the colours seemed more vivid than ever before. My face felt it would split from grinning. I expect Clotilde beamed back at me. If she did I didn't notice. I couldn't take my eyes off the dear little babe I'd somehow brought into the world.

Until she spoke I hardly noticed Joan Searle the midwife filling the doorway with her plump, reassuring figure.

'You're one of the lucky ones, mistress,' she pronounced. 'That babe was eager to be born and no mistake. Your pain was short.' She surprised me by wiping away a tear as she gathered up her belongings. 'Don't matter how many babes I see, how many new mothers, 'tis always a wondrous thing to behold,' she grinned. 'I will leave you now. Mistress Raleigh knows well what to do.'

'Do you have children of your own?' I called. She turned back with a broad smile.

'Oh yes! Two maids, grown to fine women both. Margery will follow me soon in this work and Agnes is skilled in the still room. There's not a herb our Agnes don't know the use of. I'm a lucky woman indeed, Mistress Champernowne.'

'Perhaps I'll seek your Agnes's advice in my physick garden next year. She might teach my still-room girls a thing or two,' I offered, but the fleeting thought was lost as I turned all my attention back to my baby.

'I would let you hold her, Bess,' I said as she sidled up to the bedside, 'but I can't quite let her go to anyone else just yet.'

'That's all right,' she beamed, with a slightly anxious look at the red-faced baby who at that moment decided to exercise her lungs to the limit.

'Is my husband come? Does he know? Is he pleased?' I asked. I spotted the look that passed between Bess and Katherine, although they tried to hide it.

'He's with Sir Arthur now. I left them raising a glass of the best Rhenish to wet this little maid's head,' Katherine said, trying to deflect my question.

'I was afraid he'd be disappointed,' I murmured.

'All men do wish their first child will be a son,' Katherine admitted. 'Gawen will come to accept it. You're both young, Roberda. He knows there's plenty of time to bring an heir to Dartington.' Her voice was soft and reassuring as she perched beside me on the bed and smiled down at my baby. I was too besotted with my daughter to allow any disappointment Gawen might feel to shake me for long. My eyelids fluttered and I drifted into contented sleep with my baby still cradled in my arms.

Next morning Bess brought me a dish of pottage which I wolfed down hungrily.

'Has a name been chosen?' she asked.

'Gawen sent word she's to be called Elizabeth, for the queen. I'm more than happy that she'll be Elizabeth – but in my eyes she'll be named for you, Bess. You've been my greatest friend since I came here. Will you mind?'

'I will be honoured indeed,' she said, dimpling.

'So Elizabeth she will be. But I shall call her Lisbeth,' I crooned as I stroked the soft curve of her cheek.

My baby was three days old when she was baptised in the little church only a stone's throw from my window. As was usual the parents did not attend. It felt as though a part of me was being ripped away when Bess breezed in to take her. I didn't know what to do with myself while my baby was being welcomed into the family of the church. I sat up in bed and studied my hands, surprised to see both still in their place at the end of my arms. Without my baby by my side I felt as if some part of me, a limb at the very least, had been removed. I heard her cries long before Bess marched in and handed her back to me.

'She was crying for her mama,' Bess chuckled as the baby settled instantly in my arms. 'All went well. I'll leave you now, for here comes Gawen.'

He hesitated on the threshold so I called out, gay as you please, 'Come, husband. Is our daughter not the most beautiful babe you ever saw?' But Gawen made no move. His eyes were fixed on the swaddled baby as I lay back on the pillows in the bed we had shared.

A slow grin spread across his face, a flash of pride and wonder as he looked at our little girl. He reached into the cradle, touched the tiny fingers and sighed. But then he straightened up, and gave his shoulders a little shake as though he had just remembered something. When next he spoke stern lines had chased away the joyful countenance of a new father.

'Looks as red and wrinkled as any newborn babe to me!' he answered gruffly, pulling his fingers through his disordered hair. 'I rode hard to be here in time, thinking to welcome my son.' My head jerked up as though he had struck me.

'She is a fine healthy child and we are young. Boys will follow,' I snapped.

'Hmph! Perhaps… I leave at first light,' was the only reply he gave.

'So soon? Why?'

'Walsingham has need of me.'

'Walsingham? So you go to France?'

'Walsingham was recalled months ago,' he sighed wearily. A vein stood out at his temple, a sure sign Gawen was not in a good mood. 'He's to be appointed to the Privy Council and made Principal Secretary to the queen. 'Twill be interesting to see how that goes!' He flopped into a seat by the window.

'Why? What do you mean?'

'She laughs at his sober ways and labels him a rank Puritan. Even calls him her moor for his dark dress. We'll see some sparks fly, no doubt.' Gawen looked up and gave me a gloomy stare. 'Dale is the new ambassador in Paris. I can't say what that may mean for me.'

'I'm sure you'd rather be aboard ship,' I answered and then, casting around for safer ground, 'Jacques said your mission to relieve La Rochelle went well.'

'Jacques! Pah! That fool!' he exploded, tapping his fingers on the windowsill. 'I expect he's told you a fine tale!'

'That your fleet took prizes but was forced back by bad weather,' I answered.

'The truth of it is that your father blundered!' he growled as his chin went up. 'Completely misjudged the strength of the French fleet that opposed us. We had to turn tail and run for Belle Isle! Put into Plymouth briefly, after that on to Jersey.' I remembered how he hadn't even bothered to come to see me while he was in Plymouth.

'Pah!' he exclaimed again. 'The relief of La Rochelle was no great success and I will forever be associated with it.' He crossed his arms over his chest. 'It will be the other Champernowne who is remembered there. Henry! The heroic soldier who would die for his cause, not Gawen the failed sea captain who ran before the wind.' Gawen's expression became even harder and I could see the tension in his shoulders. With sudden clarity I understood how dark a shadow Henry Champernowne had cast over my husband's young life. I ached to soothe his hurt, if only his pride would allow it.

'I've got your father to thank for that disaster. It will forever hang round my neck! And on top of that he sent your brother to William of Orange, not me!' A sudden cloud blotted out the sun, pitching Gawen into murky shadow. I shifted my position on the bed and waited for him to speak again.

'Your father's plans for the next sally had better be good,' he said at last.

'What, more war? I thought after La Rochelle there was another peace agreement in France?'

'It only grants limited freedom of worship to Protestants; only within three towns, and even then only in their own homes. Not enough to satisfy your father and others like him.'

'So what does it mean for you? Will you be able to come home to Dartington?'

'I doubt it. I must report to Walsingham. He might want me to keep watch on your father.'

'You would spy on my papa?' I snapped the question at him and he leaped up and crossed the room. With a face like thunder he picked up Diane the doll and turned her over in his hands, then looked at me. I shifted on the bed. I could feel Gawen's angry eyes boring right through me, dissolving the spark of sympathy I'd felt for him just a moment earlier.

'Pah! French fripperies!' he snorted as he set the doll down. 'Spy on your father? You could say that, I suppose,' he said. 'They might send me to France to act as messenger boy again, but I'd far rather fight. Better still, I'd rather sail with Francis Drake.' I sighed. *So he's still going on about that jumped-up sea captain,* I thought wearily.

'It all sounds dangerous to me!' I commented. He threw back his shoulders.

'Perhaps, but I'll go to serve my queen, whatever they ask of me.' I closed my eyes briefly then watched as he approached the bedside. As his eyes rested on Lisbeth, I thought I detected a change. I was convinced I saw a tiny gleam of warmth in the murky depths of his slate-grey eyes. But not for long; his face hardened and he gave an impatient shrug.

'Your father's raised a loan to pay for ships and men. So there's not much hope that he'll pay what's due on account of our marriage,' he growled. 'The dowry has still not been paid. My father thinks he'll get his money and all that's been promised. I'm not so sure. And I have a daughter!' The words *and not a son* remained unsaid, but his meaning was clear. Lisbeth gave a little mewling cry and I took her from the cradle and started to rock her in my arms.

'I've told you more than enough,' he muttered, pulling at his cuff. 'I must be away tomorrow.' He turned abruptly and almost collided with Katherine Raleigh.

'Aunt,' he nodded to her. 'I am grateful for your care of my wife and this daughter she has given me. I'd rather it was a son, but there we are!' He threw a glare over his shoulder, and I bit my lip. A nagging germ of worry was burrowing its way into my mind. Other men had cast aside unwanted wives. Lord Seymour's mother had been locked away in a convent, left there to die; King Henry was quite happy to dispense with Anne Boleyn in the most horrific fashion when she didn't provide a son. I raised a shaking hand to feel my neck.

I came back to the room with a start to hear Katherine answer Gawen brightly.

'It has been my pleasure. I'll stay until we are sure all danger is past but then I must be gone. Your cousin Philip Cole has come from the Slade. Says his mother, your aunt Elizabeth, is ailing. I must go to her.'

'As you wish,' he replied, and with that he was gone.

Next morning Katherine Raleigh came in with her face wreathed in smiles.

'There's a rather bashful young man below,' she chuckled. 'Sends his and his father's good wishes. Says he's lately returned from Chartley where your brother thrives. He brought this letter.'

'That will be Christopher Melhuishe,' I smiled with an approving nod. 'Clotilde, will you go down and thank him? Tell him to call again when I am up and about. Oh, and Clotilde, send some honey for his father, will you?' I explained to Katherine how Christopher had stepped in as young Gabriel's tutor and how it was Christopher and his father who'd inspired my interest in the new physick garden.

She nodded and smiled. As she held out the letter Lisbeth stirred.

'Is it from my mother?' I asked as I lifted the baby from the crib. 'I do so want to tell her about Lisbeth!' Despite our differences I still yearned for Maman's approval.

Katherine shook her head and I sagged back onto the pillows.

'From Madame de Beaufort,' she said. I brightened a little. Charlotte was the next best thing to Maman.

'Will you read it to me, please? My hands are rather full at the moment.' I held Lisbeth against my shoulder, rubbing her back to release the wind trapped after her last feed.

Katherine opened the packet and started to read in her low, sweet voice, and it was almost as good as having Charlotte there in the room with me.

'*We are all well. Papa has been with the queen and my lord of Leicester. Word is that we're all to go to Syon House in December and stay there for Christmastide at the queen's pleasure. I think Sir Arthur and your husband are to join us so, dear Roberda, you may have a quiet time of it at Dartington. I trust and pray that you and the babe do well. I can say no more of Maman and Papa's plans for, in truth, I do not know them. I have seen Anne Cecil who will write. Her father has been ailing, but now seems recovered.*'

Katherine looked up with a puzzled frown. 'She adds a postscript, but I'm not sure I understand it.'

'Read it then,' I smiled. So she took up the page again.

'*I went to the church as you asked. Most of those who arrive in London are tradespeople from Paris or from Flanders, but there are many in the plight you imagine throughout France. They say you may be able to bring some to Devon from Dieppe or Le Havre or even from Ducey.*'

So I had to explain all about my idea to help women left without menfolk because of the wars. I settled Lisbeth back while Katherine listened patiently, questioning me a few times.

'This idea does you much credit,' she declared, tilting her head to one side. 'You will have my support, for I have always stood by those who suffer for their Protestant beliefs. I will never forget poor Agnes Prest. It is to the eternal shame of Exeter that she met her dreadful fate in the flames when Queen Mary was on the throne.' I had heard how Katherine had kept vigil with the poor Cornish woman in the prison cells below Rougemount Castle. Suddenly Katherine's eyes opened wide. 'Hmm … why not?' she exclaimed, clapping her hands together. 'An idea has just come to me! I have lands in East Devon where many work to make cloth … aye, and some are learning the new way to make fine bone lace from the flax that grows so well on my estates. There may be work for nimble fingers. I will speak to my brother to see what we can do to bring some of your French women to Devon.'

'Thank you, thank you,' I breathed and felt all the tension go out of my body. But then a picture of Rist strutting along the kitchen table leaped into my mind. 'But what if these women do not find a warm welcome? They will know neither English words nor English ways. What if they suffer as my servants did in London?'

'That's true,' she conceded. 'If they had some education so they could speak the language they might not seem so foreign to their neighbours. It's a pity we have no teacher here.'

'But we do have a teacher at Dartington!' I chuckled. 'Master Melhuishe! If Sir Arthur would house them here for a few weeks, Christopher could teach them before they come to you to find work.'

And so it started.

Wrapped up in contented motherhood and planning my refugee scheme, I buried my fears about Gawen's wish for a son and his resentment against my father. Even the rare sight of Bess with her mouth turned down could not throw me off course. She shambled dejectedly into my chamber on a December morning as I watched the steady rise and fall of Lisbeth's little chest.

'Father's making heavy weather with Lord Seymour!' she announced. 'Edward and I have been betrothed since we were children. But I begin to wonder if we'll ever be wed!'

'I'm sure it will be settled soon,' I offered, with more conviction than I really felt.

'Father says old Seymour's after a bigger dowry. He doesn't think we can afford it.' Bess impatiently pushed a strand of shining hair back from her forehead and paced across the bedchamber. 'I hate to mention it, but I think my father's relying on that money coming from your people in France.'

I didn't want to talk about my own unpaid dowry. That brought too many reminders of Gawen's harsh words. But I did want to cheer poor Bess up a bit.

'So, do you like the look of young Edward Seymour now?' I asked. Bess blushed and a weak little smile brightened her face.

'I saw him in Totnes when I went there with Father the other week. He's grown quite a bit since last you saw him. Becoming quite the courtly young man. So what if he's so much younger than me! He's a fine-looking fellow.'

'Let's hope your father will seal the contract with Seymour before you're too much older then,' I chortled. Bess squinted at me and her bottom lip went out. Then she looked down at Lisbeth and her hand fluttered over my sleeping baby.

'She's beautiful,' she breathed the words in a voice so soft and wistful I was taken by surprise. 'I wish I had a babe of my own.'

'You will in time, dear Bess. I'm sure you will,' I said in the most reassuring tone I could manage.

I doubt I have ever been so contented. Sunshine filled my soul at each little milestone as my daughter grew. I rejoiced in Lisbeth's first smile and the soft gurgles she made as she kicked her chubby legs free of swaddling bands. I clapped my hands when her dimpled little fingers clutched an amber rattle for the first time. Even a few sleepless nights when her cheeks grew fiery red as the first tooth came through did nothing to dent my joy in motherhood. I had little time to think of the wars my father might be plotting. Neither did I spare much thought for my absent husband.

As the cold days of winter gave way to breezy March, whatever spare time and energy I had went into finalising plans to receive the first women from France. Sir Arthur lent his support and a small group from my father's estates in Ducey and Pontorson sailed on a merchant vessel bound for Dartmouth at the end of March. Christopher met them, brought them to Dartington and set up his schoolroom overlooking the courtyard.

I waited at the door under the white hart badge as the cart to draw up. The first woman climbed down, set down her bundle and held her hands up to receive a small child only a few months older than Lisbeth. The child's wide eyes locked on my face and I smiled at her. It was pure joy to see the answering smile slowly dawn on that little one's face.

'You are welcome,' I beamed, feeling as though I could easily fly up to the rooftops. The woman stepped a little closer and I saw how her cheekbones stood out sharp as razors and her clothes hung loosely about her.

'*Je suis Madeleine et c'est…*' The woman pointed to the child, a beautiful little girl with white-blonde curls, but I shook my head.

'*Mais non*! Speak only in English now. This is,' I said slowly, 'now tell me her name.'

'Madame, she is Marguerite.'

'Ah, like the flower, and she is just as pretty,' I replied with a smile as the little girl dimpled. 'Off you go. There is food for you all.' Tears brimmed in Madeleine's eyes as she picked up her bundle and followed the others.

When I looked into the schoolroom next morning, four women and seven children, including Madeleine and Marguerite, were chanting English words with huge eyes fixed on Christopher's face. They all scrambled to their feet and sang out a greeting.

'That is good progress after but one night,' I laughed, catching Christopher's eye. He held my gaze and nodded.

I visited the schoolroom room every day, often taking Lisbeth with me so the women could fuss over her. One morning Sir Arthur climbed the steps to the door and had the little ones shrinking in fear to see such a fine English gentleman.

'You are welcome here, be in no doubt, for your menfolk have given much to the cause of the true church in France. We will do all we can to help you settle here,' he reassured them. 'Melhuishe? I trust you keep them to Master Calvin's teachings? I have instructed our rector to assist … and you may also call on Pastor Forêt.' With his bluff manner, I sometimes forgot how staunch a supporter of the reformed church Sir Arthur was.

I followed him to the door and my cheeks glowed warmly as he congratulated me. The children learned very quickly, the women stumbled over the strange English words a little longer. I walked taller with a spring in my step as I saw new hope replace fear on their pinched faces.

Pierre found time to sit and talk with the new arrivals, making helpful suggestions drawn from his own experience as a young man suddenly pitched into a foreign country. Often music floated from the schoolroom windows, sometimes songs of their homeland, sometimes English dance tunes.

It became my habit to take my sewing up to the schoolroom. I felt the tension leave me, my heartbeat slow as I sat quietly stitching, listening to the day's lesson. Madeleine had great skill with a needle and I wrote a letter of recommendation for her to take to Katherine Raleigh when the time came for her to leave us.

At the end of the allotted six weeks, Christopher's relaxed smile told me he was as pleased as I that our venture had got off to such a good start. But despite his best efforts, despite Sir Arthur's stamp of approval, my refugee women did not receive an enthusiastic welcome from everyone. Rist could often be heard moaning about having too many mouths to feed. One morning I came upon him laying down the law to the obnoxious Gatchell. They did not notice me in the doorway and went on talking.

'Now mark me well. These strangers will take work from the hands of good Devon women,' he fumed. 'We don't want them here.' Gatchell was too busy leering after one of the younger women as she walked across the courtyard to reply.

'This is what you get when a hoity-toity French woman like Madam has her way,' Rist growled. 'I've got enough to do without having to provide food and lodging for the likes of them. I'll be glad to see the back of 'em.'

'Oh, I don't know,' Gatchell replied as his eyes raked over the girl. 'That one looks a pretty enough package to me. I might make her acquaintance.' He slicked his hair back and set off in pursuit.

'You will leave these poor women alone, Master Gatchell,' I ordered, narrowing my eyes as I erupted from the shadows like an avenging angel. 'They are in no need of your attentions. Have you no work to do?' He turned back, gave me a most insolent stare and sloped off in the direction of Sir Arthur's study.

'And you, Master Rist, get about your business.' Rist scowled and disappeared through the buttery door, slamming it behind him with more force than was necessary.

When the cart came to take them to Exeter, Madeleine said her goodbyes in English with barely a hesitation, little Marguerite grinned up at me and I promised to visit them when they were settled.

As they left, Gawen arrived home, back from one of his missions for Walsingham. I received him with glowing cheeks, flush from the success of my little project. But he barely acknowledged me and was soon locked in heated discussions with his father and a stream of visitors, including the rather handsome Sir Richard Grenville, burly John Hawkins and that bumptious little man, Francis Drake.

A warm April breeze, early messenger of summer nights to come, crept in through the open window as Gawen, who had resumed his visits to my bedchamber with alacrity, lay beside me. I'd almost convinced myself that something more than duty brought him so often to my bed. But that night his mind was on other matters.

'He's still in high favour,' he announced in a voice warm with admiration.

'Who?' I murmured sleepily.

'Francis; my friend, Francis Drake!'

'I've heard enough about this paragon, this Master Drake,' I grumbled, turning my back on him. 'I'm surprised he needs a ship to carry him across the ocean. You always make him sound as though he could walk on water.'

'He's the finest sailor I've ever known,' Gawen enthused. 'I'd give a lot to be able to sail with him.' I buried my face in the soft down pillow. He bored me to sleep most nights with tales of his hero's exploits.

I shut my ears to their talk of the ships they pretended were being prepared for some voyage to far-off lands; I hadn't even heard of Labrador, nor of any North-West Passage. I never discovered what was decided but the sea captains departed, leaving my husband dreaming of ships and adventures. He was champing at the bit for action, desperate to prove himself as good a sea captain and soldier as any; and as good as his dead cousin, Henry Champernowne.

The buds had long since burst on the apple trees and the bees were busy with the bounty of a new season when word came that Gawen's aunt Elizabeth, a woman I had never met, had died. Gawen and Sir Arthur left in a hurry for Cornwood, the manor near Ivybridge where Elizabeth had lived, to settle her affairs and see her buried. It was not far distant, no more than fifteen miles from Dartington and I expected Gawen to return. But he did not. Spring drifted into glorious summer and I supposed he'd been called away again on the queen's business. My life soon settled back into a happy, comfortable pattern with Lisbeth at its centre.

Chapter Seventeen

La Place de Grève

Summer 1574

June; high summer in Devon. As I headed for my physick garden, I took a brief peep upwards. Beyond the highest window Lisbeth slept in her crib, watched over by Jeanne. I allowed myself a little smile; she would not wake for another hour or more.

The air was thick with the nectar-rich perfume of honeysuckle, and sunlight danced on an explosion of colour; roses, marigolds, camomile and feverfew, all in glorious bloom. I bent my head over a full-blown red rose and buried my nose in the velvety petals. After a giddy, heady rush of scent came a sweet memory of the garden at Ducey.

I tripped lightly along, noticing the leaves were lightly dusted with summer pollen. I meandered between the clipped hedges, humming a little tune, ran my hands through lavender buds almost ready to burst and made my way to the arbour. I sat down, let out a deep satisfied sigh and allowed my head to rest on the smooth wooden strut that formed the high back of the bench. The sun was warm on my face and I squinted between my lashes as Agnes Searle explained to one of the younger maids how to gather the unripe seeds of sweet cicely. Vaguely aware of the soft rhythm of her voice and the gentle buzzing of regiments of bees, my eyelids began to droop and I drifted off into a contented doze.

All at once my eyes flew open. I cocked my head to one side

and listened; voices from the courtyard. With a longing look at the sunlit garden I dragged my feet along the path and in through the open door. Within the walls the air felt pleasantly cool and I paused, blinking hard to adjust my eyes to the sudden darkness. Sir Arthur was leaning on the jamb of the opposite door, breathing heavily and clutching his side. I stepped closer and searched his face. The cheery countenance I had come to know so well was gone, replaced by the careworn features of a much older man.

'I'm come from Southampton,' he groaned as he stumbled forward, hardly glancing at me. 'I'll leave it to you to greet our visitors. I must make ready to go to France.' With that he plodded across the hall as though he had the weight of all the world on his shoulders. Bess appeared and offered her arm, but Sir Arthur shook her off with a weary gesture. Nothing daunted she continued to walk purposefully beside him towards his study.

I turned to see John Gatchell saunter in from the courtyard carrying a saddlebag stuffed with papers. I stiffened and folded my arms across my chest as his insolent eyes strayed over me before coming to rest somewhere between the top of my gown and my neck.

'Make haste, Master Gatchell,' I hissed. 'Look to Sir Arthur. I fear he is unwell.'

'Weary after a long journey,' he drawled, still eyeing my bodice. 'And had enough of all this French nonsense,' he added, under his breath.

'That will do,' I blazed. 'Go at once to your master!' I turned my back on him and nearly jumped out of my skin. Maman was framed in the doorway, tall and starchy in her customary black silk. Beside her stood another woman. At first glance, I hardly recognised Charlotte.

'Charlotte? What have you done to your hair?' I tittered, running forward to greet her after a perfunctory curtsey to my mother.

'It's … er … the latest style,' she faltered, looking anxiously at Maman. With a little shrug Charlotte turned her head so I could admire the waves of hair swept up from her face beneath a heart-shaped headdress. 'All the ladies fashion their hair so. Some even wear wigs if their own is not enough – we all follow the Queen of England…' Charlotte's voice trailed off, sounding flat and dull.

Again she flicked her eyes towards Maman who was looking at me as though I'd committed some heinous crime. Sir Arthur's haggard appearance; Maman's pinched face; Charlotte's quavering voice; all pointed to something amiss.

'Whatever is it?' I croaked. 'What is wrong?'

Maman turned a glacial stare on me, but said nothing.

'Perhaps we should go inside,' Charlotte stuttered. 'We have much to tell you.'

As we started across the hall I noticed Rist loitering in the shadows, trying to eavesdrop on our conversation.

'Have you nothing better to do than stand and stare, Master Rist?' I snapped, narrowing my eyes. 'Bring refreshments to the parlour and have the Countess's Chamber prepared.' I realised too late I had fallen into the trap of ceding ownership to my mother by giving the room that label.

Maman did not touch the wine Clotilde poured for her but sat staring blankly ahead as she twisted a kerchief in her fingers. A few beads of sweat stood out on her lip and her eyes were unnaturally bright. Appalled, I realised that what I saw on Maman's face was fear. Clotilde saw it too.

'Madame la Comtesse,' she ventured. 'Perhaps you would prefer to retire now? I can set your chamber to rights for you.'

Maman gave a tiny nod, rose from her seat and walked stiffly after Clotilde just as Jeanne rushed in carrying a bawling Lisbeth. Even the first opportunity to meet her granddaughter made no impression on my mother. She moved on without so much as a glance at the screaming bundle Jeanne held out. I took the baby and sat down to unlace my gown.

'Goodness!' Charlotte exclaimed, raising an eyebrow. 'Did Gawen not insist on a wet nurse?'

'Gawen was not here,' I replied in a rasping tone. 'Now whatever is wrong with Maman? Why is Sir Arthur in such a state? You must tell me all, Charlotte.' Her face paled and she swallowed hard.

'Papa is taken,' she whispered. My brain stuttered and a wash of cold flooded through me. Lisbeth must have felt me flinch, for she started to mewl and fret in my arms.

'Where? How?' I stammered, gaping at Charlotte. I clamped my mouth shut and felt a pain at the back of my throat as if my heart had jumped up there and I was trying to swallow it. 'What did you say? Papa is taken?' I repeated. Charlotte confirmed it with a nod as a tear slid down her cheek and splashed onto the front of her fine gown.

'I've taken no heed of events in France since this little one was born. The last I heard you were all at Syon House. I should have asked…' By now Lisbeth's little fists were clutching at the air and her face was as red as the apothecary's rose in my physick garden. Charlotte bowed her head and her shoulders trembled as she waited for me to deal with my baby. Once the child had settled a little I turned to my sister.

'Please, Charlotte, will you start at the beginning?' I pleaded.

'Well, even you must know that Papa wanted to tackle the Catholics in France again?' As she shot the words at me she rubbed the back of her neck and then let the air out from her lungs in a weary sigh. 'The memory of St Bartholomew's Day remained fresh in his mind, as it did for many people in France.'

'People are still shocked by it in England too,' I replied defensively. Charlotte sighed again.

'Papa reckoned he'd found the perfect time to launch an attack,' she continued in the same dull voice. 'Alençon, King Charles's younger brother, was held captive at court along with Henry of Navarre and Prince Condé. Papa hoped to split the royal army by coordinating his assault on Normandy with an attempt by other Huguenot leaders to set them free.'

'I can see the sense of that,' I interjected.

'He was relying on support from Queen Elizabeth,' Charlotte went on.

'Now I think of it, I remember something Sir Arthur said about seeking permission to arm ships. I didn't pay much heed …' I murmured as my insides twisted into a knot. Charlotte wrinkled her nose.

'Yes, Sir Arthur and John Hawkins were kitting out their ships and Queen Elizabeth might have turned a blind eye to that. But she could make no public commitment. Instead, when Papa went to Jersey in March, she pretended she had merely allowed him to go there to see to his affairs.'

In a rare flash of insight I understood the queen's dilemma.

'I suppose she dare not go to war openly with France. Gawen always says Spain is getting stronger and the Catholics in France are becoming more extreme too. If those nations joined forces, what chance could there be for little England?' I pondered.

'I suppose you're right,' Charlotte went on in the same flat, tired voice, 'but it makes no difference to what has happened…'

'No, no. Go on,' I prompted.

'Papa put it about that he would give up the wars and retire to a quiet life on the islands. He took them all with him; Jacques, Gedeon, Giles, Suzette, Pérronelle and the girls. Of course, he was really planning an attack on Normandy.' She paused and shook her head.

'I was so wrapped up in Lisbeth…' I muttered to myself. My voice cracked as I spoke louder. 'I had no idea this was happening… Is my husband with them?'

As Charlotte took a sip of wine her hands were shaking.

'That I don't know, but Jehan de Refuge, Elisabeth's husband, joined Papa in Jersey.' I looked at her sharply.

'I was wrong about him,' Charlotte conceded. 'He only made a pretence of converting and hearing the mass so he could claim the protection of his family who remained true to the old ways. He was just as strong in support of Papa as were our uncles Louis and Jacques.'

'Trust Papa to make war a family affair,' I said bleakly. 'No doubt Maman made it a crusade!' I could never forgive her for dragging us all to Rouen.

'Now, now, that's not fair,' Charlotte retorted. 'Maman and I remained in Southampton.' But she admitted they only stayed behind to gather more Englishmen to join those Papa had already taken to Normandy.

'She did it too!' Charlotte cried. 'She had another contingent all ready to put to sea. Maman was only waiting for Papa's order to send them, although Queen Elizabeth made a show of putting a stop to it.' Charlotte lapsed into silence and stared at her hands. The silence lengthened and I was still no wiser as to how Papa had been taken.

'So you remained in Southampton? What happened in France?' I prompted gently.

Charlotte took a kerchief from her sleeve and dabbed at her eyes, then continued, sniffing loudly between the words.

'I think Papa became even more determined after Uncle Louis was murdered at the Abbaye Saint-Jean de Falaise.'

I drew my head back sharply. 'Murdered? No!' At my anguished cry the baby let out a loud scream. I shook my head from side to side and rocked to and fro while Lisbeth went on bawling. For the first time since her birth I was overtaken by other concerns and waved to Jeanne to lift her from my arms and take her away.

All I could think of was the last time I had seen my two uncles, laughing together at Elisabeth's wedding, Louis with his violet robe straining over an ample girth and Jacques dressed for action in leather jerkin and boots. The scene was etched in my mind of both men, so full of life. I stumbled across the room and picked up the carved ivory ink horn, the one Uncle Louis had given me all those years ago.

'It can't be true!' I whispered as I turned it in my hand and traced the carved angels with my finger.

'I don't think he was ever forgiven for opening the doors of the abbey and letting Papa's troops in when the fighting started again – you remember – after Elisabeth's wedding? Killing Uncle Louis was a way to get at Papa, I suppose,' Charlotte murmured. I felt tears welling up in my eyes and sat down abruptly. Charlotte took a deep breath.

'Despite that, things seemed to be going well. Papa seized a few towns,' Charlotte continued. 'Baron Colombières – remember him – Papa's friend?' I nodded. 'He held St Lo. The royalists surrounded the place, but St Lo held firm.' I could picture the city and its strong walls. It was where I'd first met Béatrice. I shuddered. It had been bad enough when we were confined there in that little house; how much worse it must have felt to have the enemy bombarding the walls.

'Papa managed to slip away to Carentan, where he set up a base. I think our brother Jacques was there with him. It's all a bit confused.' She fumbled for the words between sobs.

'I'm sorry, it must be hard for you to tell, but I must know,' I whispered.

'Why Papa left Carentan is a mystery. Somehow he became trapped at Domfront. I think he held out there for a while. Perhaps he didn't have enough men or arms. Perhaps his soldiers deserted or too many were killed. Perhaps they ran out of food and water. Whatever the reason, Papa was forced to surrender.' I raised trembling fingers to my mouth. I had not forgotten Domfront; a dark and dismal place, filled with menacing shadows, where the candle flame had guttered in the night.

'That's the last we've heard. He's been taken. No one knows what will happen to him,' Charlotte wailed. I felt sick and was shaking as I put my arms around her. I don't know how long we clung together.

The next few days dragged by. Maman kept to her room and Sir Arthur never stirred from his study, his plans to go to France abandoned. Messengers came and went every day but they brought no more news of Papa. I tried to hold on to the hope that Queen Elizabeth would petition for his freedom; that King Charles would listen to her entreaties. But then we heard that the ailing King of France had died and his brother Henri was now King, though he was in Poland. That meant my father's fate rested in the hands of the Queen Dowager.

Through all those dismal days Charlotte sat biting her nails, while a strangely silent Bess put a few listless stitches into her embroidery. I tended Lisbeth automatically while my mind ran through every possible outcome. I could find no break in the dark cloud that hung over us all, no shaft of sunlight to relieve our misery.

Maman's scream did not come from her mouth and lungs. It was a primal shriek wrenched from somewhere deep within her soul. It shook the very walls of her chamber and echoed all the way through the hall into the parlour where we sat. I knew instantly what it meant and yet I put my hands over my ears, trying to shut it out. I did not want to acknowledge the certainty that scream brought. It was over. Papa was gone.

Sir Arthur stumbled unsteadily down the stairs still holding a crumpled paper in his hand. He joined us and, ashen-faced, said the words I dreaded to hear.

'He died bravely. In the Place de Grève in Paris on the twenty-sixth day of June… Go to your mother. She has need of you.' He gave no details and I had no wish to hear them.

Maman stood at the window staring out with unseeing eyes. Pastor Forêt bustled in with his Bible under his arm. He read from the scriptures in French and soon had Maman praying beside him, though I couldn't think what good that would do.

I wanted to blurt out the words racing through my mind. T*his is where your religion has brought us! Papa is dead, and all because he fought for this new way.* But I knew in my heart it was not only his wish to promote the new ways of Master Calvin that had made my father risk all. Ambition, pride, recklessness, enmity, politics – all had added to his fervour to make a toxic brew. I didn't know whether to blame Maman or to run to her arms to comfort her. I felt numb, empty. I couldn't even cry.

More details dribbled in like icy water dripping from a pail with a small hole in the bottom. My blood ran cold to think of the cruelty and waste of it all. St Lo had fallen and Baron Colombières had been put to death along with his sons before my father's eyes. They had taken Papa there in chains, before he was moved to Caen for trial and then to Paris. I couldn't bear to think they'd made my papa stand there and watch his friend die.

All this time I had no word of my husband. As the days passed, Maman recovered herself a little. Soon she was busy with her pen or reading letters that came with increasing frequency. That was during the daylight hours. At night I heard her footsteps. Up and down, up and down, her heels click-clacking on the creaking floorboards in that lonely room. I doubt if she slept at all. I found myself stumbling over my words whenever I spoke to her, forever apologising for silly little things. Trying to come to terms with Papa's death was bad enough, but the nagging feeling that I had let my mother down in some way was even worse.

But the world did not stop. The sun went on shining down from an azure sky. The birds sang in the morning. Lisbeth continued to thrive. One sunny afternoon I sat on a blanket spread on the grass near my physick garden while my little girl gurgled joyfully as she played with Diane the doll. Beyond the lavender hedge the steward and John Gatchell lolled in the shade of the apple tree. Rist was leaning up against the trunk while Gatchell stretched out on the grass. Perhaps they did not see me sitting there with my daughter, though I could see them, so they must surely have known I was within earshot.

'So the Frenchman met his end,' Rist declared in a voice just a little louder than was necessary. 'Those French royals know how to dispatch a man, that's for sure.'

'Aye! They do say he was racked and tortured first, but would not confess his sins, nor receive the last rights from any Catholic priest,' Gatchell replied. 'And so he went to meet the headsman. But they were not content with chopping off his head. Oh no! They cut him into four pieces and nailed bits of him to the city gates. A lesson for all traitors!'

My body froze. I opened my mouth to scream, but no sound came. I picked up Lisbeth and pulled her close. I felt as though my chest was caving in. I could not breathe. The blackness descended.

I don't know who found me, who cared for Lisbeth while they carried me to my bed, or how long I lay there. The dreams of Rouen were back. The old woman's screams were louder. An endless stream of scarlet blood spurted from the soldier's shattered head. Sometimes in those nightmares I saw Papa. But his face wasn't there. I couldn't remember Papa's face.

Chapter Eighteen

Aftermath

1574–1575

It was Lisbeth who helped me push my demons aside. Clotilde brought her to me every day and gradually I regained my senses. I tried to banish it all from my mind and focus my attention on my daughter. Lisbeth took her first steps; more teeth appeared; she started to chew on crusts of bread and take stewed apples mixed with milk from a spoon. Tired out from spending my days running after my growing daughter, I began to sleep at nights. The disturbing dreams came a little less often.

I took great comfort in the women who came every few months from France for a brief interlude of learning with Christopher before they set off for East Devon where Katherine Raleigh reported they settled well. Sir Arthur barely noticed them and the cost was not great. How my heart swelled when one young woman stopped me in the courtyard after I'd accompanied Clotilde as she delivered bolts of cloth so that they might make shifts for themselves and their children.

'How may I ever thank you, mistress?' she whispered timidly, in heavily accented English. ''Tis the first clean linen I've had for my baby in many a long month. I shall never forget your kindness.' She turned and ran back to the others and a thin-faced child with curly brown hair peeped from behind her mother's skirts and waved to me. I waved back and lifted my head, basking in a tingling warmth that spread all though my body.

Maman and Charlotte returned to Southampton several months after we heard of Papa's death. I was not sorry to see them go. Maman's presence set me on edge. The grey shadow of her misery lingered long after she had left us. I could never go into the room that would forever be called the Countess's Chamber without feeling an icy shiver trickle down my spine.

Jacques had been there in the Place de Grève at the end. He had been allowed to write to Maman. He told her Papa had lain down a challenge to his children as he mounted the scaffold in front of the baying Catholic crowds. How cruel it was that in those last moments of Papa's life a royal edict was read out; his lands were to be confiscated; his children would not inherit his titles. Jacques said that Papa had shouted, 'Tell my children, if they are not able to reclaim their position, I will curse them from the grave!'

That was all Maman needed to set her off on another crusade. Everything she did would be to one end; to have Jacques' inheritance restored to him. Left destitute in a foreign land, she started to lobby Lord Burghley and Walsingham and, through them, the Queen of England.

I saw little of Sir Arthur, who came and went about some business of his own. If he knew where Gawen was, and when he might return, he did not tell me. I was surprised when he called out to me in the hall one autumn morning.

'Good news! Your mother has been called to court for the yuletide season.' He smiled weakly, but looked at the floor as if unwilling to meet my eyes.

'Thank you, sir,' I replied as my heartbeat slowed. I wasn't sure if I had hoped or feared he had news of Gawen. He touched his forehead, nodded, and speeded away down the hall as if the dogs were after him, leaving me gawping. I couldn't fathom why it was that on the few occasions I actually saw Sir Arthur he seemed so very uncomfortable.

After the year turned I heard from Maman that the queen had presented her with a gilt bowl as a New Year gift. Maman wrote that she might be able to sell it. It sounded as though Walsingham might be kindly disposed to her. But no offer of tangible support was mentioned. I ground my teeth, thinking it a pity that those who could have done more to aid my father were now doing only a little to support my poor mother.

February, always a dismal month, saw heavy snow in Devon and patches still lingered under the hedges when the battered letter came. Charlotte had forwarded it enclosed in a sealed package from London. It must have taken months to come from France. I huddled near the fire as I broke the seal and read Charlotte's note first.

'*This is more for you than me,*' I read. '*Every time she writes she says she is in your debt…*' I unfolded the creased paper and could almost imagine Béatrice's long fingers holding the quill as she wrote.

> *My dear sisters*
>
> *I share your grief; so much so that I fear my tears will fall and blot out these poor words. I can bring you little comfort.*
>
> *When I heard he was taken I went to the Queen Dowager on my knees to beg for his life. My uncle Tavannes has been dead these twelve months and more, so there was no one to prevent me. I had to go.*
>
> *I was surprised she agreed to receive me. Her son, King Charles, had only just departed this life. She recognised me instantly, even in my present garb. I sat with her; I prayed with her; I begged her for mercy. Her eyes were hard as flints. This is what she said.*
>
> *'In this last act he has committed treason against the Crown of France. He came with force of arms against us. The sentence is clear. But it is not for that I will see the sentence carried out. It is for what he did all those years ago. It is for that lance that shattered my husband's eye and left my life in tatters. Since that day I have lost three sons. France has been split asunder by these accursed wars. Gabriel de Lorges is the cause of all my sorrow. Now I shall have my revenge.'*
>
> *She waved a badge in my face; her badge of the broken lance and commanded me: return to your abbey and pray for his soul.*
>
> *It was clearly of no use to ask that she take council of her son, King Henri.*
>
> *So, my dear sisters, I tried, but I have failed you.*
>
> *Written in sorrow,*
> *your sister before God,*
> *Béatrice*

A strangled sob burst from somewhere deep inside me.

'At least Béatrice tried,' I cried out. 'She did all she could.'

As I folded the page another scrap fell to the floor; a note also written in Béatrice's hand, but less clear, as though she had scribbled it as an afterthought.

> *I discovered what became of your servant, Alain du Bois. Monks found his body where he lay beside the road along with others slain with him. They gave them good Christian burial in their small priory nearby. I send monies for prayers to be said for their souls. I know your beliefs are different, but it is all I can do. He was a good man.*

I laid the letter on my coffer next to Diane the doll and, grabbing a warm cloak, ran down to my physick garden. Sitting on the bench I put my hands together and tried to pray. But no words came. I was not thinking of Papa but of Alain, the man who had been my anchor through the storms of my childhood years. I would never forget him, but Béatrice's letter had brought me some small comfort. As I sat in front of the stone carved with Alain's name the memories came thick and fast. I did not stir until a bat flitted out from the window high above the kitchen as dusk fell. Then moving stiffly, for I was chilled to the bone, I returned to the welcoming warmth of the candlelit hall.

Several weeks later Bess ran in with her arms full of nodding yellow cowslips.

'Have you been out to wash your face in the morning dew this May morning?' she giggled. 'It's too late for us to make a ball of these cowslips; no use for you and me to play titsy-totsy! You're already married and I've no doubt that young Edward will be my husband one day, though that day does seem a long time a-coming.'

'Whatever are you talking about?' I laughed. When she was in high spirits Bess was the best tonic in the world.

'It's a game the village girls play. They make a ball of the cowslips and throw it one to another singing, *titsy-totsy, tell me true, who shall I be married to*?'

'As you say, it's too late for me. But I do sometimes wish your brother would act more like a lovelorn swain,' I sighed. Bess was good company, and I loved my daughter to distraction, but the truth of it was that I was lonely. I didn't hold out much hope that I would be any less so if Gawen was at home.

'You could make a love potion,' she chuckled, holding the bunch out so that I could see the dew still glistening on the clusters of trumpet-shaped flowers. 'Put some in a pot with fresh rainwater and leave them in sunlight. Then sprinkle the sweet essence on his pillow. In less than a month his heart will melt for sure.'

'Well, that's not much use, Gawen's not even here. I've no idea when I'll ever see him again. Better let Agnes have them for the still room instead.'

'I'll see what she can do,' Bess declared with a little frown. 'A cure for headaches and melancholy would certainly be good for my father.' She was nearly out of the door when she turned. 'Oh, here's a letter from Jersey,' she called.

Charlotte's letter brought news of my family. Jacques had arrived in Jersey in time for the birth of another daughter. I gave a wry smile as I read how he claimed he had made a miraculous escape from his captors hidden in a beer barrel. I suspected it was one of those tales that grows more with the telling.

All through that summer of 1575 I hardly had any speech with Sir Arthur. He was always in a hurry with no time to talk, running a hand through straggly, unkempt hair as his eyes darted everywhere, never meeting mine, until one morning as I sat in my physick garden watching Lisbeth swishing her feet among piles of scrunchy fallen leaves. I glanced towards the house and saw Sir Arthur advancing on me with a spring in his step such as I hadn't seen for a long time. Pulling the cloak more tightly round my shoulders to ward off the chill, I smiled a welcome.

'You'll want to know, of course. I've heard from Gawen. He will be home by Christmastide,' he exclaimed, grinning as he settled back onto the bench beside me. I looked at my hands, making no comment, though my stomach turned over at the thought of my husband's return.

'He'll be surprised to see how that young maid has grown,' Sir

Arthur beamed, nodding in Lisbeth's direction. My heart lifted to see a smile on his face again. Perhaps Gawen's return would put an end to the uncomfortable distance that had grown between Sir Arthur and me since Papa's death. I drew my brows together in a frown. Now I thought of it, the frosty atmosphere had started even before that. It went back to that day Sir Arthur had returned with Maman and Charlotte; the day I first heard Papa was taken. Among all the grief and confusion I had shrugged it off, but deep down I knew on that day something had changed.

'That is good news, sir,' I replied, forcing the smile back onto my lips. 'I hope he will bring word of my mother. She must have found it hard to manage these past months.' His face changed in an instant. The autumn sun still glinted on ember-red and gold fallen leaves, but it was as though a cloud passed over his face, snuffing out all the joy that had shone there at the prospect of Gawen's return.

'Things must be difficult for all of your family,' Sir Arthur breathed, staring down at his boots. 'Gawen reports that the walls of Ducey have been pulled down and reduced to rubble.'

'What? Surely not,' I gasped as an image of Alain du Bois in front of Ducey's solid walls rushed into my head; Alain, the rock of my childhood, staunch, steady and strong standing before walls that would be there forever. Even when we went home after Rouen, those walls had remained firm and protective among all the devastation. I felt my stomach clench and reached an imploring hand towards him. 'Did you say they've reduced my home to nothing but a heap of stones?'

'I'm afraid that is exactly what they have done,' he nodded gravely. 'I'm sorry … it was a wonderful place.' I shook my head from side to side slowly, just little movements at first, then wider and wider as the news sunk in.

'Is there nothing left?' I stuttered. Sir Arthur took my fluttering hand, tilted his head and looked into my eyes.

'The land alone, that is all, and that taken from your brother. Your mother works hard for his sake.' For the first time in many months I looked into Sir Arthur's face. My gaze wandered uncertainly over his dark-ringed eyes, his pallid, sunken cheeks, his pinched mouth. I suddenly felt cold, my own distress forgotten. He sighed and cleared his throat.

'You must know that everything I have ever done has been for the best of reasons,' he quavered. I blinked at him and my mouth dropped open, but before I could ask what he meant Lisbeth came racing down the path, tripped on her skirts and fell headlong. I rushed to pick her up to soothe her affronted screams and add balm to her wounded pride. When I looked again Sir Arthur was plodding ponderously towards the house.

I stared after his retreating figure until he disappeared through the open door. I pondered for a moment then, leaving Lisbeth with Jeanne, I set off in search of Bess. I found her in the parlour frowning over her needlework.

'I've just had the strangest conversation with your father,' I said. 'Ever since that day he brought my mother here when we heard Papa had been captured I've felt he's been avoiding me. But I really don't know why. Just now in the garden I thought he was about to tell me something. Do you know what's on his mind?'

She sighed, put down her sewing and patted the seat beside her. Bess shot anxious glances at me as I sat down and made a fuss about arranging my skirts.

'Oh, my dear Roberda! It's always the same. It's always money at the bottom of everyone's troubles.' She fumbled uncertainly for the words. 'It's your dowry, you see. I think he feels bad about it, knowing your family have lost so much.' Bess's voice sounded brittle as she added, 'He tried to get it from the French Crown. They haven't paid up.'

Chapter Nineteen

Wifely Duty, Family Affairs

1575 and 1576

A bitter winter arrived early in Devon that year and with it came Gawen, home after so many months in France. As I steeled myself for our first meeting I tried to summon the sort of excitement a young wife ought to feel at her husband's homecoming. But my palms were sweating as I shifted my weight from foot to foot as I waited for him in the bedchamber. There was an empty feeling in the pit of my stomach when I turned to greet him.

Without a word Gawen crossed the room to the window and stared out as little specks of white fluttered gently down to fall on the snow-covered gardens that gleamed faintly silver in the fading light. Beyond the ill-fitting window a robin poured out his wistful winter song; at first a few long notes then a burst of rapid burbling melody. It reminded me of the pool near the holy well, still and calm until it suddenly overflowed and spilled down the hillside. The robin repeated his sad little tune once more before the tomb-like hush descended again; a silence so deep, so pure, it felt as though the world was holding its breath as each snowflake fell. Gawen remained silent with his eyes fixed on the white world beyond the window. Inside the room the silence grew to fill the space between us like a thick, prickly hedge.

When I could wait no longer I leaped in to break that awkward silence, speaking too fast with my hands fluttering in the French way as they always do when I'm agitated.

'Welcome home,' I chirped in a forced voice. 'I hope your journey was good. Fancy coming home in the snow. Were the roads bad?'

'Am I welcome indeed?' he murmured without turning. 'There's not much welcome in a pile of debts that grow by the day. Debts from kitting out our ships to support your father in France. All in vain!'

'I am sorry for the loss of your coin,' I lashed out, unable to keep the annoyance from my voice. 'As you know well I have lost something of much greater value.' He started as though I'd hit him and at last he turned and looked at me. The tense muscles of his jaw softened a little and I thought I saw a glimmer of sympathy in his eyes, as if a kindly grey smoke had drifted over the flinty steel.

'I am sorry for your father's loss,' he said, swallowing hard. The words were formal; condolences offered to an acquaintance, not the warm words of support a man should use to his beloved wife.

'Our daughter has been a great comfort to me,' I answered with the cold edge still in my voice. I waited in silence, trying not to shiver as a chill draught nipped at my ankles. At last Gawen heaved a long sigh and stepped closer. His gaze strayed to the top of my shift and he stretched a hand forward to touch my neck.

'Then we must do our duty and see if this time we can get her a brother,' he murmured in a low, thick voice.

Gawen's visits to my bedchamber became part of our daily routine. For the most part I think the intimacy we shared was of no more consequence to either of us than eating or breathing. But there were times when I saw another Gawen; times when I felt a little closer to him; times when he let down his stern defences, relaxed and even smiled. He really was quite handsome when he smiled. On one winter's night as we clung together for warmth, my head resting on his chest, he spoke of his childhood in the shadow of his cousin, Henry Champernowne. Even with his lips close to my ear I could detect the resentment in his muffled voice.

'When I was fifteen I took charge of one of my father's ships and sailed across to France,' he murmured. 'I was quite terrified, of course,' he added with a nervous chuckle. 'But I was determined to show him what I could do.' In that rare admission I glimpsed the boy he must have been, forever striving to impress his father. How I yearned to comfort and reassure him. But he soon remembered himself and turned away from me, pulling the bedcover up to his chin. When, propped on one elbow, I leaned across and peered into his face it was as if an iron grille had snapped down over his features. The lines had returned around his eyes, his mouth taken on its usual set line. Whenever I felt I was getting closer to him, my husband shied away like a frightened horse.

It was a quiet Christmas at Dartington Hall, with as few neighbours and tenants invited as courtesy would allow. At the end of January, on a day when snow was piled into huge drifts against the courtyard walls, whipped up and deposited there by a relentless wind, I sat close to the fire in the parlour. Gawen had also retreated from the cold and was huddled over the blaze, sorting through a pile of papers and letters recently delivered.

'I was amazed to see a messenger,' I chirped. Gawen merely grunted without looking up. I made another attempt at conversation. 'The poor man must have ridden into the very teeth of the blizzard to reach Dartington. I've instructed Rist to give him food and dry clothing.'

'Hmm… This one's addressed to you,' he muttered, turning a letter over in his hands. He did not hesitate to break the seal and peruse its contents. I choked down the protest that rose in my throat. There was no point in jeopardising the fragile cordiality that now defined our time together. He would soon be on his way back to France.

'Oh … it's from Anne Cecil,' he said with a sly little smile. 'Had a child last year, didn't she? Word is there's bad feeling between her husband and her father. Oxford's a bad-tempered sort, too full of himself, if you ask me. I suspect he's got Catholic leanings. Petitioned for Norfolk, didn't he? He's gone off and left her. He's living a high life in Italy! I wonder what Lord Burghley thinks of that!'

'What? She has a child? Is she well?' I reached for the letter. He held onto it a little longer, taking his time to read it to the end.

'Here,' he huffed, passing it over at last. 'Read it for yourself.'

Poor Anne was still besotted with a husband everyone else thought impossible. She had given birth to a daughter in the autumn of the previous year. Edward de Vere had gone off on a tour of Europe, flinging accusations that the child was not his. She said her parents were looking after her but she was devastated to have such things said of her. The queen continued to receive her at court where she had seen my mother and sister at the New Year's gift exchanges. She and Charlotte had both received gilt bowls made by the same London goldsmith from the queen.

'She says my mother and Charlotte have exchanged gifts with the queen again this year. Surely that is a good sign that Queen Elizabeth might help us to get our estates in France restored?' I spoke my thoughts aloud. At the mention of the French estates, Gawen's eyebrows came together in a bristling black line.

''Tis to be hoped so! The dowry is long overdue. No son either!' He stared pointedly at my stomach then stomped off carrying the rest of the letters with him. I called for ink and paper and started to write a sympathetic reply to my friend, thinking how we could both have been better served in the choice of our husbands. But, despite all that encouragement from poor Uncle Louis all those years ago, I was no scribe. I threw the pen down in disgust as a blot of ink spoiled the page. I looked up to see Christopher hesitating at the door with a book in his hand.

'I'm sorry to disturb you. My father thought you might enjoy this,' he said with a shy smile. 'It's written in French.' He blinked several times as he took in the ink blot on the page and the disordered papers. 'But I can see it's not convenient. I will call on another occasion.' He wheeled round as if to bolt for the door.

'No, Christopher! Please stay,' I pleaded. 'I wanted to write to Anne Cecil, but now I've ruined my letter.' I crumpled the spoiled page, threw it into the fire and took the book from his outstretched hand. As the book passed between us our hands touched just for an instant. Christopher jumped back, cheeks flaming, but not before I saw the tender look in his eyes.

'*Mirror of the sinful soul*,' I exclaimed. 'Written by Margaret d'Angoulême? Mother of Jeanne d'Albret and grandmother of Henry of Navarre?' He nodded briskly.

'Maman has a copy,' I murmured as I ran my finger over the embossed leather binding then raised the small volume to my nose and breathed in the intoxicating woody scent of the pages bound within. 'To think of a woman writing something like this! I know my mother admires her.'

'I will leave it with you then?' he quavered, hovering on the point of flight.

'Yes, but please stay! As you see I am in need of assistance,' I pleaded, waving my hand across the scattered pages. 'Will you act as my clerk this morning?'

'I must return to the schoolroom. I have left Pierre with our latest students.' Christopher's eyes flitted round the room anxiously.

'Pierre can hold the fort a little longer,' I smiled. 'Have no fear, my husband has taken his spite elsewhere.' I knew I should not have spoken so, but Gawen and his moods were wearing me down.

So Christopher shuffled to the table, rubbing his hands together, for the room was icy cold. He sat down heavily, tidied the pages and picked up the pen to write at my careful dictation. Gawen insisted on seeing every letter before it was sent and would check I hadn't given away any secrets. *That would be difficult since I know so little of his plans*, I thought with a little snort.

The letter completed, Christopher handed me the pen. I leaned over his shoulder and signed with a flourish, then stood back. We spoke of inconsequential matters a little longer.

'How is your father?' I asked.

'He's well, but he's all in confusion. His hound Bella has whelped a litter, but every pup looks different. Not at all what he expected of a mating with Sir Arthur's best hunting dog. It seems Bella may have had another suitor!' We both laughed. 'Perhaps Miss Lisbeth would like a puppy when they are old enough to leave their mother?' he smiled. 'She could come and choose one.'

I clapped my hands together. 'Oh, she would love that. Just let us know when.'

Gawen was away again when, a few weeks later, I took Lisbeth to the parsonage to choose her puppy. She squealed with delight to see the wriggling mass of furry bodies squirming in the basket. One adventurous little fellow, white with a rakish black patch over one eye, struggled free of the others. With his stumpy little tail waggling and his head on one side he wobbled towards Lisbeth. One look into those molten brown eyes, one touch of that silky fur, and my daughter was smitten with the adorable little scrap.

'He shall be yours,' I smiled, and my eyes misted over as I remembered my own Fifi. From that day Lisbeth and her puppy were inseparable.

That wet springtime of 1576 brought an explosion of new life to my physick garden. On a rare sunny morning I was enjoying a mug of ale on the garden bench, listening to Lisbeth's happy prattle as she helped Agnes Searle pick some early gillyflowers. I raised my head to see Gawen marching along the path as though on a mission. I set down my cup and, as I stood to greet him, I put a hand to my back and eased the laces of my gown as the baby growing within me gave a healthy kick. This one was certainly a lively child. Gawen was certain this time it would be a boy.

'There's a new Edict in France,' he announced with a broad grin. 'Signed at a place called Beaulieu-lès-Loches. Things may be a little quieter over there now.'

'Does that mean you'll be home more often?' I asked, not at all sure how I felt about that prospect.

'Perhaps. There's still a need to gather intelligence and pass it back to England. But others can fulfil that role now. My father has need of me in Devon.'

'I am sorry your father has not been in the best of health of late,' I replied. 'I will ask Agnes to recommend a draught to ease his pain.'

'He's made of stern stuff,' Gawen bristled. 'No need to make a fuss, woman.' His face darkened and he ground the next words out between his teeth. 'Peace in France means your mother and that stupid brother of yours should be able to get their lands back. Then they'll have no more excuse. I expect them to pay what's owed.' I said nothing. That unpaid dowry always hung between us, stifling any chance we would ever be happy together.

His face cleared when he looked up to see Lisbeth running towards him, Patch the puppy hard on her heels. Gawen took us all by surprise when he grabbed the giggling girl and threw her high towards the blue sky above. Delighted by the unusual attention from her father, Lisbeth gazed adoringly at him.

'Have a care,' I muttered under my breath, 'don't drop her!' I shivered as his shadow fell over me.

Only a week later I held another daughter in my arms. She had come a little before her time, but though small, was healthy. We named her Mary for Gawen's mother.

'I've engaged a wet nurse,' Gawen informed me as he stood over my bed.

'No! It's best that I, her mother, should feed her...' I started to say, but my voice trailed away and my head dropped. In Gawen's eyes, people like us did not feed our own babies at the breast. That was for those less fortunate. I simply did not have the energy to argue. My eyelids felt as though they were weighted down with lead. I rested my head on the fine pillow and snatched what rest I could.

Some weeks later Bess bounded into my chamber before it was fully light.

'Wake up! Wake up!' she shouted. 'There's news. I'm to be wed at last!'

'Have the queen and Lord Burghley finally written in your favour?' I muttered, rubbing my eyes. 'Has Edward's father agreed?'

'I don't know how it's come about,' she shrieked, 'but what does it matter! I'm to be wed on the thirtieth of September!' Bess picked up Diane the doll, threw her high in the air, caught her and danced round and round my bed.

It was one of those days when autumn has yet to get into her stride and the air holds more than a memory of summer's warmth. July and August had been disappointingly cold and wet and the harvest had been poor. But a fortnight of fine weather in September had come as a welcome treat. We were all relieved to feel the sun on our backs as we stood by the door of St Mary's. I have never seen so happy a bride as Bess as she stood next to her young husband. Sir Arthur was cock-a-hoop.

'There now,' he chuckled, enfolding Bess in a bear hug. 'I told you all would be well. Now off you go. I'll look for Seymour grandchildren soon!'

Bess blushed and took her young bridegroom's arm.

'I know my duty well, Father,' she giggled. 'With Edward at my side I will be sure to make you proud.'

How I missed her bright face when she left for her new home at Berry Pomeroy. Life was dull indeed after the excitement of the wedding. The arrival of a letter was always a pleasant distraction. I clasped my hands together to stop them trembling as Rist brought in a sealed package on a pewter tray. Clearly some weeks old, the letter from France was addressed to me. But with a smug, triumphant look on his face, Rist offered it to my husband. As had become his habit Gawen opened my letter and I cringed to see his vindictive grin as he read the closely written lines.

'I don't know how she's done it,' he said. 'Your mother has got the Montgomery titles and most of the lands restored. Now they must pay up!' He threw the letter towards me and I snatched it and started to read.

'Charlotte says Jacques will return to what little is left of Ducey with Pérronelle and the children. My mother has signed all her wealth over to him. She's gone to live at Pontorson, where we used to visit when I was little.' I paused, thinking of Maman on the polished staircase Elisabeth and I used to play on. 'But how will she manage to pay her servants?' Gawen's brows beetled together and he threw me a furious look as I read on. For once I took the risk of speaking up.

'It looks as though the latest edict hasn't brought peace to France at all! Jacques will soon be fighting alongside the Huguenot forces once again.'

'Pah! Your brother with all his fine stories,' he exploded. 'That nonsense about his escape after your father went to the scaffold! I can tell you he merely bribed his captors; nothing more exciting than that. No barrels involved. Though where he got the coin I can't imagine. Now he's off to find glory, is he? Well, he'd better be sure to pay the money he owes first!'

'You are insufferable. Jacques takes up the cause my father died for; the cause of the true religion your father supports. But all you care about is money!' I yelled. With an angry swish of my skirts I whirled round and stalked away.

I missed Bess's merry face that Christmastide. I'd hoped we might visit her and Edward Seymour for the season, but Sir Arthur was loath to make the short journey through the Devon lanes. Lisbeth was old enough to enjoy all the sweetmeats, the players and singers who came to our door. But my heart was not in it.

Chapter Twenty

Sorrow and Resentment

1578

I paused to listen at the firmly closed door where Gawen and his father were closeted in heated discussion. Even through the heavy oak planks Gawen's petulant words carried to my ear.

'Drake will be gone again soon and he'll get the queen's backing,' he ranted. 'Men like him can make their fortune claiming new lands for the queen, and bringing back gold and silver. Cousin Humphrey Gilbert only waits on her command. They'll get all the glory and riches.' A low murmur from Sir Arthur was all the answer I could hear. 'Well, what about me? Eh?' Gawen demanded. 'All I do is kick my heels here hoping by some miracle our ambassador to France will succeed in pursuing our claim to Montgomery's money through the courts.' Another unintelligible reply from Sir Arthur, then Gawen's voice loud and shrill. 'It'll come to nothing! What will we do then? We've little enough left in our coffers.'

More muttering and then what sounded like a chair clattering to the floor.

'Well, you're Vice Admiral of the Fleet of the West. You're the one with oversight of all shipping around the coast,' Gawen shouted. 'Foreign vessels are fair game.' Again Sir Arthur's reply was muffled. All I could make out was something about a Dutchman. I had to scurry away quickly to avoid being discovered as my husband exploded from the room, slamming the door behind him and stalking across the empty hall. The staccato rhythm of his boot heels on the stone flagged floor echoed long after he had disappeared from view.

That spring another girl – we named her Katherine for Gawen's aunt – joined Mary in the nursery.

'Another girl,' I murmured wearily to the midwife. 'Can your daughter Agnes not give me a potion to make sure the next is a boy?' Her eyebrows shot up to where her crisp white cap covered her hair.

'Madam, I will pretend I did not hear that,' she cried. 'For such talk sounds much like witchcraft to me.'

I was relieved we could still afford to have the wet nurse live in, so I saw something of my daughters. I don't know how I could have borne it if I'd had to send my babies out to board with some strange family, as happened in some households. But, though they were bonny girls, I left much of the care of my younger daughters to their nurses, while I kept Lisbeth at my side through a hot and sultry summer.

A storm was raging when, a few days past Michaelmas, Sir Arthur staggered in, returned from Plymouth. Though soaked to the skin he was beaming like a full moon.

'Ah, my dear,' he purred, then clutched his chest as a sudden wave of pain contorted his face. He struggled to get his breath back and gasped between the words. 'Good news! As Vice Admiral of the Fleet of the West I've stayed fifteen sail of French shipping in Plymouth. Sold off the cargo. That should please Gawen! Help with some of our debts.'

'I know nothing about these matters,' I replied, scanning his flushed face anxiously. 'But, Sir Arthur, please do take your ease. Take off your wet cloak and rest a while.' His face clouded as he peeped into the cradle where Katherine slept soundly, oblivious to the wind that was howling so fiercely the nurse had brought the children down from the nursery.

'A bonny child,' he sighed. He didn't need to say the words to tell me how much he hoped for a grandson. He sank onto the settle, wheezing a little.

'Where is he? Where's Gawen?'

'Gone to Exeter, sir. He'll be back tomorrow.' The sigh he heaved made the settle shake beneath him. I felt an unexpected urge to pour some balm on the troubled relationship between father and son, to put in a good word for Gawen.

'I am sorry to see you at odds with my husband, sir,' I offered. 'He is like most young men, he looks for the chance to shine; to make you proud.'

'He's been doing vital work in France. Walsingham and Burghley value his efforts.'

'But, sir, acting as spy and message-carrier cannot compare with clearing the way for the Huguenot armies at Montcontour, as his cousin Henry did. It cannot compare with sailing off to unknown lands to bring back cargoes of gold like his idol, Francis Drake.'

'Hmph! Perhaps. Harrumph!' he muttered and his shoulders began to shake. The fit of coughing that followed was most alarming.

'Let me call Agnes to see if she may prescribe a draught,' I offered. But Agnes's potions and poultices had little effect. Worn down with all his money worries, Sir Arthur was fading away before our eyes.

I greeted Bess fondly when she arrived, large and beaming from ear to ear, later that month. She had begged to come home to Dartington for the birth of her first child.

'You didn't warn me how tired I'd feel,' she laughed after we'd exchanged the latest news. 'I'm off to my chamber to rest after the journey.'

So she left me snug by the fire in the parlour where I sat with Lisbeth who held a horn book on her lap as she traced the letters through the cow horn covering with her finger. She was a quick learner and needed little prompting. Suddenly Lisbeth jerked her head up at a crash beyond the door. She squirmed on her cushion and raised fearful eyes to my face as Gawen stormed in wearing a scowl as black as a lawyer's robe: a bad omen. Determined to shield my daughter from whatever had sparked her father's temper I stretched out an arm and cuddled her.

'*Bon travail, ma petite*,' I cooed. Without thinking I spoke in French. 'Well done! Now go to Clotilde and see if she can find you a sweetmeat.' The little girl peeked anxiously at Gawen but trotted off dutifully with Clotilde.

'Gawen, whatever has brought you to such a fury?' I asked. 'You look so fierce poor Lisbeth was quite frightened.'

'I've told you before to speak only English to my daughter,' he said as he crossed the room and perched in the window seat. 'She speaks French like a common servant. Does she learn it from them?' He waved vaguely in Clotilde's direction.

'You know very well I've instructed Clotilde to speak only in English. But if I do choose to teach my daughter languages, that is my affair. There's no one but Christopher can hold a proper conversation in my native tongue,' I muttered, filling a mug from the jug and handing it to him.

Gawen gulped down the ale, slammed down the mug, wiped his mouth on his sleeve and sat in silence as I busied myself tidying Lisbeth's lesson books. I had rearranged her belongings several times before he spoke again.

'I'm come from Plymouth,' he said, his tone suddenly matter of fact. 'My good friend Francis Drake sailed today in the *Pelican* with four other vessels. He's off to follow the call of adventure and opportunity!' His lip curled, revealing even white teeth.

'Well, you've made plenty of trips to France,' I answered without thinking.

'Foolish woman!' he said with a dismissive wave of his arm. 'Do you think being on the sidelines over there, skulking in corners and listening in on conversations so that I can send word home, compares in any way with sailing for the Americas to plunder Spanish gold? The most action I've seen was on the edge of a few skirmishes. That and the failed attempt on La Rochelle with your father. That hangs round my neck even now. Without the money your family owes I'll never have a chance to sail the high seas!' He stood up abruptly and huffed out of the room without waiting for me to give him an answer.

I sighed. Despite his bad temper I felt a pang of sympathy. It wasn't really Gawen's fault that he'd found so few chances to be hailed a hero. The secret role he'd played in service of Walsingham had been important – at times probably vital – but it had none of the glamour and glitter of discovery and plunder that seemed to fall so easily about Drake's shoulders. Now his father was ill and the weight of coming responsibilities must be heavy on his shoulders. I heaved another weary sigh, fearing the distance between us had grown too great for me to reach him.

Gawen's mood improved slightly when, a few days later, just before Bess's daughter was born with very little fuss, we heard that Drake's flotilla had been forced back to Plymouth by heavy seas. My husband managed a smile when Bridget Seymour was baptised in St Mary's Church behind the hall on the first day of December. Rist grumbled as I chivvied him to roust the servants to provide a splendid feast for all the godparents and well-wishers.

Sir Arthur looked much brighter as he stood by the fire with Sir John Gilbert and Sir Edward Seymour. His face was all smiles as he threw back a glass or two of good Gascon wine to wet the baby's head. But I noticed he was breathing heavily when he left the hall later that day.

A few days later Gawen stomped in, back from Plymouth with the news that he'd waved Drake off once again.

'The weather's set fair, so he'll make it this time!' he said, taking the mug of spiced ale I offered with no thanks. When Lisbeth danced in, a French song on her lips and Patch a pace behind her as usual, Gawen's face grew even darker.

'I've told you,' he shouted. 'She must speak in English.' He spat a mouthful of ale into the fire. 'This ale's past its best. Can you not make a better job of overseeing the servants?'

As that winter ground on, more dull and wet than icy cold, it was clear to everyone that Sir Arthur was ill. But he would not admit it. He insisted on riding out to visit his nephew Philip Cole on a blustery day as March slipped into April. The sad news came from Cornwood. Sir Arthur had been taken from us.

I felt as though all the energy had drained out of me as I waited for them to bring him home. Although we could all have seen it coming, Sir Arthur's death was a blow that sent us all reeling, struggling to grasp the sudden finality of it. Rist went about blank-faced, as though he wore a mask. Even Gatchell lost his swagger. The whole household was unnaturally quiet. Pierre's face was as long as the fiddle he'd learned to play so well. Food was prepared for the mourners by snivelling kitchen maids. Even the cook wiped a tear from his eye. Sir Arthur had been well loved by his people, and a good friend to me. My own grief came in waves, sometimes little, sometimes so strong I felt I must be swept away.

My husband was called back from the Lent Assizes to see his father laid to rest in the little church behind the hall he'd loved so much. To my disappointment Katherine Raleigh remained in Exeter where her husband was ailing, but Sir John Gilbert came as did Richard Champernowne of Modbury. It was the first time I'd met Henry's eldest boy who would soon come into his majority and take charge of the old family home beside St George's Church. Fair-haired and slender as a gossamer thread, the boy did not resemble his illustrious father at all.

The day before the funeral, Gawen and his brothers spent hours discussing the will Sir Arthur had signed in his final hours at Cornwood. Gawen emerged looking rattled.

'God's wounds! My hands are tied!' he cursed that night as he untied his hose. I hoped it was more than habit that brought him to my bed. I yearned to comfort him, but I could see I was going to get the rough edge of his anxiety. 'I am the heir, but he's left everything entailed for whoever is next in line. Doesn't look as if that's likely to be a son of mine, does it? Parcel of girls! That's all you've given me. I'll have to provide marriage portions for them all!'

'It is not for want of trying,' I observed bleakly. 'Since you've been back from France there's been few days when I haven't been carrying a child of yours in my belly.' He went on as if I hadn't spoken.

'There are annuities to find for my brothers. I'm left with the estate, but with that come all of the debts my fool of a father has racked up.'

'Please don't speak ill of the dead, Gawen. Sir Arthur was a fine man and I'm sure he did what he thought was best.' I echoed Sir Arthur's own words in that strange conversation we'd had.

'He was so hot to support your people in France! Not just for religion, though he was always staunch in that. But he also had some foolish dream of taking our family back to our roots in Normandy. Wanted to be a mighty landowner over there. Why couldn't Dartington be enough?' He sat down on the bed and his shoulders slumped.

'This is not the time to think on these things,' I said wearily as I slipped between the sheets. 'It has been a long day. Tomorrow will be another. Rest now.' My eyes felt dry from the tears I had shed for Sir Arthur and I ached to curl up and sleep.

'I always said it was a mistake to trust your family!' Gawen muttered. Understanding fell on me like a stone dropped from a high place. His father was hardly cold and he was already going on about my dowry.

'My father tried to strike a deal with the King of France before yours went to the scaffold, you know,' he sneered. 'He hesitated for a long time, but I persuaded him.' My mouth dropped open then snapped shut again. 'Well, it was clear that the French Crown was going to have all your father's lands, so why shouldn't they pay his debts?' he went on as he pulled a clean nightshirt over his head.

'Are you saying your father would have betrayed mine for money?' By now I was bolt upright and feeling a bit light-headed.

'You could put it that way, I suppose,' he drawled.

'So you would have betrayed my father? Denied my brother his inheritance?' I said in an icy voice, leaning across the bed to jab my finger in the direction of his face.

'You'll never know! But it's all water under the bridge now, my dear,' he scoffed. 'The Queen Dowager denied all knowledge and however many letters Walsingham or Dale wrote on his behalf, my father got no satisfaction. Now he's gone and here I am with a wife who hasn't yet managed to produce a son, still no dowry paid and all I've inherited is a pile of debts.'

'Money!' I shouted. 'It's all you care about! What about your daughters? What about me?' I buried my face in the pillow, sobbing my heart out. Gawen clambered into the bed beside me and turned his back.

As I lay there in the darkness, turning it over in my mind, it all started to make sense. No wonder Sir Arthur had been in such a frenzy to go to France as soon as he heard Papa was captured. He didn't go; someone must have persuaded him it would do no good. But it must have lain heavily on his conscience, that he had wanted to get his hands on the money. Now I could understand why he'd avoided my company all that time, why he'd spoken as he had.

I couldn't find it in my heart to blame my father-in-law, now gone to his grave. He had been kind to me and I knew he was a good man at heart. But my husband was another matter entirely.

I did not go to the church. That was customary. But I did hear the music Pierre had composed especially for the occasion as it drifted in through the windows. When they gathered in the hall I flitted round, checking that all the mourners had sufficient food and drink and chivvying the servants to bring more. To my surprise I came upon young Richard Champernowne in deep discussion with Pierre. I hung back, making a show of collecting empty mugs, and listened.

'I mean to have a troop of musicians and singers at Modbury. It will be the best in all the land,' the young man boasted. 'My great-grandfather loved music and his singers even entertained King Henry. Now, is it true you composed that melody yourself?' Pierre gave a shy little nod. 'You have an unusual talent, boy. Don't waste it here,' Richard Champernowne went on. 'There will be opportunities at Modbury for your talent to shine. Think on it!' Pierre shuffled from foot to foot as Richard hailed a neighbour and moved on. I stepped forward and Pierre shot me a look as sharp as a needle piercing linen stretched tight on a frame.

'I'll not leave you, Mistress Roberda,' he whispered. 'My place is here, helping Christopher with your women from France. There is still much to do.' I shook my head and my voice broke as I answered him.

'I fear he is right. My husband cannot offer you much. You'd do well to think on what Master Champernowne said.'

Chapter Twenty-one

Wings Clipped, But Still I Will Fly

Summer 1578–1579

After the funeral, and to my relief, Gawen left for Exeter with his brothers and everything settled back into a more usual pattern. I often looked in at the classroom where Pierre was helping Christopher with the latest group of women from France. On my way across the courtyard one morning in June I nearly fell over Alice Blackaller, hovering behind the door.

'Alice? What are you doing there?' I cried. It was not the first time I'd stumbled over her in unexpected places.

'Nothing, mistress,' she mumbled and ran off before I could say anything more.

'What was that woman doing?' Christopher asked.

'I have no idea,' I shrugged. 'Lately she seems to make a habit of being in my way.'

A week later the latest group of French women and children piled into an oxcart with their few belongings ready for the journey to East Devon. Christopher was about to signal to the driver to move off when a horse galloped into the courtyard. Sparks flew as hooves skittered on the cobbles and flecks of foam from the poor beast's mouth came to rest on Christopher's doublet. Gawen threw himself from the saddle and stormed up to the cart until he loomed over

Christopher in his seat up front. Gawen was raging like a bull escaped from the pound on market day.

The startled driver called out, 'Have a care, sir, you'll have us over!' But my husband paid no heed.

'That's the last, Melhuishe,' he shouted as he jabbed a finger towards Christopher's chest. 'Your services are no longer required. My coffers will not stand the cost of these women. There will be no more. Now be gone.' Christopher raised a hand in protest, but Gawen motioned impatiently to the driver who flicked his whip and the cart jolted forward. I called out and ran from the steps where I'd been waiting to wave them off. But Gawen grabbed me roughly by the arm and marched me back to the hall as the cart rumbled through the archway.

'A woman has no business in this sort of charity. Certainly not any wife of mine!' he blazed. 'We can't afford it. It must stop now! Besides which, it's come to my notice you've been spending far too much time with Melhuishe. It is not seemly. I won't have it. It must stop.'

I lifted my head and looked him in the eye.

'Are you suggesting there is something improper between me and Master Melhuishe?' I hissed with hands gesticulating wildly. 'How could you think such a thing of me? Christopher Melhuishe is a good man. He has been a good friend to me and my family. God knows I am in sore need of friends in this dreary place!' I paused for breath and licked the spittle from my lips and drew myself up in a manner Maman would have been proud of. 'Let me remind you I am a Huguenot lady of noble birth. I am your true wife and mother of your daughters. How dare you insult me so in front of the servants! Now, allow me to pass!' With a withering glare I swished past him, leaving Rist, Alice Blackaller and a gaggle of other servants gawping after me.

For three days I sulked; I stamped my feet; I barked orders at the servants. I challenged Gawen as he wolfed down a hasty meal before setting off again for Exeter.

'Will you not reconsider?' I asked, trying to keep my voice calm. 'There are many more women displaced by the war in France and in need of help. Your father was happy to receive them.'

'My father is no longer here and I can't afford it,' he answered gruffly and started for the door.

'But the cost is small,' I shouted after his retreating back. I thumped my fist down on the table, and bowls scattered as my anger boiled over. 'You have no right to curtail me so! My work must continue,' I yelled as a round-eyed servant scrambled to pile up the dishes I'd knocked askew. But Gawen had already stormed out.

I could not even offer an apology to Christopher. I heard from Clotilde that he and his father had gone to visit relatives in North Devon. When my husband next came home we tiptoed around each other, icily polite in front of the servants, hardly exchanging a word in private. It was quite a relief when we rode over to Berry Pomeroy for a visit.

Devon looks its best in high summer and I was looking forward to seeing Bess. It was a wrench to leave Lisbeth on the steps in Jeanne's care, even for a day or two, but I was determined to enjoy the rare excursion. Gawen, however, maintained a brooding silence for the entire journey. He barely doffed his cap when we met neighbours as we passed though Totnes. He took no notice of the men, women and children stooking wheat in the fields we passed. He hardly glanced at Thomas Wright, the vicar, who hailed us by the lychgate of the Church of St Mary in the little hamlet of Berry Pomeroy. Gawen's face remained set and stern. Only when the Seymours' great castle came into view did my husband speak.

'Impressive, isn't it?' he remarked as we emerged from the piney shade of the trees and trotted up to the formidable gatehouse. 'Built for defence, I suppose, though they could have chosen a spot on even higher ground over there.' He waved an arm. 'Look at that portcullis!' I looked up dutifully at the iron gate that could be slammed down to keep intruders out. 'Seymour kept the walls of the Pomeroys' old fortress, but he's made a new palace within. 'Tis all for show!'

As we emerged from the shadow cast by the gatehouse, I caught my breath. I dismounted, handed the reins to a waiting man, and stood stock-still.

'It would rival many houses I saw in London,' I exclaimed, raising my eyes to the top of the magnificent facade of Seymour's new house. Gawen let out an oath then sucked in his bottom lip as he squinted up at the dressed stone walls studded with tiers of elegant glazed windows; windows that reflected white clouds scudding across a clear blue sky.

'Hmph! Fine indeed. It's all right for some!' he grumbled, as his envious eyes roamed over the grand building. 'You might think Bess has come off well in this, but old Seymour's brother, the Earl of Hertford, has kept the plum properties. If it weren't for John Thynne of Longleat aiding him, he'd never have got his hands on this place at all. Thynne was once old Seymour's steward. Look how he's risen!' I made a business of smoothing my skirts and didn't answer.

Bess came hurtling out of the door and embraced me before leading us to a splendid hall where long tables were set for a feast. The Seymours, father and son, greeted us courteously and we were served a lavish meal, with meats of every sort imaginable. Gawen kept throwing black looks around and demanding his mug be filled rather more often than was good for him. Bess raised an eyebrow enquiringly but I merely shook my head.

After we had eaten, she drew me up the stairs to a room lit by a large window that gave wonderful views over the Gatcombe Valley. A meandering brook shone like a thin sliver of silver at the bottom of the steep slopes.

'My, you have quite a viewing point here, Mistress Bess,' I laughed. 'Are you happy?' She dimpled, took my hand and drew me towards an ornately carved cradle.

'How could I be anything but happy with this dear little girl,' she grinned, pulling the coverlet up over the sleeping child. 'Edward is a good husband. I have no complaints. But what of you?'

'Least said the better on that score,' I muttered.

'Gawen? Oh dear! I noticed how he was at dinner – he used to get like that when we were children if he didn't get his own way. Things build up until he's like a great cauldron of pottage set too long on the fire; he'll boil over, spluttering and spitting at the slightest provocation.'

'He's become quite insufferable!' I exclaimed. 'Since your father died he thinks of nothing but money. He lashes out at those who are nearest.'

'Edward says he's being pursued about some ship business. Something about my father and a cargo of salt.'

'He does have money worries, I suppose,' I sighed. 'Oh, Bess, let us hope your husband and father-in-law take Gawen out hunting, for he surely needs to relax.'

While the menfolk were so occupied, we spent a pleasant time catching up with all the news and walking along the steep paths beyond the old walls where Sir Edward was making a garden. As we passed a tower that remained from the Pomeroy's old defences, Bess chuckled.

'Look! Down there! That's where the White Lady walks!' Bess pointed to the steps leading down into the darker recesses below the tower. 'It's called St. Margaret's Tower. People say they see her there. They say she was starved to death; shut up by a jealous sister. A fight about a man! Oh it's scandalous indeed.'

I laughed rather nervously and a chill ran down my spine.

'Oh, Bess, to think of being locked away like that. Poor woman!'

'It's only a tale, Roberda. Don't worry, I've never seen or heard her!' We went on to talk of other things but I couldn't shake off the anxious feeling the ghost story set running through my mind. My sleep was disturbed by dreams, not this time of Rouen, but of being shut into a small space, confined within stone walls behind a locked door.

Our remaining time at Berry Pomeroy passed pleasantly enough. Gawen brought down a fine stag and was a little less prickly. Soon Bess and her Edward stood framed in the doorway to wave us away.

'We're off to Longleat for a visit and then on to Maiden Bradley, Edward's father's place in Wiltshire. I'm not sure when we'll be back,' Bess beamed, laying her hand on Edward's arm. I gave a half-hearted little shrug and felt my ribs squeezing. I would have given a lot to have Gawen look at me the way young Edward Seymour looked at Bess.

'Lucky you!' I called as we set off for home.

We had only been home a few weeks when I cornered Gawen as he was preparing to leave for Exeter where he was often called to serve as Justice of the Peace. I asked to accompany him.

'Why would you need to go to Exeter?' he asked. 'I will be there but a few days and then you'll have to make the journey back again.'

'Gawen, I must visit the tailor,' I insisted. 'Lisbeth grows so fast she's in sore need of new gowns. Would you have her look like a pauper child with skirts so short you can see her knees? And it's high time I visited your Aunt Raleigh.' I did not add that I wanted to talk to Katherine about the refugees. Gawen huffed and puffed a bit but eventually agreed, I sent word to Katherine and we set off in fine style, Lisbeth and I in the carriage, as she was too young to ride so far in the rain. At the last minute Patch the dog leaped up after Lisbeth as she climbed the steps. Remembering Fifi, I didn't have the heart to evict him, so we had an extra passenger on our journey.

While Gawen did business with the aldermen of the city, Katherine welcomed us at her town house by the Palace Gate. She made a fuss of Lisbeth and led us to the kitchen to find a bowl of water for Patch. The door creaked open and we found a woman seated on the settle. When she raised her head from her needlework I threw up my hands.

'Madeleine? Is it you? I hardly know you for you look so well,' I exclaimed in shaky voice. She dimpled prettily, stood up and drew Marguerite from behind her skirts. Lisbeth and the little girl eyed each other until Katherine distracted them with a litter of kittens in a basket under the table. They got on famously after that. Madeleine told me in much improved English that she was working as a needlewoman for a tailor in the town of Honiton, a place Katherine had found for her.

'Madeleine is too skilled with her needle to toil in the flax fields on my lands near Axminster,' Katherine commented. 'Many of the merchants' wives are keen to have her needle-lace to trim their collars and cuffs.'

'I'm learning the new way of bone lace too,' Madeleine added. 'Without your aid, mistress, I would not be in such case. Please, take this for the little one,' and she pressed a bundle of fine lace edging into my hand. I felt my chest swell with satisfaction.

Later that day I settled in for a cosy chat with Gawen's aunt. Never one to mince matters, she came straight to the point.

'How do you get on with your husband now? Have you forgiven him for curtailing our efforts to aid those poor women?' There was no avoiding her piercing blue eyes. I ground my teeth and I felt my muscles tense. I had no need to speak; my face told its own story.

'My advice is to be happy in what you have achieved, rejoice in all the women like Madeleine you have helped. I would wait a while before you tackle him,' she advised with a conspiratorial grin. 'Let him simmer; he may run out of steam and then we can continue. But in the meantime there are others to whom you might bring comfort. I think of one your husband could have no objection to your befriending. Why, I believe you and poor Anne Cecil are already acquainted.'

'Anne? I haven't heard from her for some time. Is all not well with her?' I asked.

'I only have the reports my boys bring me, but it seems her husband treats her most cruelly and makes vile accusations against her. She might appreciate your friendship at this time.'

'I never did like that man she married, though she doted on him,' I said with frown. 'He made my skin crawl.'

'If the reports my sons bring me be anywhere near true, then your distaste for him was well-founded. A friendly face would no doubt cheer Anne through a difficult time. We women must support each other in this world men construct around us. See if you can find excuse to visit her.'

'Thank you,' I mused. 'I will think on it.'

Next morning I stepped with purposeful stride to the tailors and ordered Lisbeth's new gowns, which would be trimmed with the finest needle-lace. On a whim I also ordered one for myself, thinking I might have need of it should I visit Anne.

Even Gawen's complaints on our journey home about the money I'd spent could not dampen my joy in seeing Madeleine. On top of that the germ of an idea was forming in my mind. I was determined to find a way to persuade Gawen to let me visit my friend Anne.

As it happened, Gawen gave me the perfect opportunity. We had retired for the night but he could not settle.

'Whatever ails you?' I cried peevishly. 'You fidget like a cat that's burned its paws on a bakestone.'

He sat up and pushed his nightcap back from his brow.

'There's been a lot of fuss and bother about a cargo my father seized. He disposed of it but now I'm being chased for recompense by some merchants of Dieppe. I might have sought advice and help from Lord Burghley or Walsingham, but I have little contact with them these days.' He swung his legs from the bed and started to pace the floor in his nightshirt. I sat up and rubbed the sleep from my eyes.

'What do you mean?' I murmured.

'Others have stepped in to spy for them. Another Champernowne – Henry's second boy, the valiant Arthur of Modbury – he is one of them. As a second son he's not tied to an estate and an inheritance like me.' I bit my tongue. He had complained often enough of being used as a messenger and spy. Now he was jealous that others had taken that role! To be replaced by the son of the illustrious Henry was sure to stoke up his bitterness.

'I'd go to court, but as you know I'm short of money.' An edge in his voice reminded me of the missing dowry. 'And I have no real excuse to go.' By now I was wide awake.

'You could take me to visit Anne Cecil,' I said softly. 'She might be persuaded to invite me to stay. I could listen and bring back the latest news for you. Or you could use the excuse to make your own approaches. The girls, even Lisbeth, can remain here in Jeanne's care.' His silence told me he hadn't thrown my suggestion overboard.

Next morning he had me write to Anne and within the month we were on our way to London, with Gawen to visit Walsingham after he'd left me at Burghley House. Anne's father was otherwise engaged so we soon settled down to talk. I was shocked to find my friend in sad case.

'He has left me,' she wailed, clinging to me. 'He says vile things about me, but he's the one who leads a dissolute life.'

'Oh, Anne,' I cried. The tears welled up in my eyes to see her so. 'Men will always try to put the blame on we poor women when they are the ones at fault. Worse still, oftentimes other men choose to believe them. But I thought Edward had returned from his travels? Can he not be persuaded to be reasonable?'

'Now he's back I really wish he'd stayed away. Scandal follows him wherever he goes. My father is beside himself!'

'Tell me more,' I whispered, patiently patting her hand.

'I don't know where to begin,' she sighed. 'He's back in London and he's accused of just about every crime you could think of. Even murder, though Father managed to get him off by putting the blame on a servant. But, Roberda, he claims that I'm the one who's been unfaithful – and then he sets up house with a Venetian boy. A boy! Why, the lad must only be fifteen, if that. A chorister with a wonderful voice, apparently!'

'You don't mean…?' I asked, cocking my head to one side.

'I do! I Most certainly I do! Father's incensed and the boy's a Catholic besides.'

I sat back in my seat and my mouth opened and closed several times with no sound coming out. Suddenly my own marriage difficulties and my unfeeling, controlling, bad-tempered husband seemed of much less moment.

'But it seems there are girls too!' Anne's lip curled. 'And debts and charges against him from half of London.'

'Oh, Anne,' I murmured, taking her hand and holding it tight to stop her picking at the tapestry cover on the chair cushion.

'It is such a relief to have someone I can talk to,' she whimpered. 'I don't think he ever cared for me a bit. I think he only married me so Father would pay his debts and get his uncle Norfolk off. Well, despite Edward's pleadings that old fool went to the block for plotting to marry the Scots queen. Edward's never forgiven my father for that and he's using me to get at him.'

'Men!' I exploded. 'Why does God send such fools of men for us women to deal with!'

'I write to him constantly … for the sake of our daughter; my little Elizabeth. Even now I would take him back for her sake. And for the sake of my good name, if anything is left of it!'

'No one believes for a moment that you are the guilty party, dearest Anne,' I soothed. Then, thinking to distract her from her worries, 'Oh you are brave to say you'd take him back. Perhaps I can distract you from your troubles and share some of mine? Let me tell you about my scheme to help poor women from France. My lovely scheme that my fool of a husband has just put a stop to.'

I spent a week with Anne giving what comfort I could.

'Your friendship has come as balm upon my woes,' she smiled

shyly as I waited for Gawen to collect me. 'You'll think me foolish, but sometimes I find solace in writing. Poems! Oh they are probably poor efforts, but I can pour my feelings into the words.'

'I most certainly do not think you foolish,' I exclaimed. 'Why should a woman not write poems as well as a man? I hear it's quite the thing for men like Gawen's cousin Walter Raleigh to write. And your old suitor Philip Sidney, does he not wield the pen? Why not you, Anne?'

'Your confidence in me encourages me to try,' she laughed. 'I will start with keeping up my correspondence with you, for it seems you'd welcome that when back in deepest Devonshire.'

'Let's keep writing and support each other as we may, dear Anne,' I replied. As we travelled back to Devon I resolved to complain a little less of my own lot in life.

Chapter Twenty-two

A Son Is Not Enough

1580

Crouched on the floor, I clutched the bed post with all my might.

'Will there ever be a time when I am neither swelling like a fat cow nor pushing another child into the world?' I grunted through gritted teeth. The wave of pain passed. I straightened up and climbed unsteadily onto the bed, hoping to snatch a brief respite from the waves of agony that had been racking my body for so long. The room was stifling, the shutters closed to blot out bright May sunshine. Margery Searle put on a brave smile as she wiped the sweat from my brow, then busied herself mixing a cream infused with brandy and saffron.

''Twill help you bring forth this babe, mistress,' she crooned, as she rubbed the mixture into my belly. I'd had no need of such when my other children were born, nor the cordial of meadowsweet and almonds Margery's sister Agnes had sent to ease my pain.

'Take a breath, my lady. I'm sure it won't be long now. My mother always said you were one of the lucky ones.' Joan Searle had passed the mantle of midwife to her daughter and now spent her days knitting in her little cottage in Staverton. Margery chattered on about her mother, told me how Agnes enjoyed working in my physick garden and said how pretty and clever Lisbeth was. Anything to distract me.

The midwife's eyes darted this way and that, never still, all through those long hours. If she slept at all it must have been in snatches so short I didn't notice, for she was ever at my side, willing me to stay strong for the child.

'Oh! I wish my mother was here! Or my sister! Or Bess! Or Anne! Or any other gentlewoman! I'm all alone!' I screamed as yet another wave seared though me. At Berry Pomeroy Bess was as near her time as I; Katherine Raleigh was tending her ailing husband; Maman and Charlotte were far away in France; Anne was in London where her husband's behaviour had not improved. I had no gentlewomen to bear me company for the birth.

'I am here,' Margery soothed, but her soft calm voice barely registered.

The pain of my other labours had been intense but short-lived; not this time. My mind closed. The room around me faded. The midwife was little more than shadow; I barely registered the little gasp as she sucked in her breath, the rhythmic beats as she tapped her finger on the top of my bedside coffer. Soon there was no other world beyond the pain.

Margery Searle knew her business well, but despite all her efforts a day and a night passed before, as a shaft of early morning light crept between a gap in the shutters, a mewling cry told me the child was born.

'A boy,' I murmured, hardly able to believe it. 'Perhaps now he'll be happy.' Drained of all energy I could hardly raise my head enough to drink from the cup Margery offered before I sank into oblivion.

How long I slept I will never know, nor how faithfully Margery tended me and the babe. Days may have passed before I came to my senses and I stirred a little when a tap came at the chamber door. Bleary-eyed I watched the midwife open it a crack, peered past her shoulder and saw my Lisbeth, begging to come in.

'Let her come to me, Margery,' I croaked, my vocal cords strained by all the screams I'd let pass my lips. The midwife put a finger to her lips and in they trooped, Lisbeth followed by four-year-old Mary, round-eyed with wonder as she crept up to the cradle, holding her sister Katherine by the hand. With but a year between them those two girls were inseparable. The nurse puffed along behind them with little Ursula in her arms. I struggled to sit up and beckoned to Lisbeth. I opened my arms to her, but she was hanging over the crib. My eyes were heavy and Margery soon shooed them away to let me rest.

When I woke again, still feeling muzzy-headed, I called for Clotilde. But it was not Clotilde who came clattering into the room, rattling a tray of dishes. A sour-faced maid charged in, set the tray down and turned away without a word, leaving me again with Margery Searle who'd stayed to watch over me and the baby.

'Where is Clotilde?' I shrieked. 'Who is that miserable-looking woman?' Margery pressed her lips tight together and looked away.

'Now, don't distress yourself, mistress. Have you forgotten? She is the woman Master Gawen has engaged to be your maid.'

Then I remembered it all.

Three months had passed since my husband returned briefly from Ireland where he'd been sent on the queen's business. Gawen was in a foul temper and remained at Dartington for only a few days. Long enough to order that my Clotilde and Jeanne be put into a cart, carried to Plymouth and from there shipped to France. I pleaded with him to let them stay, seeing I was so near my time. But he would not listen, saying he could no longer afford to keep them. My last lifeline, my last link with home, had been severed when Clotilde's tear-stained face faded to a blur. Pierre was also gone. I'd known I must act when Gawen started muttering about the cost of keeping musicians and threatening to set Pierre to work in the kitchens. With a heavy heart I had secured a place for him with Richard Champernowne, who was now of age and in command of his own estate at Modbury and delighted to take my gifted protégé. Pierre had protested, but I insisted he go. The hall was deathly quiet without his music.

'Has any word come from Charlotte or Maman to say Clotilde arrived safely?' I whimpered as a tear squeezed its way from my eye and trickled onto the pillow. Margery Searle laid a cool cloth across my forehead.

'Shh! Rest now,' Margery soothed, as she shook her head.

I drifted in and out of sleep for several days, and managed a little of the broth the surly maid Marie Weare brought to me. As the days passed I began to feel a little stronger.

The wet nurse pulled up her apron and set the baby in the crib next to my bed.

'He's a well-contented babe,' I murmured, easing the binding on my own breasts which were aching painfully. I had not argued when Gawen engaged her before he left for Ireland. But with a son in the cradle, I wondered if he'd be in such a hurry to return to my bed.

'May I go to the kitchen for my dinner now?' she asked, and I waved her away. She had to veer round Gawen who loomed in the doorway. Without a glance in my direction he strode purposefully across the room and peered into the cradle. A rare smile briefly touched his lips.

'A boy!'

'And a healthy one too,' I ventured.

His brow furrowed. 'There's plague in Plymouth, so I hear. Who knows what fate lies in store for the boy, or for any of us.'

'Gawen. We have a son,' I soothed. 'Surely we may celebrate and be happy now.' The urge to comfort outweighed my exhaustion and any anger I harboured against him. I reached out.

'One son after all these years!' he grunted, and shook my hand away. 'Ireland's a hellhole! I'm merely a messenger boy again. I have to see Walsingham, then I'll be here for a while by the looks of it.' Any hopes I had cherished that he'd be better tempered now he had a son seemed likely to be dashed.

Not three months after Arthur was born, Gawen returned to my bed. By October he was back in Ireland with his cousin, Walter.

'I've seen no one apart from Lisbeth for months. No one visits us. Dartington might as well be an island in the middle of the ocean, cut off from the world. I don't even receive letters any more,' I complained as Christopher sat formal and correct in my parlour.

My isolation had been so complete I seized on Christopher when he and his father returned to the parsonage. He brought me up to date with happenings beyond my closed Devon world; how Queen Elizabeth still kept the Duke of Anjou dangling in hope of marriage; how the Earl of Leicester, Lord Robert Dudley, who had fallen out of favour when he married Maman's old friend Lettice, would never quite regain his place and his wife was still banished from the court; how my brother Jacques had been appointed Governor of Brouage and young Gabriel had left Cambridge, where he'd studied with the young Earl of Essex, and joined Jacques in France as his lieutenant. I'd wept to learn that poor Pérronelle had died of the plague and Jacques had already taken a new wife, and was shocked when Christopher told me that my sister Elisabeth's husband, Jehan de Refuge, had been murdered in the street in Paris. I gnashed my teeth and cursed Edward de Vere when Christopher told me that Anne Cecil's husband was the talk of the court because he'd fathered a child on one of Queen Elizabeth's ladies–in-waiting.

Sometimes Christopher helped the girls with their lessons. He was the only one who brought news of my family. He was the only one I could speak to in my native tongue. Gawen was away, perhaps in Ireland; I had no knowledge of his whereabouts. When he did appear for brief visits I found him engulfed in the blackest of moods .

Awakened by the March wind rattling the glass in the ill-fitting window, I hauled myself from the bed and called for the close stool. Marie Weare shuffled in to give grudging assistance. Too tired to reprimand her, I lay back on the pillows and laid a hand on my stomach, cursing Gawen for leaving me with yet another baby in my belly. Later I had Marie bring out my clothes and help me to dress.

'I will remain in my chamber,' I told her as, with a heavy sigh, I settled myself on the cushions beside the window. 'I'm too exhausted to bother to come down.' I picked up a book, but could not concentrate, and instead sat listlessly staring at the rain running down the panes. Marie reappeared some time later with a malicious grin on her face.

'That Master Melhuishe is below, mistress. He's wet to the skin but still he insists he must come in. I don't know what I should do, mistress; I fear he's followed me up the stairs.'

'I don't see why that's put you in such a pother,' I snapped. 'Master Melhuishe is always a welcome visitor here. No doubt he's on his way to the nursery to seek out Miss Lisbeth for her lesson. Tell him to look in on me, will you, for I'm too exhausted to stir.' Since his return Christopher had become a regular visitor. His visits were a treat.

'*Bien rencontré*,' I cried – we had quickly slipped back into our habit of conversing in French. 'You are well met, Christopher,' I repeated. 'I'm in sore need of someone to cheer me up. What a day! But Marie is right; you're soaked.' He had discarded his cloak and boots below and stood in his stocking feet, leaving wet marks on the floorboards.

'Marie, Marie! Find some dry stockings from the master's coffer that poor Master Melhuishe may change.' She bumbled off, and I heard her calling to someone on her way.

Christopher made to protest but I called out breezily, 'You can change your stockings out there in the antechamber. I shall close the door, have no fear. Knock when you are decently clad.'

The knock came and as I opened the door I saw that, beyond Christopher, Marie had one of the laundry maids at her elbow. She gave the girl a shove.

'M-m-mistress. Will you have me t-take your night stuff for washing,' the woman stammered as she gawped at Christopher.

'Why would you come at this time to take it?' I asked sharply. 'You know well enough 'twas already taken this morning.'

'Yes, mistress,' the girl muttered and bolted for the door. I raised an eyebrow and gave Marie Weare a stare, then shrugged and thought no more about it as I ushered Christopher to a seat by the window.

'Marie? Come and sit in the corner here,' I commanded and she took the seat I indicated and sat, eyes screwed up, mouth puckered as if she'd sucked on a lemon.

'When you have given me all the news I'll have Lisbeth brought down. She has made good progress with the book you left for her. But, oh, what a pleasure it is to speak with you in French!' I smiled my encouragement as he brought me the latest news of my refugee women. I felt a rare glow of satisfaction when he told me that two had found husbands and taken English names already. All were in work and the children were well fed. I clapped my hands when he told me that Madeleine was flourishing in the employ of the Honiton tailor who had a steady stream of customers for her fine stitch work. But for me she would still be in France struggling to feed her little girl.

June, and sweat trickled down my cheek as I lay in the stuffy room. My sixth child had come too soon, slipping into the world so fast Margery had only just arrived in time to cut the cord.

'Oooh! He's so tiny!' Lisbeth gasped. I managed a fragile smile and nodded.

'Hush! Quietly, children,' Margery Searle whispered as she ushered them in an echo of the scene barely a year earlier. 'Your mama and your new brother are tired and need their rest'.

'Baba! Baba!' Ursula shrieked, paying no attention to the midwife. Lisbeth lifted her youngest sister up so she could see into the crib and the little girl squealed with delight. Named for Walsingham's wife, Ursula had the healthiest pair of lungs of any of them. The midwife allowed them no more than a peep then chased them all out. Lisbeth threw an anxious look over her shoulder but was pushed aside by another plump young woman. I recognised her homely face, dark kirtle and freshly laundered apron. She looked as neat and efficient as I'd thought her when I interviewed her for the post of wet nurse barely two weeks earlier.

'Begging you pardon, mistress, with your permission I will take the baby now,' she announced. Margery bent forward over the cradle and gave a slight shake of her head.

'You may try, but he's fair worn out with his coming into the world,' she said. The midwife's brow was furrowed as lifted the child into the wet nurse's waiting arms.

'You must pray, my lady,' she murmured, her voice hardly more than a whisper. 'His grip on life does not seem strong, though he breathes. It is in God's hands.'

I nodded my agreement, sighed and lay back onto the soft down pillow. Margery had replaced the clammy sweat-soaked sheets with crisp clean ones that smelled of the outdoors and sunshine. I rubbed my eyes.

'That little scrap has cost me dear, Margery Searle,' I murmured. 'He slipped into the world fast enough, unlike his brother Arthur! But I was not ready to bear another so soon.' Margery put a hand to my brow then smoothed the sheets. I squeezed my eyelids together then forced them wide open in an effort to stay awake. It was no use. My eyes felt as though lead weights rested on them. My lids drooped again and I drifted away.

'Is my husband not come yet?' I demanded angrily when next I woke. 'To think he left me so. Surely Gawen will return to see he has another son. Perhaps he'll be satisfied now!'

'Be calm,' Margery soothed. 'I'm sure he'll come when he can.'

But I was fired up with resentment and she was the only one there to hear it.

'Is it my fault that he's so envious of men like his cousin Humphrey Gilbert?' Margery drew up a stool and took hold of my hand to stop it feverishly clutching at the sheet. 'Humphrey's first attempt might have failed but he's still got the queen's letters patent. No doubt he's itching to sail away again and establish a new colony across the sea. That's sure to add fuel to the flames of resentment in my husband's heart!'

Gawen's brother Charles had put money into Humphrey Gilbert's first abortive project; money that Gawen had had to find in accordance with his father's will. How Gawen had cursed that he could not go adventuring but must remain in Devon to 'see to his affairs' as he put it. Perhaps he'd got his chance in Ireland.

'And then there's that Francis Drake! Sir Francis Drake he is now! The great circumnavigator of the globe!' The midwife's eyebrows shot up.

'Now, mistress,' she coaxed. 'Be calm. Will you not drink this? 'Twill help you sleep.' But I pushed the draught away, my mind trapped in vivid memories of a September night a few months after Arthur was born. Just before Gawen returned to Ireland.

'He'd seen Drake's ship come into Plymouth with its cargo of riches.' I spoke softly. 'He looked so gaunt and haunted with that vein on his temple throbbing, ugly and purple.'

'Don't distress yourself so,' Margery murmured. 'You need to rest. There are some things best forgotten. Sometimes bleak thoughts do bother a new mother. It will pass. Now please, mistress, will you drink?' I sighed and raised my head a little to take a long draught from the mug she held to my lips.

'He couldn't get his boots off!' A hysterical little laugh rose in my throat. 'Rist sidled up and managed to pull them off, all caked in mud as they were. It was Drake's glorious return that upset my husband so.' Margery offered the mug again and I drank deep.

'It was envy that drove my husband into melancholy. Your sister has no cure for that, does she?' Margery patted my hand as I bit my lip and my shoulders trembled. I was growing drowsy again but memories continued to flash through my mind. Memories of the night he'd returned from Plymouth having seen Drake fêted and applauded on his triumphant return. I could almost feel the hard wooden surface beneath me as I remembered how I'd sat on the edge of my seat, waiting for an explosion of jealous ranting. But Gawen had not spoken. He'd slumped on the settle before the fire staring empty-eyed into the flames. When I'd reached a hand towards him he'd slapped it away. It was then that I'd realised my husband was truly lost to me. Worse still, it was then I realised that despite his prickly, proud, surly moods, despite his constant nagging that my family's failure to pay my dowry was the root of all his woes, I cared for him. Beyond my wifely duty, beyond the forced intimacy that had produced all those children, a tiny flame flickered in my heart. There in the birthing chamber with the midwife still holding my hand, I acknowledged it. But I feared Gawen would never allow that flame to grow into love.

My thoughts returned to the clammy room where I lay exhausted and bereft. Margery managed to raise my head, and again held the cup to my lips, and soon her soothing potion brought oblivion.

Gawen arrived next day. Somehow the news had reached him as he conveyed another message back from Ireland. He strutted about the hall, overjoyed to have a second boy to his name, for two sons equalled the achievement of his cousin Henry. How proudly he arranged the baptism; we called the boy Philip after his great-grandfather. A scant three weeks later my baby boy returned to the little Church of St Mary's behind the hall.

I couldn't take it in. One moment the world was full of joy, the next pitched into the blackest sorrow. My mind was in a fog, the days passing, one upon another, without my notice. I could not even weep for my baby who lay, not warmly swaddled in a crib, but in a cold tomb beside his grandfather.

In his own grief Gawen lashed out at everyone. I felt he had added the poor babe's death to the list of crimes he held at my door. He snarled and cursed every time he saw me. It was a relief when he left for Exeter, muttering about it being 'time to put an end to all this nonsense'.

Chapter Twenty-three

The Interview

Spring 1582

Sir Robert Denys swaggered into my parlour, raised a nonchalant hand to stroke a fashionable pointed beard and turned a steely gaze upon me. His piercing eyes moved slowly from the top of the little cap I wore tipped back to show off my upswept hair, over my starched ruff and modest partlet, right down to the hem of my gown of emerald silk, only to crawl up over me again. My flesh crept too as he looked me up and down as if assessing a cow at market. The dapper little man's unrelenting appraisal set me instantly on my guard.

'Sir Robert,' I said, blinking fast. 'To what do we owe this unexpected visit?' It took all my self-control to keep my tone even and welcoming. I glanced at Sir Robert's companion, a black-clad crow of a man with sunken cheeks and a great hooked nose. He stood motionless on spindly legs, poised like a heron waiting to strike. I suppressed a shudder, but it was not the chilly February morning that sent shivers running down my spine.

It was many months since we'd received any visitor at Dartington Hall and the Exeter City Recorder's unannounced arrival was beyond unusual. I shot Gawen an enquiring look but he hung back by the door with his eyes cast down as a flush crept up his neck to flood his face until he was as red as the ruby ring that flashed on Sir Robert's finger. I waited, feeling a sudden tightening in my chest.

At last Gawen raised his eyes and spluttered a bit before the words were out.

'I'll call for refreshments, Sir Robert.' Then to my amazement my husband turned and made a dash for the door, calling loudly for Rist as he went. I'm surprised he did not fall to the floor there and then, for the look I threw at his back was deadly as any dagger.

After some clattering and banging beyond the door Rist bumbled in, his footsteps sounding unusually loud as he fussed around offering wine and honey cakes. But Sir Robert waved away the platter and mug with an impatient hand. Disdaining to take the seat I indicated, he stood with hands clasped behind his back, oozing patrician confidence as he peered at me from beneath brows bristling with straggly grey hairs. Rist threw a knowing look over his shoulder as he shuffled out, leaving the door open a crack. No doubt the odious fool had his ears flapping to hear whatever was to follow.

I forced myself to relax the muscles that had stiffened defensively at the insolence of Sir Robert's appraisal, trying to keep my eyes still. But the temptation to dart anxious looks at the men standing before me was overwhelming.

Sir Robert pulled his shoulders back and I thought he would speak. But it seemed he had not yet finished his inspection. I felt his cold eyes studying me again, as though he thought I had just crawled from beneath a stone. The other man clasped the leather pouch he carried tighter to his chest and I noticed the ink stains on his bony fingers. As I waited in vain for my husband to rejoin us, it felt as if the very air in the room crackled with menace. If the cook had come in carrying a cleaver I swear he could have brought it down and cut right through the silence.

I thought of Maman and determined I would not wither under Sir Robert's condescending gaze. Since he had yet to answer me I lifted an eyebrow expectantly, stared back into Sir Robert's face and pursed my lips. At last Sir Robert broke the silence to introduce the other man.

'This is Thomas Trosse, your husband's proctor, brought here to note down our words.' He motioned to the man to sit at the board. 'Trosse will represent Mr Champernowne in the case before the Consistory Court.'

'What case?' I snapped as the other man perched a pair of spectacles on his beak of a nose, took out his ink horn, dipped his pen and began to scribble. 'What case can be of concern to me?' Silence, but for the scratching nib.

I struggled to call to mind what I knew of Sir Robert; a well-connected man who had followed his father to become Sheriff of the county. Gawen, of course, knew him. They had served together for years as Justices, though I had met him but once or twice. Oh yes, Sir Robert knew Gawen and his family well. Not for the first time I remembered I was a stranger in a strange land. The men of Devon would always stick together.

After much throat-clearing, Sir Robert found his voice again.

'Madam, I am here to question you in the matter of your marriage,' he announced in clipped tones. 'I do not approach the task with relish, but I am charged to do it.'

I whirled around to face him. The obnoxious little man had the decency to flinch as I spat out in a voice icy cold, 'What concern can this be of yours, Sir Robert? It is well known that my marriage to Mr Champernowne was contracted before the Queen of England herself. What question can there be of it? How dare you stand before me and question my marriage!'

'I am here to hear the truth, that is all.' Sir Robert's face had turned mottled and red. He cleared his throat again.

'It has been put to me, madam, that matters between you and Mr Champernowne are not as they should be.' He pronounced the words with all the pomposity of a sitting judge. 'You should be ashamed, madam. You should be 'shamed. It is no mean thing. Now, give me your answer. What do you have to say?'

I opened my mouth to speak but instead a hiss crept between my teeth like the sound of a goose threatened by the fox. I turned away, fighting hard to quell the anger boiling within me. Some instinct for self-preservation screamed at me that I must remain calm. I took a breath and turned back to Sir Robert. To his credit he was now fidgeting from foot to foot and swallowing hard. Perhaps for all his haughty show he was embarrassed by his task.

'Sir Robert, I am sorry you have been put to such unnecessary trouble,' I said, sweet as a sugared almond. 'Has some complaint been made of me? If I have offended my husband in any way I would surely ask his forgiveness, aye and God's forgiveness too if that was warranted. But, in truth, I have no idea what has brought you here.' Sir Robert took a breath.

'Madam, it has been put to me that you are not a true wife to Mr Champernowne; that you have shown to others the favours a wife may bestow only upon her husband. In short, that you have known a man's body other than your husband's.'

That was too much for me. I could contain the seething fury those words provoked no longer. I exploded with a tirade of French, flinging my hands from side to side. In my native tongue I denied such calumnies and fervently maintained my innocence. When I stopped to draw breath I flicked a poisonous glance at the proctor and felt my gut tighten as it dawned on me that Sir Robert and Trosse might not be fluent in French. When I had recovered a little I spoke sharply, this time in English.

'Sir, pray tell me when I am supposed to have committed these offences?'

'Mr Champernowne has told me it was clear on the first occasion he met you that you had eyes for other men,' Sir Robert answered. Emboldened, he threw his chest out and nodded vigorously as his voice rose. 'Mayhap you had known another even before you were wed. I am told many have noted and will testify to your behaviour since. The evidence that you are no better than a strumpet is clear.'

'Sir, you insult a well-born lady,' I cried. I took a step forward, raised my hand and came within the breadth of a hair of striking him, so strong was my desire to wipe the condescending sneer from his face. I pulled my hand back just in time, but Sir Robert had seen it.

'See how she behaves!' he scoffed triumphantly. 'Trosse! You saw it yourself and you heard her Frenchie words too. She has confessed. You've heard it from her own mouth. Mark it down.'

'What do you say you've heard from my mouth? I admitted nothing,' I started to say. But Sir Robert Denys was already on his way out of the door without so much as a nod in my direction.

Back in my chamber I twisted Diane the doll in my hands as I tried to understand what that pantomime might mean. I dared not think what Gawen might mean by bringing the supercilious fool to question me.

After we lost baby Philip, Gawen had sunk into the darkest despair. I had hardly seen him in weeks, barely exchanged two words with him since Christmastide. I knew my husband was in sore want of money, hard pressed by debtors and envious of his cousins and other men of Devon who went off adventuring. But I couldn't see what he hoped to gain by pursuing some outrageous claim against me. Perhaps he thought the threat of some public hearing, some foolery that demeaned me, would prompt my family to pay what was due. I shifted uncomfortably on the velvet cushion in the window seat and hugged my arms tight round my middle, rocking to and fro. A memory surfaced through the fog of panic and confusion that gripped me; a day when I'd walked in the sunlit garden, not long after I first came to Dartington. I could almost hear Bess's light voice telling me about Protector Seymour's first wife, sent to a nunnery and locked away.

That night a new dream came to haunt me. First it was the old one of Rouen, but this time I followed the old woman, heaving myself up the steep steps, weighed down by the rough-hewn stone I clutched. When I reached the top I peered over the battlements to see a soldier poised below, an arquebus raised to his shoulder. The man holding the weapon, pointing it straight at me, was my husband. In the dream I stepped back and found myself shut up in a tiny cell with neither window nor door. I clawed at the stone walls. I looked down and saw that my hands were bleeding.

Chapter Twenty-four

The Case

Early summer 1582

In the days and weeks that followed that dreadful interview I slept only in snatches, fearing the torment of my terrifying nightmare. I picked at my food. Dark rings formed under my eyes and my cheekbones stood out like a barber's blades. I wept into my pillow wondering how we could have come to this.

The battle lines were drawn. Marie Weare announced to me one morning that she had been told she would be called as one of the witnesses when details of my alleged marital infidelity were to be aired for all to hear at the Church Consistory Court.

'What is this court?' I snapped.

''Tis the Bishop's Court. It rules over the clergy and parishioners alike. It's where all those who have done wrong in their marriage are judged.' I took a step back and waved at her to be gone. But Marie had not finished.

'Alice Blackaller,' she informed me, 'she's called as well, and ever so many of the servants. And Master Rist too, of course.' I did not give her the satisfaction of a reply but kept my face set like a mask until the door closed behind her. Then I collapsed in a heap and wept, constantly asking myself how he could do it. Did he not care that it would be the talk of the county, if not the whole of England? He branded a cuckold, me an adulteress.

I was to have proper representation. How Gawen could afford

to pay for that was a mystery to me. But if his plot was to succeed I supposed there must be no suggestion that I'd not been given opportunity to put my side of 'the case'.

At our first meeting I took an instant liking to Jasper Bridgeman, the proctor assigned to me. He was a man well past the first flush of youth, balding and somewhat stooped, but I thought his face open and honest-looking. I took in his neat attire; shoes clean of any mud; cloth of good quality; well-made clothes but by no means ostentatious; all to the good. I was lucky to have been assigned a man with a university education, though it must have been many years since he last trod the corridors of learning. Beside Bridgeman sat Nicholas Wyatt, a more flamboyant man with overlong, rather theatrical hair, who must have gained his experience in the law more recently. Nicholas would be my advocate when the case was heard in the Church Court.

Bridgeman rested his elbows on the table and considered the pile of documents, all closely written in a spidery hand, strewn on the table before him. He sat back and regarded me over steepled fingers, sucking his teeth.

'We can do nought but answer the charges truthfully. Do you maintain there has been no improper behaviour on your part?' I nodded and he sighed and looked down at the floor. 'I am sorry to tell you the questions that will be put to the witnesses – the articles Trosse will present from his little black book – may have been so framed as to beg answers that are not helpful to you.'

'Witnesses? What witnesses are these?' I protested, shaking my head so vigorously I had to put up a hand to right my headdress. 'Who can be a witness to what has never happened!'

'Nonetheless, those called will make depositions before the court,' he sighed. 'We will have but one chance to give answer. These are the charges.' He passed a paper across the table. I took it up, scanned it and threw up my hands, letting it fall, so that I must then scrabble among the heap to clutch it again and read on.

'What foolishness is this? Gatchell? That arrogant whoreson knave!' I shrieked. 'I would have that man come no nearer to me than Staverton Church is to this house, and then I'd wish him further. Lies, Master Bridgeman! A story concocted between them to humiliate me.' I read on, hands shaking. 'No! Not this! How can they say such things? Christopher is a good man.' I threw the paper down and the proctor regarded me carefully.

'It is the nature of these cases that names are bandied about,' Bridgeman said. 'You stand accused of adultery with two men. Witnesses will be produced. Oftentimes men are paid to say what is needful.' He paused and frowned. 'I know both of the men accused with you. That two men so very different in nature and repute are named smacks to me of false charges. One man might have been believable. But two?' His brow wrinkled. 'Though the charges against Queen Anne Boleyn were no more believable all those years ago, but it did not aid her cause,' he mused. 'I fear we must await the depositions to see what these servants say.'

'This will wound old Master Melhuishe to the quick.' I rasped the words out, feeling as though my breath was trapped in my lungs. 'Such lies about his son. Christopher has never been more than a true friend to me. He taught my brother. He shared my determination to aid poor souls uprooted and left destitute by the French wars. We worked together to aid those poor women. Since he returned he has helped my daughters with their lessons. I need say no more of Gatchell, for all of Devon knows him to be an arrogant braggart who preys on young women. Do you tell me my husband actually believes these lies?'

'It is he who has brought the case against you,' he answered with a nod. I picked up the Bible that lay on the table and placed my hand firmly on the leather binding.

'I swear on this holy book: never has there been any impropriety with these men, or indeed with any other man. I swear I have known no man but my true husband.' Bridgeman flushed and Wyatt shuffled the papers, not meeting my eye.

'That being so we must find our own witnesses to counter these claims,' Wyatt advised. 'What of your maidservants?'

'Sent back to France by my husband two years since. Replaced by his lackeys.'

'Ah, so this has been a time in the planning.' Bridgeman sighed heavily.

'We will do what we can,' Wyatt assured me, though the shake of his head suggested he was by no means hopeful. He jumped to his feet and started to gather the papers, giving me the distinct impression he would rather he had not taken on my case.

'And then the dragon breathed fire and ate them all up,' Lisbeth chirped as she lifted her eyes from the Bible and studied my face.

'Yes, that was well read, Lisbeth,' I murmured as I stared past her to the trees waving in the rough winds beyond the chamber window.

'Mama! You are not listening!' she giggled nervously. 'I just read to you about a dragon. There are no dragons in the story about the feeding of the five thousand in the New Testament, are there?'

'What? Um … er … no,' I stuttered, hauling my thoughts back into the room. Mary and Katherine, seated on cushions and applying themselves none too diligently to their needlework, nudged each other and tittered. Lisbeth swallowed and stared at me, biting her lip. She put up a hand to brush away a stray lock of hair that had escaped her cap and I noticed my daughter's fingernails were bitten nearly down to the quick.

'Mama, whatever is wrong?' she asked as she clutched the Bible. 'It's as if you are somewhere else. Did those men who came yesterday upset you? Is there bad news? Why is Father never at home?' I squared my shoulders and tried to concentrate. My thoughts had been as confused as the tangled threads of an unravelling tapestry since I learned that my own husband sought to make a case of divorce against me. How could I explain to my dearest daughter, only nine years old, why her father would do such a thing? I had been as good a wife to him as I could. I had born his children, run his household and tried to love him. It was Gawen who had rebuffed all my attempts to bridge the gulf between us.

'Lisbeth, er … um … I am indeed distracted and … um … those men did not bring good news,' I stammered a little, unsure how to protect my beloved girl. 'Events are unfolding that I would never have wished to see. People may say things you find difficult to understand. Do not believe what they say of me.' I gasped as a sudden dark thought struck me. 'They may even ask you questions about me.' Her face flushed and her finger went to her mouth. She chewed on her nail and raised her beautiful eyes to my face. After a moment she cuddled up to me and lay her head in my lap.

'Mama, once Alice came to me,' Lisbeth whispered. I searched my mind. Ah, yes, she must mean Alice Blackaller who worked in the kitchens.

'Mama, she asked me strange questions.'

'What questions, *ma petite*?' I asked as I stroked her hair.

'It was a long time ago, when Father was away in London or Ireland or somewhere. She asked me if I had seen a man in the little room next your chamber, or perhaps she meant my father's room – I didn't really understand her. I said no, but I did tell her that once I had thought someone was there. I was only remembering a time when I was frightened in a storm long ago. Did I do wrong, Mama?'

I pursed my lips. 'Alice should not have asked you such a thing. You did not do wrong for you answered with the truth, as you have been taught,' I soothed, and planted a kiss on her nut-brown curls.

'Mama, she asked me about Master Melhuishe who used to come and help me with my reading. She said strange things about him.'

'Alice has been foolish. Pay no heed to what she said. Christopher Melhuishe is a good man and a fine teacher. Now, try to forget all about that woman and her nonsense. Let us put on our cloaks and walk in the garden before the rain comes again. Now, see that you put on your pattens to keep your feet clear of the wet.'

Lisbeth was easily distracted, soon charging headlong through the garden despite the despised pattens, with the wind lifting her hair behind her like a banner. Patch lolloped along close at her heels. She'll be glad of the companionship of that hound in the difficult months we must face, I thought, as she nearly barrelled into Agnes Searle coming in the opposite direction. Head down, battling against the wind, Agnes approached, shifted the basket on her arm and addressed me directly.

'You need not speak of it, mistress. I fear it is the talk of the village. Be assured that I know you for a true and honourable lady, ma'am. You may look to me to speak up for you.'

'Thank you, Agnes. I will tell Master Bridgeman. He will speak to you.'

I hardly noticed that bees were busy among the blossom or that the birds sang out joyfully in the morning sunshine. Despair took root within me and like tangled weeds in a neglected garden it grew until it smothered all my hope. The weeks dragged by.

Bridgeman came again, this time alone. He held out a paper.

'These are the ones who will be called to give their depositions in Staverton Church. Having the hearing close to home rather than dragging them to Exeter means they will all happily attend.' I ran my eye down the list as he took a seat at the table opposite me.

'Sir Robert Denys? Must I face him? Will he be there to say his piece and shame me with his misunderstanding of my words? For it's certain his version will be accepted above mine.'

'Mayhap Sir Robert will give a written account,' Bridgeman replied evenly. I read on.

'Marie Weare? Why, she's been in my husband's employ but two years. Alice Blackaller – now that name does not surprise me! But who are these? John Evans, Walter Winsor, John Chittle, John Chinnor; these must be my husband's men, for I know them not. Ah, and here's one at the heart of matters. Hugh Rist!'

'A long list indeed,' Bridgeman muttered, shuffling his papers. 'I understand that Rist will give account of his conversations with Gatchell. That may be difficult to counter. I'll warrant he's rehearsing before Trosse and Weston, the advocate for your husband. They will coach him to deliver his account in a way that will be most convincing.'

'Then I fear I am lost. Rist has ever resented my presence here. His father died at the hands of a Frenchman,' I moaned. One look at the proctor told me there was little hope. His shoulders were hunched, his face a blank mask.

'We have little to set against it,' he confirmed bleakly. 'I have spoken with Agnes Searle. She is willing to speak for you but I must tell you, the woman will take a grave risk should she do so. She is known as a wise woman, I believe? Known for her skill in healing? One who mixes many potions and salves?'

'Why yes, she has great and valuable knowledge of such matters. She assists my maids in the still room. Ah, it is a relief to see none of their names are listed,' I commented, waving the paper. 'Agnes is often here. She sees to my physick garden.'

His expression was baleful, his tone solemn, when he spoke again.

'It is being put about, good mistress, that this Agnes will be decried as a witch should she give her deposition in your favour. The woman is courageous. She says she will appear. But I fear the consequences.'

'Would they stoop so low?' I gasped as tears welled up in my eyes.

'Mistress, simple people are easily led. Once they take into their heads such a notion they may turn on Agnes. You know the treatment of those so accused may be harsh indeed.'

'That I do. You must dissuade her. Tell her I forbid her to speak. I will take my chances upon my own truthful answers. She must not put herself at risk for my sake.'

Bridgeman's eyes misted over.

'So be it. 'Tis shameful to think that you, a noble lady of great compassion, must endure such humiliation at the hands of those who should value you more highly.' The table jumped as his fist came down hard on it. 'There, I've spoken my mind when I should not.' He paused to recover himself. 'If it should go ill with the court there may be recourse to appeal to the Court of Arches in London. But I can hold out little hope. I take it you've written to your family in France?'

'I have, but I doubt the letters will ever reach them. I've had no word from them in months. Master Bridgeman, be assured I will withstand whatever may befall alone.' I spoke the words with some determination, as if to comfort him, though in truth I had no idea how I could survive the horror my husband was bent on inflicting on me.

Chapter Twenty-five

The Bishop's Court

July 1582

The fourth day of July dawned; the day appointed for the depositions to be heard in Staverton Church before Richard Mindall, the bishop's representative. I could hardly bear to look at Marie Weare as she laid out my clothes. I had chosen a dark gown of good quality, but not too fine, a modest partlet and simple coif for my head. I would have them see me as a respectable matron.

'You had best hurry, Marie,' I snapped. 'The cart is waiting to take you all to the church. I shall be there betimes.' She said nothing as she laced my gown. 'You may go,' I ordered, determined to maintain my dignity. Without so much as a nod she was gone and the door closed firmly behind her. I heard a man's voice then a sharp metallic click.

I screamed, bounded through the antechamber, leaped to the door and tried the latch. It was held fast. The key had been turned in the lock. I rattled the handle and beat my fists on that door until they were raw. I shouted and I yelled and I screamed. But no one came. Eventually I sank to the floor, sobbing and defeated. I would not be going to Staverton Church to give my carefully prepared answers after all.

I wept until I could weep no more, then moved to the window and sat looking vacantly at the bright garden, all the time clutching Diane the doll to my breast. The afternoon shadows were growing long when I heard the click and knew the door to be unlocked. But I did not stir.

Much later I heard a commotion below and tried to gather my scattered wits. I poured water from the ewer and soaked a cloth to dab my swollen eyes. I smoothed my gown and waited. It seemed a long time before Marie Weare slithered into the room. To my surprise I could see Master Bridgeman standing at the top of the stairs behind her. But there was someone else concealed behind the door. The sound of their heavy rasping breathing gave them away.

'A man to see you, mistress,' Marie squawked, shooting rapid glances at me.

'Marie, as you know very well it is not my custom to receive men in my chamber. That would be most improper,' I announced loud and clear. She looked baffled and turned as if to seek advice from whoever stood hidden beside her. I went on imperiously, 'Pray tell Master Rist, if it is he who lurks behind you, that I will come down and greet Master Bridgeman in the parlour. Light the candles and ask him to wait for me there.'

I took a few breaths to calm my beating heart and then went down. The proctor bowed to me and darted an anxious look at Rist, who had followed me in. I invited the proctor to sit, offered him refreshment, which he declined, and took a seat opposite. Rist made as if he would remain but I hurled such a look of fury in his direction that he turned to go.

'Leave the wine and cups and be gone,' I commanded. 'Be sure to close the door this time, Master Rist.' The weasel of a man flushed, scuttled out and the door slammed shut.

'Why, Mistress Champernowne,' said Bridgeman, his shrewd eyes studying me. 'I am pleased to see you are well. It was given out you had a fever.'

'No fever detained me! It was a locked door that kept me from Staverton Church this day. I have no doubt Master Rist had a hand in it.'

'Then matters are indeed most serious, my lady,' he said. The sorrow in his eyes was genuine. 'I have brought you the notes I made of the depositions they laid before the Bishop's Court. It is only right that you should know what has been said of you.' He took a bundle of papers from his bag and pushed them across the table.

'Will you take a glass of wine while I read?' I asked. This time he nodded, took a sip and settled back in his seat while I perused the crumpled papers. The glass was drained before I looked up.

'You will understand that I must ask this question?' he said gravely. 'Is there any truth in anything that has been put to the court?'

I considered carefully before I replied.

'Sir, I will speak clear. I have known no man but my husband. I believe this so-called case against me has been cleverly conceived. My husband despatched my faithful servants to France and brought people into our household with one intent. To spy on me. Why, now I think it's been going on for years. How often have I fallen over Alice Blackaller in passageways?'

'Ah! So they can all say truthfully they were in these places?' sighed Bridgeman as he pointed to the long list of statements.

'I suppose that may be so,' I answered. Suddenly I felt cold and heavy, as though I was in the cell I'd dreamed about so often lately, with the stone walls closing in around me, crushing me until I could no longer breathe. I gripped the table and raised my eyes to see the anger written large on Bridgeman's flushed face.

'Ah, it is shocking! Perhaps now you may understand what they have done? It is clever indeed,' he fumed. 'Mistress, the most convincing of lies are those that hold a germ of truth at the kernel.' Bridgeman's eyes narrowed as he jabbed a finger towards the papers. 'Do you see? They have gone to great lengths to present themselves as honest, to present accounts that will seem credible,' he declared. He spoke more quietly now, more like an impatient but kindly teacher explaining a difficult lesson. 'Let us take the most damning – the words of Master Rist.' I took a deep breath as the bile rose in my throat.

'Sir, there is no truth in it,' I stammered.

'Yes, yes, it is clear to me. But Rist is a clever witness and well schooled. He limits himself to what he has himself observed and gives much detail to make it sound all the more plausible.'

'I pray you will explain it to me,' I said, with a shudder. I wondered if it was my husband who'd had the man so well prepared or if it was some scheme hatched between Rist and Gatchell.

'Rist deposes that on one occasion Gatchell woke him late in the night having returned unexpectedly from Exeter where he had left your husband at the court sessions. He claims Gatchell insisted that he, Rist, go with him to your chamber door on the pretext of fetching some paper or other. We will leave aside why Gatchell was so insistent that Rist accompany him. Surely this Gatchell, who has been in your husband's and his father's employ these many years … surely he knew his way around your house?'

'He did indeed. I cannot think why Rist would need to show him the way,' I exclaimed. 'And good Master Bridgeman, if any of what Gatchell is supposed to have told Rist about his intimacy with me were true, then he would certainly have no need of Rist's direction to my chamber!'

'Ah! Indeed! Do you see it now, my lady? Next Rist says he observed Gatchell knock at the door and be admitted, though he's careful not to say it was you who admitted him. He says he saw the man, Gatchell, approach your sleeping chamber, even saw him go to your bedside. Note he does not say that he saw you, or that you were awake or that he heard you greet the man. Rist then says he left Gatchell, who implored him not to tell his wife that he had seen him there. These details all add credence to the tale. They state little of fact, but they imply much.'

'I do begin to see that,' I muttered, feeling quite sick. 'Such a tale, so cleverly concocted to deceive!'

'Rist asserts that Gatchell had called on you in your chamber three or four times in the previous three years—' I snorted so loudly that he paused. 'But he states that on only one occasion did he himself witness the man go there. He then adds more to his testimony by recalling a separate occasion when he and Gatchell discussed you. There is such a level of detail…' He pushed back his seat with a clatter and walked round the table to point at the paper.

'Do you see here? Read what is written. All this about going with Gatchell to the house of John Towpes in Staverton for breakfast and his conversation with Gatchell on the way. It is a trail laid to establish how reliable a witness he is. No doubt it can be proved they did go there. No doubt John Towpes would confirm it.'

'Ah, I see it now! The event cannot be disputed so that makes the rest of what he says the more believable? He throws in the name of this Towpes who will corroborate his story!' I brought my fist down on the oak boarded table with a thump. Like a pot on the fire my anger passed simmering point and was boiling over. 'Rist is a devious knave!' I spluttered.

'That is it exactly. Towpes can only confirm that they visited him, but it will be assumed that he confirms the rest of the story. Rist has established himself as a credible witness, so when next he alleges that Gatchell took him into his confidence and admitted to him that he could have his pleasure of you whenever the master was away, that will also be taken as truth.'

I leaped up from my seat and for a moment I was so incensed that I resorted to French, hands flying wildly. Master Bridgeman's eyes opened wide and I remembered that, educated man though he was, he might not fully understand my words. I wanted no repeat of what had happened with Sir Robert Denys. I spat out my next words in English.

'Gatchell is a bragging, boasting, lecherous, arrogant pig of man! It is just what he would say! It is all lies!' I cried. The very touch of the paper felt sharp and brittle as I turned it over in my shaking hand.

'Yes, madam, but they weave many convincing insinuations on small grains of truth. I fear all who hear them will put the worst interpretation on your supposed involvement.'

'Now I remember! In the days running up to Christmastide the year before Arthur was born, while Gawen was gone to Exeter to meet with the mayor, I actually found that oaf Gatchell in the little anteroom next my sleeping chamber when I woke in the early hours one morning. I ordered him gone and took to bolting the door after that. It caused a great to-do when Gawen came home and found the door barred.'

'Ah! If you search your memory you may well find that those things alleged of Master Melhuishe are also rooted in some perfectly innocent occurrence.' I picked up the paper.

'This nonsense about his hose being undone! I do remember a time when Christopher came to help Lisbeth with her lesson. I had kept to my chamber, for I was ailing; I was carrying our poor boy who went too soon to his grave.' I paused and swallowed hard. The reminder of the swaddled bundle in his tiny coffin had thrown me and my heart was beating fast. Bridgeman waited while I gathered my wits. 'I did receive Master Melhuishe in my chamber that day. With a maidservant present, I might add; Marie Weare if I'm not mistaken. He had been caught in a sudden downpour and was soaked to the skin. I had her give him a pair of Master Gawen's stockings and insisted he change in the privacy of the antechamber. I kept the door closed tight the whole time. That such a small thing could be so overblown!'

'It is how men like Trosse win their cases and claim the fee. But I have never seen it so blatant as this,' he said with a rueful shake of his head. I ran my eye over the other accusations.

'The laundry maid. Hah! That same day she came saying it was to take my night things for washing. But she had taken them already! She came to my chamber that she may say she saw Christopher there.' I read on. 'Alice Blackaller did indeed question my daughter and left the poor mite confused and upset by it. That woman should be dismissed.'

At the next accusation I threw my hands in the air. 'His hands in my ruff? Now that goes too far!' I gasped. 'Once my hair was caught in the wire rebato that held my ruff. It was painful and Christopher did step forward to release me. Could that be it? But that was in the parlour, not in my chamber, and he certainly did not sit in my lap, as she alleges.'

Bridgeman shifted in his seat.

'Now this is beyond belief!' I exclaimed as a brittle cackle of laughter escaped me. 'It seems I am under suspicion because I speak in my own native tongue. I see no reason to apologise for speaking French with Christopher, or with anyone else. As it happens he speaks French fluently and is the only one with whom I can converse in the language of my birth, my husband being always from home and my maidservants despatched.'

'Madam, we both understand what has happened here.' Bridgeman gave a weary sigh.

'Yes, indeed! But was my husband complicit in these damning insinuations? Did he truly care so little for my honour?'

'That I cannot say. All I can say is that he has brought this case and the depositions placed before the court are likely to bring forth a damning verdict. Rist's final allegation that Gatchell said he would have five thousand pounds of you should your husband die, introduces a sinister motive. It is calculated to cast you in the worst light. And then to add that Gatchell has promised Rist a new pair of hose and doublet if he keeps quiet!'

'And the money Gatchell is supposed to have paid to this woman named as Marie – I take that to be Marie Weare – does she confirm she had that sum of him?' I peered at the writing. 'That is a vast sum indeed! Am I to believe he actually paid her forty pounds as stated here?' Bridgeman shook his head. 'I doubt that such a sum changed hands.'

I hurled the paper across the table and paced the floor. I could feel my pulse thumping, hear it pounding in my ears.

'Rist suggests here that Gatchell told him he paid Marie to keep his secret, the secret of his supposed intimacy with me,' I bellowed. 'In truth she was paid to provide her own malicious false testimony! And to keep her counsel on what she knew; that those rogues had set this trap for me.' The candle flames flickered as I swished past, casting eerie shadows on the walls. I could feel the hair sticking to the nape of my neck.

'Madam, I implore you, be still,' Bridgeman pleaded.

'Master Bridgeman I am rocked to the core by this. I'll own I am beyond fury!'

He took my arm and guided me back to my seat . When I was a little calmer I began again.

'Forgive my angry outburst, Master Bridgeman. Sir, I cannot believe my husband could have ordered this. But to my great sorrow I do believe he has been fooled by their lies. What is to be done?'

The lawyer resumed his seat and seemed lost in thought. At last he replied.

'You were denied the opportunity to speak in person, though Wyatt did his best on your behalf. If the bishop's representatives had seen you, madam, had they heard you speak, the scales might just have fallen from their eyes. For who, after meeting you, could doubt that you are an honest and noble lady?' His hand fell to his chest. 'Would there were another chance for you to be heard! I am sorry, madam, but the Church Court will reach its conclusion on the basis of the statements given.'

'May we not prove their duplicity, as you have revealed it to me this evening? You mentioned an appeal?'

He shook his head. 'It would take a clever lawyer to do so. If your family in France would pay for it, perhaps. But your husband has many friends in high places. You must consider this very carefully, my lady.' After a long silence he looked up. 'I have done my best, The court will, I fear, find you guilty as charged. Send word to me if it is your wish that I appeal the matter in the Court of Arches.'

My head was pounding as I bade him farewell and made my way to my chamber, relieved that Rist was nowhere to be seen. I dismissed Marie Weare with a flick of my hand; I could not suffer to be served by one whose false words had condemned me. I fumbled to manage my undressing without her, put on a clean smock and curled up into a ball in our marital bed. I lay there hugging Diane the doll, trying to make sense of it all. It was a long time before sleep came and when it did I was tortured by the most evil nightmares ever, so vivid, so real, that I could hardly distinguish their torture from the hopeless reality that was engulfing me.

Chapter Twenty-six

Desolation

Summer 1582–1584

The silence slid snakelike into my consciousness, sucked the breath from me and smothered me like a veil of fog. I staggered from my bed and clung to the windowsill straining my ears. No birds sang. My logical brain argued that the sun was already up, that I was too late for July's muted dawn chorus, that the swallows' first noisy brood had long since flown the nest beneath the eaves. I cocked my head to one side and listened again. With a jolt I realised not only birdsong was missing. No squabbling children's voices, no joyous shrieks of laughter echoed down from the nursery above. Yet surely my children should all be up and about by now.

I tried the door, half expecting it would be locked again, but it opened at my touch. Still in my nightclothes, I set my foot on the bottom step of the stair. I peeped into Lisbeth's room. The bed was tidy; there were no books strewn across the coffer, no discarded clothes, no work basket with silks spilling in confusion all over the floor. Only a faint scent of lavender lingered in the air. A lump came to my throat. It was the perfume my Lisbeth loved most. Heart pounding, I raced on to the nursery where my younger children should be at their lessons. But that too was empty. As empty as the swallows' nest.

I backed up against the wall, trying to ward off a sudden overwhelming dread. My fingers felt cold and a sour taste came into my mouth. In my head I already knew the truth, but still my heart resisted. I convinced myself they must be somewhere in the house. Flinging myself headlong down the stairs I tripped and cut my knee, scrambled up and raced on into the parlour, the hall, and the kitchens where I found only one white-faced maid who looked up from her task and screamed at the sight of me. I rushed on. *Yes, of course,* I thought, *I will find them in the garden.*

Barefoot up and down the paths I flew, snagging my shift on thorns, impervious to sharp stones, searching in vain. How I got there I cannot recall, but of a sudden I found myself in the church porch. Confused, I peered up at the carved vaulting above my head, then set my hand on the iron ring, lifted the latch and stumbled through the studded door. The church felt cool, but welcoming. I inhaled deeply; a faint fusty smell, a mixture of dying flowers and earthy honeyed beeswax with pungent hints of ancient incense. I paused beside the reassuring bulk of the eight-sided font where our children had been baptised. I ran my fingers over the rough granite surface and a teardrop splashed onto the stone floor. I took a few hesitant steps towards the carved oak screen, feeling the stones smooth and cool beneath my bare feet. A refrain shouted loud in my head – I have failed them; *I have failed them all. My Lisbeth, my babies … I have failed them all…* Oblivious to the hard floor I fell to my knees near the place where baby Philip lay; the only child he could not take from me.

It was Agnes Searle who found me there, stiff and cold, and brought me gently back to my chamber. It was Agnes who bathed my cut knees, rubbed salve into my bruised and battered feet and it was Agnes who offered the bowl with its sedative draught and rocked me in her arms until I slept.

I drifted in and out of consciousness, escaping only briefly from the world of nightmares. Whenever I opened my eyes I found Agnes at my side. Many days must have passed before she coaxed me to eat more than a mouthful, to speak again and to begin to face up to the aching emptiness that was all I had left. I felt hollowed out, as though my insides had been scooped from me when my children were taken. I wept, I ranted, I raved and sometimes I tried to pray.

Agnes kept Rist beyond the door and for a time she could resist his demand that she leave me with Marie Weare to tend me.

'I will stay as long as Mistress Champernowne has need of me,' she insisted. But as I regained some control of my fragile emotions I started to worry that it would go ill for her should my husband choose to return.

'Let us face that when we must. Let us bring you back to health so that you may deal with the master when he comes, as in time he must. If he then orders me away I will have to go. But I can at least stay until then and help you heal and prepare.'

It was September, and I was stronger, much stronger, when he came.

I hardly knew how to speak to him but there he was, desperate eyes blazing, with Marie Weare a step behind. Agnes took a stand beside me and smiled her encouragement.

'Madam! Have no fear. I am by your side,' she whispered.

'I'm told you've run quite mad. Barefoot and in your nightclothes scaring the servants and making a fearful din,' Gawen said in a shaky voice. His breath was coming in short gasps and his gaze flitted round the room, never settling, never looking directly at me. 'You need to be locked up for your own safety.'

'Where are my children?' I demanded, keeping an iron control over my voice lest it rise, become shrill and give credence to his accusation.

'They are safe where they will be well cared for,' he replied, thrusting his chest out in a parody of pride.

'Where could they be better cared for than here with me, their mother?'

'Roberda, you must see that I cannot leave them with you. After all the evidence presented at the court you cannot be considered a suitable person to have the children in your care.'

'Evidence?' I cried. 'I have heard of no evidence; merely packages of untruths concocted to deceive.' Agnes put a steadying hand on my arm.

'The court's judgement is known, the sentence given. I have laid an Act in Parliament. I have divorced you from my bed and board,' he announced, crossing his arms across his chest. 'And now I'm told you rant and rave and run around in a state of undress. I'll not have my children near you.'

'In my shock and terror I did run in search of them. But you will find me calm and in my right mind now, as Agnes will testify.' Faithful Agnes stood her ground under his cold stare and nodded. I adopted my mother's most domineering voice. 'I have a mind to ask Master Bridgeman to take my case to the Court of Arches. It would be a simple task to expose the lies that were set before the Bishop's Court.' Gawen blanched while Marie Weare flushed and studied the floor.

'You will do no such thing,' he snorted, but I could hear a slight tremor of uncertainty in his voice. 'That I cannot allow.'

'Ah! That is because you know in your heart that what was said of me was all a tissue of lies. Any good lawyer could disentangle it,' I fired back.

'The time for appeal has expired. Bridgeman failed to act in time,' he said with a note of triumph. I had not expected that. I had sent a letter to Bridgeman but had no response. I kept my face set. I would not let him read any disappointment there.

'Ah, I suppose you intercepted my correspondence again,' I accused. He could not meet my eyes. 'Did you think me too simple to realise that you have prevented me having word from my family for many months? '

'They have other concerns. Your brother fights again for the cause of the reformed religion with Henri of Navarre. Queen Elizabeth is desperate to keep relations sweet with the other Henri, the one who is King of France, while the threat from Spain grows ever stronger. She's kept Anjou on a string long enough.'

'I don't see how that may concern me,' I said, hoping that might provoke some further explanation. I had a vague suspicion that the queen's advisers, Walsingham and Anne Cecil's father, might be somehow involved in my plight. But I couldn't see how. Gawen did not reply so I tried another tack.

'Gawen, husband, can we not stop this?' I beseeched. 'What have you gained by destroying my honour so? You will not be able to remarry. I know the law of this land. Master Bridgeman explained to me the case of John Stowell, who thinks he can remarry after setting his wife aside. But the law does not allow it. You will not be able to find another dowry, much less a willing bride.'

Gawen's face grew red and he looked at his boots, but said nothing. Next I tried appealing to him as a father.

'To separate me from my daughter is beyond cruelty. The others will survive, but Lisbeth is of an age when this will damage her. Where have you sent her?'

'She is cared for by those who may teach her to become a lady,' he snapped. At this point I noticed that, though the day was not overly hot, he was sweating. He turned away so I could no longer see his face and shuffled his feet.

'The dog is dead,' he muttered. 'Run over by the cart wheels as they left Dartington.'

I thought my heart would burst. That my dearest daughter should suffer just as I had when my Fifi was no more.

'My poor girl! I should have been there to comfort her. How will she manage?'

'It was no more than a dog. She can have another.'

I let out a roar as my anger boiled over.

'You really have no understanding of the hurt you've caused, do you?' I snapped. 'Another dog will not heal Lisbeth's wounds. And those things said of his son are like to kill old Master Melhuishe.'

'You spent too much time with Melhuishe. You were too close to him these many years past.'

'You were jealous?' I yelled, then drew in a breath and lowered my voice. 'There was never any cause. And that story made up by Gatchell and embellished so cleverly by Rist! You cannot have believed that I, a noble woman, would have sullied myself with the village lecher? Such things as were said of me!' He looked distinctly uncomfortable.

'I did not know they would go so far…' he mumbled, shaking his head.

'So far as to lock me in my chamber so I could not come to Staverton Church to give my side?'

He swayed on his feet as though I had hit him.

'What? They told me you had a fever! That was why you did not appear…'

'If you believe that you're a bigger fool than I thought!' I had found a raw nerve, for he turned on his heel and marched from the room.

Agnes was dismissed and Marie Weare was left to see to my needs.

It was several days before I saw him again.

'So, how do we proceed, husband?' I used the word deliberately, my voice cold and cutting. 'Must I return to my family in France?'

'That I will not allow.'

'Then what?'

'You might retire to a nunnery,'

'Like old Seymour's mother? Oh no, sir, I will never agree to that.'

'The Act is passed. You are divorced from my bed and board. It is too late. It cannot be undone. But I am a compassionate man. I will allow you to remain here well fed and housed. But you will not see your children.'

'I will find them,' I screamed after his departing figure.

'No, Roberda, you will not.'

And so my imprisonment began. Marie Weare was my gaoler. She appeared well suited to the task; big boned with muscled arms that looked as strong as many a man could boast. She gave me food that was delivered daily to the door. She saw that I had clean clothing. When the weather was fine she accompanied me for short walks in the gardens. Men stood by to make sure I spoke to no one, made no attempt to escape. The key was turned in the lock from the outside when we returned. Marie was as much a prisoner as I. She sat and sewed. We exchanged few words.

I wondered if my tongue would remember how to form the sounds if ever I had someone to speak to again. Diane the doll was my only comfort and I confess I talked to her at times. I struggled to fight off my nightmares, but resolved that though I might be bowed by the loss of my dear ones, I would not buckle under his cruelty.

Empty days passed. One morning I studied Marie's sullen face as she hunched over her work.

'Are you happy, Marie Weare?' I taunted, thinking to vent some of my anger on her. 'Is this what you were promised? To spend all your days watching over me? I hope you are well paid!' She did not lift her head.

'Forty pounds is no small sum. I hope Gatchell paid up.' I saw her stab her finger with the needle.

'I had need of it,' she said, keeping her eyes cast down. But I saw how her lip trembled.

'Are you from one of the villages nearby, Marie?' I asked, my interest engaged.

'No, ma'am, from Exeter,' she replied in a flat voice.

'So what was this need of yours? What did you need so much that you were prepared to condemn me?'

She hesitated, brushed a tear from her eye, and swallowed hard.

'I have a daughter, ma'am. I was only fifteen years old and in the service of a merchant. A young man came to my master's house. I was not so strong then as you see me now. He forced himself upon me. I lost my place when they saw I was with child.'

I gasped and felt my cheeks burning. I had cast her as an evil villain, but the sour face I had taken to signify a malicious nature could equally be a mask of pain. I waited for her to continue.

'She is well grown. I took the post here because I needed money to apprentice her to a glover that she might rise above the rank of mere serving woman. I was desperate to make sure she did not suffer at the hands of men as had I. The glover is a kindly man, he treats her well and watches over her. She is safe, though she hates the work.'

'I had not considered what might have prompted you to act as you did. I am sorry, Marie. But am I correct in thinking you were set to spy on me?' She nodded. 'And the money from Gatchell?'

'I had given my report of your doings. They taught me a way of saying it that would discredit you. I am sorry, ma'am. That is what I was paid for. I needed it to pay the glover.'

I turned away and we spoke no more of it for a day or two as I turned her confession over in my mind. If what she said was true then I could understand her motives. Marie was forever shifting in her seat and wringing her hands. I knew I must give her some reassurance.

'I wish you had come to me, rather than take money from that fool,' I said. 'But here we are, we two. We must make of it the best we may.' I still found it hard to forgive her, but from that day the atmosphere was a little less strained between us.

Each day I watched Marie's needle catching up a hem, mesmerised as it pulled the thread in and out of the cloth. I decided that I must find employment for my own hands. Lisbeth must be growing, I would embroider a new smock for her.

My request for a supply of fine linen and skeins of black silk was granted. I remembered how Béatrice's elegant fingers used to work their magic and prick out her pattern on the crisp white fabric. I lost myself in concentration, striving to make the stitches neat. The rhythm of the thread was a welcome balm. My thoughts dwelled often on Béatrice, serene in the cloistered life she had been constrained to follow. I wished I could come to a similar calm acceptance of my fate.

Christmastide went unmarked, though I thought once I heard the singers at the door, muffled and indistinct. Marie was replaced by Alice Blackaller for a few days. I guessed that Marie had gone to visit her daughter, and was glad for her. I could hardly bear to look on Alice who sat sullen by the door until relieved.

Grief and anger were my bedfellows, consuming me in successive waves as the months rolled round. The absence of my children crept up on me through many small reminders as I watched from the window; piles of autumn leaves beside the path with no little feet to scrunch through them; bluebells under the trees with no little maid to run among them; feathery heads of dandelions with no little mouths to blow them away.

The days merged together. Only the changing weather gave any indication of the season. On days when it was too wet or cold to walk in the garden I took to pacing round and round the room, prowling like a beast in a cage. I told myself it was for the exercise. My heels clicked impatiently on the floorboards, just as my mother's had all those years ago. It was the thought of Maman, so strong against all adversity, that pulled me thought my darkest hours.

One dark dreary morning I brushed past a pile of books as I stalked to and fro. I coughed as a cloud of dust flew up and stooped to wipe it from the topmost volume. It was the book Christopher had brought me long ago, Marguerite d'Angoulême's poem, *The Mirror of the Sinful Soul.* I began to read. Oh, the joy of hearing in my head the French words but oh, the challenge the author had laid down for me. As I followed the speaker through the roles of mother, daughter, sister and wife I was reduced to tears as I recognised my own failings and omissions.

As a daughter, sister and mother I had certainly been far from perfect. As a wife I could hold my head high in the knowledge that

I was innocent of those sins laid at my door in that parody of a court. But as I held a mirror to my own life I wondered if I was truly blameless. I had tried to be a good wife to Gawen, tried to love him. But perhaps I had not tried hard enough. Certainly in those last years, worn out by childbearing, I had not made time for my husband when he returned from France or Ireland. We had not come together to comfort each other when baby Philip passed away. Perhaps he would not have treated me so callously had I tried harder.

Through that spring, through another summer and winter, I studied. I read the book over and over and I read the Bible. Gradually I made peace with myself. Though it might be too late to repair my marriage I hoped for another opportunity to be a better mother. My resolve to survive and be ready for that day remained strong. As I became quiet in my mind I even found smiles to brighten the days Marie and I must share.

Chapter Twenty-seven

Redemption

July 1584

The scent of roses hung heavy in the morning air as I walked in my physick garden with Marie Weare at my heels like a faithful hound. I bent to pick a posy, thinking to bring some cheer within the four walls that had been my prison for so long. I held the delicate purple and yellow blooms to my nose, turned them over in my hand; they looked like little faces.

'Some call them heartsease,' I sighed. 'Would that they'd bring ease to my heart!'

Marie gave an understanding little nod.

'Let me pick more for you, mistress,' she offered.

As I straightened up I froze, my muscles paralysed at the sight of a tall woman at the end of the path. She was dressed all in black and her head was held high. A gasp caught in my throat and I stumbled back, recoiling from the force of the shock. Marie put out a hand or I would have fallen. Recognition fought with disbelief a heartbeat longer – and then I picked up my skirts and broke into a run, paying no heed to the flowers that fell from my grasp and scattered the path as I hared along. I tumbled headlong into Maman's arms.

'My dear child,' she laughed. 'Be careful, or you will knock me from my feet.'

'Maman? But…' I quavered, blinking furiously. As she held me close I felt hot tears filling my eyes to the brim.

'No more tears, my child,' she declared. 'You are free.'

'I can't believe it!' I cried, dabbing at my eyes with my sleeve. 'Is it really you, Maman?'

'I am as real as the walls of this fine hall.' Maman's voice was warm and reassuring as she waved vaguely towards the house. 'I am come to tell you that your ordeal is over. Queen Elizabeth has revised the sentence your husband obtained against you. His cruelty is at an end. Your children will soon return.'

Maman stood back, held me at arm's length and peered into my face. Trembling, I raised my face for her inspection. She puckered her brow as she studied me, turning my cheek to one side and then the other, with a soft touch of her gloved finger.

'It is not quite so bad as I feared,' she muttered. 'Thank God you seem whole and healthy.'

'I-er-I don't understand,' I stuttered, feeling my stomach all a-flutter as I tried to marshal my addled wits. 'How can it be so? Maman … how have you brought this about?'

'The power of a woman with a pen is indeed a wondrous thing! You owe your freedom to a sisterhood of women who have each taken up the pen on your behalf.' Maman grinned and went on with a touch of her more usual imperious tone. 'But I am merely one of them.'

I wanted to ask what she meant, but the words stuck in my throat. I shook my head, turned aside and closed my eyes then, taking a deep breath, I turned again, opened my eyes wide to stare, disbelieving, at my mother.

'Come, let us sit here in the sunshine while I tell you a little more.' My legs felt wobbly as she took my hand and led me to the bench in the scented arbour overlooking my garden. Maman sat beside me, took off her gloves and clasped my hand between hers.

'There is one woman who has done more than any other to set you free,' she explained softly. 'One who never doubted your innocence. One who walked many miles to find your brother and persuade him to intervene.'

I wrinkled my brow. 'Whoever can you mean, Maman?' I croaked, gripping her hand tight in an attempt to stop the feverish shaking that had overtaken me. 'Who? Charlotte?'

'No! It was Béatrice, your sister, Béatrice! When she heard of your appalling situation from Charlotte, who'd been acquainted with the facts by Bess Seymour, Béatrice knew just what to do. She went to find your brother Jacques.'

'Jacques ? Why? How?…' My voice trailed off as I struggled to understand her words.

'Béatrice knew that Jacques was the only one who might bring about your release. You know he has sworn allegiance to Henry of Navarre?' I shook my head and Maman narrowed her eyes. 'Ah, I had forgotten. You had little news of us in these past years.'

'Even before—' I started, but Maman jumped in impatiently.

'There has been another uneasy truce in France. But it will not last long now the Duke of Anjou is dead.'

'Anjou? Dead?' I asked. 'The one Queen Elizabeth seemed so like to wed?'

'The same, though the English queen decided not to have him a while ago,' she answered. 'His death means Henry of Navarre, a true follower of Master Calvin, is heir to the throne of France. That has put the Catholics in a stew. No doubt they will rally under the Duc de Guise, break the peace and try to remove the Protestant heir.' I shook my head. Maman's words were not penetrating the fog in my brain. She tried again to explain.

'The details don't matter, Roberda. Your brother has been trying to restore our lands while serving Henry of Navarre. He was so caught up in preparations for the conflict that will surely follow that he heeded no letters from any of us. Not even letters from me!' Maman threw up her head and twisted her lips into a familiar disapproving grimace. 'Béatrice thought if she could see Jacques face-to-face she might persuade him. So she left her convent and walked – yes she walked – halfway across France until she found him.' My mouth fell open.

'Her convent is wealthy and she is at its head,' Maman continued. 'No doubt she offered Jacques a good deal of money. A contribution to the Huguenot war chest from a Catholic convent! Oh, that's rich!' Maman was laughing now, but I was none the wiser. She might have been speaking in ancient Greek for all the sense it made to me.

'You say she walked? Why would she do that?' An image of

Béatrice slipping her pretty little feet into a pair of velvet slippers all those years ago in St Lo flashed into my mind. I couldn't imagine her walking so far.

'Béatrice is a pious girl,' Maman replied. 'She has been brought up in the old superstitious ways. Apparently she felt she must do penance for some debt she still owed, and for giving the convent's money to her brother.'

'She did this for me?' I could hardly breathe as I stammered the words. 'I don't deserve it!'

'Nonsense!' Maman snapped. 'Béatrice went down on her knees and implored him. It was not the bag of gold she took him that won him over. She reminded him of your dear papa's last words on the scaffold in the Place de Grève. She reminded Jacques that he was charged with restoring the family estates and lands, and she told him in no uncertain terms that your papa would have also expected him to restore his sister's honour.' Maman paused and squeezed my hand.

'So, at Béatrice's insistence, Jacques wrote first to Walsingham's man de Brumen, who in turn raised the matter with the English. The spy wrote that you had brothers who stood ready to avenge you. But in the end it was Jacques' direct appeal to Walsingham that tipped the balance.'

Again, I could find no words. I squeezed my eyes shut and tried to steady my breathing.

'Oh, I wrote as well,' she went on. 'And I think Katherine Raleigh got her boy to raise the matter with Walsingham – she would have acted sooner but she lost her husband just before this all came to a head and has been in deep mourning.' My eyes flew open.

'I will write to her, Maman. I did not know. She will feel his loss, for I saw the true love between them.'

'That is a kindly thought, my dear,' Maman beamed. 'But, to return to your release. I am in no doubt it was Jacques' approach to Walsingham that did it. And it was Béatrice who persuaded him to it.' I shook my head, still confused.

'Don't you see?' Maman persisted. 'My appeals were not enough, though I did write to both the queen and Walsingham. After your brother wrote, Walsingham persuaded the queen who instructed her judges to review your case. Jacques would never have approached Walsingham as he did had Béatrice not persuaded him.'

Hot tears welled up again and I clung to Maman's hand. I still didn't understand why or how Walsingham had persuaded the Queen of England to reverse the judgement Gawen had secured against me. But I was beginning to see how important Béatrice had been. She had repaid her debt ten-thousand-fold.

'So here I am,' cried Maman, 'come from France to bring you news that Queen Elizabeth has fully understood your plight and righted a heinous wrong. But I am not come alone.' A movement on the path caught my eye and another woman stepped forward.

'Clotilde! Oh, Clotilde,' I cried. I leaped from the seat, stumbled forward and collapsed into my old nurse's arms. Clotilde held me so tight I could barely breathe as she whispered in French all her love and care for me. All the little sayings from my childhood days fell in my ears as the sweetest balm. Maman wandered off and Clotilde sat close to me on the bench for a long time. Then, the three of us together, we walked along the path and picked up my scattered posy.

'They say they are Queen Elizabeth's favourite flower,' I smiled, handing them to Clotilde whose old eyes sparkled with joy. 'From today they are mine too.'

For the first time in nearly two years I walked into my own parlour. A maidservant I did not recognise bobbed a curtsey.

'Bring refreshment for my mother and I, and some for Clotilde too,' I ordered with a grin so wide I felt my face would burst open. 'Bring the best you can find, my girl, and see that the countess's room is well prepared!' Over the most delicious caraway biscuits I had ever tasted Maman explained that her friend Lettice, Countess of Leicester, had secured a place for Christopher as a tutor with a family far from Dartington.

'I will miss his friendship,' I sighed. 'For though there was nothing amiss between us, I will confess to you, Maman, that his conversation helped me through some dark times. But I can see it will be for the best.'

Rist and Gatchell had been dismissed.

'I insisted to your husband that they go forthwith. You will also wish to dismiss this woman,' Maman said sharply, pointing to Marie Weare who was hovering uncertainly just beyond the door. 'Is she not one of those who decried you?'

'Marie will remain at Dartington, Maman,' I replied, loud enough for Marie to hear. 'Clotilde will attend me, but she is not so young as she was…' At this Clotilde made to protest and I chuckled. 'Marie can assist her and she is most skilled in needlework too. Marie, please come in.' She wobbled unsteadily into the parlour and waited, wringing her hands in her apron.

'Now, Marie, you have nothing to fear,' I cooed. 'How old is your daughter now?'

'Near twelve, mistress,' she stammered.

'Then you may fetch her here, for Miss Lisbeth will be in need of a maid when she returns. I will see that the glover is paid to release your girl from her apprenticeship.' Her round face lit with a bright smile and she stammered her thanks. Maman put her head on one side and gave me a quizzical look.

'It seems, Roberda, that you have learned much in your solitude,' she commented with a wry smile. 'Perhaps God has shown you the way to forgiveness.'

'Perhaps that is so. I have had much time to reflect, Maman, and my books have been a great solace,' I replied, marvelling that I could speak so openly with my formidable mother. 'I will need to consider carefully what to do with the others who spoke in that so-called court, but Marie will stay.'

Later that afternoon Maman and I walked again in the physick garden. She nodded towards the stone with the name Alain du Bois inscribed on it.

'You held me responsible for his death,' she said quietly. 'It has long been on my conscience. Can you forgive?'

'Maman, I can,' I answered, keeping my voice low and soothing. 'As would Alain. He knew the risk he took. He would understand and be glad you were safe. I'm so pleased that Béatrice has his grave tended.'

'That girl has earned her place in our family,' Maman sighed with a wistful look in her eyes. 'Her father would be so proud of her.' We walked on, step for step, my arm through hers.

Bess arrived the next day, bouncing in as full of energy as ever, though I had learned she now had three children in the nursery at Berry Pomeroy. A light breeze stirred the topmost leaves as we walked in the direction of the holy well.

'It is the only time I have been at such difference with Edward,' she confided. 'He sided with his father and would not allow me to interfere! Men will always stick together, you know; they took Gawen's side. You'd have thought they'd have more sympathy with you, given what became of Edward's grandmother, Katherine Fillol.' Bess had a point. Katherine was the woman accused of adultery, put aside and sent to a nunnery. If that had not happened Edward and his father would have kept their titles and estates intact.

'It took me a long time to pluck up the courage to defy Edward and write to Charlotte,' Bess continued. 'I had to smuggle the letter out with my tailor when he came to Berry Pomeroy to measure me for new gowns – I've become so fat since I had the children.' She giggled nervously and then turned an anxious face to me. 'It was when your musician, that boy Pierre, turned up at Berry Pomeroy that I knew it had gone on long enough.'

'Pierre? But he's at Modbury. I trust he's in no trouble.'

'No indeed, he's doing well there. But when he heard what my brother had done to you he came to me, so angry I was afraid he might do something foolish. Together we devised a plan to get word to your family. We arranged the trick with my tailor, then Pierre was able to get the letter into a messenger's pouch – I think perhaps one in the employ of young Arthur Champernowne of Modbury who now serves Walsingham in France. I was so very worried my letter might not reach your sister. I am so relieved it did!'

We sat down on the grass beside the holy well. I lay back and relaxed, listening to the drowsy buzzing of bees busy among the oxeye daisies that nodded in the sunshine. But Bess fidgeted, patted her skirts and fiddled with the pomander at her girdle, her hands flying to and fro. At last she lifted her head and looked into my face.

'Oh, Roberda, how can I ever make it up to you?' Bess's eyes had a haunted look and her voice cracked. 'I knew what they said of you was all lies. I should have acted sooner. I should have been stronger.

I so wanted you there with me when my babies came, but I was forbidden that too.'

'Bess, please do not upset yourself,' I soothed, offering her my kerchief to dry the tears running down her plump cheeks. 'I understand. It took real courage to go against your husband like that, and to plot with Pierre. If it were not for your letter to Charlotte and for Béatrice's action, I would be imprisoned still. I am free now and all will be well.'

'I don't think I will ever speak to my brother again,' Bess announced, looking fierce as she struggled to her feet. 'Gawen has treated you shamefully. Whatever would my father have said!'

I remembered Sir Arthur on that afternoon in the garden all those years ago; the time he had looked so uncomfortable as he tried to apologise for chasing my dowry. Kindly Sir Arthur would surely have been dismayed beyond measure at what had happened.

'Gawen seems to have completely lost his senses,' Bess continued. 'There was a great quarrel between him and Sir William Courtenay earlier this year. Gawen hurled insults and one of Courtenay's men barely escaped with his life. Why my brother, who claims to be so strapped for money, should think to take such a childish matter to the Queen's Attorney I cannot think. Patched up now, though Gawen was found to be at fault. I do believe my brother has run quite out of his wits.'

'I fear you may be right,' I responded with a smile. 'Shall we cast off our stockings and paddle?'

A few days later Thomas Trosse, Gawen's proctor in our supposed divorce proceedings, stood before me in the hall. His long face seemed more cadaverous than I remembered; pale parchment-thin skin stretched over razor-sharp cheekbones. He kept his eyes cast down and his hands shook as he held out a paper – a letter from Gawen.

> *'Madam. The sentence against you has been reviewed. It seems I was misinformed. I am instructed that I must treat you better. That will best be served by my absence. I am bound for Ireland again in the service of my queen. You are re-instated as my wife*

and mother of my children. You will have charge of the household and estate in my absence. Trosse will assist.'

'Quite right too,' said Maman triumphantly when I passed the missive to her. 'Now you can show that foolish, misguided man what a ruby he has in a virtuous wife who will manage his affairs.'

'Are there matters I should be aware of, Master Trosse?' I enquired. 'Any pressing matters concerning the estate?'

'Master Gawen was here last November sorting out the muster returns and arrangements for the defence of Plymouth and Dartmouth. He set all to rights. The rents are all in order, madam,' he croaked. I jerked my head up and had to choke back an angry retort. It cut me to the quick to learn that my husband had been at Dartington and brought me no news of our children.

'My first task will be to appoint a new steward of the household, and then you may bring me the account books. But that will be all for now, Master Trosse.' It gave me such pleasure to dismiss the man who'd portrayed me as a harlot before that court. Perhaps he had only served my husband; perhaps he had been taken in by lies. But he had been glad enough to profit from my downfall and I would find it hard to forgive him.

All the colours of Devon in summer seemed brighter, more intense; I felt weightless as I floated through those next days in a haze of happiness. Maman would stay for a few weeks. Long enough for the children to return to fill Dartington once more with laughter and happiness.

The day came at last. The morning sun danced on the grey stone walls as I waited at the door under the white hart badge. My heart was light as those sunbeams as I stepped out into the courtyard to welcome my children home.

Author's Note

The Dartington Bride is a work of fiction inspired by a scandalous divorce that occurred in sixteenth century Devon. While most of the characters in the story are real people, a few, such as the French servants and named refugee women, have been added to enrich the narrative. Although the historical record offers some glimpses into the lives of these individuals, it does not provide a complete story. I have respected events that are backed by reliable sources, but this interpretation is entirely my own. Through extensive research, I have laid the foundation for Roberda's story and then used creative imagination to shape the thoughts, intentions, and dialogues of the main characters.

Lady Gabrielle Roberda Montgomery merits no more than a brief footnote in the historical record. On the few occasions historians specifically mention her, it is as the daughter of the French regicide and Huguenot leader, the Count of Montgomery, or as Gawen Champernowne's adulterous wife. It has generally been accepted or implied that Roberda was 'guilty as charged'. But it seemed extraordinary to me that a woman of such noble birth, daughter of the formidable Isabeau de la Touche, a staunch and valiant upholder of the protestant faith, would actually have behaved in such a scandalous way. I rejected an alternative explanation — that Roberda's promiscuity may have been a reaction to her traumatic childhood in war-torn France, and was an act of rebellion — since it seemed to me most unlikely her mother would have been so vociferous in pleading Roberda's innocence if that were so.

In sixteenth-century England, divorce as we know it today was not an option. The Church of England did not allow full divorce for reasons of adultery or desertion, unlike some other Protestant churches in Europe. Separation from 'bed and board' was permitted, but remarriage was only allowed after the death of the other party. Cases of adultery were handled by Church Consistory Courts, which supervised the moral and religious behaviour of clergy and laity. High-profile cases, like Gawen Champernowne's in 1582, where a husband sought an Act of Parliament to divorce his wife from bed and board after a ruling in the Consistory Court, were rare.

As I studied the records of the Exeter Consistory Court[1] detailing the depositions given by a long list of servants, my doubts grew. When I discovered that the statement made by Hugh Rist was quoted in a book on Elizabethan rhetoric[2] as an example of carefully constructed narrative delivered in such a way as to be convincing, I became even more suspicious. The servant, Rist, seemed to have been well coached to make his testimony seem credible. He limited his account only to what he himself had observed and provided circumstantial detail that made it seem all the more plausible.

Rist relies heavily on what I think might now be termed *hearsay evidence*. He reports the conversations he had with Gatchell, one of the men accused of adultery with Roberda. As I have Roberda's proctor (legal representative), Jasper Bridgeman, say of Rist,

> *'He says little but he implies much.'*

Numerous serving people, including some in his employ for only two years, came forward to support Gawen. It is not surprising that maidservants were called to give depositions. They would have regular access to Roberda's bedchamber. However, it was strange to discover that numerous men, who appeared to be grooms and estate workers, were often near her sleeping chambers as part of their duties. It is tempting to imagine them gathering outside her room to eavesdrop.

Jasper Bridgeman had trouble getting witnesses to give evidence

---

1 Devon Archives, South West Heritage Trust, Chanter 783 and 861.

2 *Elizabethan Rhetoric Theory and Practice* by Peter Mack, Cambridge University Press, a book which explores the use of language in the sixteenth and seventeenth century, includes a full transcript of Rist's deposition.

in favour of Roberda. She was supposed to attend Staverton Church to present her side but it is not clear from the records whether she actually did so. A supposed confession reported to the court by Sir Robert Denys appears somewhat problematic for my alternative interpretation that maintains Roberda's innocence. I did not want to suggest that Sir Robert, JP, MP, nine times Sheriff of the county and an upstanding member of the Devon gentry, deliberately misled the court. Instead I've sought to explain his evidence as a language-based misunderstanding that conveniently supported Gawen's case.

In some accounts, the men accused with Roberda, Melhuishe and Gatchell are called grooms, but their identities are uncertain. I found out that a gentleman named Thomas Melhuishe rented the rectory and parsonage at Dartington from Sir Arthur Champernowne for 99 years starting from 1 September 1566.[3] I have depicted Thomas as Christopher's father and allowed them to live in the parsonage. Additionally, considering Christopher's ability to converse in French with Roberda, as mentioned in the depositions, I have portrayed him as an educated man.

An exchange of letters[4] between Roberda's brother, Jacques, her mother Isabeau, and Sir Francis Walsingham in the spring of 1584 gives credence to the claim that Gawen treated Roberda cruelly after the divorce. The Countess wrote that:

> *"What her daughter is accused of is pure calumny, far from all truth, invented by her husband in his transport of unbridled passions."*

At the end of June 1584 Roberda's mother sent a request to Walsingham via a French Huguenot apothecary, Geoffroy de Brumen, who may also have acted as a spy. She asked that the sentence delivered against her daughter be reviewed and set aside. Isabeau evidently came to England and eventually Walsingham was persuaded to act, for de Brumen writes on 16 August:

3 Devon Archives SWHT Ref Z15/2/3

4 Calendar of State Papers France

"Madame de Montgomery has gone, who is greatly obliged to you".

Although I have not been able to trace documentary evidence, it is almost certain that the 'sentence' was overturned, but Roberda continues to carry the label of *adulteress.*

In the Champernowne family a tradition has been handed down that a woman was once kept locked up in a room at Dartington Hall. According to family records it was believed that this woman was Roberda. We cannot know for certain whether Gawen actually went so far as to lock his wife away after the divorce proceedings, but records show that she did remain at Dartington after the divorce.

A number of ghost stories have been attached to a room at Dartington Hall, known until quite recent times as the Countess's Room. One story holds that the room is haunted by Roberda while another suggests that the ghost is Roberda's mother, the Countess of Montgomery.

After the jousting accident in which King Henri II of France died, Roberda's father converted to the Protestant faith. He became a military leader in the *French Wars of Religion,* a series of eight conflicts between Huguenot and Catholic factions in France that started in 1562 The *Huguenots* followed the teachings of theologian John Calvin and were often persecuted by Catholic French governments, causing many to flee the country. The first wave of refugees from religious persecution in France arrived in England during the reign of Edward VI who, in 1550, acknowledged the existence of the Church of Foreigners (Strangers' Church) in London.

The *St. Bartholomew's Day Massacre* on 23/24 August 1572 was a targeted group of assassinations, followed by a wave of Catholic mob violence directed against the Huguenots gathered in Paris for the marriage of the Protestant Henry of Navarre to Marguerite de Valois, sister of King Charles IX. In the following days the violence spread throughout France. An estimated 3,000 French Protestants were killed in Paris, and some estimates suggest as many as 70,000 in all of France. Many others fled to safety overseas. They joined others fleeing persecution by Catholic governments in the Low Countries.

Some refugees settled permanently in England, mainly in Kent and London.Others are thought to have come to Devon, though it is not known if any unaccompanied women were among them. The strangers, as they were known, were generally tolerated, but not welcomed by everyone. Some people were concerned that they would take work from locals, while others were suspicious that the refugees came, not to escape persecution, but to seek a better life with more lucrative employment than they had at home. By the 1580s harsh social, legal, working and taxation conditions were placed on the new arrivals. Some London citizens even blamed them for an outbreak of plague in 1593 and attacked their homes.

The French Wars of Religion lasted for 38 years. A second, larger influx of Huguenot refugees arrived in England after October 1685 when Louis XIV revoked the Edict of Nantes, increasing levels of persecution on France.

Queen Elizabeth's relations with France were complicated. She inherited a bad relationship with France from her predecessor Queen Mary. The strategic town of Calais, which had been ruled by England for hundreds of years, had been lost. France now controlled the entire northern coastline of France leaving England more vulnerable to attack. Mary, Queen of Scots whose mother, Mary de Guise came from a powerful French Catholic family, had been married to Francis II, King of France until his death in 1560. So the French supported Mary, Queen of Scots and her claim to the English throne. One reason why Elizabeth was hesitant about ultimately executing Mary was the fear of possible French retaliation. But while England and Spain maintained a good relationship, France could not afford to antagonise England for fear of attack from Spain from the south west.

In 1562/63 Queen Elizabeth and her chief adviser, William Cecil, wanted to reclaim Calais and to end French interference in Scotland. They sent a force to France in the hope of securing a foothold there by aiding the Huguenots in their fight against the powerful Catholic faction. The attempt came to nothing when Catherine de Medici, Dowager Queen and Regent of France, managed to negotiate a settlement (which proved short-lived) between the warring French factions. In the years that followed, Queen Elizabeth continued, spasmodically and often surreptitiously, to support the Huguenot cause while also courting good relations with France.

In June 1584 at the time Roberda's family were petitioning Queen Elizabeth, Francis, Duke of Alençon and Anjou, youngest son of Catherine de Medici and former suitor to Queen Elizabeth, died. Henry of Navarre became the Protestant heir to the French throne. This may have increased Queen Elizabeth's fears that the Catholic Duke of Guise might persuade the childless King of France, Henri III, to join forces with Spain. Walsingham, a staunch Protestant, finally persuaded Queen Elizabeth to act to overturn the sentence of divorce. By this time Roberda's brother Jacques was a prominent supporter of Henry of Navarre, and Walsingham may have seen benefit in keeping Roberda's family 'on side'.

Readers may also like to know that :

- Isabeau took her children on the campaign trail in France, even during the siege of Rouen.
- There is mention of an illegitimate daughter named Béatrice, possibly the child of a woman named Diane de Tavannes. However, I haven't been able to confirm her identity.
- I have moved Isabeau's first visit to Devon forward by one year to 1568.
- Some sources suggest that Gawen and Roberda were married in Ducey in May 1571 when Sir Arthur visited[5]. However, other records[6] indicate that the Count of Montgomery was at court in Greenwich from November 30 to December 6 of the same year for the wedding of his daughter to Gawen Champernowne.
- An inscription on the tomb of James Rodge in Honiton churchyard describes him as a 'bone lace seller'. By the time he died in 1617, Rodge was a wealthy man, suggesting the industry was already well established. It has been tentatively suggested that the Honiton lace industry started in the reign of Elizabeth I, with an influx of refugees[7].

---

5 Calendar of State Papers Foreign, Elizabeth, vol 9 1569-1571 accessed via British History Online

6 Cofferer/Controller of the Household Accounts, The National Archives accessed via Folgerpeidia

7 The History of the Honiton Lace Industry H.J. Yallop

- A Tudor courtier›s great house would not be complete without a well-laid-out garden. While we cannot know exactly how Sir Arthur Champernowne arranged his gardens when he renovated Dartington Hall, or if he had a physick garden. Later references in Champernowne papers refer to a 'best' garden in the area behind the hall. Sir Arthur's nephew Adrian Gilbert was a renowned garden designer. He created extensive gardens at Wilton House for the Countess of Pembroke and at Sherborne for his brother, Sir Walter Raleigh. His elder brother, Sir John Gilbert, laid out gardens at Greenway Court beside the River Dart.

Acknowledgements

I have spent many happy hours sharing my love of Dartington Hall in Devon with visitors as one of a team of volunteer garden guides. It is a very special place with a long and fascinating history. I am particularly grateful to the Dartington Trust for allowing me to explore 'behind-the-scenes' parts of the house as I researched Roberda's story. I am also indebted to the staff at the Devon Archives at South West Heritage Trust, Exeter, for their patient assistance and helpful advice as I consulted the records of the Exeter Consistory Court and the Champernowne papers. Special thanks to the amazing Dea Parkin of Fiction Feedback, who has helped me to develop Roberda's story and has kept me on track, and to my beta readers for their helpful feedback. Once again everyone at Troubador Publishing has been incredibly helpful throughout the publishing process. Many thanks also to Bob Cooper for the stunning cover design, to Fiona for her unfailing support and most importantly a huge thank you to my husband David who has always believed in me.

RG 2023

Roberda's story does not end with her release ....

About the Author

Author and speaker **Rosemary Griggs** has been researching Devon's sixteenth-century history for years. She has discovered a cast of fascinating characters and an intriguing network of families whose influence stretched far beyond the West Country and loves telling the stories of the forgotten women of history – the women beyond the royal court; wives, sisters, daughters and mothers who played their part during those tumultuous Tudor years: the **Daughters of Devon.**

Her novel ***A Woman of Noble Wit*** tells the story of Katherine Champernowne, Sir Walter Raleigh's mother, and features many of the county's well-loved places.

Rosemary creates and wears sixteenth-century clothing, a passion which complements her love for bringing the past to life through a unique blend of theatre, history and re-enactment. Her appearances and talks for museums and community groups all over the West Country draw on her extensive research into sixteenth-century Devon, Tudor life and Tudor dress, particularly Elizabethan.

Out of costume, Rosemary leads heritage tours of the gardens at Dartington Hall, a fourteenth-century manor house and now a visitor destination and charity supporting learning in arts, ecology and social justice.

You can find out more on Rosemary's website:

https://rosemarygriggs.co.uk/

Follow Rosemary:

X (formerly Twitter): @RAGriggsauthor
Facebook: https://www.facebook.com/ladykatherinesfarthingale
Instagram: griggs6176

BY THE SAME AUTHOR

Few women of her time lived to see their name in print. But Katherine was no ordinary woman. She was Sir Walter Raleigh's mother. This is her story.

Set against the turbulent background of a Devon rocked by the religious and social changes that shaped Tudor England; a Devon of privateers and pirates; a Devon riven by rebellions and plots, *A Woman of Noble Wit* tells how Katherine became the woman who would inspire her famous sons to follow their dreams. It is Tudor history seen though a woman's eyes.

As the daughter of a gentleman's family with close connections to the glittering court of King Henry VIII, Katherine's duty is clear. She must put aside her dreams and accept the husband chosen for her. Still a girl, she starts a new life at Greenway Court, overlooking the River Dart, relieved that her husband is not the ageing monster of her nightmares. She settles into the life of a dutiful wife and mother – until a chance shipboard encounter with a handsome privateer turns her world upside down…

Years later a courageous act will set Katherine's name in print and see her youngest son fly high.

Made in the USA
Middletown, DE
14 May 2024

54356175R00166